I0737819

YOURS TRULY, DELLA COLEMAN

Case One: The Crunch

Written and illustrated by:

AMELIA R. RIKSTAD

*To my Mom who always loves my crazy stories. Thanks
for putting up with your wacky kid.
To Dad who always kept my goals grounded.
You helped my fantasy happen.
To Owen. You are my light. Don't let anyone take that from you.
I love you all so much.
And to God for keeping me on the right path.*

~CONTENTS~

PROLOGUE

As he fiddled with the bright yellow bow tie that kept his filigree patterned button-up together, he scrolled the many under-detailed pages on many underwhelming websites. He sat lazily at his desk, his feet propped up on the mahogany desktop as he began stroking the head of a black and white speckled cat. The cat was equally as bored as its amber eyes scanned the computer screen intently. Would it kill these people to do a little extra research? He studied each page for less than a second, but somehow, he gathered all the information he needed. Sighing heavily, he moved on to the next page, not bothering to remember the one he had just read through. The cat hissed at him before he could click onto yet another page. It was such a slow reader.

"I swear. . ." The man breathed. He may have been past his prime, a little out of the loop some might say, but he was dead sure not once in any lore did it state that Bigfoot was created when a man fell into a vat of super-glue and got covered in hair. He shook his head angrily, clicking onto an open tab that read *Yours Truly, Della Coleman.*

His sagging gray eyes scanned the newest article; *Champ; Myth or Monster?* He yawned, scrolling through. At least this one could spell. That was more than he could say about half the people working for him. He read on, nodding in approval about the facts this girl had found. Yes, Champ was said to be twenty feet long, yes, the creature was documented in stories in *Samuel de Champlain's* journals. His lips twitched into a smile. Had he found whom he was looking for?

Quickly moving his cursor towards the menu on the right side of the page, he clicked on the tab that read 'about.' Instantly captivated by the short paragraph that filled his eyes, he leaned in closer. There was something in the way this one wrote; something that made him, a true believer, question things.

In bold, jagged writing, the page read; *Delphee C. Coleman, eighteen, Amateur Paranormal Investigator. Take a step inside the world of things the government would love not to have discussed. Area 51? You have read about it, yes? Why else would you be here? Nevertheless, do we really know what is going on in there? Is that really where they keep extraterrestrials? Bigfoot? A monster or a cursed soul? Is he the only one? What about Yetis? Were the witches of Salem really witches, or were they wrongfully accused? Were their accusers the real evil? These subjects and more discussed below. New article every Tuesday.*

The man scrolled through post after post on her site, swelling with pride. She pulled no stops, did not cut any corners, did not hire an executioner to rid herself of facts, all the while adding her own little dash of imagination to the subjects.

Even the cat seemed impressed.

The man stopped petting him, leaning forward and adjusting his thin-framed gold glasses. Down in the corner, purposefully written backward and upside down, was an address—a mailing address.

The man stood, smiling slyly to himself. He waltzed over to one of his old filing cabinets and produced a set of medieval-looking stationery from it. He wrote a simple letter—a little lie here, a little lie there—baiting her to come to his neck of the swamp.

"Can you mail this?" He asked the cat, who watched him with a very human sort of judgment. It did something akin to an eye-roll, then stretched, waiting for the man to hand it the letter. The man hesitated, a wry smile pulling at his lips. "And please, do not 'lose it' like you did last time." He instructed, making a show of air quotes.

The cat hissed, but seemed to comply, taking the letter in his mouth and running out of the office.

"To new beginnings." The man said wistfully, dusting off his suit pants. He grabbed his tweed jacket and top hat, leaving his office.

As he walked through the halls of his little business, he heard typing and the incessant beeping of printers. Voices fluttered into his ears. He could just make out the whispers and gossip from the night shift as they chatted about the newest politics of this strange little town. He smiled, looking over his shoulder, waving at the shadow of a person leaving the communal kitchen.

"Goodnight, Mavericks!" Their voice rang.

"Same to you, Elanor."

His old loafers caught on the steps of the basement like they always did, giving a pleasant little squeak that resonated through the silence like waves crashing against the shore. As his hand rested on the door above him, he felt a presence. He scowled, pushing open the door.

"What's done is done, Richmond." He called wistfully to the young man standing in front of the door.

"You cannot do this. Not again." He began, ignoring the old man as he tipped his invisible hat to him and made for the door. "This isn't a game. This isn't poker or chess. You cannot manipulate people just because you are bored. Not anymore." His tone was almost pleading.

"I can do whatever I damn well please." The man snapped, rounding on him.

Richmond scowled, stepping forward. His cousin—Lenora—stood, watching the scene unfold before her with a look of terror on her face. Richmond glanced at her, a low, rumbling growl resonating in his throat.

Richmond rolled his eyes. "Please. Just listen to Lenora and I. Stop searching for another set of pawns."

"Oh! But I have! Not ten minutes ago, I found a suitable benefactor! Milliano is sending a letter as we speak." Mavericks smiled.

Richmond stared at him in disbelief, his mouth hanging open. "You didn't. You sick son of a—"

"Careful now, wouldn't want to anger me." Mavericks winked, once again making to leave.

"When this all blows over, I hope you know my loyalties have *never* lain with you," Richmond said, and with that, he vanished—disappearing as if he had never set foot inside the building.

Lenora picked up her leather jacket off the back of her chair, smoothing out her peplum dress nervously. "He's right y'know. About certain parts. We're supposed to care." She said quietly. Mavericks stood at the doorway, staring out at the world through the circular stained-glass window above it.

"If you were anything like me, Lenora, you would have stopped caring a long, *long*, time ago." He whispered an ounce of sadness in his voice. "Tell your cousin that if the girl is harmed, there *will* be a war. Furthermore, it *will* be my fault."

She nodded, her shiny ash-blonde hair rippling like the ocean waves she once drowned in. He nodded as well, grabbing an umbrella out of the lion-footed stand near the door, hearing a small squeak from Lenora as he opened it carelessly indoors. He laughed coldly, stepping out into the moonlight.

"New beginnings indeed."

~CHAPTER ONE~

How do you tell if someone is a monster? Is it by the way they walk? The way they talk? The way they look at you when they think you are not paying attention?

Should you base your opinion on your first impression? I should think not. You'd miss out on a lot of good relationships if you did. Still, why is it when we see a man who drives a motorcycle, full of tattoos, we think of a wife-beater? Why is it when we see a celebrity, we assume they can do no wrong? Why do we believe a Priest is as holy as God?

Now riddle me this; are they monsters if we do not believe in the same things? Do they drive white vans and kidnap children if they do not have the same political views you do?

Maybe.

But why do our minds jump to conclusions? Why do differing opinions make the world so gloriously chaotic?

The answer is quite simple. There is a set of rules given to us at birth, by the country we live in, the parents we were born to, and the color of our skin. We all have morals, beliefs, and values. Three words that at first glance seem precisely the same, but in reality, are drastically different. We would not be very human without them, now would we? It should be an easy task figuring out the difference.

However, common sense *should* be simple. Too bad so many people lack it. Maybe if they did not, the world would indeed be as safe as we like to tell preschoolers it is.

To put it in perspective, the wisest preacher, one who knows the Bible cover to cover and back again, still does not know everything. He believes what mom and dad told him, believes that God exists because a book and two people told him so. He believes that the reason there is so much evil in the world is because the first humans sinned. He believes that no matter how many times he takes from the tithes, he will still go to Heaven. He is only doing it because he can't afford an extra lunch. Not that he has food at home or anything. Of course, he will get into Heaven! Didn't Jesus die for our sins? Surely that means we don't have to put in any extra work?

Those are values, beliefs, and morals.

Even a criminal has their own little set of them. Whether you believe it or not, they are still human. They may value being a cut-purse or rebelling against the law. Their morals may consist of being untrustworthy, and they may believe in doing wrong for reasons unknown by others.

They aren't monsters.

Or are they?

They do not have tentacles or horns or hairy backs, they have two legs, two arms, two eyes, and a brain.

So how do we find the real monsters?

I guess that is up to you and what you've been conditioned to perceive. Are you willing to challenge your own values, beliefs, and morals? Or will you turn a blind eye and conform to the everyday narrative?

~ ~ ~

"Miss Coleman, don't you think this is. . . a tad too *political* for a creative writing assignment that is meant to be published in the school paper? A paper that is mailed to the entire town?" Ms. Durnell, Sycamore High's principal, asked loftily as she looked over the top of the thin stack of papers she had been reading. She stared lazily into eyes of a young woman whose hair was dyed neon green at the ends. The girl sat across from her in Ms. Durnell's brightly lit office, looking bored out of her mind.

"Oh, yes, I quite agree. Expression of belief is *very* political. It is quite offensive to most, actually." Delphee 'Della' Coleman said politely, smiling. Her cheeks hit the rim of her clear-framed glasses, the cold plastic sending icy darts through her burning cheeks. She had been waiting to say that all day. She narrowed her eyes at the young principal, incredibly proud of herself for not chewing Patricia Durnell right out of her ugly citrine pantsuit.

Her eyes darted up to look at the clock above Ms. Durnell's head. It had only taken her four hours to call Della in. That had to be a new record. Though she could not quite remember, she was sure the last time she had been in this much trouble; it had taken Patricia an entire day to gather enough strength to face Sycamore High's brightest delinquent.

Pulling at the hem of her plaid skirt, she smoothed it gently, letting Ms. Durnell stare at her forehead. Della knew she intimidated the young principal. Every part of her had to be unnerving, right down to the way she sat perfectly straight on the edge of her seat, ankles crossed.

"That's precisely why you are in my office," Ms. Durnell exclaimed, biting her tongue as best she could. "Delphee, I admire you. You are a very talented writer, you always have been, but your writings are rather. . . *mature* for the minds of your classmates and their parents. It would be in your best interest to dial it back. Just a little?"

Della thought for a moment, staring off into space, then shook her head. She took off her glasses, using her skirt to clean them. There was this one little smudge that just would not come clean.

"This paper was for my Philosophy class, Patricia. As you can see, I received a very large, gleaming, red 'A' for my work. It was your employee who suggested I turn it into the school newspaper." She nodded to herself, fact-checking her thoughts. "I do recall it was an Advanced Placement Philosophy class. None of my classmates would be in it if they were not—" She held her glasses up to the light, satisfied with her work. "—*mature*." She finished.

Ms. Durnell stared at her blankly as Della replaced her glasses on her heart-shaped face, a blank smile on her lips, her eyebrows raised slightly, making her look like nothing but a statue.

"I do believe the paper is to be edited by one Sebastian Breckenridge, who is *also* in that class. You should really be talking to him." Della added.

Ms. Durnell opened her mouth slightly.

"I do believe we have been over this, but I prefer *Della*, not *Delphee*." Della said, letting her tone go an ounce sourer than it should have.

Ms. Durnell inhaled sharply, reminding Della of an angry dragon.

"I have spoken with Mr. Breckenridge. He said you told him you had been reinstated to your position at the paper. You even went so far as to give him a note with 'my signature' on it. You are lucky you aren't sitting in detention right now." She said, raising her eyebrows.

Della's blood boiled at how unfazed this woman was. "If you did not want me to forge your signature, you should not have sent my parents letters with it."

Ms. Durnell scowled. "Do you know why you were removed from the paper?" She asked, leaning back in her chair, eyeing Della coldly.

"Among other reasons, the school board does not particularly enjoy freedom of speech nor the fact that I am not a childish lackey they can manipulate. Honestly, who wants to read about the statistics out of one-hundred and seventy-two that Lorelei O'Malley will win Homecoming Queen?" It had taken her years to master that flowery little tone. No matter how harsh her words were, it always saved her.

"No, Delphee, it is because you have a tendency to hurt people's feelings." Ms. Durnell snapped. "Do you not remember forcing Mr. Breckenridge to print that article about the old Chem teacher and the janitor having an affair?"

Della squinted at her in disgust. "If I must step on a few hands and feet to get to the top, I will. Their families did not deserve what they were doing behind closed doors, and guess who had the power to stop it."

"Delphee, those aren't things you need to write about. It isn't your place. I had to make a public statement and fire both of those people. Not to mention, two divorces happened afterward!" Ms. Durnell exclaimed.

Della was aware of that. The janitor's wife had asked her to testify in court and had paid her a nice fee too.

"Yes, well, the truth hurts. Has anyone ever told you, *in truth*, how that beehive looks sitting on your head?" She shot back, losing her temper slightly. "And what of my feelings? Don't they matter?"

Ms. Durnell clutched the arm of her chair. She glanced

in the mirror that hung on her office door, thinking Della would not see. However, Della did see, and she reveled in the distressed look Patricia had on her face. Insecurity happened to be a high leverage point.

"Ms. Durnell, are you aware that the government loves to silence people young and old who know exactly what they are talking about, so they keep the world from thinking for itself? And in fact—"

"Miss Coleman, you know very well I do not tolerate your theories."

"*And in fact*," Della continued, raising her voice as much as she dared. "That you work for the government?"

"Delphee—"

"So, therefore, whether you know it or not, you have been conditioned to make sure my voice is never heard." Della finished.

Ms. Durnell stood briskly, her beehive hair shaking, the hem of her jacket getting caught on her chair, nearly causing it to topple over.

"DELPHEE COLEMAN!" She screamed. "How *dare* you talk back to me!"

Della sat back, stifling a laugh, crossing her legs and putting her fingertips together in a menacing triangle. To think that this woman— this woman that wasn't old enough to be her mother—had any say over anything she did was perplexing to say the least. Some people do have *such* a superiority complex.

Ms. Durnell tugged her jacket from the grip of the chair, straightening her suit. Her face glowed red with rage as Della stared at her. "If you would stop your silly little games, you could hear the real reason why I asked you to come see me! The reason I would've called you down here *without* your stupid paper!" She screeched.

This intrigued Della greatly. Ms. Durnell usually took every precaution to avoid her unless she was in trouble. Della nodded, showing she was listening.

"Your mother called me. Are you aware you received a letter yesterday?"

Della frowned, furrowing her eyebrows. She shook her head curtly, waiting for further information.

"You have been looking for a job this past year, one that involves your interests, correct?"

Della nodded, trying to suppress the excitement that began to rise in the back of her throat.

Ms. Durnell smiled. "Your mother brought me this letter," She pulled an intricately designed envelope out of a drawer on her desk. "There is a newspaper in. . . Moss Hollow—I believe that is somewhere near New Orleans—that has been watching your blog. They have offered you an internship."

"In Louisiana?" Della asked dumbly for clarification.

Ms. Durnell nodded, rolling her eyes. "Seeing as it is only a month into the final year you will grace me with your presence, you may be surprised to hear I am allowing you to go." Ms. Durnell smiled as if she had the upper hand on the situation.

"I am not surprised at all. It's a miracle you have not found a way to get rid of me sooner. Poor planning on your part." Della smiled, regretting it slightly. Patricia leered at her as she sat back up.

"Your mother and I think it will be good for you. I admire you Delphee, I know you won't listen to me, but maybe you will listen to her? You are incredible. You just need to realize that and put that awe into something more productive." Ms. Durnell's face softened slightly.

Della stared at her in disbelief, forcing herself to subdue all the sarcasm she wanted to use. "Will I come back to school after the internship?"

"It's a short offer, but if they like you, they will offer you a job. If not, well, your grades are high enough that I couldn't care less whether you come back or not. We'll call this a gap year, shall we?"

High enough? Della thought with a scowl. She had one of the highest GPAs of the entire school, as well as the entirety of the school's records. She could have dropped out years ago and still gotten into whatever college she wanted. Not that her father would have let her. . . the family plan and all.

"This is a one-time offer, Miss Coleman. What do you say?" Ms. Durnell asked, a hopeful look on her face.

"I say it's sad you despise me so much that you have convinced my mother to let me fly halfway across the country for 'X' amount of time." She smiled, adjusting her glasses again as she stood. "But how can I refuse?"

Relief flooded over Ms. Durnell's face. She handed Della the letter with such excitement you would have thought she just won the lottery.

"To a year of no issues?" She asked, holding out her hand, but Della made no move to shake it.

Della nodded, tucking the letter inside her book bag. Whatever the letter was made of, it was not paper. The paper, or rather parchment, was speckled with gold, the fibers coarse, the ink shining like it was made from ground-up gemstones. Newspapers do not tend to spend such money on things like this. She wondered what exactly she was getting herself into. Grabbing her jacket she walked over to the door. Smiling over her shoulder, her hand hovering above the door handle, she cleared her throat.

"Oh, and Patricia? 'You're' sounds sloppy. 'You are' is much more eloquent. Furthermore, you should never use the same sentence twice. 'I admire you' is so cliché. A good writer knows how to change things up." With that, she left Ms. Durnell's office, never to see it again.

She stood in the hallway of Sycamore High, smiling widely. She inhaled deeply, trying to contain her happiness, jogging in place with excitement and squealing with delight.

~ ~ ~

Sitting at her sticker-covered laptop, Della typed out the title to her latest blog post; *Proof Higher Education Wants to Silence Us*. She smiled to herself as she pushed the 'publish' button, swirling around in her office chair, leaning back and placing her arms behind her head.

Her suitcases were packed, her tickets were in her wallet, and her book-bag had been cleared of anything and everything school related. The entirety of her eighteen years of life had been packed up into those four beat-up suitcases. Her room was nearly bare, leaving nothing but the furniture and the larger decorations on the walls. The apartment she was going to rent had a couch, a bed frame and mattress, and appliances, other than that she would have to buy everything on her own.

Knowing she would be able to live on her own was exhilarating.. Her parents hadn't even moved out at eighteen. Neither of them had been this independent. Her father had been a lackey, complying with the rules of his family, her mother nothing but a wallflower. There was quite a legacy to 'live up to.'

When she arrived in Louisiana tomorrow, she would finally get to be a writer. Sure, it would be as dull as Hell having to write epitaphs, local interviews, and other mundane articles, but the hauntings and legends of that state would be more than enough to keep her—and her readers—occupied. She would have to come up with an excuse to knock on each and every door, asking whether they had seen a strange and glorious anomaly, but eventually, she would figure it out.

She turned back to her computer, opening a new notes page and quickly writing out some good excuses off the top of her mind. Potentially, she could say a 'gas leak' had occurred in a nearby neighborhood. She could play the part of a concerned citizen merely asking if anyone had felt the effect. She could just about imagine what the responses to 'Hello there, have you been hallucinating any swamp monsters lately?' would be.

A knock on her door startled her, causing her to slam her laptop shut. The poor thing had seen many hardships while belonging to Delphee C. Coleman. It was a miracle the screen wasn't cracked.

She turned, acting as casually as possible. Her door opened slightly, a pimple-covered face peeking through the doorway. There in all his glory stood Sebastian Breckenridge. His dirty blonde hair fell into his sad eyes as he stared at her through the crack in the door.

"Hey, Seb." Della said, smiling slightly.

"Coleman." He sighed.

Sebastian Breckenridge was her inside man. The only reason he wasn't in trouble was that it was common knowledge they weren't exactly friends. They did not talk outside of school; they did not hang out; they did not do anything ordinary people did. They were strictly business. Strictly acquaintances and nothing else—though, she was sure that only half the party was okay with those rules.

"What's up?" She asked, nodding to allow him safe passage into her room.

He shrugged, throwing the door open with the force of a gale-force wind. Good moods rarely graced him, his face usually adorned with the look of sucking on a lemon, and today was no different. "I was just wondering who was going to bring the heat when you are gone." He said sourly. He was sad, which meant he was angry.

Della rolled her eyes, returning to her computer. "You make it sound like I am dying, Seb." She chuckled. Would the people of Moss Hollow fuel her imagination if she said she was writing a book?

"You might as well be. I am never going to see you again." Seb said. She heard him plop down on her bed, the sleeping bag she used as a comforter making an annoying crinkling sound.

"Ominous. What makes you think that?" Della asked, peering at his reflection in her secondary monitor. It saddened her she couldn't bring it with her, but it was much too old and fragile to travel with.

"Because, mark my words, within your second week they will offer you a position as an editor or whatever, and you will get attached to your office and say something like 'Oh, how can I leave now,' and then once again, I will be alone." Seb exclaimed, adding a little *humph* at the end for effect.

Della rolled her eyes. "And that my less-than-friend," She said, hammering down on the 'enter' button. "Is why they made video calling a thing." She cared about him a lot, though, in her experience, friendships only ended in sorrow. In fact, this was the first time he had ever come over, even though Della's mother had invited him over many times.

"When you're famous, do not forget about me—er—us. All of us. Like. . . Like your family and me. Mostly your parents, I mean I don't matter in the grand scheme of things." Seb said coldly, though she could hear the smile in his voice. She nodded, finally turning to meet his eyes.

"You'll get a four-page thank you note in my biography." She smiled.

He thought for a moment, smiling mischievously. "You have to write it like I died in some tragic accident though, I want to be a man of mystery. And say something cheesy like, 'always and forever, my one true love.' That will get their heads spinning." He ruffled his blond hair, his cheeks reddening. She stuck her tongue out at him playfully, tossing a loose sock at him.

Della checked her watch—along with the time, it showed what phase the moon was in, the date, and what Zodiac was currently guarding the earth. She frowned. Sebastian was going to be late for band practice. She flashed her watch at him, nodding her head at the door.

He scowled for a moment, standing and adjusting the wrinkles on his white-washed *Star Wars* tee. "Come here." He said awkwardly, and they hugged for less than two seconds before he hobbled over to the door. "I'll see you around, Delphee. In this life or the next."

Della saluted him, slumping back into her chair. Although she hated to admit it, she was going to miss his melancholy personality.

~ ~ ~

". . . and for the love of God, don't fall in love." Jasper Coleman sighed, watching his daughter tear the 'BEWARE: AREA 51 CONTAINMENT UNIT' sign off her door the next morning, her head pounding.

Hopefully, she had enough medication left in that ugly orange pill bottle to last a couple of months. Della had suffered from chronic migraines for as long as she could remember. *Painful* chronic migraines.

"It's perfectly okay to fall in love." Kimi Coleman, her glorious mother, the person Della would die for, corrected. She held a paper sack out for Della as she brushed by, smiling sympathetically. The squishy sack probably contained blue corn scones, something Della would miss greatly.

"You make it seem like I'm running away to Paris to pursue my art career." Della smiled tightly.

"Don't be stupid. Carry—"

"Carry pepper spray always, use your keys as brass knuckles, know where the local police department is, and carry a cross with you." Della said, finishing her father's rules. Half of the stuff her father said sounded like a joke, but make no mistake, he was dead serious.

Jasper nodded curtly. "If you run across any heathens, shout the name of God in their face and run in the opposite direction, you hear me?"

"Sir, yes, sir." Della said lazily, shoving her sign into her bag. She planted a kiss onto her tiny, half Native American mothers' forehead. Exchanging a roll of the eyes behind Jasper's back.

Kimi pulled her into a hug, whispering in her ear. "Stay safe. No matter what happens, you can always come home."

Della nodded, making her way through the house. Her younger siblings Cassandra and Leonel were playing in the living room, waving goodbye at her. She was pretty sure they didn't quite understand what Della leaving really meant.

Perhaps Della didn't either.

Last night, Della had realized there was some truth in Sebastian's words. Though she had plenty of beautiful Tarot cards to predict her future, fate was still unsure. What if this was the last time Della was going to see the irritatingly picturesque town of Sycamore Heights? Even though she hated the picket fences and white-washed walls, this place was meant to be home. This place had formed her very being. It had made her who she was in every aspect of the phrase, right down to the shoes she wore and the beanies that kept her sensitive ears warm. What would she amount to now that she was leaving? Would she be something or nothing at all?

Deciding that whatever the universe wanted to happen, it would be for the best, she had gathered up the last of her belongings, said her goodbyes to her parents and younger brother and sister, then headed off, making a small pit-stop before reaching the airport. She picked up a can of bright, neon-green spray paint from the local hardware shop and drove around the town, looking for the alleyway all the seniors painted once they left school. She had been wondering for months about what she would paint, but she thought it was pretty obvious now.

As the cold, early September winds blew her hair in every direction, she spray-painted a simple set of words over several people's paintings: Delphee C. Coleman was here. Do not forget it.

~CHAPTER TWO~

The dingy yellow taxicab rattled its way into the parking lot of the old apartment building. The cab's windows—so crusted that they didn't roll all the way up or down—reflected the words 'Ambrose Apartments' in bright red light onto Della's face. She slid a few dollars onto the dirty middle compartment between the front seats and got out of the taxi. The driver smiled and waved as he pulled away, the engine giving a small *POP!* as he drove, leaving her alone in the cold, dark, damp Louisiana air. He had been nice. . . for a creepy old man that is. Della shrugged to herself, turning on her heels to examine the building before her fully.

It was a quaint little building, six stories tall, and at least three semi-trucks long. All it needed was a paint job and some flowers, and it would look a little less foreboding. At least it would be a roof over Della's head, and at the moment, that's all she needed.

Della turned to her left, struggling to get her four heavy suitcases up over the curb of the sidewalk and in through the gigantic glass double doors that led inside. A strong, musty smell filled her nostrils as soon as she heaved her way inside. Torn bright red velour carpet shifted beneath her sneakers, causing her to be over-aware of her footsteps. Candles in rusty old candelabras lined the loose furniture around her, and the occasional broken oil lamp adorned the walls—which were covered in a rather old and ugly floral wallpaper. On top of it all, the welcome mat lay askew, pointing out into the world rather than inside.

That was almost poetic.

Della smiled slyly, staggering over to the front desk with her luggage, flipping her short brown and green hair behind her. She had pinned a bright purple extension in on the right side on the way here. Its cheap silicon fibers poked her cheek as she smiled with what little dignity a person who was going to call this place 'home' could.

A young man sat at the front desk, feet on the counter, reading a magazine. He had sandy blonde hair and pale, almost ashy, skin. He looked away from his magazine briefly, revealing a pair of bloodshot blue eyes as he observed her. His eyes traveled over her entire body, lingering on her heather-gray shirt that read 'Bigfoot: Hide 'N Seek Champion.' He rolled his eyes, shaking out the magazine, making little clicking noises with his tongue.

"Name." He demanded lazily.

"Delphee C. Coleman." She replied sweetly, peering behind him. Behind him, the wall was lined with rusty old hooks. Only four of them did not have a silver key hanging from it.

The man looked blankly in front of him for a moment, his magazine sagging onto his chest before he begrudgingly removed his muddy shoes from the counter. Tossing his magazine aside, he typed something into the old computer opposite him, spinning around in his chair to grab a pair of keys off the wall. As he spun back around with absolutely no emotion, he slid the keys across the counter and gave Della a somewhat irritated look.

"Here are your keys, you can provide first and last month's rent in the morning. Derek will take it." He said breathlessly, yawning at the end.

Della cleared her throat as he began to turn away. "I paid over the phone about a week ago." She said in a corrective tone, taking the keys.

The young man sighed dramatically, typing away at his computer again. Della stood on her tiptoes to see what he was writing, but he swiveled the screen away from her prying eyes. After a few minutes of him squinting at the screen, his scowl deepening, he held out his hand, wriggling his fingers, looking up for only a moment.

Della furrowed her eyebrows.

"Keys." He yawned.

She nodded, handing him back the keys. Once again, he spun around in his chair, replacing the keys and reaching for another set. He hesitated, then grabbed for another, checking his computer screen one last time before he handed them to her.

"Each month, you have a two-day grace period, or you will be evicted. You are apartment two-o-three on the left. The elevator is stuck on the third floor. Have a nice night." With that, he dismissed her, replacing his feet on the counter with a thud, snapping his magazine open and continuing to read.

"Thank you," Della said, rolling her eyes as soon as she turned away. No wonder this place was so run down, what with employees like him. The thought of meeting his coworkers drained all the energy out of her.

She heaved her luggage up the stairs, not bothering to ask for assistance even though she struggled terribly. She had a feeling it would have been a lost cause. Climbing the steps, panting with the effort it took, she reached the second floor, realizing that there were three different two-o-threes. Thankfully, only one happened to be situated on the left.

Her keys slid into the lock, unlocking the door with a satisfying little click.

Hers was a tiny abode. No balcony, no dishwasher, there weren't even glass panels on the windows. Only shutters. The tiles in the kitchenette were stained and crusted, the carpet two distinctly different shades of yellow. The couch she had been left with was an old, frayed excuse for a loveseat, reminding her of something that her grandmother would own. She suddenly dreaded knowing what the bedroom looked like. She groaned, turning to the fridge and prying it open. Surprisingly, it was the only clean thing in this wretched place.

A cold draft flew in through the shutters, blowing them open gently. Although this place was meant to be far warmer than Sycamore Heights, Della had little faith in the weather. She shivered, shutting the fridge and pulling her suitcases into the living room.

After ten minutes of struggling to loosen a wheel on her suitcase from the threads that connected the two carpets, she gave up, going instead to close the shutters. She gripped them tightly, looking out over the bayou below. In the distance, she could see a small dock and a rope swing. Through the cracks in the densely growing oaks, the lights from the town of Moss Hollow flooded through, illuminating the stagnant swamp.

Della swore she saw something lurking beneath the murky water, creating tiny ripples near the bank. She shook her head, smiling. This place was going to fuel her imagination and then some.

She closed the shutters, latching them together. She strode through the living room, grabbing a suitcase she hoped was full of clothes as she walked down the hallway. She yawned loudly, jetlag and exhaustion finally catching up to her. She pushed open the door to the bedroom sleepily, plopping face-first onto the bed. Della was beyond caring at this point, though she noted with appreciation that the bedding looked brand new. Rolling over, she stared at the ceiling, listening to the croaks of frogs and the buzz of passing cars.

Even with all that was wrong or missing, this place seemed like it could be quite a perfect fit. Better yet, here she had free internet.

What more could she ask for?

~ ~ ~

Della woke early the next morning, partially from excitement and partly from the fact that she had slept with a spring poking into her rib cage for seven hours. She showered and dressed, put a few things away, then headed for the bus stop she had spotted the night before, counting her pocket change as she went.

The bus ride around the town was choppy and full of colorful characters, but short. Honestly, Della would have loved to stay on that bus all day just watching the world go by, but alas, she only had a small amount of change and a destination that was eagerly awaiting her presence. She hopped out of the bus, lingering for a moment, the rising sun casting an orange glow on the town.

Just outside of New Orleans, the slowly disappearing town of Moss Hollow stood. The pictures Della had seen were nothing compared to the sight that greeted her eyes. Moss Hollow was a stereotypical Louisiana town, full of historical buildings, voodoo shops, and horse-drawn carriages. All ironically situated around a cemetery.

She smiled, forcing herself forward, digging in her book bag for the letter that had prompted her journey to this masterpiece of a town. The letter gleamed in the sunlight as she opened it, scanning it for the address of the newspaper; One-Eight-Three, South Berkshire.

One-Seven-Five was to her left. A small little convenience store that was currently having a sale on all the busted cans of soup from the last delivery. She walked on. One-Eight-Zero was a thrift shop called *The Dusty Attic*. She walked a tad more, her pace quickening as her destination neared. She stopped in front of the door, looking up at the sign above her. One-Eight-Three South Berkshire! The place where she would finally—

A long resounding honk filled the air from a steamboat that was drifting along the long bayou ten miles behind her as she stared at the crooked sign above her in bewilderment.

The sign clearly read *P.J. Mavericks Law*, though Della

did not believe it. She looked down at the letter in her hand, checking to make sure she had not misread the address. To her confusion, the addresses matched each other. This was the place.

But why on Earth would she be sent here?

Curious, she stepped inside the law firm. A black and white cat hissed at her as she walked towards the line of chairs to her right. A short, stocky lady sitting at the front desk waved at Della, beckoning her forward. Della looked around nervously. She immediately appreciated the cleanliness of her surroundings. The walls were painted with a rich olive lacquer, and as she walked towards the woman at the front desk, the wood floors sparkled. The patrons that sat behind her all looked equally bent-out-of-shape that she had been called directly to the front desk. She smiled apologetically over her shoulder, though she took joy in their disgruntled faces.

The lady at the front desk smiled, chewing very miasmic smelling bubblegum.

"P.J. Mavericks Law, how may I help you?" She asked. She had the same bloodshot eyes and pale skin as the young man that worked at Ambrose Apartments, only she was much more cheerful.

"Hello, Miss. . ." Della scanned the woman for a name tag. "Miss Ambrose, I have a letter here with an address, but I think—" Della began. The two must be related.

"Name?" The woman asked kindly, cutting her off.

"Oh, but I don't think—"

"It's all right suga,'" The woman said, blowing a rather large pink bubble and popping it with her bacon-grease-glossed lips. "Name please."

Della sneezed. The black and white cat had jumped up onto the desk, watching her. Its face was almost human-like, and it stared at her with a rather judgmental look. Della shooed it away from her. She was slightly allergic to felines. She sneezed again as the cat reached out to claw her hand.

"Name please," Lenora repeated, patting the kitty lightly on its head.

Della looked around exasperatedly, rolling her eyes. "Delphee C. Coleman." She sighed.

"Oh! Yes! The intern!" The woman exclaimed with a tiny clap of her pudgy hands. She stood revealing just how short she really was. She only came up to about Della's shoulders, and Della was neither exceptionally tall nor average height. The woman swung her way out from behind the desk, her long poodle skirt swishing behind her. "Right this way, honey."

"I think there has been a mistake," Della said, following reluctantly, the cat at her heels, growling quietly.

Ms. Durnell knew how much she hated the thought of working a nine to five office job. . . If this was some cruel prank to scare her into being a 'better student,' she would have Patricia's head before she even left the airport. Possibly not metaphorically.

"P.J. Mavericks neva' makes mistakes," Lenora informed her, seeming slightly offended. Her accent seemed to be growing with every sentence.

Della smiled weakly, following the woman down a flight of stairs and into a thin room that resembled the first, only it was lined with many bookshelves and display cases. Some of the shelves were lined with stacks of leather-bound journals, others housed encyclopedias about everything and anything you could imagine. Between the shelves and cases were cork boards, full of red string, newspaper clippings, and photos. Some had giant gold stars on them, others had a note that said whoever made the boards could do better.

In the distance, Della could hear the dull rumble of muffled voices and the click-clack of computer keys.

Della peered through an open door to her left, seeing a tiny, grungy kitchen. Through another door, she could see a little library, and behind another, there was a room full of suits, ties, scrubs, and other government official outfits.

Della's heart skipped a beat. *Where the Hell am I?* She wondered.

Lenora turned sharply down another hallway that ended with a large mahogany door. She knocked several times in an out of sync pattern, then turned to leave.

"He will be with you in a moment, dear." She smiled. As she walked away, she stopped abruptly, turning back around to stare into Della's eyes. She seemed to have lost her cheerful demeanor. "Do not touch anything. Do not move." She hissed, then picked up the hem of her skirt and left, blowing another bubble with her stinking gum. "Have a nice day!" Della heard her call as she rounded the corner.

Della shook her head in disbelief, leaning casually against the wall behind her. The cat had jumped up onto a nearby pedestal below an intricate painting of a pilgrim. It observed her, still growling. Della nodded in its direction, turning her attention towards the display case in front of her.

A rather strange arrangement of items filled it in a haphazard looking way. An otherwise ordinary-looking sandstone rock had a plaque beneath it that read 'Lincoln Valley, Nevada.' Behind that hung a small, black and white photograph of an eccentric looking man—even by Della's standards—sporting a tinfoil cone on his head. He pointed behind him at a heavily guarded facility, giving the photographer a thumbs up. Hanging above the rock, suspended only by a bent piece of thin fishing line, was a crudely constructed model of a UFO. She leaned in close to the glass, ignoring Lenora's cryptic warning, reaching out to touch it.

The door next to her opened with a bang.

The cat hissed, jumping off the pedestal, running from the scene, smashing into walls as it scurried away. Della turned to see the same man from the photograph standing in the open doorway. His head tilted to the side as he looked over his half-moon spectacles, a dazed, open-mouthed expression on his face. He looked as eccentric as ever wearing a brightly colored collared shirt paired with a pair of expensive suit pants. Stranger still, he was barefoot, his toes wiggling up and down as he squinted at her. He had dark spiky hair, and his face was slightly wrinkled, though he carried himself with an air that made him look older than he was.

"Yes?" He asked wistfully, scratching his untamed beard.

Della straightened, holding out her hand. She had been practicing what she was going to say since the moment she left Ms. Durnell's office. Nowadays, first impressions are everything. "Delphee C. Coleman, you are?" She asked, hoping her smile wasn't too big. She didn't want to look like a hopeless fool.

The man smiled. "Splendid! Delphee C. Coleman!" He paused, adjusting his glasses with nothing but two fingers that left greasy stains on the lenses. "What's the 'C' stand for?"

"Uh. . . Chrysanthemum, my middle name." Della replied, twiddling her thumbs.

The man's smile faded. "Poor thing. Must be the least favorite child. What a shame. . ." He said quietly.

That little statement was, in fact, truth, but Della was too prideful not to prove it wrong, nonetheless. "My parents thought they'd only have one girl. Therefore, I got the street my grandmother grew up on and her favorite flower." She explained, somewhat absentmindedly.

She was very engrossed in the things in the display case next to her. A ceramic footprint balanced near the top of the case, showered in green light from a cheap-looking Bigfoot nightlight.

The man leaned forward, dropping his voice to nothing but a whisper. "Were you made fun of a lot?" He asked, looking thoroughly concerned.

"No," Della said, smiling tightly. "Everyone calls me Della. There's less shame in it."

"Della! Yes, that rolls off the tongue much better! Well, why don't you come in?" He turned on his heels, whispering

'Della' under his breath several times.

Della inhaled quietly, weighing her options in her head. Eventually, she let her stiff shoulders relax and walked inside his office, making sure to leave the door open.

Just in case.

The man's office smelled strange, like all the smells she associated with her childhood had been mixed up into one ugly potpourri. Every inch of his office was lined with brightly colored candles, but Della had a feeling that the smell was not coming from them.

The man skipped over to his desk, spinning a giant globe as he went, chuckling to himself.

"I am Percival James Mavericks. Pleased to meet you." He bowed deeply before taking a seat behind his desk, whose legs were all mismatched. "I also prefer a nickname. You may call me Mavericks."

He sat patiently for a moment, waiting for Della to respond.

She smiled like she would have if a small child had told her something important in a voice she couldn't quite understand. "Oh, good to know." She despised children.

Mavericks wiggled around in his chair, smirking happily. "As you can see, this is no ordinary law firm." He gestured around him. "We may make bank above, but down here—here we make people's dreams come true!" He kept nodding at the patchwork chair in front of his desk, gesturing for her to sit, but in reality, it looked like he was having a stroke.

Della sat, taking in the rest of his office. Everything in there would have seemed out of place if it wasn't for the thing you saw before it. A reptilian armchair stood ominously in the corner, shrunken heads hung from the ceiling, old jukeboxes and arcade games hummed low, dying music, the maps crudely taped to the walls depicted all the strange and unexplainable creatures of the world and next to his desk sat a cotton candy machine. It looked like he had raided some freak show that had gone out of business.

Della found that absolutely wonderful.

"Della, I spend hours a day searching for talent like your own. Someone who writes as if the words they type are the breaths they breathe." He made an odd typing motion in the air, his eyes crossing outwards. "That they can write as well as they believe." Mavericks leaned forward, crossing his fingers in front of him. This motion reminded her of Ms. Durnell, which suddenly sent her on edge.

Della rolled her eyes, leaning back in her armchair. "I believe I write better than I believe." She said, gesturing to her shirt, which gave yet another nod to her obsession with cryptozoology. She suddenly realized why this man had called her here. "What's your story? Did you get abducted by aliens? Family drowned by merpeople? Oh no, I see! A lone yeti flogged you in the Himalayas!" She said facetiously. "Listen, I have heard it all before. Let me guess; you want me to write a little snippet about your tragic experience on my blog. Maybe even write you a biography? Let me guess; you want to pay me to make you famous then sue me in the future? Fat chance." Della said calmly.

"Although a biography would be nice, that is not why I have brought you here. Before you, beneath the law firm, just outside the door you left open, is a printing press. The old-fashioned kind. We call her Linda. . ." His eyes trailed off for a moment. He shook himself, returning his gaze to her. "My people scour the world for the strangest, most outlandish stories out there. My dear Della, this is the home of *The Utopian Courier!*" Mavericks exclaimed.

Della forced her face into a false look of confusion. She had been following *The Utopian Courier* since she could read. To say she was excited to be sitting in front of this man was an understatement.

It was common knowledge among the people of her expertise that a mysterious newspaper that refused to go digital floated around the south. This paper compiled stories from throughout the world, covering subjects from *JFK's* assassination to accounts of the Mongolian Death Worm. *The Utopian Courier* was a prestigious paper, and there was no way to sign up to receive it if you lived outside of the South. On the offshot chance, you received the paper, it was because it found you. Not the other way around. Della had been dying to get her hands on *The Utopian Courier* for years, and now she was sitting just shy of where it was printed.

Della cleared her throat to keep from squealing with excitement. "I've caught wind of your paper. But of course, I could not get a copy, you know for obvious reasons." Della sighed to herself.

"It would be different if we had better funding," Mavericks explained, nodding sadly.

". . . I thought you said you made good money upstairs?"

"No, no, no! . . . Well yes. . . But you see, I do not collect much of that money. Just enough to keep the lights on and feed myself. Everything is under my name, of course, but do I look like the type of person that would spend his days working for a law firm? For the government? Selling people's souls?" He shook his head. "No, I am sure I don't. I would be awfully disappointed in myself if I did. I promised an old friend that when he passed on, I would take care of his children. I pursue my dreams down here, and Miss Lenora Ambrose keeps up the front, hiring ignorant lawyers and whatnot." He smiled wistfully. "It's genius, really. Who would expect a hole in the wall place like this to house such a secret beneath its floorboards?"

Della nodded. "So, what's the problem? Why do you need my expertise?"

"To put it simply, I work with a babbling band of blubbering baboons!" Mavericks whispered energetically. "And you say we didn't evolve from monkeys. . ."

Della shrugged, sitting forward. "No ape-like creatures have webbed fingers and toes. Except us."

"Agree to disagree." He said kindly, though his eyes told her he was extremely offended.

Della looked him up and down, wondering very seriously if there was something wrong with this poor man's brain.

"So, you need me to write?"

He nodded vigorously, his glasses falling off. "The way you write is captivating, even for someone like me who knows everything about everything and then some. Our Cryptozoology Department lacks in people as well read as you. Right now, we have my. . . *son* . . . and two others. All of which cannot write and do not necessarily believe. I mean, the way you covered the broad topic of Nessie was beautiful! You really put the 'spiracy' in 'conspiracy.'" He laughed to himself, causing Della to raise an eyebrow. He looked up, clearing his throat, his face darkening. "Truth be told, my company is dying. My readers are getting bored; they are starting to think my paper is a joke. I fear that if I do not find— excuse my pun—fresh blood, then countless people will stop reading, causing countless others to lose their jobs."

Della looked away, taking in his office again. No one other than her mother had ever truly encouraged her to write about stuff like this. This could be her big break. Plus, unless she was mistaken, it sounded like this was an actual job. Not just an internship.

"If I agree," Della began, putting her fingertips together like she did whenever she was going to make Ms. Durnell an offer she could not refuse. "I work by myself. No common office, no 'partner,' no one to help me. And no candles." She said quickly. The odd smell in the room was giving her a headache, and she did not want to take any chances.

"The only private office is upstairs. It has been a massive junk drawer for quite some time, but I think I can find someone to help you clear it out." He winked.

Della stood. "And the candles?"

"None shall grace your presence."

She smiled slowly, holding out her hand for him to

shake.

He snorted. "Oh, no, I don't touch people." He lowered his voice to a feverish whisper. "People carry diseases."

Once again, Della nodded like she was talking to a child.

Mavericks smiled brightly, bowing. "I'll see you tomorrow, Miss Coleman."

~CHAPTER THREE~

This morning, Della had time to enjoy and soak in the town around her thoroughly. Upon further investigation—just like her fridge—it seemed the 'law firm' was the only immaculate business in Moss Hollow. Even the cobblestone sidewalk she was jogging along was falling apart. Stones the size of potholes were missing here and there, and immense quantities of this strange, lime-green moss grew between the cracks—and just about everywhere else she looked. Half the streetlamps were busted and full of cobwebs. The bus stops and fire hydrants should have been taped off; they were absolutely a safety hazard.

The buses she had reluctantly used did not fare any better. Their paint peeling, their hubcaps rusted to the point where they were cracking apart, and the seats inside were duct-taped together to keep stuffing from falling out.

As the town whizzed past her, she saw the manicured swampy lawns of colonial houses that looked drastically out of place next to the crumbling town and bubbling swamp.

Stopping herself from squealing with excitement like an idiot, she smiled at the person sitting next to her. A young girl with a pair of old yellowed headphones. She nodded to Della, giving a weak thumbs up before turning away.

Everything was overwhelming and exciting at the same

time. This place was such a drastic change from her home-town. . .

She couldn't be happier.

Apart from the scenery, Della was still trying to wrap her head around the fact that she was going to be writing for *The Utopian Courier*. She could not help but smile as she strolled the aisles in the little convenience store, picking up something for breakfast. Although Ambrose Apartments was well catered, Della—impatient as ever—didn't have time to wait for Richmond 'Richie' Ambrose to show up for work. Something cheap and ready-made would work just fine. Ramen noodles counted as a breakfast food, right? Della sighed. Her mother would be very disappointed in her choice of food.

~ ~ ~

Days in Moss Hollow were wonderfully warm, the hot end of Summer breezes carrying banjo music and the pick-pick-picking of guitars. Smiling, Della made her way up to her new office. Back in Sycamore Heights, she would have done away with her camouflage shorts and tank tops on the last day of July, but here she would have at least another month to reign in warm weather. There was already sweat forming on her forehead, but she didn't mind.

Though it seemed Mavericks had tried, no one had agreed to help her clean out the storage room, leaving Della to sift through decades of junk. The room was gigantic, filled to the brim with water-stained boxes and miscellaneous junk. It had taken half the day just to make a path to the window at the back of the room.

Most of the boxes were full of old police reports that needed to be filed away or simply tossed since they were covered in coffee stains, but there were a couple of boxes full of odd stationery and other things she kept to fill her office. There was even a tiny jukebox that Mavericks had most likely thrown in here once he got the bigger ones. With her headphones in, Della danced around her new office, cleaning, sorting, and labeling. There were tall inset cabinets on the walls that she used some spare yellow masking tape to label, placing all the old reports inside. She had no idea why Mavericks had not done this to begin with; she never understood people who threw things away, especially when those things could help you with future research.

Occasionally, she would take large boxes full of things she did not need down to the sidewalk with a sign labeled free, taking care not to step on the tail of the paint-splattered black and white cat. She was pretty sure it didn't like her, but it did love to watch her from the hallway, following her up and down the stairs. Lenora had helped her a couple of times, chatting Della's ear off as they carried the heavier boxes between them. Lenora, Della realized almost immediately, was not the person you should entrust secrets to. Her lips were looser than the baggy t-shirt Della wore. She had covered everything from the love triangle in the common office upstairs, to the fact that Richie was her cousin in excruciating detail, but Della didn't have the heart to ask her to stop talking.

When the last of the heavy boxes had been brought downstairs, Della quickly thanked her for her help, then returned to the mess in her office, somewhat irritated to find another helpful soul working in there. He nearly plowed into her as he struggled with a stack of boxes Della knew was packed with dirty old plates, which fell from his arms and crashed to the floor. He automatically lunged to the floor, mumbling under his breath as he picked up the broken pieces. Della sneezed as she bent down to help, but he ripped a large piece from her fingers.

"Ei've got it. . ." The boy sighed.

He looked up, running a hand through his short curly black hair. He had splotches of tan on his rich chocolate skin—he obviously had vitiligo, a condition in which the pigment is lost from areas on the skin, causing whitish patches to appear. His eyes were a very striking amber color, and he had very thick eyelashes, probably a result of allergies. He smiled feverishly, looking embarrassed.

"Sorry, it's been a rough day." He admitted, taking hold of Della's hand as she offered to help him off the floor.

"No harm done." Della smiled.

The boy shrugged, brushing off his pinstriped pants. The longer she stared at him, the more he reminded her of someone, or rather something, but she could not quite put her finger on what.

"Ei'm Maximilian." He smiled, shaking her hand. He had a thick, high-octave Irish accent and smelled strongly of cologne.

In turn, he stared at her, his eyes lingering on the blue hair extension she had pinned in today. He furrowed his eyebrows in a sort of detached confusion, rubbing his shadowy muttonchops.

A sneeze. "I'm Delphee, but you can call me Della." She smiled sweetly as she rubbed her nose with the back of her hand. It seemed this town wanted to suffocate her with all these horrible smells. His cologne was positively gagging her.

Maximilian slowly let go of her hand, smiling awkwardly. "So," He began, walking over to the nearest garbage can and throwing away the broken pieces of stained fine China. "How are ya settlin' in?"

Della shrugged. It had only been two days, and she had not taken the time to ask herself that question. Maximilian smiled, nodding to himself. They stood awkwardly for a moment, ignoring the snobby passing lawyers as they spilt their coffee on the floor.

Or had they?

There certainly were not any coffee stains, though one guy had spilled half his cup on the intricate rug before them.

"Do ya need help with anythin'?" Maximilian asked rather quickly after a moment of staring at the spot Della's eyes were fixed to. "Mavericks said Ei had tuh, but Ei don' want tuh bother ya."

Della appreciated honesty. "If you have time, I guess it wouldn't bother me too much."

They worked together over the next few days, Max—as she had begun to call him—filling the silence by telling her a little about himself. He was the I.T. guy for both the newspaper and the law firm, much to his disdain. He told her—the tan parts of his face glowing red—that he had grown up as a street rat until one-night Mavericks found him breaking into his car. Instead of taking him to the police, Mavericks had welcomed him into his family with open arms, offering him a place to stay and work.

Max had a very soft aura to him; the kind that made you think he wouldn't hurt a fly. He shared his love for science whenever he found it necessary, and although he grew up believing in the strange wonders around him, he kept himself and others grounded.

Della found that once he finished talking, she had nothing exciting to say about her life. Though Max thought otherwise. After some prompting, she told him about the defining moments in her life that led up to her coming here. Things like her grandmother dying, or how many times the school had threatened to expel her. Her short existence seemed very monotonous, but he hung on her every word as if he was watching an action movie. He took particular joy in the retelling of all her arguments with the school.

He asked again how she was settling in, and she answered with sincere honesty that she was quite enjoying herself. She had not done much exploring just yet, but she loved this little place with all her heart. And the people were not too much of a hindrance.

~ ~ ~

Now that her office was cleaned and decorated to her liking, Della could finally get to work. This morning she sat downstairs with the rest of *The Utopian Courier* employees at a gigantic round oak table. Mavericks paced back and forth in front of them like King Arthur, his eyes closed in concentration. Max stood leaning against a bookshelf in the corner, trying to stay awake as were most of the non-caffeinated employees. Lenora was behind Mavericks, a sparkly pink clipboard in hand, awaiting instructions. Mavericks stopped abruptly, turning to face the table.

"In just a few short weeks, begins our busiest time of the year, October. People are going to expect the goriest, bloodiest, scariest articles of the year." He roared, smiling as the room filled with quiet claps of approval. "In saying that," He began, looking nervously over his shoulder at Lenora. "We will be putting other projects on hold."

Every person besides Della looked to the person next to them, a look of confusion on their faces. A woman near the front of the group raised her hand. Mavericks nodded.

"I have been working on an article about the Salem Witch Trials for the past month. I have spent far too much money and time on it. You cannot expect me just to put it on the back burner." She said. It seemed she was biting her tongue to keep from saying what was really on her mind.

"My dear, witches are a large part of Halloween, aren't they? All I am saying is that things like assassination theories, secret service interviews, modern mysteries, and things like that, will not be published until November. You may continue any project you are working on in your free time, but when you are here, you will be working on something downright spooky." Mavericks explained rather coldly.

Max yawned loudly, causing several people to roll their eyes. Obviously Della was the only one excited to be here this morning. Maybe she was the only one excited to be assigned a topic, too.

"Lenora and I have compiled a list of topics for each of you to begin work on. Finish whatever you have started for next month's issue, but come October first, I expect you all to be in the All Hollow's Eve mood." Mavericks said, gesturing for Lenora to start handing out papers.

When the person next to Della—a burly looking man who had been typing away on his computer—received his paper, he practically spit his coffee on everyone in the room.

"You want me to stop researching the Illuminati to begin writing about the difference between modern murder and Pagan rituals?" He asked in disbelief.

"Someone had to do it, Howard. It's not like you have anything going on." Mavericks laughed, eyeing him oddly. "Join up with Frankie, please. I'm sure she will be of some assistance."

The room filled with muffled snorts of laughter. The burly man shook his head, scowling deeply. He angrily folded up his piece of paper and stuffed it in his pocket, grabbing his laptop and leaving.

"Here you go, suga'." Lenora said, handing Della her paper.

Her assignment was to research the cryptids of Louisiana. Especially the lesser-known ones. She looked up at Mavericks, who smiled and winked, turning around to open the tin cabinet behind him. Inside the cabinet hung a beat up old whiteboard marked with sporadic instructions and lists.

"Week one's issue will be called Murder Market. Howard, Frankie, Lisa, and Gabriella will be our featured writers. Irene, you will be head editor for most of the month, but I know you have a weaker stomach, so Norman will be taking over for the first week.

"Week two will be called Origin of Holidays: Halloween and will cover—well the name is explanatory. Nick, Rosa, Anderson, I'm leaving this to the three of you after your beautiful reports on Saint Patrick's Day earlier this year. Feel free to write about the coming harvest and traditions of famous places throughout the world.

"Weeks three and four will be Witch Weeks. Samuel, Gloria, Alexis, and Sue will be featured. Interview the local practitioners, voodoo shop owners—even go to churches to ask opinions. Readers love drama. If you need bus fare money or plane tickets, go ask Milliano. We have about three hundred set aside for travels through November." Mavericks explained, then caught himself. "And Sue, please keep the arguments with Pastor Davis to a minimum. We don't want a repeat of last year."

This time Della's coworkers did not try to hide their laughter. The room burst into noise immediately, leaving an older woman in the corner red-faced, though she smiled.

"He was a righteous asshole! It's not my fault those teens egged his house." Sue laughed.

"Really? Are you sure you didn't give them his address?" Mavericks asked, smiling kindly. Everyone laughed louder, whispering to each other. "All right, everyone settle down. Week five is Cryptid Corner!" There were cheers. "Featured writers will be Alexis and Bart. Oh! I can't forget the other one. I would like you all to give a warm welcome to Della, the newest addition to our little company!"

The room exploded in applause, the nearest people coming over to shake Della's hand and introduce themselves. She smiled, feeling her cheeks catch on fire. She hadn't expected Mavericks to do that, she obviously underestimated his opinion of her.

"Alright Couriers, go team go!" Mavericks shouted.

The room emptied quickly; some people were still laughing about Sue as they made their way back to their desks. As Della stood to leave, Mavericks caught her by the arm, spinning her around to face him.

"I am counting on you, Miss Coleman." He said, staring at her in a way that made her feel like he could see into her soul. For some odd reason, she felt he wasn't talking about the paper.

"I will not let you down," Della said with a confidence she had never felt before.

Mavericks nodded. He stared over his shoulder for a moment at Lenora, who was cleaning up empty coffee cups. He looked back at Della, lost in thought.

"I—Since you are new to this little town, I would suggest looking into our strange events first. Maybe even the most recent ones? Maximilian can show you to the man who gets us all our police reports." He smiled, then shook his head. "Of course, only if you need him."

With that, he swept past her. Lenora looked up from the table, eyeing Della with trepidation. She looked back at Max—who had curled up in a ball, asleep on the floor—then walked over to her.

"Be careful, dear. Don't stay out too late." Lenora said, her eyes full of worry.

~CHAPTER FOUR~

Strangers

Found in the rubble of things Della and Max had cleaned out of her office, was a giant swiveling chalkboard. Della had opted to keep it and was extremely glad she had. She stood, leaning casually against her desk, arms crossed over her chest, staring at the things she had taped, tacked, and hammered to it.

She squinted at the newspaper clippings and articles, her 'thinking eyebrow' raised. Louisiana was one of those states that had a plethora of weird and wonderful. From creatures like the Louisiana Thunderbird to swamp monsters and spirits, it was a cryptozoologist's Heaven. Or at least it should be. How was she going to pick which creatures to add to her article? How was she going to write a cohesive piece without stealing things she had already written on her blog? She glanced at the tea-pot shaped clock on her desk, pulling at her fingernails nervously.

The world knew of Thunderbirds, the Lizard Man of Scape Ore and Skunk Apes. She needed something different, something exciting, something new.

Maybe she could go with a precautionary tale of Rougarous, Werewolves, and general lycanthropy. But would the rest of her coworkers and Mavericks see that as a safe option? Furthermore, hadn't Mavericks said he wanted the lesser-known creatures? Rougarous were technically lesser known. . . A giant wolf-man that supposedly fed on disobedient Catholics? Pretty intriguing.

Maybe the Honey Island Swamp Monster would be a better bet. Who wouldn't want to read about a hairy, gray, manlike alligator?

She rubbed her temples, sourly staring at her 'evidence board.' Her head began to pound, forcing her to look away. At least for now, she would go with the Rougarou storyline. She turned on her heels, swirling her computer towards her. She had saved a couple of local conspiracy blogs to her home page, scanning them for recent sightings. Interestingly enough, it was fabled that there was a werewolf run bookstore right here in town. It wasn't exactly what she was looking for, but it would work for now.

Tomorrow would be a day of discovery. One she hoped would put even the greatest adventurer to shame.

~ ~ ~

Della had printed out the map of Moss Hollow as soon as she got to work the next morning, determined to learn her surroundings so she could walk instead of taking the bus everywhere.

Standing in the dingy communal kitchen, she examined the map, all the while making herself a coffee cut with Holy Water and hot chocolate. The whole town was a perfect circle. Right down to the way the streets curved around the businesses and all the cul de sacs full of homes. All of which surrounded the cemetery.

The bayou was the most prominent thing on the map, taking up most of the town. It made a swirling pattern that reminded Della of a hypnotic swirl. Staring at the map, she began to wonder why Mavericks had told her to research the town when there wasn't much about it on the internet. Della leaned forward, distractedly reaching for her steaming cup of joe. Ambrose Motel was not listed on the map; neither was P.J. Mavericks Law.

She made a mental note of this as she left the law firm, stuffing the map in her pocket. She walked along in the Louisiana heat, her glasses slowly transitioning into sunglasses. Irritatingly happy passersby waved to her as she walked, making her quicken her pace. A restaurant called *The Burning Tankard* tried to beckon her and the general store offered her a sample of cheesecake. She politely refused, keeping on until she turned into a small bookstore. She had left all of her 'frivolous possessions' at home and was in dire need of something to keep her occupied. Plus, she wanted to pick up a small gift for Max to thank him for helping around her office.

The book shop was nice enough, though it was nothing compared to the ones in Sycamore Heights. It had no cafe, no reading area; it was just full of books and odds and ends. The books were organized by author and color, sprigs of delicious smelling herbs hung near the doorway, and displays of local candy and soap companies dotted the floor. She walked along the shelves, running her hands along the titles of the glorious tomes before her, searching for something that piqued her interest. Surprisingly enough, Della had never been one for history unless it was oddball history. Glancing around the store, she walked on until she came to a section full of puzzles and games, finding a rounder full of tins that contained word magnets. She smiled, grabbing one full of Shakespearean words and phrases. Max ought to enjoy that.

Della walked past the fantasy books—though she longed to buy one—watching as a young man around her age struggled with an armful of books. As he tried with little effort to steady the books and grab another, someone bumped into him, sending his books to the floor, the paperbacks bending, the dust jackets of the hardbacks ripping off. What angered Della was not the fact the books had been ruined, but the fact that the person who had bumped into him didn't stop to help or even look back.

She audibly rolled her huge brown eyes. She had no idea why her parents had wondered why she didn't have faith in humanity.

Irritated, Della took it upon herself to help the young man, forgetting her own endeavors, which consisted of begrudgingly searching through local pamphlets on tourist traps. The boy's face burned with anger and embarrassment.

"Thanks." He mumbled as she handed him a book that had strayed a little too far.

She nodded, scooping half of the books into her arms. He looked up at her with a strange, sorrowful look, like no one had shown him this kind of simple kindness before.

Della shrugged. "No problem. Need me to help you get these up to the cashier?" She asked.

He nodded apologetically, starting to smile. This melancholy little smile of his was quite infectious, seemingly spreading over and onto Della's lips. Her cheeks and ears flushed red. Many boys had done that to her before, but none had done it with just a smile.

He led her to the cashier with the expertise of a mountain man who knew the woods like—maybe even better than—he knew his reflection. He paid, the woman at the counter offering him a box for all his goods, then thanked Della yet again as she paid for her tiny tin of magnets. She shrugged again, assuring him that it was her pleasure.

"Plus," She said as she dug into her martian-head-shaped purse for change. "I'm willing to help anyone with your taste in books." She smiled, nodding towards his box. It seemed he had a thing for fantasy romance.

"I have high expectations." He explained, opening his jacket to reveal a *Twilight* shirt that showed which love interest he had voted for like it was a college football team. "Most of which are caused by the blasted words authors pour their hearts and souls into, but it's worth it." He tapped one of the books he had bought, his smile brightening.

Della chuckled. "You must be reading wrong because clearly, the vampire was the superior choice."

The boy rolled his eyes. "Yeah, and pigs can fly."

"You never know, genetics is a growing field. I bet you in ten years that little statement will be invalid." She said as she walked past him.

"I will hold you to that." He called after her.

By now, Della had utterly forgotten what her reason for taking a walk around town was. No one had ever done that to her before. He waved at her as she left the shop, his eyes losing their shimmer with her every step.

~ ~ ~

No one had ever cared about his well-being like that. Not Pops, not his mother, and most likely not his father. That girl with the green hair did, however. She had a fiery spirit to her. He smiled wider.

What was he doing with his life, sitting here, spending

his paycheck on such a frivolous purchase? This was about as useful as undoing a paperclip and shoving it in the eraser of a pencil. He barely had time to sit and read the texts he received each morning, let alone read all these. There just weren't enough hours in the day, not enough days in the week, not enough weeks in a year, not enough years in a lifetime.

He sighed.

"Mind if I leave these here for a moment?" He asked the cashier. She shrugged her approval, and he ran out of the shop.

Things hadn't changed for him for a long time. It was always the same thing every day. He got up, he helped his grandfather around the mortuary, dug a few graves with his mother, got some groceries, helped at the police station, came home to make lunch, then did it all over again. Same old same, like some sort of torture.

As he walked along the streets, following loosely behind the girl with the bright green hair, he realized just how done with the concept of his life he was. What was the point in getting up every day just to repeat the same events the next?

No one ever gave him answers to that question. All they ever told him was to do his job and stop worrying so much.

"Stop thinking Porter; you'll get yourself killed." They would say.

Jokes on them, Porter was thinking very hard right now. Thinking about all the things he had done in the twenty years of life he had lived so far. Sometimes it felt like he had done far too many bad things for all the things he had done right.

He was smiling despite himself as he followed the crowd of people around him, trying to catch up to her. She walked along, completely unaware of her surroundings, texting away on her phone.

If only the girl with the neon green hair knew that Porter had never been so excited to talk to someone in his entire life.

~ ~ ~

Della's phone buzzed in her hand again. Sebastian hadn't spoken to her in a week, which meant he was not going to leave her alone for the next two. She walked along the sidewalk, rolling her eyes as she replied to his dumb little GIF from one of his favorite television shows. She paused, leaning against the stoplight, lazily pressing the pedestrian crossing button as she typed away on her phone. It beeped, making her think she could cross. She hit the little paper airplane send button, smirking at what Sebastian was saying about his day.

He had stuck up for himself in P.E., talked one of his peers into holding a D&D meetup at his house, and found— halfway across the street, someone grabbed her around the midriff as a car zoomed past her.

She fell backward, landing on top of whoever had saved her, staring blankly in front of her. She would have been a Della-shaped pancake if it was not for her savior. When that piece of information finally clicked in her brain, paranoia and panic kicked in, which prompted her lungs to forget how to work. She looked around in horror, breathing heavily, shaking all over. Her mother was going to finish the job that speeding Subaru hadn't when she told her what had just happened. Della made to stand, crushing her savior's fingers as she did.

"Sorry," She said breathlessly, slightly dizzy from the lack of oxygen currently reaching her lungs.

"It's fine, are you all right?" A voice asked.

Della nodded, shrugging to herself. "Oh, yes, I'm perfectly wonderful." She said wistfully, unable to move her eyes away from the road. "Marvelous, sublime, delightful." She said, counting all her fingers.

Her savior grabbed her loose hand, pulling her out of the road and safely back onto the sidewalk. She finally looked up into his face, realizing it was the boy from the bookstore. For some reason, this horrible near-death experience had forced her into observing his features. Della's only defense mechanism was to observe every tiny detail of her surroundings.

The boy's skin was the color of sand, his hair was so black it absorbed the same sunlight that made his green eyes glisten with worry. He wore a pair of dirty black jeans with holes in the knees and a dusty green denim jacket. Obviously, this was a cold day to everyone but Della.

Della wobbled on the spot to both their surprise as she stared at him. He caught her, looking around with a terrified expression on his face.

"Are you sure you are all right?" He asked.

She nodded, gently pulling away from his grip, snapping out of her trance. Handsome, prince-like guys had never been her type. Though she was grateful he had just saved her life;

she found him quite repulsive at the moment.

Book taste aside.

He sighed, beginning to smile again. She really wished he would not do that. It melted her a little bit.

"Thank you." She said, her rapid breaths finally slowing.

"It was the least I could do; you carried at least ten pounds of books for me." He said, scratching the back of his neck. "I'm Porter, by the way."

Della held out her hand for him to shake. He looked at it with a confused expression, then shook her hand roughly. His hands were soft, but they were dreadfully filthy and covered in small scrapes. He seemed to be examining her hands, as well. There was a purple gemstone on her middle finger, and her nails were painted with a glittery maroon lacquer. Once he finished his observations, he reluctantly released her hand.

"I'm Della." She stuttered. *Get it together*, she told herself.

There was a moment of awkward silence before he cleared his throat, smiling widely.

"Uh, do you need me to walk you anywhere?" He asked.

She stared at him for a moment, not knowing what exactly to say. ". . . No, I can handle myself. Thank you, though." She replied.

"You're welcome." He said with a curt nod. "Well . . . I have to go. Hey Max." He said, then left, once again looking forlorn and atrabilious.

Max appeared at her left, startling her right out of her black floral boots. He stood casually, holding a paper coffee cup in his trembling hands. He stared at Porter's disappearing form as he spoke. "What happened?"

"Nothing," Della said before she could stop herself.

~CHAPTER FIVE~

Curious, Is the Mind

"Hey, Coleman! Get run over recently?" Norman, one of the editors of *The Utopian Courier*, asked as he walked past Della, pushing her away from the sink in the community kitchen as she filled a soap stained glass bowl full of water.

She did not respond; instead, she emptied the shrimp flavored seasoning into the water, threw dried noodles in after it, and slammed the bowl full of ramen into the nearby microwave. People would not stop teasing her about her accident at the beginning of the week. These people seemed to care more about others' blunders than their jobs. She had begun to lock her office door since even the passing lawyers would tease her.

To say Della was annoyed was an understatement. Her head was pounding again. The bottle of sumatriptan she kept with her always was running low. Trying to save as much of her precious medicine as possible, she had resulted to using ibuprofen. Not that it helped.

"Awe, come on, Pluto, it's funny," Max said in his high, melodic, melancholy accent as he crept up behind her, watching her stare down the microwave. He had a bag of 'tayto' chips in his hand that he was munching away on.

"It is always funny when you are not the punchline," Della said through tight lips, wondering why Max had called her that.

Max giggled quietly, opening the mini-fridge and searching for his mason jar full of apple cider vinegar and fruit. Della grabbed her ramen, waiting for him to get some cereal.

"You are disgusting." Della breathed, catching a whiff of his tonic as he cracked the lid open.

He rolled his eyes. "Ya eat ramen every day. Breakfast, lunch, and dinner. Ei do believe ya cannot judge me on this one." He said as he followed her out of the kitchen and to her office.

It had come along quite nicely. She had found some old furniture at a local thrift shop for both her office and apartment and even got a couple of band posters to put up. If she was honest, she was overly proud of the work she had accomplished here. Max plopped down onto the little chaise lounge she had bought, kicking back and chowing down on his cereal. Della shook her head, sitting down at her desk.

"Do you know where the cat is?" She asked, opening her laptop. Her article was going pretty well. She had written about twenty-thousand words on the wolf-like monsters of the south, though she wasn't necessarily ecstatic with the topic.

Max choked on a blueberry from his apple cider vinegar.

"Hmm. . . That's what you get." Della said lazily.

When Max had stopped choking, he turned around to face her. "W—Why do ya ask about the cat?"

Della shrugged. "Animals help me de-stress." She said, scrolling through the Moss Hollow Tribune. Nothing unusual was ever posted, but she checked it anyway. Better safe than sorry.

"Ei—Ei haven' seen 'im—er—*it*, in a while." Max said.

Della peered over her glasses at him, raising a thin eyebrow. Max was chewing on the sleeve of his sweater, causing the wool to break apart. He had ruined many sweaters with that sick nervous habit of his.

"Right." Della said skeptically.

Not even an animal attack was sprinkled in between the reports of pie-eating contests and historical reenactments over the Summer. What kind of town was this? Della was thoroughly disappointed.

"Do you—" She stopped scrolling aimlessly through the Moss Hollow Tribune. "Huh." She said, reaching for her own lunch.

"What?" Max asked.

"There have been a couple of disappearances over the last few months, nothing strange really, just a bunch of kids, but today, one of the victims' parents were found stabbed to death in their home." Della said, reading through the article.

"Aye, Ei read 'bout that. Sad, really." Max said, though there was no emotion in his eyes.

Della sat back in her chair, munching away at her ramen. "Week one is murder week, right?" She asked, already knowing the answer.

Max nodded, scrolling through his phone.

"And we can. . . contribute to the issue even if we aren't featured writers?"

"Yeah, why?"

Della smiled, discarding her ramen and grabbing her holographic roller skates. Della was nothing if not a shoe connoisseur.

"Wait, where are ya goin'?" Max asked through a mouthful of cereal.

"To go ask Norman and Irene to call a couple people." Della replied, jotting down a few names.

"Why?" Max questioned, sounding a little alarmed.

"I'm going to go pay the people who found the bodies a little visit." Della responded, lingering in the doorway. "Don't leave the door open, thanks."

~ ~ ~

In her humble opinion, Norman and Irene were the most valuable members of *The Utopian Courier*. Without them, Della would not have been able to find the group of people who found the dead bodies. Better yet, she wouldn't have been able to arrange a meeting with them. They had asked to meet at a park during their outing today, which surprised Della. For a group of people who had found dead bodies, they seemed rather unperturbed.

Interviews had always bored Della. She was on the bird watchers time, not her own, and it irritated the Hell out of her. Back in Sycamore Heights, she would have gotten all the information she needed out of this ragtag group within ten minutes. Apparently, being the daughter of one of the most respected— feared, actually, not respected—men of a community helped you get your foot in the door.

The bird watchers led her through the park, stopping occasionally, to take pictures of herons, cranes, and other birds, until they turned off the path and into the tall grass, completely ignoring her.

"So," She said, tapping her foot a couple of times and clearing her throat to get people's attention. "As my associate said over the phone, I work for the Moss Hollow Tribune. We wanted to do an in-depth report on what you all witnessed." Della explained. Norman had even gone the extra mile to make her a fake name tag that read *Della Coleman, MHT Reporter*, which she wore on her dusty gray tweed jacket proudly.

Only half the bird watchers had heard her; the others were too engrossed in photographing a heron near a murky puddle. Della cleared her throat again, scaring the bird.

"Sorry, Miss Coleman." An older gentleman at the front of the group said. "Do—Do we *really* have to relive what happened?"

Della nodded sadly. The elderly man sighed.

"It was just a normal day; we were waiting at Bayou Gil's for a while—we usually meet there for breakfast before going bird watching. Manny Dixon and his wife were late, which we all agreed was unusual since they are usually here with their daughter before the rest of us." The man shook his head. "The girl went missing the other day. Her poor parents. Anyways, we all thought it would be best to check up on them, given the recent events." At that, he got choked up and could not continue speaking.

"It's all right Jimmie. . ." A woman that looked only slightly younger than him said. "Long story short, we arrived at their house. We knocked a couple of times, but they didn't answer, so I tried the door handle. It was unlocked, so we all went in." The woman inhaled sharply. "We found them in the kitchen."

Della was writing down essential parts of the story as the woman spoke. She looked over her shoulder at the trees, wondering how not to upset these fidgety people.

". . . Did your friends have any. . . enemies?" She asked quietly, clicking her pen a couple of times.

"I thought you said you were a reporter, Miss Coleman." The woman said.

"Eloise, she's just trying to help." A younger woman at the back said irritably.

Della nodded her agreement, eyeing the woman now known as Eloise. There was something odd about her. The way she wrung her hands nervously, the way she didn't blink as she stared at Della, the way she kept shifting her weight from one lousy ankle to the other. An average person would have chalked it up to her nerves, but Della was very far from being an average person.

"The Dixon's were nice people," Jimmie assured her.

"Some might say too nice," Eloise added, her eyes going cold.

Della locked eyes with her. "Why would you say that?"

Eloise opened and closed her mouth a couple of times, taking a half step back. "W—Well, everyone has their secrets." She stuttered.

Della nodded slowly. In the distance, a steamboat blew its whistle, startling the remaining birds. The birdwatchers gave a collective sigh, stowing away their cameras and 'Birds of The South' guides.

"What about their daughter? What was she like?"

Jimmie smiled. "Hyper little bugger, but sweet, nonetheless. They have an older daughter too. She lives somewhere in town. Hasn't talked to her parents in years, I suppose." He said sadly.

"Why not?" Della asked. "I don't mean to pry, but it might help."

"Didn't have a good relationship. Never talked about it much." Jimmie explained, scratching his short beard.

Della nodded, scratching away at her notepad. She could relate to that. Family was both a blessing and a curse. She was lucky to have the mother that she had, but the rest of her family was another story. However, no matter how annoyed she had ever gotten with her siblings, she would never stop talking to them. She couldn't imagine it. Her father was another story, though. One for another time perhaps. . .

Something was off about this whole situation. Every fiber of her being was telling her that.

"One more thing," She began. "Did you see, smell, hear, or find anything weird around the house?"

"What kind of question is that?" Eloise asked.

Jimmie sighed heavily. "Nothing much, although. . . Naw, I'm sure it was nothing. . ." Della looked at him expectantly, prompting him to continue. "I swore I saw a shadow around the corner. The police said they weren't dead for long before we arrived. . . I thought I saw someone lurking around back. Well maybe it was more of a. . . some*thing*."

Eloise went white. "I—I saw it too." She said quickly when she realized Della was staring at her again.

"Can you describe to me what it looked like? Did you notice leathery skin? How tall do you think it was?" Della asked.

"About four feet." Jimmie said.

"I saw it too, in the window. It was hideous! Looked like a monster." A man at the back said.

"I saw it's huge clawed hand! It looked all hairy and bloody." The woman who had been short with Eloise added.

"Did you tell the police any of this?" Della asked skeptically.

There was a collective shaking of heads.

Jimmie looked lost in thought as he rubbed his chin. "Y'know, that was another thing, wasn't it Glenn? There were scratch marks on the floor, weren't there? Almost like an animal had made them?" He asked, looking over his shoulder at one of the guys.

Glenn nodded.

Della furrowed her eyebrows. "How big were the markings?"

Glenn held up his arm—which was very thick and round, due to the fact he was well fed—and shook it. "About the size of my arm. But I doubt the animal was that big. It looked like the thing was digging."

"And you are sure these markings were new?" Della asked. Everyone nodded. "So, you think an animal broke into their house, grabbed a knife from the kitchen and stabbed the Dixon's to death?" She questioned skeptically.

"Stabbed?" Jimmie asked. "The poor Dixon's were ripped to shreds." He said, laughing darkly.

It seemed no one wanted to talk much after that, all the birdwatchers wallowing in sadness.

Hairy hands? People ripped into pieces like roast beef? Unless Della was mistaken, this was no ordinary murder. Perhaps she had rightfully chosen lycanthropy. And what of the missing girl? How did she tie into this?

"Well, thank you all for your time. I will be in touch." Della said politely, bowing to them all.

She stuffed her notebook into her book bag, turning

away from them all with a satisfied look on her face. All her life, she had had these odd sorts of feelings. There was no other way to describe it. These strange feelings were why she was so good at this little job. It gave her great joy to know that her gift wasn't tied to the town she hated so much, that it was still alive and thriving here in Moss Hollow.

To put it simply, Della Coleman just stumbled onto a huge mystery.

~CHAPTER SIX~

Emotions Are Fickle Things

Mavericks was standing outside her office door when she returned, an odd look on his face. Della smiled nervously, digging inside her pocket for her keys.

"I heard you went to chat with some witnesses. Find anything interesting?" He asked, stepping out of her way as she unlocked the door. Today he wore a pair of cargo pants, a high collared suit jacket, and a filigree patterned button-up. Still no shoes, however.

Della nodded. "Lots."

"Do I get the inside scoop?" He asked kindly, his eyes glowing like a child waiting for their Christmas presents.

"Several people saw something out of the ordinary. A furry hand?" Della said, telling him everything the birdwatchers had said. He listened intently, a look of concern on his face. "Personally, I think it's a Lycan. Rougarou maybe. I'll have to check some things out."

"Good thinking." Mavericks said, though it seemed like he wasn't truly standing in front of her right now. "There was another kidnapping a couple of days before you came here. You should see if there is any connection. You might want to ask Milliano for some help—"

"No, I'm good." Della interjected. "I don't play well with others." She laughed.

Mavericks nodded. "You've done well so far. It is good to have friends, you know, they can help you out of sticky situations. Especially Max. He is quite gifted." There was an air of sadness to Mavericks' tone.

Della played with her keys, staring down at her sneakers. "In my experience, friends are only good if you want someone to throw you to the curb when they are done telling you about their day." She looked up to meet Mavericks' gray eyes. "They dispose of you, moving on to the next, more popular, or nerdy, or attractive soul."

"I'm very sorry you feel that way." Mavericks remarked.

Della forced herself to smile. "I've been like that for a while. I wouldn't change it for anything." She said, her voice strained as she tried to hide her sadness.

"Hmm." Mavericks said, taking off his glasses and adjusting the nose pieces. "Well, now that you're done gallivanting around the village," He smiled. "I have a job for you."

Della leaned against the doorway, watching Mavericks dig into his pockets. He pulled out old candy wrappers, neon paperclips, and other odds and ends before finally producing a crumpled piece of paper.

"What kind of job?"

Mavericks smirked, handing her the paper. The note was a crumpled black and white photograph of a crumbling mausoleum with giant scratch marks on it. "Those appeared this morning. The police looked over it, said it was nothing. What do you think?"

"I think it's strange." Della said. The markings looked like the ones on the trees surrounding Sycamore Heights. The town had a massive bear problem, and they loved to use the trees as scratching posts.

"I've already called ahead, informing the residents of Garroway Mortuary that you are on your way. Better hurry." He said.

Della gave him a thumbs up, folding the paper up and shoving it into her pocket, closing and locking her door.

"And, Della," Mavericks began.

"Yeah?"

"Even if you hit a dead-end, do not stop searching. It will be the death of you." He continued, a look of worry flashing behind his irises.

Della raised her eyebrows, her eyes widening slightly.

"Good to know." Was all she could muster up.

~ ~ ~

Porter watched her struggle with the humongous castle-like gate through the window, wondering what she was doing here. She did seem like one of those punk freaks that used to hang around, but then again, they were banned from his humble abode. Maybe she had family buried here? If that was the case, wouldn't they have met before? Her tiny form flew through the cemetery like the ghosts that like to push over flowerpots or hide his keys.

Their eyes locked onto each other for a minute, him staring open-mouthed, her cheeks slowly flushing. He walked away from the window, letting the dusty white curtains return to their preferred positions, and opened the door.

"Hi." He said awkwardly, standing to his full height and letting his broad shoulders block her from his mother's sight. Della was tall, but the top of her head only came to his chin.

She shook her head, snapping herself out of her thoughts. "Hello. . ." She looked over at the dirty gold plaque near his head. "Mr. Porter Garroway." She paused. "I'm Delphee Coleman," She said stupidly. He already knew her name by heart. "I'm with the local paper. My boss called your residence and left a message telling you that I would be coming to examine the damage you reported this morning."

Porter rolled his eyes. "Yeah, my mom's boyfriend saw something on his way home this morning. He was scared out of his mind, but I'm sure it was just a bunch of raccoons." He said sweetly, smiling in a way he thought was convincing.

Jedidiah 'Jed' Oye, the bane of Porter's existence, never listened to him. He hated his mother's boyfriend with all his heart. He was an outsider, and all outsiders brought trouble since they did not understand this town. They didn't know when to keep their heads down, when to speak up, when to smile and nod. It was ridiculous. Even this Della girl would eventually ruin the carefully crafted hierarchy of the town.

Especially her, Porter thought, slouching a little bit to see her better.

Della squinted at him, pushing up her thin-framed glasses. He had allowed himself to forget about her pretty eyes. However, here she was, standing before him, utterly unforgettable, enabling him to be a hopeless romantic.

Hopeless indeed.

He shook his head, still staring at her. He had not noticed until now just how pretty she was. He cursed his brain for taking in her tiny details. Her skin was almost translucent, and her hair was the perfect shade of brown. Her tiny, veiny hands looked so soft and fragile. She dug a piece of paper out of the pocket of her oversized blush-colored corduroy jacket, watching him examine her with a blank expression. Well, her soft features were set in a blank expression, but her eyes, the beautiful brown ones he was gushing over, were not empty. They were full of perplexity.

"With all due respect," She began, tearing her eyes away from him and looking at the paper she held. "The reported marks do not look like a mere raccoon could have made them." She turned the paper around to reveal a black and white picture of the mausoleum that had been destroyed.

Porter stared at her. He had no idea how she had gotten that picture, but he did know he would get nowhere by trying to tell her to leave, so he stepped past her, nodding in the direction of the cemetery. Thank the Lord above he didn't have to take her through the house. His mother was preparing a body for an open-casket viewing. The poor Dixon's. To be murdered in your own home. . . had to be terrifying.

Porter would honestly love to be in their position. Of course, he only *half* wished he was dead; he was just feeling very tired. The coffins the rich people bought were extremely comfortable. The padding was made of fine silk and down feathers, and it muffled all the outside sound perfectly. He sighed wistfully.

Porter took naps in them occasionally.

You know, *as you do.*

He shook his head again, looking over his shoulder. Della was following him obediently, not trying to make small talk or anything like that, which he was grateful for. He stopped abruptly, causing her to walk into him. He couldn't tell whether he did that on purpose or by force of habit, but it made him smile, feeling her brush up against him.

He turned slightly, enjoying watching her scowl at him. "This is it." He said, pointing to a mausoleum to their left and stepping out of her way.

The scratch marks were about as long as Porter's arm

and just as thick as his muscles. She took a step forward, snapping a picture of the markings with her phone. She had one of those silicon cases that made it so your phone wouldn't fit in your back pocket. He smirked to himself. Shaped like a bottle, the word 'nightshade' written on it, it described what she would be to him. Poison.

He smiled to himself. She was strange. Eccentric even. The way she carried herself made him feel at ease, even though she seemed as nervous as a child alone on a Ferris wheel. It made him feel funny inside. Playful was the word he was looking for. Care-free was a synonym.

She reached out to touch the scratches as he watched her, looking at the rubble beneath her feet. The place was a wreck. There were pieces of rock, dirt, and moss strewn at the bottom of the crypt.

"How have you been?" He asked her.

"*Swell.*" She took a double take at a piece of rubble, kneeling to look closer at it. "Can you get me a pair of tweezers and a Ziploc bag?" She asked.

He nodded. "Sure thing, ma'am."

~ ~ ~

Porter returned after a moment, kneeling next to her and handing her the items she had requested. A piece of dark green leather was stuck between a piece of rubble and her shoe covered in a thick slimy substance. She grabbed it gingerly with the tweezers, holding it up for him to see.

"That's not raccoon hair." He said, seeming very proud of himself for that comment.

Della glared at him.

"Yeah." She said, standing. Idiocy wasn't a trait she found to be attractive. "I will have to keep the tweezers, sorry about that." She placed the leathery skin and the tweezers in the Ziploc bag and stuffed them in her bag. Her hands were shaking slightly; the night air was frigid with the promise of autumn. The sun had just set, casting the world into blue-purple light.

"That's fine." Porter smiled, but he had a quizzical look on his face.

"Does your mother's boyfriend happen to be Catholic?" Della asked with great dignity.

". . . No?" Porter said confused.

"You said he was scared?"

Porter nodded.

"Interesting." Della yawned. "How scared?"

"I've never seen a grown man cower in fear like that. Ever." Porter smiled.

"Hell hath no fury like that of a mutant beast hiding in the woods waiting to rip your face off."

Porter stared at Della in confusion until her face turned red and she cleared her throat.

"Yours isn't the first strange occurrence." Of course, that was not a lie, but somehow when that sentence flew from her lips, it sounded like one. "My department is teaming up with the police to find out what is going on," Della said quickly.

Porter nodded. "Right, right. You know, at the paper."

They stared at each other, both equally wondering what the other was going to say. Not once in her life had Della met someone who could see through her carefully crafted lies. She had a gift. If only others would realize that. Maybe then she would not have gotten in so much trouble back home.

"Yes." She said, holding her head high. "At the paper."

He smirked. "Well, Miss Delphee Coleman," He began, stepping closer to her. "If you need any other pieces of whatever that is, you can come pick them up anytime." He smiled.

For some reason she could not quite figure out, this irritated her more than anything else had in her entire life. She put her nose up, squinting at him. That was a bad habit of hers. If you were lucky enough to pick up on it, you would know that she did that when she was on the verge of her sanity. Sadly, no one had ever figured that out either.

"Thank you, Mr. Garroway. You've been a great help." She snapped.

That just made him smile bigger. He leaned down to Della's eye level; their noses nearly touching. Her heartbeat was betraying her. She could hear it as it thumped against her rib cage so loud, it sounded like thunder. She really hoped he couldn't hear it.

"Anytime." He didn't seem to want to move.

Her cheeks were glowing; she could practically see their reflection in his emerald eyes. She took a step backward, turning and hitting him with her hair. She heard him stifle a laugh as she walked away.

"Oh, and by the way, nice shoes!" He called after her.

She looked down at her feet as she walked. Today she was wearing a pair of chunky lavender heels. The part that covered her toes was covered in thin feathers, all of which caked in mud. Her blood boiled as she stared down at her feet, stomping away. She took off her glasses, cleaning them on the faux sheep fur that lined her corduroy jacket. She wanted so badly to walk out of the cemetery with a relaxed air about her, but unfortunately, the universe had other plans.

Delphee C. Coleman, the clumsiest girl on the face of the earth, walked right into the rusty gate of the cemetery, her glasses poking her in the eye as she tried to replace them on her face and the edge of the gate tearing into the thin skin on the bridge of her nose. Her ankle rolled to the side, her thin body slamming into the ground. She screeched with pain, shoving her glasses into her pocket and rubbing her nose.

She looked at her fingers, wanting to gag.

She was fine seeing other people's blood, for some reason, that did not bother her, but when she got hurt, the sight of her blood spilling out of even the tiniest wound made her queasy.

Porter was by her side instantly, reaching out and turning her face towards his. She pushed his hand away, fuming.

"I—I actually refuse to believe that just happened." His voice was strained, like he was trying desperately to keep from laughing. She glared at him, almost in tears. His face darkened, full of self-loathing. "Come on, let's get you patched up." He took her by the hand, hoisting her up off the ground and leading her back to the house that was the mortuary with minimal effort.

He was exceptionally strong. She dug her muddy heels into the ground, trying to pull away from him, but he held her in a gentle, yet firm grip and didn't budge.

"Hey Pops?" Porter asked as he led her inside the mortuary.

The entryway had been converted into an office, complete with a sizable front desk where an old man lay passed out on top of a stack of papers. He was snoring softly, drooling all over the documents. An open casket stood in the corner where an older woman was messing with the corpses suit. The woman seemed completely unaware of her surroundings, and her face looked just as dead as the corpse. Della shivered. The place smelled of evergreen car fresheners and death. Della almost preferred the smell of Mavericks' office to this.

"Pops." Porter said sternly, still gripping her hand. The old man at the front desk didn't move. "Grandpa." There was a loud, long snore. "MOM I THINK HE FINALLY DIED! BETTER START DIGGING THE GRAVE!" He screamed, much to Della's chagrin.

The old man sat right up, rubbing the sleep from his sunken eyes, acting like he was doing whatever job he was meant to do.

Porter smirked deviously. "Hey Pops, this is Delphee. She had a little mishap with the gate, I'm going to bandage her up and send her on her way." Pops grunted his approval, waving them upstairs. "Come on, we've got some bandages up in the hall closet." Porter whispered.

He led her upstairs, into a room which looked like an ordinary house. There was a kitchen and a living room, even a little balcony that resembled the porch beneath it. Porter sat her down on a stool at the breakfast bar, then disappeared behind a wall only to return moments later with a bottle of hydrogen peroxide, cotton balls, and band aids.

When he sat down, forcing her to look at him, she realized his left eye was bruised, though it was barely noticeable.

"What happened to your face?" Della asked quietly.

Porter smiled. "Back-alley catfight. Those Maine Coons are strong little fellas." He laughed.

She rolled her eyes. Something about him was off, but she tried to play it off as his nerves.

He sat in front of her on the barstool, calmly cleaning her wound with innate expertise. That kind of bothered her; he probably learned how to clean wounds from working and living here.

In a mortuary.

With his mom and grandpa.

Alone.

The only company being corpses.

She shivered, a cold sweat playing across her forehead.

"Sorry." He said, thinking the cut on her nose had stung. He was using an excessive amount of hydrogen peroxide. "Does it hurt?"

She nodded. It stung dreadfully but she kind of forgot that was the reason she was sitting up here with him. He looked extremely concerned as he placed a bright pink band aid over her nose, gently pressing down the edges.

"Did your glasses break? I could try to fix them." He spoke so quietly, so softly, his expression full of compassion and concern.

She shook her head, pulling her glasses out of her pocket to show that they were still in one piece. He smiled his melancholy little smile, sitting back to examine his handiwork.

"Thank you." She said quietly, crossing her legs and pulling her skirt over her knees.

"Don't mention it," Porter said, echoing her tone. He leaned against the counter, propping his head upon his fist, his fingers curling around his bruised cheekbone. He was so *very* handsome.

No, she told herself. *You tried being in love; it didn't work. It almost broke the only stable relationship you have. Pull yourself together, go home.*

"Everything all right?" Porter asked, furrowing his eyebrows.

Her face must have given away the emotions she felt dwelling deep inside her heart. She nodded, shrugging, and sliding off the stool, smoothing out her skirt. "Thank you for fixing me up and allowing me to snoop around your property. I must be going." She said, holding out her hand for him to shake.

He did something quite surprising. He stood, grabbed her hand, and walked her back down the stairs and to the nearest bus stop. He waited with her until the bus came, handing her some change and gently pushing her up the stairs. The doors began to close, but he put a hand up to stop them.

"Try not to die anytime soon. I probably won't be there to stop fate from wrapping his cold hands around you." He laughed.

He smiled, but there was a gravity to his words that made that beautiful smile irrelevant. He looked down to his lower left for no apparent reason. Nevertheless, there was a reason, and Della knew it. He was reliving some emotional memory. She made him meet her eyes and nodded.

"I will." She assured him.

He stepped back from the bus, waving her away with a tiny look of satisfaction. Her cheeks burned red as she took a seat. Her lips broke out into a smile.

She was so mad at herself, but very, *very* happy.

~CHAPTER SEVEN~

Troubles

Della's cheeks hadn't stopped glowing since she went to bed last night. The heat of her cheeks didn't bother her in the comfort of her own home, but now, walking briskly past Max, it was a nuisance. He was staring at her, jaw dropped down to the floor. Lenora was taking her own sweet time trying to find the paper Della had to sign to get a package from one of the bird watchers. She crossed her arms, refusing to look at him.

"How did yer little meetin' go with Venus?" Max asked.

Lenora quit looking through her papers, looking up to gaze at Della with a look crossed between sympathy and something of a warning.

"Who?" Della asked.

"Porter Garroway," Max said sourly.

Della turned to look at him. "How did you know—"

"Everyone knows the Garroway's," He said abruptly, missing the point. "Some of us better than others. Some of us even have a vendetta against 'em. Some come home with a bruised nose because of 'em." There was red-hot fire in his eyes.

"Porter didn't do this to me. I did it to myself." Della said, trying to sound casual. For some reason, she felt it her civic duty to stand up for Porter since he was not here to do it himself.

"They all say that." Max snapped.

Lenora finally found the paper she was looking for. Della quickly signed it, taking a small, beat up, soggy box from her outstretched hands. "Thank you." She said politely. Max followed her up to her office, waiting for her to open the box.

Inside was a tiny letter that she read out loud. "'My brother wanted you to have this, he says it might help with your research. Sincerely, Jimmie Heiser.' He's one of the bird-watchers." Max came around to peer over her shoulder. Under the letter, there was a plastic container wrapped in pink bubble wrap. A piece of what looked like a horn about the size of Della's hand was inside it. The horn looked about as ancient as her grandfather and just as fragile. It crumbled little by little when she moved the box. How could this help her?

"Heiser. . . That name sounds familiar." Max breathed.

"I'm surprised he's trying to help me. I wasn't very popular with the rest of his friends." Della admitted.

Max snorted. "Ei'm pretty sure ya aren' popular with anyone."

Della whipped her head around to look at his cheeky little smile. "What's that supposed to mean?" She snapped.

Max rolled his eyes, nodding at the specimen in her hand. "Can Ei take that to my lab and test it?" He asked, holding out his hand for the tiny container greedily.

"You have a lab?" Della asked, handing him the container as well as the Ziploc bag full of squishy green skin.

"Aye, Ei have a lab, but ya didn' let me finish." Max scowled, examining the evidence. "Ei will test these samples if ya tell me what happened last night."

"You just asked me for these." Della laughed. "You can't make a deal now. Mind finding out if this matches any local lizards? Alligators maybe? Crocodiles?"

He scowled at her, crossing his arms and tapping his foot, waiting for her to keep up her end of the bargain.

"Alexithymia." Della said coldly.

"Uh, bless ya?"

She sat up straight, reveling in the fact that she knew something he didn't. Maybe she should have bought him a dictionary rather than a tin full of poems. "Alexithymia. The inability to describe emotions verbally." She explained.

"Okay." Max said blankly. "Ei guess Ei'll just throw these away then." He made to toss the specimens across the room and into the waste bin.

"NO!" She screamed, falling out of her chair, reaching for the precious specimens. Was it her imagination, or did they hover in midair a second before her fingers curled around their containers?

"Fine, start talkin'." He hissed.

Della weighed her options for a moment, then sat back down. "I. . . ran into a gate and got hurt, and Porter insisted that he helped me." She said simply, hoping she would still have some dignity left after this conversation.

Max burst out laughing. "Ya—Oh, *wow*. Ya ran into a gate? Oh for the love of God Della. . ." he exclaimed in his thick Irish accent. He made a show of wiping away tears, then started laughing again.

"You can go now." Della snapped.

"As ya wish." He grabbed the specimens from her, then skipped out of her office, still laughing.

~ ~ ~

The cat scurried through the alleyway, a tube of green skin in its mouth. As quickly as possible, the cat scurried behind an old dumpster, peering inside Moss Hollow Police Department through the only window in the basement. *He* had his back to the speckled kitten, sitting there cleaning a scalpel. The cat shivered. It hated mortuaries and morgues and death in general. Thank God the poor thing still had seven of its nine lives left. . .

Making a noise akin to a sigh, it scratched at the window, causing *him* to turn. At first, he looked surprised, looking around the morgue, wondering where that incessant little scratching noise was coming from, but realization quickly dawned on him. Looking like someone had just asked him to clean a stable full of horse poop, he rolled his eyes, begrudgingly walking over to open the window and let the cat in.

"You are going to get me fired," Porter said, hurrying over to the box that controlled all the security cameras and shutting them off.

The cat jumped up onto one of the empty metal gurneys, spitting out the test tube and shaking. His fur fluffed up, crackling with electricity as his features melted. Slowly, he turned back into a boy. When the last of his bones had cracked into place, he sat cross-legged on the gurney, scowling at Porter.

"I'm serious, Max. People are going to start getting suspicious if the cameras keep getting turned off." Porter hissed.

Max yawned, stretching out his fingers. His knuckles cracked loudly, sending shivers up Porter's spine.

"Technically, Ei own this place," Max said matter-of-factly. Technically, Maximilian and Mavericks owned the whole town, however, they didn't have the money they needed to keep flaunting that.

Porter rolled his eyes. "You have a day, Milliano. *One day*." He said, pointing at the container of slimly green skin.

Max smirked. It amused him that he did not bother to ask what it was. It could have been drugs for all he cared, and Porter wouldn't mind. He would tear apart this whole town if it meant Max would get off his back.

Max nodded, vaulting off the gurney. He turned away, hearing Porter's footsteps growing softer and softer.

"Hey, Porter?" He called, his face set in a deep scowl.

"What now?" Porter called back exasperatedly.

"Stay away from Della," Max said simply, looking over his shoulder at the boy he used to look up to.

Porter turned around slowly, squinting at him with a disgusted look. "I didn't hurt her, Max. She tripped." He assured him.

Max rolled his eyes, dismissing him. However, he didn't hear Porter's feet shuffle across the floor.

"Trust me, Milliano, it was pretty obvious she wanted nothing to do with me." There was such sadness in his voice. Max almost felt sorry for him.

They could have been as thick as the thieves they were. Could have ruled this sorry excuse for a town together. Nevertheless, Porter was too broken, and Max had never been able to find his way through the rubble. Their lives were full of could-haves, should-haves, and would-haves. Full of despair and sadness.

Some people were just that unforgivable.

Some people could not be glued back together.

Some people should not be able to see the light of day.

Some people would not know what to do without setting the world on fire.

However, here he was, working for MHPD and living his

best life. All the while, Max was stuck fixing computers and running errands. He hated Porter. Hated him more than the parents that left him for dead, hated him more than the lawyers, hated him more than every bully that used to torment him at school.

No one was ever going to fix that.

~ ~ ~

Whatever tests Max was doing on the specimens were taking forever. Della decided that instead of twiddling her thumbs and waiting around for *hopefully* exciting news, she would talk to the only person that would be able to give her answers.

Della knocked on the Dixon's eldest daughter's door. She lived on the outskirts of town in a small blue house. The lawn was untidy, the hanging plants were withered, and garbage littered the porch.

A girl only a couple years older than Della—maybe in her early twenties—opened the door. Her face was tear-stained, her silky red hair untidy. She held a baby against her hip, bouncing up and down to keep the tiny thing from crying.

"Hello, can I help you?" She asked, brushing her hair from her face.

Della smiled kindly. "Hi, I'm Della. I work with the paper. I have a few questions. If now isn't a good time, I can come back later."

Clara thought for a moment, then nodded. "Now is fine, come on in."

She led Della through her messy house—toys here, dirty dishes there, baskets full of laundry everywhere. Clara set the baby down in an old crib near a window, sighing heavily. She brushed off her t-shirt and jeans, smiling as best she could. She looked much sadder than Della had expected. The way Jimmie had made it seem, Della thought she would be less friendly. Less beaten down.

"What can I help you with?" Clara asked.

"I'm working an article about what happened to your parents," Della explained.

"Right, Mrs. Heiser called me earlier," Clara said, gesturing for Della to sit on an empty armchair. "I'm sorry about the mess, I've been stretched thin lately." She laughed darkly. "Feels like everything is going wrong. . ." She whispered.

Della stared at the disarray the house was in. She had a feeling that Clara tried to keep things as clean as possible. Seeing the house like this must be extremely rare.

"Do—Do you need help with anything? I can whistle while I work." Della said kindly.

Clara's eyes filled with tears. She shook her head, blinking the tears away. "That is very kind, but I couldn't ask that of you." She said.

"It's no trouble for me," Della said insistently. If you wanted information, all you ever had to do was be kind. Many people seemed to forget that.

Clara smiled weakly, pointing over her shoulder. "If you could do some dishes, that would be great."

Della stood, grabbing a few dishes off side tables as she made her way into the kitchen.

"The soap is below the sink," Clara called.

Della got to work, not bothered by having to do this little chore. She cleaned a brownie pan in silence for a while, before mustering up enough nerve to ask what was on her mind. She stared out of the window above the sink, looking into the dense willows that lined the backyard.

"Any word on your sister?" Della called.

"Not yet." Clara's voice rang through the kitchen like a Church bell. "Me and my parents were supposed to go looking for her today."

Della scraped at a plate covered in dried spaghetti. "Did you see your sister—it's Anna, right—before she disappeared?"

Della heard Clara blow her nose. "I see her once a month. My parents drop her off. They travel a lot. Last time I saw her was two weeks ago." There was a wave of anger in her words.

"Do you know anyone that would have been close enough to kidnap Anna?"

There was a pause. "The cops said she disappeared after school. It could be anyone. I just don't understand who would, or why." Clara's footsteps clicked into the kitchen. She bit her lower lip, lost in thought.

Della put the clean dishes aside, drying a coffee cup that read 'best mom ever' on it. She smiled.

"The little one in there, he yours?" Della asked.

Clara's eyes brightened. She nodded. "Turned one a week ago. His name is Everett."

"He's a cute little thing." Della smiled.

"Thank you. Takes after his father, just a little too fussy." Clara allowed herself to smile, pointing at a picture on the wall above the oven. Clara and a young man with brown hair sat in a forest clearing, smiling happily. "Arthur and I are set to marry this spring."

"Wow, how did you meet?" Della asked, thankful Clara wasn't picking up on the reason behind her questions.

Clara blushed. "High school sweethearts. He came here during the foreign exchange program when I was sixteen. Came for the sights, stayed for the girl." She said wistfully.

"You guys live together?" Della asked.

Clara nodded, looking around her home. Despite the mess, the mold, the water damage, the burns on the floor by the oven, she looked happy. She smiled, wiping the tears off her face.

"Four years." She announced.

Della smiled back, nodding to herself. "How'd that happen?"

Clara looked away. "My home life wasn't great. I turned eighteen, and I left. Mom and Dad couldn't stop me. I would not. . . I wouldn't change it." She said, more to herself than to Della. "Arthur and I may not be as wealthy as my parents, and our house needs work, but we are happy. We don't lack in the places that are important."

"If you don't mind me asking, what happened at home?" Della asked.

Clara shook her head. "Rebellious teen, strict parents." She said, tears watering up in her eyes again. Her face darkened as she stared past Della into the willows and oaks.

Della finished cleaning the dishes, setting the rag she had been using in the empty sink. It made a loud splash, startling Clara. She reached up to rub her left eye. Della noticed her left eye sagged a little like it wouldn't open all the way. Clara looked away, peeking around the corner into the living room where Everett lay asleep.

"I'm sorry, but I'm going to have to cut this short. Thank you for your help, if you need anything, stop by." Clara said.

Della pulled a dark purple business card out of her back pocket, offering it to Clara. Clara read it, her eyebrows furrowing.

"Personal hot-line," Della explained quickly. "Side business. If you need dishes cleaned, or laundry done, I'm here." She assured her.

Clara nodded, pulling Della into a loose side hug as she led Della back through the house.

"Thank you." She said again when she opened the front door for her. "You have no idea how much this meant to me."

~CHAPTER EIGHT~

Werewolves of London Avenue

Della paced back and forth in the hallway that housed the conspiracy boards and books, scanning each of the projects, looking for anything that could help her with her investigations. Mavericks was right; the Cryptozoology Department was lacking. These lazy idiots didn't even know their Chupacabra from their Jersey Devil. And Max's board. . . There was a time and place for science and conspiracy to mix, but not when you were blatantly trying to disprove Nessie. This was ridiculous. Della leaned in closer, looking over another board, shaking her head.

"Like?" A voice rang through the hallway.

Della turned around to see a girl with bright blue hair leaning against the door to the 'Disguise Room.' Alexis Martin— one of the other two featured writers in the Cryptozoology Department. She was smiling widely, looking a little too proud of herself.

"I worked really hard on that one," She explained, gesturing to the board Della had her nose stuck to. "Mavericks flew me to Mexico to research Quetzals."

When it came to things Della was passionate about, she was extremely competitive. She smiled tightly, standing to her full height.

"For one, it's not Quetzal, it's Quetzalcoatl, and no, I do

not like it. You didn't even interview any Aztecs. Most of what you wrote was pulled off Wikipedia, I doubt you even did anything in Mexico besides sip on cocktails." She said, lifting a picture off the board. It wasn't even an actual photograph. It was nothing but a stock photo that still had a watermark on it, printed on cheap printer paper. Absolutely ridiculous.

Alexis just stared at her, the strings from her hoodie hanging from her fingers. She opened and closed her mouth, then stood up straighter, swishing her electric blue hair behind her back.

"I did interview an Aztec. I held a séance." Alexis said defensively.

"Yes, because Spirits are always the most trustworthy sources. How do you even know it was an Aztec? Could've been some homeless guy that died near your campsite the night before for all you know." Della snapped.

"What about you, 'Miss-I'm-The-Favorite?' Don't expect to come in here and wiggle your way into our lives so easily. People can't just be replaced." Della thought that an odd thing to say. "You haven't even written anything yet. Word on the street says you are working two cases. That never ends well." Alexis said, smiling slyly.

"Maybe that's because I don't cut corners," Della said, sweeping past her, making towards the door. This was why she hated working with people.

"Maybe it's because you really don't know what you are talking about. You're doing an article on Lycanthropy? Can you say snooze fest? Trust me, this town has had far too much of Werewolves. Have you even talked to Bayou Gil?" Alexis looked all too proud of herself. Della scowled at her. That was twice that name had popped up.

"Not yet. That was my next stop." Della lied.

"Yeah, I'm sure it was," Alexis said. "Mind the steps." She called just as Della tripped. Alexis laughed as she made her way down to the common office, leaving Della burning with anger.

Della stood tall as she walked by Lenora at the front desk, smoothing out her black and green tights and pulling the edge of her purple skirt down. Della always made a note of the people she would have to prove herself to. It was a habit her father had accidentally started.

Alexis was four on the list for Moss Hollow.

Right after Max.

~ ~ ~

Bayou Gil, as Della found, was not only a person but a place. Sitting between the bayou itself and the crossroads of a lonely street called London Avenue lay the sleepy crab shack.

Della stood; her head tilted to the side as she stared at the rickety bridge before her. She had not expected this. "This is how I die." She whispered. She was pretty sure she saw an alligator swimming near the shore next to an old suburban full of happily squealing hippie children.

Somewhat reluctantly, she followed the bridge, the stinking swamp water seeping up through the cracks of the knotted wood, drenching her velvet boots. She made a noise halfway between a *humph* and a groan, holding her head high. The bridge was illuminated by lanterns full of fireflies and spiders, but the light was very little. It was two in the afternoon, but the fog was so thick that she could barely see two steps in front of her. Every couple of steps she tripped on loose planks, her faced screwed up in concentration and embarrassment. Soon enough, as the pathway curved through the swamp, a low, red light began to fill Della's eyes.

A crudely built shack, or rather a poor excuse for one, stood before her. A flickering old neon red sign adorned with a crab read *Bayou Gil's Crab Emporium Est.1837*, above the slouching door frame.

Yes, that was an alligator sitting beneath the foundation of the shack, eyeing Della's boots with hunger in its eyes. Anywhere else, perhaps at a zoo, Della would've stopped to observe these beautiful beasts.

Not now.

Now she felt like dinner.

It was almost enough to make her become a vegan.

Almost.

"You have got to be kidding me," Della said breathlessly as a group of older gentlemen made their way around the creaking porch of the shack, waving at her. They looked utterly drained of life, and not because they all looked older than dirt. She stood at the doorway, the smell of old seafood and beer stinging her nostrils. Looking back over her shoulder, her face contorted with disgust, she finally allowed her muddied boots to cross over the door frame.

Several patrons waved to her, saluting her with their mugs full of water. She sincerely hoped that it was just the cups that were dirty, not the water itself.

"If you are allergic, you have to sign a waiver." Someone said. Della turned to her right to see a woman in a dark red dress and dirty apron, holding out a clipboard with a flower pen. Della smiled through tight lips, taking a step back.

"Not allergic." She said, hoping her facial expression was cordial and pleasant, hoping it didn't mirror the utter disgust that was brewing in her chest.

The woman sighed, shoving the clipboard under her arm, arranging her face in a smile. "Hello, my name is Cheryl. I will be your server today." She said in a tone reminiscent of a growl. She pushed the flower pen into Della's shoulder, making her turn towards a nearby table. "Today's specials are Crayfish ala' Carte, Roadkill Pizza—flavors vary—and a house favorite, Bottom of The Pot." She explained as she forced Della to sit, shoving a menu in her hands.

Della thought that if she opened her mouth at this very moment, she would be the newest flavor on the Roadkill Pizza. Instead, she looked down at the crusty menu, hiding her face behind her hair. Her eyes widened at the names on the menu:

🦀 Bayou Gil's 🦀 Crab Emporium

~Sun Up til Sun Down~

Daily Specials:

Crayfish ala' Carte $11.99
Roadkill Pizza—Flavors Vary . . . . $7.99 a slice
Botom Of The Pot . . . . (seasonal prices vary)
World Famous Gumbo—Cup/Bowl . . . . $5.99/$8.99

House Favorites:

Alligator Stew—Your Choice of Gator . . . . (prices vary)
Cornbread & Grits $8.99
Grits $2.00
Crayfish & Grits $8.99
Grits $2.00
Lobster Bisque—Cup/Bowl . . . . $5.99/$8.99
Lobster & Grits $8.99
Grits $2.00
Crab Cakes & Curly Fries $11.99
Crab & Grits $8.99
Grits $2.00
Lazy Susan—Your Choice of Susan . . . . (prices vary)
Steve Sauce Over Red Beans $10.99
Did We Mention Grits? $2.00

Desserts:

Homemade Beignets:
    Chocolate Filled/Raspberry Filled/Plain $4.50
Bread Pudding $5.99
Custard Pie . . . . $5.99 a slice

Della swallowed hard as Cheryl watched her expectantly. "Uh—do you have any salads?" She asked politely.

The woman scowled at her. "Freak." She whispered under her breath, then snatched the menu from Della's hand.

Della pinched the bridge of her nose, instantly regretting it. The cut on her nose burned like someone had pured hot oil over her face. Part of her wondered if that was what Cheryl was imagining herself doing.

Della sighed, looking around at the tables—which were a mix of palettes attached to the wall with a layer of thick blue-green glass set upon them and giant empty wooden spools—feeling as if she was being watched. Sure enough, a few tables away, two men with bloodshot eyes and ashy skin were staring her down. Della smiled, nodding to them. They must be Ambrose's as well.

An arrangement of candles reflected in the dirty windows, distorting their faces. If Della didn't know any better, she would have assumed they were demons. Her eyes twitched. Perhaps they were.

The floors were covered in peanut shells and discarded shellfish carcasses that cracked as people walked by. The ceiling hung low, the boards bending under the pressure of the chandeliers they tried to support. Oddly enough, those magnificent chandeliers were shimmering and spotless.

Cheryl returned moments later, throwing a plate full of wilted lettuce in front of her. By throw, Cheryl tossed the plate at her like a frisbee, so the lettuce spun off the plate and into Della's face.

"Thank you for that, Cheryl." Della smiled, pulling a piece of spring mix off her glasses.

"Much obliged." She rasped back. "Can I get you anything else?"

"Yes, I was wondering," Della began, picking a piece of lettuce from her hair, scowling in disgust. "If I could speak to the owner of this establishment?"

Cheryl scowled, blinked several times, then nodded, turning away. She disappeared behind the front counter. Della noticed the restaurant had fallen silent. The pale men that had been staring at her were now looking at the counter, utterly confused. They glanced back at Della, then whispered to each other. Cheryl soon returned, a hobbling form following her. She led an old man to Della's table, a wry smile on her lips.

The old man wore a jewel-encrusted eyepatch, dirty overalls without a shirt, and wore his long white hair and beard like a crown. He smiled at Della, revealing a mouth full of missing teeth.

"Naturally." Della smiled, gesturing for the man to sit down.

"'Ello." The man said, his lips twitching. He shook violently as he climbed into the seat across from Della. "Said ye wanted to speak with the man'a'ger?" He asked.

Della stared at him for a minute before nodding, holding out her hand for him to shake. He didn't even look down at her hand, he just stared at her. Della slowly moved her hand, nodding at him.

"Yes, I have a few questions about—"

"About my wolves?" The man asked.

"Yes. . . no. . . what?" Della asked, blinking away her confusion. She had come here intending to ask how the Dixon's treated their daughters, or whether anyone had seen anyone watching them, whether they had come in recently or not, and other boring yet mandatory questions.

"Alexis told me ye were researching us. I assumed." The old man smiled again. He had several gold teeth, yet no silver.

Cheryl nodded. "I can assure you that none of the Lupine's have murdered anyone." She spoke very loudly, tossing a look over her shoulder at the demon-like Ambrose's. They rolled their eyes.

"I'm sorry, I think you have mistaken me for—" Della began.

"Although, der was dat incident wit the kickens. . . Some of duh youn'ger ones. . . dey just don't listen." The old man said, shaking his head.

Della squinted at them. She had a feeling she knew what these people were talking about, though she had no idea whether she should be excited or terrified.

"You, and the Lupine's, you haven't murdered anyone?" Della repeated.

"That's what Cheryl said." The man smiled.

"Right," Della said, reaching into her bag to grab her notebook and write some stuff down. "And you are?"

"Seventh generation Gil Lupine, of Bayou Gil's. Alpha of this pack." Gil said with pride. "Cheryl is my granddaughter, my Beta."

Della clicked her pen a couple times, nodding to herself. "Okay, now that we have that out of the—"

"Ye know, I didn't see the Dixon's come in with the rest of the birdie watchers. Haven't been in since the girl went missing, I suppose." Gil said.

Cheryl nodded. "They were devastated. . ."

"Right, do you—" Della tried to cut in.

"They didn't have too many enemies. Just the people they bought out of house and home." Gil continued. "I assume only the Ambrose's would want to harm 'em, but then again, they can't feed on the living. Only the bagged stuff."

Della looked between Cheryl and Gil blankly. "And the Ambrose's are v—"

"Pesky little vamps, yep." Gil nodded, lifting his eyepatch to reveal a large scar over an empty eye socket. "Did this to me eye about twenty years ago."

Della glanced at the table where the pale men had been. They were now gone. She inhaled sharply. "Right. Okay, thank you for your time, Mr. Lupine. I will be in touch." Della said, standing.

"You gonna pay for that?" Cheryl asked.

"Hmm?" Della looked down at her plate of untouched greens. She sighed, digging into her purse for her wallet, taking out a ten, and placing it on the table. "Uh, keep the change."

Cheryl smiled, taking the bill and stuffing it in her bra as Della walked away. "Oh, Della, is it?"

Della stopped, turning back. "Yes?"

"We don't want to end up in your paper, okay?" Cheryl said sweetly, lifting her dress a little to reveal a thigh holster and a gun.

"I can assure you, you won't," Della said, smiling. She'd been threatened before, but somehow when you were being threatened by a werewolf, it was different.

"Good, see you around." Cheryl smiled.

Della gave a curt nod, then left the restaurant, standing outside the door. Her lips pulled into a little smile. If only the people of Sycamore Heights could see her now. She would love to shove a vampire in their faces, stick a howling werewolf on their tails. Her dad would have a heart attack if he knew what she had gotten herself into.

"Holy *shit*." Della breathed, running a hand through her hair. "I'm not crazy."

~CHAPTER NINE~

Apologies Are for The Weak

Dead end. Della shook her head, crossing that word out of her notebook. She had a feeling that 'dead end' in Moss Hollow meant you were dead. Like six feet under, flowers next to a slab of concrete dead. Not emotionally or mentally or internally, like Della felt today.

Stuck.

"Yes, there we go, that's better." She whispered as she wrote that word down.

So, she couldn't do a piece on Lycanthropy. Well, at least not safely. No amount of silver was going to protect her from Cheryl. That woman haunted Della's waking dreams. She shivered.

Vampires were out of the question, they weren't cryptids. Technically neither were werewolves but believe it or not they were still less human than an immortal, blood-sucking, albino.

Funny how once you are finally handed your hopes and dreams, you can't use them for personal gain.

For now, it seemed Della would have to choose one of the other mysterious creatures that roamed the swamp. Perhaps she would be writing about Lizard Men after all. She rolled her eyes. If she was to create a list of all the glorious weirdness she loved, Lizard Men would be behind the Congolese Giant Spider. And Della *hated* the Congolese Giant Spider.

Not to mention this town and its resident weirdos were under lock and key. Would it kill the Moss Hollow Tribune to give her any piece of information? Would the planet explode if a line that resembled 'strange creature spotted somewhere in town' suddenly appeared? How was she supposed to do her job? What was she to do in the meantime? Read a book? Yes, Della was a true bibliophile, but she was beginning to grow restless. One could only read the same book so many times before going insane.

Yawning, she looked through her notes in her bedroom. She had asked her faithful readers their opinion on her article, but most them were of little help. She sighed, hoping it would be the least of her worries when there was a knock on her door. She crawled out of bed, not bothering to put on her glasses. It was Max who was at the door, his face split into a broad, toothy grin.

"It's not a lizar', at least not fully," Max said, pushing his way into her apartment.

Della crossed her arms over her chest for multiple reasons; one, it was midnight, and she was angry at him for coming around so late, two she was cold due to the fact she had no glass in her windows, and three, she was in her pajamas. She tapped her foot a couple times, looking around awkwardly.

"What?" She asked exasperatedly, trying not to look so embarrassed.

"Both samples carry the same DNA—human, goat, gator, everything—and the sludge is a composition of some sort of animal triacylglycerol and get this; crystalline sulfur." He smiled expectantly.

"English, please."

"Right, sorry. Fat and just. . . sulfur." He smiled, prompting her brain to start thinking with a wave of his hands.

"So that means. . . ?" Della yawned.

Max furrowed his eyebrows in disappointment. "Ei was hopin' ya could tell me that."

Della thought, rubbing the sleep from her eyes. "A Golem, maybe?" Della asked as he placed a piece of paper with the test results in her hands and began rummaging through her refrigerator.

"Potentially. When Ei spilled some water on the horn, it didn' do anything." He said in a corrective tone, taking out a carton of almond milk, looking slightly disappointed. "If it was a Golem, wouldn' Ei had found clay? Wouldn' the clay start to melt?"

"It's a possibility. Sulfur usually means demons. Did you use *Holy Water*?" Della asked. He shook his head. "Cereal is in the cupboard—no, not that one, the other one. The clean bowls are next to the oven." Della sighed. "That doesn't disprove that it isn't a Golem." She leaned against the counter, watching him fumble around her kitchen.

"But think about it! Yes, Ei'll admit that this whole thing is goosed, but what if someone is tryin' tuh make us believe it is supernatural? There be many soils and rocks that carry small traces of sulfur, and animal fat isn't exactly a rare find. It could all be a hoax." Max said sternly. "Ever watched *Scooby-Doo*?"

"Alright, say it is a hoax. That still presents the question of why. Why make it look like hoodoo? Why kill the Dixon's? Where's Anna?" Della asked.

"We should talk to her older sister, Savanna, was it?" Max asked.

"*Clara*, and I already did." Della corrected.

"Alone?" Max asked.

Della raised an eyebrow. "Yes. . . ? Like always."

He scowled. "Ei thought Ei was gonna help out?"

"You volunteered yourself, I never asked." Della pointed out. "I can't get work done when I'm distracted."

"But, we're friends." Max said, smiling widely. "Crime fightin' friends." He pointed his fingers like guns at her, amused.

Della snorted. "We are not friends, Max, we are coworkers." Della said, speaking out of experience. Max opened his mouth to contradict, but she held up a finger. "I'm done with this conversation. To you good sir, I say, take your bowl of cereal and go home. It's one in the morning, I'm tired and frankly," She paused, yawning. "I would not like to see your glorious face until tomorrow. At work."

"Ya know earlier, when Ei said no one likes ya? Maybe this is why." Max snapped.

Della was taken aback. She shut her eyes tightly for a minute, biting her lower lip. "I've made my peace with that. I don't do the whole 'friendship' thing. It's a waste of my time, and frankly I find people annoying. It would help if you were happy. I let you follow me around twenty-four-seven. That's more than a lot of people get, Max."

Max ripped the DNA results away from her, stomping over to the door. "This is the *last* time Ei help *you*." That last word vibrated through the air like a missile.

Della rolled her eyes. "If you think you are inconveniencing me, you would be wrong. See you at work." She said as he ripped open her door.

He mumbled under his breath, cursing her out like the sorry excuse for a leprechaun he was. She shook her head, mocking him.

Richie, who had been vacuuming, smiled at her. "Finally, something we can agree on." He said maliciously, then continued cleaning.

She slammed her door shut, took a nice hot shower and then climbed into bed, fuming.

Maybe she shouldn't have said that. Maybe she should've just nodded and gave him a little thumbs up. But even Delphee Coleman got tired of lying. Even Delphee Coleman was tired of being hundreds of different people at once.

~ ~ ~

Max refused to look at her as he followed her down to Mavericks' office. Max had blabbed to him about their little argument, and now they were both in trouble. Every time Ms. Durnell had called Della to her office, she had not been scared like she was now. If she had gotten expelled or suspended back then, it would not have been the end of the world. But here, it was like there was a noose tied around her neck. If she stepped too far out of line, the rope would tighten, and she would die, which meant being forced to go back home. She knocked on Mavericks' door, absentmindedly examining the trophy case. She was pretty sure that 'unicorn horn' had not been there last time she came down here. Mavericks opened his door, lacking his typical gusto. He leered at them both, gesturing for them to come inside.

The reptilian chair had been pulled up to the desk, along with the patchwork one Della remembered. Max jumped past her to claim the patchwork one, smirking. Della reluctantly sat in the reptilian armchair, trying to look professional. She could feel Max's eyes on her as she stared down Mavericks. Her heart was pounding in her chest, but not like it had when she had been face to face with Porter. No, this made her feel like she was having a heart attack.

"I'm assuming you both know why you are here?" Mavericks asked, leaning on his desk like a disappointed father of two delinquent teens.

Max nodded, slouching in his chair.

"You do know that I value a very professional workspace, don't you?" Mavericks asked.

"And so do I." Della said, shooting Max a look out of the corner of her eye.

Mavericks put his head in his hands, grumbling as he shook his head. Della was pretty sure she saw a streak of pink in his dark gray hair.

"I swear." He whispered. "Alright, here is how we are going to do this. It is a team-building exercise. Max, you go first and tell me why Della's words hurt you."

Max looked at her for a moment, sinking further into his chair. "Because Ei took time out of my week tuh test her stupid samples, and now she is treatin' me like the pavement beneath her tie-dye sneakers." He said sternly, though he too seemed to be afraid of Mavericks. Maybe even more so, which made Della's heart beat even faster.

"Good, now Della, how does that make you feel?" Mavericks asked.

Della rolled her eyes. "I don't need therapy." She yawned.

Mavericks' cloudy gray eyes were full of rage. "How does that make you feel, Della." He insisted.

"Misunderstood." Della said simply.

Max audibly rolled his eyes. "Honestly."

"If you have something to say, you can say it to my face." Della snapped, though she didn't waste her energy turning to look at him.

"Oh, Ei wouldn' want tuh do that; ya wouldn' be able tuh *focus*," Max said sarcastically.

"Well it's pretty hard to get some sleep when someone comes knocking on your door at midnight to have a bowl of cereal and tell me the DNA results that could have waited until morning." Della snapped.

"Ei thought ya would want tuh know!"

"Of course, I would! But I would have liked to hear

about it in the morning." Della said calmly.

"And Ei would have loved for ya not tuh have such a superiority complex. Guess we cannot always get what we want." Max spat.

Mavericks, who had been taking a sip of his coffee, began choking, sputtering dark roast everywhere in a very exaggerated manner.

Della rolled her eyes. "I'm sorry Max, I am but—"

"No yer not! Yer a walkin' oxymoron!" Max yelled, sitting up in his chair.

"And you think you are better? At least I can take a hint and know when I'm not wanted!" Della scoffed. Max's ears went back like an angry wild cat. Was he growling? Or was it the chair? Why was the chair vibrating? Why was the candle near Della's hand shaking?

"Obviously not, because as far as Ei am concerned, ya aren' wanted anywhere! Yer school sent ya away, and yer family too. Bloody Hell, Ei'm sure Mavericks and *Porter* will too." Max screamed.

The candle's flame went out as it toppled to the floor. A crack erupted on the lens of Della's glasses. For a moment, the world seemed to stop. The law firm fell silent, the birds outside stopped chirping, and Max was caught mid-expression. Even Della's heartbeat had ceased its rapid beats. Tears were welling up in her eyes as Della slapped the armrests on her chair. She swore it growled at her when she did that.

"Leave Porter out of this!" She hissed, standing and stomping out of the room, wiping away her tears with such force that her skin stung.

She stormed through *The Utopian Courier*, ignoring Norman as he came walking up to her, as joyful as ever, asking her about her recent research. As she stomped up the stairs to her office, she stopped. An unimaginable amount of anger was welling up inside her chest.

What if Max was right?

What if no one wanted her around? Maybe that is why so many people left. Maybe that is why she didn't have any friends.

Screw Sebastian's theory about how she pushed people away. She was not the problem; it was the rest of the world. They didn't understand her; they didn't care about her; they didn't want her around.

And she didn't want them either.

All she had in this wretched, wretched world was herself. She didn't need validation from anyone any more than she needed a copy of her favorite book. It was a want, not a need. She wanted to be understood, she wanted friends, she wanted people to love her, but it wasn't a need.

She was a fool to think any different.

~CHAPTER TEN~

Mistakes Were Made

A day passed. Della had been in the town of Moss Hollow for two weeks now. She earned herself a case, an article, a pair of mysteriously broken glasses, and a target on her back. Apparently, when you anger the son of Percival James Mavericks, it doesn't go unnoticed. Half of her coworkers wouldn't do so much as look her in the eye. Others whispered behind her back.

September began to present itself in an array of colors that all looked rather dull to Della. The air was still as hot as ever, though the sun was hidden behind a few clouds. Della shook her head as she walked in the shadows, pulling her brightly colored hair into a high ponytail. She was beginning to loathe the heat. Would it kill the South to rain every once in a while?

She ducked under the bright yellow caution tape outside the Dixon's household, her face set into a scary look of indifference. So, she didn't have Max to test whatever she thought she was going to find? So what? She could find someone else to help her, someone whose hand she didn't have to hold the whole way through. Surely her loyal readers knew of someone in the area that would be more than willing to help.

Pulling a thin sparkly purple bobby pin out from the front of her hair, Della picked the lock of the door. The inside of the house smelled absolutely revolting. It smelled like someone had thrown a mixture of sulfur, dirty socks, and sour milk into a blender and called it air freshener. Gagging, Della walked along, careful not to touch anything and leave behind her prints. On the surface, there was nothing odd about the house; the walls were adorned with picture frames depicting a happy family, the living room full of discarded toys. There was even a vase full of yellow carnations, orange lilies, and a striking blueish-purple flower Della couldn't name.

Covering her mouth and nose with her shirt, Della made her way into the kitchen, where evidence of murder was still afoot. She snapped a couple of pictures on her phone, examining the crime scene. Chairs around the table were upturned, showing signs of a struggle. A drawer full of knives had been thrown open, the drawer barely hanging onto the slides, its contents on the floor, labeled by the police. The smell was most potent here, Della could barely breathe.

The window over the sink was broken, the sink showered in bloody glass. Slowly, she made her way towards it. The dirty stainless-steel sink was stained with blood like someone had tried to clean their hands. Carefully, Della reached into the sink and scraped some of the gore into one of her test tubes. She turned away, capping the—a noise echoed into her ears from the living room.

The faucet began to rattle, water spraying out in every direction. As the droplets hit her, Della took several steps away from the sink, hastily taking pictures as a set of feet clapped along the hardwood floor in the kitchen. She stuffed her phone in her pocket, turning around, smashing into a broad-shouldered form. She struggled against the figure as he pushed her against the wall. She kicked whomever it was between the legs, reaching her hands around the figure's neck and slamming his head into the wall behind her.

Free of his grip, she made a run for the living room, instantly regretting it. She heard sirens in the distance, the glow of red and blue lights suddenly appearing on the cotton curtains.

". . . *Ouch*. . ." A familiar voice moaned.

Della turned around to see Porter leaning against the wall that separated the kitchen from the living room, holding his head in his hands, his ankles crossed as he bounced up and down on the spot. Boy had she gotten him good, his nose was already swelling up.

"*What are you doing here?!*" Della whisper-yelled, pulling him back into the kitchen just as heavy footsteps echoed from the porch.

"Apparently, saving you." Porter hissed back, looking over his shoulder with great fear as the front door clicked open. "What are *you* doing here?"

"MOSS HOLLOW POLICE DEPARTMENT! THIS IS A CRIME SCENE! COME OUT WITH YOUR HANDS WHERE I CAN SEE THEM!" A voice screamed.

Della glared at Porter, spinning around to observe her surroundings once again, panic and adrenaline rushing through her. There was a door to her left that led to the back yard. If they ran, they might be able to vault the fence before someone saw them. Shaking off the freezing fear that was gluing her feet to the floor, she felt around behind her for Porter's hand, pulling him toward the door, kicking it open. She made to run towards the fence, when Porter pulled her in the opposite direction towards a large patch of shrubbery. He pushed her down inside the bushes, not necessarily taking time to make sure she didn't get poked in the eye by a branch.

"Stay here; don't move." He said sternly, then pulled away.

Not in a position to argue, Della nodded, listening to his footsteps disappear in the grass. She hugged her knees to her chest, trying to be as small as possible, hoping that she wasn't visible through the shrubs. Her neon green hair and purple shirt weren't exactly hard to miss. Her heart was pounding as she sat there, listening to the voices drifting in from the front yard.

". . . Eric! What are you doing here?" Porter's voice rang, a twinge of something she couldn't quite make out fighting his tone.

"We got a call from across the street. Someone saw a woman breaking in." The man, now known as Eric said. How had he gotten here so fast? Who had been watching?

"A girl? What girl? I see no girl. Jacobson, do you see a girl?" Porter said, laughing nervously.

A long pause.

Della gulped, shutting her eyes tightly. Days like these made her question her sanity. Why on God's green Earth had she decided to come here? Of course, someone would have spotted her; it was the middle of the day! Sometimes, she didn't feel as smart as she tried so hard to portray.

Trying to calm down, she pushed herself closer to the fence behind her back. Something wet clung to her shirt. Turning slightly, she saw a small bloody handprint with only four fingers on the rotting fence. There was a massive hole in the fence covered in dried scales and slime; broken fence boards lay like corpses on the other side. The hole was most definitely big enough for a four-foot-tall monster to fit through.

The leaves of the shrubbery were ripped open, startling her. Porter's smiling face greeted her, holding out his hand for her and hoisting her up off the ground with little effort. She stumbled into him, staring behind her at the wreckage as Porter picked pieces of twigs from her hair.

"Yeesh, what's that?" Porter asked, looking over her shoulder as he dusted off her jacket.

She waved him away, kneeling. The inside of her nose stinging as she breathed. She could still faintly smell sulfur. Most of the blood was still a sticky mess, but some of it had dried, turning into an odd greenish clay that resembled the horn Jimmie Heiser had sent her. This wasn't human blood.

"It's injured." Della said, more to herself than to Porter. She looked back at him. "You wouldn't happen to have a container of mints on you, would you?" She asked.

Porter put his hands on his hips, watching her curiously. He playfully rolled his eyes, kneeling next to her.

"Humor me, Miss Coleman—after all, I did just save you from going to jail—why do you need a container of mints, and why are you smiling like you just won the lottery?"

"I just need the container, and I'm smiling because I have more proof." Della explained, holding out her hand as Porter stuck his hand in his back pocket.

"Proof? Of what?" Porter asked, handing her a container of peppermint *Altoids,* which she emptied into his still outstretched hand.

"That Max—" She began, using a stray twig to scrape some of the blood and scales into the container. "—is wrong, and I am right."

"Funny. . ." He whispered. Della gave him a questioning look, but he shook it away. "I'm more than willing to help with that." He popped all the *Altoids* into his mouth, smiling dumbly, the stench of mint replacing the smell of sulfur.

Della raised an eyebrow, snapping a picture of the hand-print, standing. "Why?" She asked.

Porter stood slowly, looking at her as if he was deciding whether she could be trusted with all the secrets of the universe. "We used to be friends, but I grew up and he didn't. Though he would tell you otherwise." He said glumly.

Della nodded her agreement with a sigh.

"Hey, were you crying?" Porter asked, hunching over to look at her at eye level.

Della straightened, her face glowing red. She had cried a lot last night. Full moons always do that too her. Or least that is what she was trying to convince herself. She sniffed a couple times, holding her head high. "No." She lied.

"Huh." Porter said. "Just wondering, since you've got an ocean of mascara all over your face." He waved his finger around her face.

"Jerk." Della snapped, brushing past him, her dry ends smacking him in the face. Okay, maybe she *had* cried a little earlier.

He sneezed once, rubbing his nose then followed her. "I'd agree with you, but then alas, we would both be *dreadfully* wrong." He said in an awful Victorian accent, complete with him sticking his nose high up in the air, his hands crossed behind his back.

Della smiled to herself, laughing quietly.

"So, what did you do? I hear no sirens; I see no police-men. You can't have possibly told them to leave." Della pointed out.

"You'd be surprised. I have connections, you see. I assured my fellow officers that nothing was wrong, and they trusted me. Awful decision, really. I'm surprised so many peo-ple trust this little face of mine." Porter explained. His arrogant humor eased her anxiety.

"You? A cop?" Della asked as he held the back door open for her.

Porter nodded proudly. "*Undercover*, dearly detested. The skillset I have acquired from growing up in a mortuary proves useful to Cheif Steiniger. Plus, on Tuesdays, if you show your I.D. down at *Bayou Gil's Crab Emporium*, you eat for free."

"Sneaky."

"Not as sneaky as you, I presume." Porter corrected. "You finally going to tell me the real reason you are here?"

"As I said, I'm proving a point," Della said simply. It wasn't a total lie.

"No, I meant here in Moss Hollow."

Della stopped walking as soon as they got to the sidewalk. An old hearse was parked on the curb. Della guessed it was his.

"Why do you ask? I fit in, don't I? Just another one of you, Louisiana freaks?" She smiled.

He shrugged. "You certainly look the part." He said, earning himself a scowl. "No one ever comes to this town without good reason. What did you do? You into fire? A couple of houses burned down in Alexandria. What about water? I hear the drowning rate has gone up." What scared her was that this didn't feel like a joke. He was dead serious, asking her if she had drowned someone.

". . . No." She said, tilting her head to the side to look at him more carefully. She suddenly didn't want to be alone with him.

Porter was staring at her quite oddly too. He suddenly went white, taking a step back. "Right. Ha-ha, gotcha!" He exclaimed, pointing finger guns at her. What was up with the men in this town using that as a defense mechanism?

Della opened her mouth to speak, but he just kept pointing his fingers at her, laughing maniacally. She let her mouth hang open, her eyebrows furrowed deeply over her eyes.

"Well. . . I'm going to go. Have a nice day, Miss Coleman." He said, then ran around to the driver's side of the hearse, quickly getting in and pulling away.

"Yeah," Della said, staring after him. "You too."

~CHAPTER ELEVEN~

Seventy-thousand people followed her blog. *Seventy thousand.* Yet not one person knew of anyone that would have the time to examine the specimens she had. What were nameless, faceless, internet stalkers good or these days?

"Hey, Norman!" Della called as she ran through *The Utopian Courier,* mint container and test tubes in hand.

She burst into the common office. Echoes of beeping printers, the clicks of computer keys, and typewriters, and the smell of hot ink overtook Della's senses. From what she had heard, the common office had been constructed out of a vast chasm in the floor caused by faulty cannons in seventeen-seventy-four. She took carefully to the zig-zagging gothic staircase, careful not to trip over the threadbare runner. The common office was full of old mismatched desks, and large bookshelves that made it look more like an old sunken library than an office space.

"What do you need, Della?" Norman asked. He smiled toothily, eyeing the vials in her hand. Norman was a short, stout redhead whose wardrobe consisted of band t-shirts, which Della respected, though did not find attractive. He reminded her of a washed-up, old, drunken leprechaun.

"Do you know of anyone who can test these?" She said, eyeing Irene—a tall, hook-nosed woman with a very fragile looking frame—who was bent over a photograph with a gargantuan magnifying glass.

"Yeah, Max is our guy for that sort of stuff. I thought you two spent a lot of time hanging around each other, shouldn't you already know that?" Norman asked, scratching his mass of ruby hair.

Della scowled, pulling the samples of moss out of Norman's sight. "Maximilian McGregor-Mavericks and I are not on speaking terms as of the moment, thank you, sir." She said hotly.

Irene looked up from her magnifying glass, her crudely drawn eyebrows raised in surprise. "I do believe you are out of luck, Miss Coleman."

Della rolled her eyes. "You seriously don't have anyone else that can help me?" They both shook their heads. "Thank you for your time, I suppose." Della hissed, turning on her heels.

"Wait," Irene called. Della heard a ruffling of papers and the scratch of chair legs against lacquered wood. "Mavericks said these are for you."

For such a tall woman, who easily looked like she could have taken on half the men and women in this room with ease, Irene shook with such little confidence that Della thought she would fall over. Her hands shaking so much that the paper she held began to rattle like thunder, Irene handed over a list of recent disappearances. Just as Della was going to dismiss it, she noticed that underneath each child's name, was a date unrelated to the date they went missing.

"Why did he want me to have this?" Della asked, visibly confused.

"Percy is something of a legend in this town. He has a way of doing the police's job for them." Norman began.

"He is smart; some might say too smart." Irene added, staring off and shivering for a moment.

"He figures out most mysteries within an hour of them being announced." Gabriella, a pretty Latina woman stated as she walked by with a box full of old *Nancy Drew* books, shaking one in the air and nodding.

"Naw, I'd say he's more of a villain out of the *Sherlock Holmes* books." Nick, a boy with long blonde hair who wore long trench coats and called himself Wiccan, corrected, scribbling away in a tiny wine-colored book.

"Quite scary if you ask me." Rosa, his partner in crime, added. The only difference between the two was height and gender.

"You aren't going to break out into a musical number, are you?" Della laughed.

The room dropped dead with an eerie silence. Della couldn't even smell ink floating in the air. Nick looked up from his book, his feather quill dropping from his hands. Irene covered her mouth, Norman gasped, Gabriella tripped over her own feet. Della looked around at the rest of the writers, re-searchers, editors, and photographers. Everyone was staring at her with looks of either terror or unbridled rage.

"I—It was a joke." Della said, smiling nervously.

"We do *not* talk about two-thousand-and-eleven that way." Rosa said sternly, picking up a pile of papers from Nick's desk and walking away.

Norman nodded his agreement, Irene whispered a little '*Well I never*' beneath her breath, and Nick picked up his quill, whispering something. Della squinted at her shoes. Never talk about musicals, or two-thousand-eleven. Apparently. She would have to add that the list of things she never thought would be forbidden.

"What we are trying to say," Norman began. He was staring at Della, death floating behind his dull brown eyes. "Is that whatever 'clue' the boss hands you, you work it out. Nothing he says is irrelevant. I've been here for twelve years, and I still haven't cracked his code. Run those numbers in whatever computer system you got. They got something to do with whatever you're doing."

The noise in the room picked up again, though most were still staring at her over the tops of their laptops.

"Got it." Della said, slowly slinking away. "And. . . sorry."

Nick slammed his hand onto his desk, rounding on her, pointing his quill at her like a sword. He opened and closed his mouth a couple of times before jumping up, looking like he had been zapped by lightning.

"SORRY ISN'T GOOD ENOUGH!" He screamed.

Della winced at the volume of his voice, turning around and quickening her steps out of the common office.

"It's okay Nick, they cannot hurt you anymore." She heard Irene say in a very motherly tone.

"I can still hear *You Are the One That I Want* from *Grease* playing in the distance." Nick cried. Della glanced over her shoulder to see him weeping into Irene's arms. "Curse you, I say! Curse you!"

~ ~ ~

It seemed to Della that the entire town of Moss Hollow hated her. Her mail had arrived soggy, thrown in her face by the mailman, she found a fly in her oatmeal at breakfast, and her fellow employees seemed to think she didn't exist.

Ridiculous.

How was she supposed to know not to say something, if no one said anything about it? This backward, backwoods, horrible excuse for a community kept pushing her closer and closer to the edge of her sanity. Della had never missed the town of Sycamore Heights so much. Even Richie was treating her differently. He was acting as though she were the villain in some grand story, she knew nothing about. Well, that wasn't that different from how he normally treated her, but still.

She had begun to give up on even toying with the fantastical idea of socializing. At this point, it seemed more like the end of the world than a simple conversation between two living, breathing, walking, talking beings.

Della sighed heavily, tapping her foot rapidly on the pavement.

She stood at a bus stop, shivering as the wind blew pouring rain into her face. A rain cloud seemed to follow her around. She looked up at the sky, furious. The scowl she wore was deeper than the depths of the ocean, and the sadness she felt was bigger than the cloudy, thundering sky above her.

As for the mysterious numbers Mavericks had given her, they were nothing but a pile of dirt with a couple of twigs sticking out of it. She had spent several sleepless nights on the Moss Hollow Tribune's page, cross-referencing the names of all the kids who were missing with the dates, but nothing extravagant jumped out at her. One of the dates was the kid's birthday, but she didn't see how that would help. Things would be so much easier if she retained everything her uncle had tried to teach her about coding. She'd just have to chock that up to her being the family disappointment.

The bus pulled up in front of her as she mulled this over in her head. It took her a moment before she realized she could finally leave this crumbling bus stop and go to work.

You'd think that she would have been more excited about all this; going to work, writing, researching. You'd be dead wrong to think that. As with all things, the novelty had finally worn off for yours truly, Della Coleman. Her dream job was beginning to feel like more of a chore to do the things she loved than a passion.

Not to mention that she had neglected her blog for the past month. All she had for her readers were questions, not stories. She had lost four hundred people. Not once had she left her devoted followers hanging. Not once. Unfortunately, here she was, at a loss for motivation and deprived of creativity.

She hadn't even bothered to make sure her socks matched this morning. In reality, no one would probably notice. No one ever did. Not even if she wore a sushi sock on one foot and a rainbow one on the other. Not even if she stood before them all, screaming at the top of her lungs.

The bus ride was nothing but a bus ride. That is, until Clara Dixon waved at her, her arms full of flowers. Della waved back, trying her best to seem joyful. Clara sat down next to her, pulling a flower out of her bouquet and handing it over.

"Good morning, Miss Coleman. How are you?" Clara asked.

"Same old same old, how are you?" Della replied, fingering the soft blueish petals of the flower between her fingers. They were the same odd flowers she had seen at Clara's parents' house.

Clara shrugged. "I'm doing better. My shop's opening back up." She smiled, gesturing to the flowers.

Della furrowed her eyebrows. "What shop?"

"I own a little flower shop in town. It's a hole in the wall, easy to miss. Arthur just got back from visiting his parents; he's spending the week with Everett while I get everything up and running again."

Della smiled. "I'll have to stop in and get some hydrangeas to brighten up my apartment."

Clara nodded energetically. "I sell seeds, bulbs, arrangements, and bouquets. I'll set one aside for you."

Della nodded, glancing out the window, twirling the flower between her fingers. She sighed, breaking off part of the stem and shoving the flower behind her ear. "These are pretty."

Della said, nodding at the rest of the strange flowers.

"They're Aconite. Or Monkshood, I guess. Want me to put some in with the hydrangeas?"

"That would be lovely." Della said, the sadness in her voice unmistakable.

"Anything you want to talk about?" Clara asked kindly.

Della shook her head as the bus pulled up to P.J. Mavericks Law. "Have a nice day, Ms. Dixon." She said as she edged past her.

Clara waved after her. At least one person still seemed to care. However, it didn't stop the smile Della tossed over her shoulder at Lenora from being nothing but a smile as she walked through the lobby. Just something she forced her lips to do. There was no happiness dwelling inside her today. The walk to her office was just a walk. Not a trot, not a promenade, not a stroll. Just a walk. One foot in front of the other.

Just as she sat down in her spinning chair, safe inside the confines of her office, her puffy eyes feeling heavy, a pain erupting in the back of her neck, the door before her opened slowly. Mavericks poked his head inside, watching her with a look crossed between fear and admiration.

"God, what now?" Della whispered under her breath.

"Do you mind if we have a little chat?" Mavericks asked.

"Be my guest." Della said sarcastically, trying to look as cheerful as possible.

Reaching into her purse, staring at the empty bottle of sumatriptan in her possession, her headache seemed to grow, almost as if her body was taunting her. She sighed, tossing the bottle aside. She'd have to call her mother and ask her to order her some.

Mavericks hesitated before swinging the door open to reveal Max standing next to him, chewing on the right sleeve of his sweater. Della didn't have enough energy to tell them to go away. She swept her hand in front of her, gesturing for them to sit on her little couch.

Mavericks smiled widely. "Now, I hear you need some help with some samples?" He asked.

Della nodded, not looking at Max.

"Well, Max is good with that kind of stuff, aren't you, Max?" Mavericks said, a hopeful tone to his voice.

"I've got it handled." Della replied. She very much did *not* have it handled, but that piece of information was on a need to know basis. And Max didn't need to know.

"Yeah, Ei'm sure ya do." Max said sarcastically.

Mavericks shot him a look, causing him to roll his amber eyes.

"It's fine," Della began, turning towards her laptop and typing away. Curse words. She was typing curse words. "Don't waste your breath trying to make the baby behave." She breathed.

Max jumped off the couch. "Ei'm a baby, am Ei? It looks like ya've been crying yer eyes out, don' babies do that? Cannot say Ei've ever experienced it, 'cause Ei'm not a baby."

Della shook her head. "You just love the sound of your own voice, don't you?"

She looked up at him for a second, exchanging looks of waspish aggravation. Max opened his mouth at the same time Della did, both launching into long-winded screaming fits. Their voices mixed inaudibly as Mavericks desperately tried to calm them down.

"CHILDREN!" He screamed, slamming his hand down on Della's desk. "I swear to the Lord above; you two are the most idiotic beings on this planet!" He shouted. "I tried to make this a *peaceful, casual* experience, but obviously, that isn't working!"

Della sank into her chair, a wave of dizziness washing over her for no apparent reason other than her tantrum towards Max. Her eyes drooped shut against her will for a moment. She leaned forward, taking off her glasses and pinching the bridge of her nose. Her head ached and throbbed. If she didn't know any better, she would have assumed it was a ticking time bomb.

"Apologize to Della, right now!" Mavericks yelled. A ringing sound echoed in her ears as he spoke.

"Fine." Max breathed hotly. "Ei'm sorry Ei said ya weren' wanted anywhere." He said.

"Do you mean it?" Mavericks asked.

Max shrugged, then nodded.

"You don't have to." Della said truthfully. It wasn't going to change anything if he did or didn't. Once you learn something, once you believe something, it's tough to change your own mind.

She knew their worried eyes were on her as she rubbed her temples. Pressure was building up between her eyes, blurring her sight. She had suffered from severe headaches her whole life, but this was the worst she had felt in a long time. Voices swirled in her mind as she sat there.

She sat there, feeling like the life was being drained from her thin veins, shaking all over, a cold sweat breaking out on her brow.

"Delphee." Mavericks' voice rang in her ears.

"Hmm?" She asked weakly, forcing her eyes open.

Mavericks was kneeling to her left, his hand gently resting on her shoulder. He looked scared, his face stark white. Max was in front of her, confusion spreading across his round features.

"Are ya okay?" Max asked, furrowing his eyebrows. "Ei'm not going tuh do anything for ya just because yer 'sick,' ya know." He said though worry was spreading over into his eyes.

Della stood. "I'm fine. Just tired." She said, her voice quiet.

"You look—you look exhausted." Mavericks said, pushing her up as she wobbled on the spot. The room swayed, her head feeling like it weighed ten pounds.

"I'm fine." She repeated sternly, more to herself than to Max or Mavericks.

She pushed her way over to the cabinets opposite her desk, searching inside them for the vials of blood and container of scales. She grabbed them, tossing them at Max. He eyed her for a moment, wondering whether to address the fact that she was clinging to the open drawer beside her for stability, but ultimately decided against it.

"Where did ya get these?" He asked, opening the mint container with a cheeky little grin on his face.

"I broke into a crime scene." Della said, smiling far too proudly.

Mavericks clapped his hands, taking a seat back on the couch. Max rolled his eyes again—that seemed to be his signature move—stuffing the samples in his pockets.

"What am Ei testin' for?" He asked, sitting next to Mavericks.

Della didn't have the guts to try and move to face them properly. If she did, she'd surely fall flat on her face.

"You're the scientist. Tell me if anything weird shows up."

Max nodded. "And the. . . What is this, clay?"

"Found it behind the house after P—when I was snooping around." Again, specific details were only on a need to know basis. "There was a handprint in the bushes. About the size of a child's, only had four fingers. I want you to cross-reference it with the horn we got sent."

"Sounds good. Lookin' for the same human DNA, right?" He asked.

Della stared at him for a long moment, trying to process what he had said. "What?" She asked. Her voice croaked as her skull rippled with pain.

Max held his hands out in confusion. "The human DNA that was intertwined in the animal fat. It's probably nothing. Ei gave ya the paper; Ei thought it was obvious."

"*I'm not a friggin genius like you are!*" Della hissed exasperatedly. She was pretty sure that made him blush.

"There we go! Two fr—two *coworkers* getting along!" Mavericks smiled. They glared at him. He put his hands up in defense, though chuckled slightly. "Now, with this new information, what are you going to do?"

"We should probably revisit the cemetery," Della said.

Max nodded. "We need another common denominator, though. Have ya found anywhere else that might be worth investigation? Ei could help ya, y'know."

Too tired to contradict, Della nodded, though it was evident she was filled with dread. She leaned back against the cabinets, thinking. She smirked. "I was reading up on a missing person's report filed last night. A teen went missing from some old butcher shop? The kids seemed pretty freaked out about what they saw. Said something about a monster in the woods? We could check out the place, and talk to the kids, get a first-hand report."

"All right, it's settled then." Mavericks said, looking between them like a proud father. "Max, get your equipment, and Della, gather your notebooks. You've got work to do."

~CHAPTER TWELVE~

Bloodshed

Killing two birds with one tiny pebble, the pair made their way to the cemetery. Max had said Porter could take them to the old butcher's shop, and that it would be safer that way. Della had tried to ask why, but he skirted the question, a dark look on his face. Della knocked on the mortuary's front door, not sure how to feel. Especially given her last encounter with Porter Garroway.

Porter opened the door, smiling widely until he saw Max's short figure behind her. "What are you doing here?" He asked, though not unkindly. He stared at the flower in her hair for quite some time, his face going through a multitude of emotions.

"We have a couple of questions." Della smiled.

"Anything for you, Miss Coleman." Porter smiled. He made a point to look only at Della. "What would you like to know?"

"You can call me Della." She said politely. Max made a gagging noise as Della got out her phone and hit record. "Have you seen any large shadows in the cemetery?" Porter shook his head. "Have you found any other pieces of whatnot or clay?" Porter laughed but shook his head. "Have you seen eyes lurking in the woods?" Another shake of his head. "Have you seen any Golems? Maybe, oh, I don't know, some strange guy in a ghillie suit messing around with sulfur?"

Porter stared at her, then looked to Max. There was an odd expression on his face. "I'm sorry, Miss Della, I can't help you there." He seemed extremely nervous. "Nothing odd since the raccoons." He winked.

Unlike Moss Hollow, the people of Sycamore Heights hadn't been big on conspiracies. It had been a quaint little town that relied on its faith in Jesus and nothing else. Any speak of witchcraft, goblins, Bigfoots, or other weird creatures was strictly forbidden. Nevertheless, Della had needed juicy information to feed her readers. It had taken a couple of years, but she knew how to get the answers she wanted from just about anyone. One time she even had to fake an incurable illness.

"Not once in your life have you seen a strange, large, human-sized mound of sludge crawling around?" Della asked, putting on a corrective tone.

Porter looked up to his right, then stared her down. "No. I haven't." He was standing as stiff as a board, rubbing his upper lip. He was blatantly lying to her. What was worse is that she was pretty sure he knew that she knew.

"If you had seen something, what do you think it looked like?" Della asked.

Porter shook his head, pointing at her. "You are a tough one, aren't you?" He smiled.

Della straightened with pride. "So, you *have* seen something?" She asked hopefully.

Porter ran a hand through his thick hair, debating his options. Max was leaning against the railing around the porch, mindlessly looking through his phone. Porter rolled his eyes, sighing.

"More scratch marks showed up." He said, his smile faltering.

"Where?"

Porter edged past her, nodding, loosely gesturing to the right. "I'll show you."

They followed him through the cemetery, a thick mist beginning to rise from the ground. Nothing but three sets of footsteps echoed through the air. As they walked on, the ground began to incline, the pathways between mausoleums turning to nothing but grass. Soon, dirty obelisks popped forth from the ground, each adorned with wilted flowers. Max quickened his pace, trying to keep as close to Della as possible. She rolled her eyes. Cemeteries weren't supposed to be scary; they were meant to be a place to visit the people we lost. A place of remembrance.

"Here we are." Porter sighed, coming to an abrupt stop. Before him stood a crumbled headstone and a giant bottle of *Wet & Forget*. He leaned down, picking up pieces of stone, looking at them as if they were diamonds.

"Raccoons, huh?" Max yawned, trying to look cool though they all knew he would've clung to Della for dear life if she allowed it.

Porter shot him a warning look, standing back up and brushing his hands off on his pants. "What are you two thinking?" He asked.

"Confidential." Della smiled. "You sure you didn't see anything?"

Porter shrugged, looking around his graveyard. "Nope. It was weird though. I heard something when I was cleaning up the moss last night, but whatever did this was gone before I got here. All they left was an odd feeling in the air. Like a odd sort of terror." He looked so sad.

"Whose grave was it?" Della asked.

"Floyd Cummings." Porter said.

"Yeesh." Max said. Something flew out of the oaks in the distance, startling him.

"You guys know him?" Della asked.

"He died a couple weeks ago. Hotel room, stabbed." Porter sighed. "No sign of a break in. Some are saying suicide."

Max watched him, his face twisting into a look of concern. "Suicide? Ya thinkin' somethin' else?" He inquired, crossing his arms.

"I think that if you two are here, something is wrong. Something that *people* can't fix." He looked at Della, waiting to see if she was catching on to what he was saying.

"Well," Della smiled, putting away her phone. "It's not the werewolves."

"It never is." The boys said in unison. Porter smiled to himself, giving her a curt nod.

Della rolled her eyes. So, this was the new normal? Normalcy was now defined as standing in a cemetery, discussing murders, assuring each other the local wolf pack had nothing to do with the recent spike in crime?

"Thank you for your time, Mr. Garroway." She said, taking a step to the side, watching Max work up the nerve to talk. Porter nodded to her, rubbing his nose and sniffing.

"We need yer help." Max said.

"I just helped you. You know, for the *paper*." Porter said, staring Della down.

"Well. . . We need *more* help than." Max said shortly. Another set of birds flew from the trees, making him yelp.

"With what, Milliano?" Porter asked, giggling. "The fact Miss Coleman has a bad omen tucked behind her ear?" Della eyed him, instinctively reaching up to touch the flower Clara had given her. He nodded, shrugging.

"Don' call me that." Max hissed. "Ya know that old butcher shop ya used to hang out at? Can ya take us there?"

Porter paled, shaking his head. He moved them aside, making to return to the mortuary. "Sorry, that place is a no go. Last time I was there, I had my first taste of tequila, and Cheif Steiniger arrested ten kids. I'm not going back."

"Porter." Max pleaded.

Porter turned on his heels, ready to rip into the scaredy-cat before him, but all he could do was point a finger in his face. They stared each other down, Della looking between them. Porter glanced at Della, having an internal struggle.

"Eventually, Miss Coleman, you're going to have to pay me back for all these favors." He said, sighing hotly.

~ ~ ~

Porter watched as she debated her answer. She looked dreadful this morning. Dark circles danced under her eyes; her skin looked a little too dull. He silently wondered if she was okay, praying that she was.

Eventually, she smiled. "I'm sure you will think of something." She said, an ounce too sweet for his liking.

Porter looked her up and down. He was suddenly regretting his decision to give in and take them to the butcher's shop as she and Max climbed into his old rusty hearse. He jumped off the porch once he finished tying his shoes, trying to arrange his face into a jovial expression.

He had an awful feeling about this little outing.

Della was watching him with a curious expression. She knew far too much about the human mind for his liking. Though she probably figured all that out because of her career, not because she hated the entirety of human existence like he did. Little did he know she felt the same way. He smiled at her in the rearview mirror, letting the old car warm up.

It was a rather blustery morning down in Moss Hollow. He loved it; this was his home. How could he not? However, at this very moment, he wished he was somewhere else entirely. Preferably on some beach in Hawaii. Maybe even the Caribbean.

The drive out of town was quiet. The tension between Max and Della, and Max and himself, was thick enough to cut with a knife, though it might have some trouble.

Porter hadn't been back to the old butcher shop since he was in school. It brought back bittersweet memories of drinking with the undesirables he would rather not relive. Parking the car, he unlocked the doors.

"I'll wait here." He said, casually leaning against his arm and rolling down the window. "Call me if you need me."

"The whole point of ya comin' was for protection," Max said. Della raised an eyebrow.

"Like I said, call me if you need me." Porter smiled, leaning across Max's thin frame and opening the door for him.

~ ~ ~

The butcher shop wasn't like anything Della had expected. It had been located off a long gravel road she believed used to lead to a farm. The butcher shop was overgrown, the walls crumbling, the ivy and moss making the broken windows look less deadly than they were. She and Max stuck close together as they examined their surroundings. Though the sky was covered with gray clouds, casting blue shadows down on everything, she was glad it was the middle of the day.

Over his shoulder, Max had a big leather bag bursting at the seams with scientific equipment. He struggled with it, placing it on a somewhat flat pile of old bricks.

"Ei'll set up here, wanna start takin' a look around?" He asked.

Della nodded, placing her own bag down on the bricks, taking nothing but her flashlight and phone to take pictures. She dared a glance over her shoulder at Porter, who was staring at her with a worried expression from the cab of the hearse.

"What's with you two, anyway?"

Max shook his head, pulling a couple of beakers out of his bag, acting like she didn't exist.

"Fine." Della said, leaving him to work and entering the rundown place.

Rundown might have been too sweet of a word. 'An absolute wreck' was more appropriate. The floor was covered in some sort of squishy foliage, the walls covered in graffiti and swear words. It looked crossed between a homeless camp and the set of a horror film. Della shivered. She continued walking on. Her nose was suddenly filled with a horrible stench, something akin to Porter's house, minus the evergreen. Trying to be quiet, as not to scare anything, she stepped around a corner to where a half-open walk-in freezer was. The lights inside it were flickering. Della inhaled sharply, taking another step forward.

A horrendous sight greeted her eyes. Animal carcasses were piled in the corners, along with foot-long scratches. Daring a step inside, Della began taking pictures, gagging on the smell. A glimmer caught her eye as she looked around. A golden watch was mixed up with all the gruesome things around her. She bent down to pick it up.

Something moved out of the corner of her eye. She screeched, running towards the door, slipping as she grabbed the door, causing it to swing back and shut before she could get to her feet. The lights in the freezer stopped flickering. They began glowing brighter and brighter, causing Della to cover her eyes as she tried to adjust. Shaking all over, she pushed herself off the floor, turning back to the door, expecting it to open.

But it didn't.

Della slammed her entire weight into the door. Were those footsteps she heard outside? She pushed against the door with all her might, feeling terror rise in the back of her throat. Though the freezer was empty, she swore she wasn't alone. She kept looking over her shoulders, waiting to turn and see a dark figure standing behind her.

As she made to run into the door again, it made a little clicking noise like someone had locked it.

"*No, no, no.*" She swore. Was Della a coward? No. Was she scared? Absolutely. You try being stuck in a walk-in freezer at an old butcher shop and see how you like it.

Every vein in her body was tingling with horrified electricity. She punched the door, hoping it would open. Her eyes closed tightly as she rest her forehead on the door. No credit card or bobby pin was going to get her out of a locked freezer. She opened her eyes, seeing her reflection in the warped surface. Was it her imagination, or was the door bending?

She banged on the door as the whir of electronics buzzed in her ear. A cold mist was forming in the freezer, chilling her almost instantly.

How the Hell is this place still working? She thought.

A long, low growl echoed into her ears.

"Oh shit. . . HELP!" She screamed, pushing with all her might on the door.

~ ~ ~

Porter stared at Max as he walked the perimeter of the butcher shop. His leg was jiggling up and down, giving away his panic. Della should have been back by now. He fought himself for a moment, then got out of the hearse, slamming the door on accident as he walked over to Max.

"Do you need help with anything?" He asked nervously.

Max shook his head. "No," He held some sort of weird device in his hands that began making a beeping noise the closer Porter got. "And Ei didn' call for ya either. Go away; yer messin' with my device."

"What kind of device is it?" Porter asked, looking over his shoulder, thinking he had heard a twig snap.

"It's supposed to pick up on ectoplasmic energy." Max looked up from fiddling with a button on the device, scowling at him. "Or in terms the likes of a gimp can understand, it finds ghosts." He said the last part in a fake American accent, his voice high pitched and slow like he was explaining to a child what two plus two equals.

"I'm a gravedigger. I know what ectoplasm is." Porter snapped.

"Aye, ya practically bathe in it. Which is why yer messin' with my readin's." Max hissed.

Porter shushed him. He heard voices.

"Don' *shh* me!" Max yelled.

Porter rolled his eyes, stepping past him to investigate the dense forest that surrounded them. He saw a small flash of light and heard footsteps as someone hurriedly ran from the scene.

"Don' ignore me either!" Max screamed.

Porter put up a finger, and Max fell silent. A flock of birds flew up from the trees in the distance. Someone screamed.

No, a *girl* screamed.

Max and Porter swore in unison, tripping over each other to get inside the butcher shop.

Nothing. The place was empty.

"DELLA?" Max screamed.

They raced through the butcher shop, ending up in front of a freezer door. Porter pushed his way past Max, his hand hovering on the door handle. He could hear Della's muffled voice coming from inside. The door wouldn't budge.

He tapped several times on the door. "Hey, we're here, it's okay." He said, hoping she could hear him. The door seemed to be locked. "Max, look for a key."

"*Stop bossin' me around!*" Max hissed.

"Are you—NOT NOW OKAY?!" Porter screamed.

After several long minutes that felt more like days, they found a key a few feet away. Porter unlocked the door, tearing it open. Della fell into his arms, nearly knocking them both to the floor. He pushed her away by the shoulders, picking her up by the waist and setting her behind him. The freezer was full of mutilated animal carcasses. He spun around, holding Della's face in his hands. She was covered in blood, which he couldn't tell whether it was hers or not.

"Are you okay? What happened? Are you hurt?" He asked. She was staring madly at the freezer door, her eyes glazed over. Max stepped past them to get a better look inside.

Della slowly pulled away from his grip, wiping beads of sweat from her forehead. "I'm okay." She said breathlessly. She winced, doubling over, gripping her forehead.

The light inside the freezer suddenly blinked off, scaring them all, though none of them would admit it.

Porter stared at her for a moment. "What happened?"

She shrugged. "I—I don't know. . . I walked in and something—moved—and—the— door—" She shut her eyes, rubbing her forehead, hyperventilating, waving her hands up and down to try to calm down. "Oh—If you—if you hadn't been here. . . If it had come back—"

Her eyes went all droopy for a minute as she swayed to the side, breathing heavily. He tried to steady her, but she pulled away, pacing back and forth in front of him, running her hands through her hair repeatedly. The boys paled, stepping away from the freezer. Max gagged, turning a morbid shade of green at the sight of it all.

Della whispered something under her breath, shaking her head. ". . . 'I' before 'e' except when your foreign neighbor Keith receives eight counterfeit beige Faberge eggs from feisty overly caffeinated atheists. Weird. 'I' before 'e' except when your foreign neighbor Keith receives eight counterfeit. . ." She kept repeating as she paced, her eyes full of crazed wonder.

Porter turned on his heels, looking to Max—who was peering inside the empty freezer—for assistance. "Is she going to be okay?" He looked back at Della, who was now laughing maniacally. He winced.

Max shook his head. "Probably not." They sat there for a moment, just watching her as she paced until she suddenly stopped and looked at them.

"Someone locked me in there." She said, the life coming back into her eyes. There was such fire in her eyes. The kind of fire a seasoned war veteran had.

"I heard footsteps I should go—" Porter paused, he smelled something. Something bitter that burned his nose. That familiar fear he had felt last night returned, this time stronger.

Max's EMF detector went off in his pocket, beeping like a bomb that was about ready to explode. He looked to Della; his eyes wide. Max had never been one to coddle ghosts and play with monsters. No matter how many times he turned into a cat or saw vampires feeding, he tried to disprove all the myths and legends that ran the world. Max found it easier to toy with the ideas of space travel then try and explain why witches didn't obey the laws of physics.

"Could be a haunting. Some ghosts look like monsters, with scaly hands, like a wraith." Della explained nervously, looking over her shoulder.

"Or a ghoul." Max added, swallowing hard.

"Guys I think we should—" Porter began.

"Do ya smell sulfur?" Max asked. "Isn' that a demon thing?"

Della scratched the back of her neck, spinning around, staring down every dark corner. She reached inside her jacket, producing a pocketknife. The blade was very old and rusted, and the handle seemed to be carved out of a deer antler. "If something possesses you—"

"Me? You're fresh meat!"

"I drink Holy Water, idiot."

"GUYS!" Porter shouted. There was a scratching noise coming from above them. He pointed upwards, and they both fell silent. He hadn't realized how much power he had by merely holding up a finger.

An otherworldly screech tore into their eardrums as Della opened her mouth to give a command. The roof showered them in dust and asbestos, the horrible scratching speeding up.

"FRIGGIN RUN!" Porter screamed, grabbing them both by the elbows and running towards the door.

Della broke free of his grip when they got to his car, her knife brandished. Max was frozen, one leg on solid ground, the other in the hearse. Porter still had a hand on him, the other hovering over Della's shoulder. He could tell that she was scared, her hands were shaking, her breaths low.

"Maybe we lost it?" Max said, his eyes glimmering with hope.

As if on cue, another bloodcurdling screech rang through the air, vibrating through them like a bass drop in a crappy rap song.

"Why on *Earth* would you say that?" Della groaned, switching her blade from one hand to the other.

A hideous form greeted their eyes, lumbering across the roof of the butcher shop, its mouth seething with foam. It had its back to them as Della took several pictures with her phone. Its body was covered in patches of different colored hair like some voodoo-hoodoo quilt. As it sat pawing at the butcher shop's roof, loose shingles and nails rained down upon them. The beast was merely four feet tall, but it cast an eerie shadow on them all. Porter grabbed Della's arm as it turned its head to look back at them, a foaming smile greeting them. The creature's eyes were glowing white as it locked onto Della, her eyes reflecting the glow.

Porter seized her as she screamed in terror and slumped against him, pushing her and Max into the car, vaulting over the hood and slamming the door so hard behind him that the windshield cracked. Max was screaming at him to drive as he fumbled with his keys, quite literally pushing the pedal through the floor. The hearse buzzed to life, wheeling back.

Porter turned around as the hearse hit a tree, catching Della's face. She looked sickly and exhausted, holding her head in her hands, her eyes shut tightly. Max didn't look any better, and he assumed his own face was pale and stricken with fear. He swore under his breath, turning back to look out the windshield. He gave the creature a rather rude gesture, then tore away from the old butcher shop.

He hated magic. He hated monsters. He hated it all.

~CHAPTER THIRTEEN~

Bayou Gil's Crab Emporium

"**Y**ou good?" Porter asked, his voice shaking. His tan skin was looking awfully pale in the late afternoon sun, an angry vein popping forth from his forehead. Maybe angry wasn't a strong enough word. After all, he had just flipped off a creature of the night.

Della gave a weak thumbs-up, her head pounding, her vision blurry. "Yeah," She croaked. "I'm fine, I'm great."

The boys breathed a sigh of relief, watching her in the rearview mirror as Porter drove. Della rolled her eyes, staring at them judgmentally. There was a moment of shocked silence, each of them sitting in their own thoughts. Della began to smile, watching Max's face in the mirror. He looked like he had seen a ghost. She laughed weakly, leaning against the old pleather seats in Porter's car. *Definitely* not a ghost.

"So," Max began, his voice shaking. "What the bloody Hell was that?"

Porter eyed Della, an odd expression on his face.

"That thing was a Grunch. Did you see it's face?" Della smiled wider, leaning forward between the two seats, resting her elbows on the middle compartment.

"No, Della. Ei did not. Ei must've missed the very thing that is goin' tuh haunt my nightmares for the rest of my life. Sorry 'bout that." Max snapped.

"What's a Grunch?" Porter asked.

For people who lived in Louisiana, they were awfully uncultured.

"The Grunch Road Monster is a four feet tall Louisiana Chupacabra." Della began. The wave of exhaustion she had felt was finally disappearing. "Stories of that creature go all the way back to the beginning of New Orleans in the seventeen hundreds. Or as you would've called it back then, La Nouvelle-Orléans." She smiled as Max shivered at the ominous tone to her voice. "Some say the settlers back then caught wind of a tiny reptilian humanoid that instilled fear into the minds of whoever saw it. Some said that the outcasts and deformed freaks of society inbred, causing the abomination." Quietly, Della crawled her fingers up the back of Max's seat like a spider. "Some say a witch had. . . *relations*. . . with a demon or made a deal with it to have the creature. Some say it does its mother's bidding. Others say it killed her." She smiled wider, lunging her fingers at Max's neck, causing him to scream like a little girl.

"No living thing can live that long," Porter said out of the blue. He was staring at the road, lost in thought, his face blank.

Della shrugged to herself. "Legend says that if you are bitten by one, you too become a Grunch."

"Welp, definitely got the whole fear thing covered. I guess the plot thickens," Porter said darkly.

Max turned to him. "Yeah, for the two of us," He scoffed, pointing his thumb back and forth between himself and Della.

"You can't bench me, Miliano. Not now." Porter smiled.

"Do. Not. Call. Me. That." Max snapped, a low rumbling coming from the back of his throat. "It would do ya good. Seein' as yer ego is an absolute problem." He continued.

"Boys," Della said sternly before any more shots could be fired.

"What?" They yelled in unison.

"Be cordial at least. Please." She said with a sigh as Porter turned down a side road that followed the bayou. London Avenue. "Especially when we go to meet the teens who saw this thing to begin with. If I'm right, and this is a Grunch, then they have had their fair share of terror. They don't need to witness you two bickering. I think it would kill them." She smirked.

Porter nodded, though reluctantly. "So, where are we

heading to meet them?"

"Norman said they would be at *Bayou Gil's Crab Emporium*," Della replied.

"*Yes!*" Max said quietly, looking quite ravenous.

"I could eat," Porter said in agreement.

Della rolled her eyes. "Work first, then food."

~ ~ ~

"I don't understand. . ." Della said under her breath. The parking lot was packed this afternoon, groups lingering around their cars, chatting away in the heat. She sighed heavily, looking down at the state she was in. Her clothes were stiff with animal blood and Lord knows what else. Somehow, she knew no one would even bat an eye.

"It's the local hotspot." Porter smiled, handing her a napkin to clean up her face. She scowled deeply. "What? I could've spit on it first." He said, somewhat offend as she roughly wiped off her cheeks.

"And they say chivalry is dead." Della said dryly.

Max choked down his laughter, sliding out of the cab as Porter came around to her side, opening her door for her. Della rolled her eyes, ignoring his hand as she jumped out of the hearse, the cabin rocking back and forth on its wheels in a way that made her wonder how it was still running. She sighed heavily again, trying to remember which of the wooden planks were loose as she followed the boys down the bridge.

"What?" Max asked, struggling to get the door open for them all.

Porter joyously entered the restaurant, waiting for Della to follow. She stood at the doorway, her face screwed up in a look of disdain. She hated this place.

"If you're allergic, you have to sign a waiver." Cheryl's voice rang. "Oh, Miss Coleman! Didn't expect you to ever come back."

"Desperate times." Della assured her. Cheryl nodded, sweeping them over to a table.

"Specials today are Jambalaya and Pecan Pie. Bottom of The Pot will be ready in half an hour. Lunch rush isn't done with their wild duck quite yet." Cheryl explained.

"Still no salad?" Della asked. Cheryl scowled.

Max stifled a laugh. "Ei'll take an order of crab and

chips, madam." He said, his eyes full of joy.

Porter rolled his. "Double helping of Crayfish and Grits for me."

Cheryl nodded, still staring at Della as she walked away, gripping the menus so hard the thick plastic bent beneath her long fingers.

"She's. . . pleasant." Della said, forcing a smile.

The daring trio sat in silence for some time, observing their surroundings, mulling over what had happened. Della was honestly quite proud of her companions. If something like this would have happened back in Sycamore Heights, she was sure Sebastian would've died.

Porter cleared his throat. "So, what do you think?" He asked quietly as Cheryl set three glasses of murky water on the table.

Della waited until Cheryl had left to reply. "Well, I'm sure this place is—" Della stared in disbelief, her words trailing off as the boys took long swigs from their water glasses. She gagged. "*How can you drink that?*" She whisper-yelled.

"Well, love, ya lift the glass tuh yer lips. . ." Max laughed. She kicked him hard under the table.

"It's not that bad." Porter smiled.

Della stared back and forth between them for a minute, shaking her head slowly. "Is everyone in this town insane?" She asked.

The boys seemed lost in thought for a moment.

"Define insane," Porter said at last with a slight scowl.

Eyebrows raised, Della sat back in her creaking seat, crossing her legs and arms. "Drinking dirty water, eating road-kill on flatbread. Eating alligators. And shellfish, for that mat-ter."

"What do ya have against shellfish?" Max asked, finish-ing off his water.

"You're kidding, right?" Della scoffed.

The boys exchanged a confused look, slowly shaking their heads.

"Crabs, shrimp, lobsters, crayfish, clams, and oysters are the devils of the sea." She declared dramatically. "They are unnatural, hideous beings. I mean come on, what animal walks sideways? It's disgusting." She couldn't stop herself from shivering, goosebumps running up her thin arms.

Porter set his glass down and turned to her. "Are you

seriously afraid of crabs?"

"*How can you not be*?" Della hissed.

"Out of all the things in this mad, mad, *mad*, world, you are afraid of a harmless crab?" He asked in disbelief. He lowered his voice. "After what we just saw, you are afraid of *seafood*?"

Della's cheeks reddened. "Childhood trauma." She said simply.

Max had grabbed her water since she wasn't going to drink it, spraying the nasty water out his nose as she spoke. Porter rubbed his temples, trying not to grin.

"Okay, you going to elaborate?" He asked, his voice cracking.

Della sat as straight as humanly possible, holding her head high. "I had family in a town called New Crest Wharf back in Washington. We went to visit them a lot. One day, my cousins thought it was a good idea to go down to the beach, and I followed, looking for adventure." The boys were watching her with blank expressions, looking utterly bored. She sighed heavily. "A crab clamped its claw on my toes, all right? Are you happy now?" She spat.

Max was now coughing, laughing so hard he couldn't breathe. Porter cupped his head in his hands, his shoulders shaking, betraying the laughter he was trying to hide.

"Mature. *Real* mature." Della hissed, looking out the window to her left, her face burning red.

"Awe, come on, Della, quit it," Porter said. She saw him smile in the flickering candlelight reflected on the window. "You have to admit that your fears are irrational."

Della mocked him in a high-pitched voice, crossing her eyes. "Your fears are irrational. Yeah? Well your face is irrational, how about that?" She asked, adding a little *humph* for effect without a second thought.

"Wow. Ei mean, honesty is the best policy." Max smiled.

Cheryl returned with heaping plates of steaming crayfish and a bowl full of bubbling gumbo. She glared at Della, setting a plate full of wilted lettuce in front of her and walking away. At least this time it was adorned with what looked like blue cheese salad dressing. Or maybe that was the kind of mold you *shouldn't* eat. . .

"The most important things you should come to accept about this town, are that we aren't afraid of the boogeyman, we know that death is more of a vacation than an end to our means, and we don't eat salads," Porter explained in a very matter-of-fact tone, squeezing a crawdad into his mouth.

Della gagged, swallowing hard. She moved around the wilted greens on her plate for a moment, before removing herself from the table. She was starving, but no one in their right mind would eat from this place.

"Where are you going?" Max asked through a mouthful of fries.

"To do my job." She said, wrinkling her nose as a whiff of Porter's fishy breath filled her lungs.

"Have fun!" Max called to her as she made her way over to the front counter.

Bayou Gil sat there, smiling his rotten little grin. Behind him, in a large glass cabinet, jars and bottles full of pickled vegetables and floating frog eyes glistened in the late afternoon sun. He wore an old straw hat over his greasy gray hair, adding to his hillbilly aesthetic.

"How may I be of service?" He asked in his pirate-like voice.

"I'm just wondering if a group of kids came in? I'm meant to be talking to them." Della asked politely, trying not to stare at his eyepatch made of thick leather. The filigree design that had been burned into it looked like some sort of family crest. Complete with a wolf.

Gil nodded "He's out back. Fidgety young fellow." He said, hopping off his stool. Della believed he would've been shorter than even Lenora. And that was saying something. "I'll show ya."

Della followed him through his restaurant, receiving odd looks from the chattering customers. He led her through a side door covered in hanging beads that jingled like bells in the wind, pulling them aside to reveal a large porch full of empty tables. Empty except for one.

"Wesley is a good kid, go easy on him." Gil said. He had this fatherly look to him today. Della smirked. Maybe she wasn't picking up on the fact that he was a good father, but rather he was an excellent pack leader.

She nodded, walking over to the young boy at the table. He held a steaming cup of hot chocolate in one hand, a half-eaten Reuben sandwich in the other. He looked up from staring at a passing gator, smiling at Della. His face was pockmarked, his blond hair untidy, his eyes full of worry.

"Miss Coleman, right?" He asked. His voice was small and squeaky like a mouse. Which now that she mentioned it, Della thought that's exactly what he looked like.

Della nodded. "Mind if I sit?"

Wesley gestured to the chair across from him, observing Della, his face reddening. "Hope you don't mind me saying this, but I was expecting someone older. Given what Uncle Norman said on the phone." He smiled, reaching up to straighten out his curly hair.

"Not at all." Della smiled. "Thank you for speaking with me this afternoon. So, you're Norman's nephew?"

He nodded. "Fifth-generation Hamilton! Uncle Norman and I don't talk much, but he is a good man. I didn't know he worked for the Moss Hollow Tribune. I never would have pinned him as a gossip." There was an odd light in Wesley's eyes.

"He's an editor," Della half lied.

"Wow." Wesley breathed. "So, what would you like to know?" He carried himself with more maturity than someone who looked barely thirteen should have. Or at least he *tried* to.

"Whatever you feel comfortable sharing. I'm on your time, not mine."

Wesley nodded to himself, looking back over the bayou. "Charity, me, and a couple of friends went to check out the old butcher shop." He began. "We are all in an extracurricular film class for the more advanced kids. Our teacher wanted us to do an amateur horror film based on the town. You know the stories; the butcher shop was the perfect place to visit."

"What stories?" Della asked, leaning across the table. She pulled out her phone and hit record, wanting to capture every word Wesley uttered.

He looked back at her. "You don't know?" He asked, his eyes widening.

Della shook her head.

Wesley smiled, his eyes full of excitement. Della had seen that look before, usually in her own eyes. It was the kind of excitement she got when someone asked her about something she was passionate about.

"Some eighty years ago, this guy murdered his family there," Wesley said, taking a sip of his cocoa. He scowled, looking inside the cup at its contents. "Well, that's what the paper said. My mom says it was just a hoax. She says the family got in over their heads in money and left. I don't believe it. Something weird happened out there, and the events with Charity prove it."

"Charity was the girl who went missing?"

"Yeah. She's my girlfriend." Wesley said. He took a bite of his sandwich, watching Della roll her eyes. "Was. I meant she *was* my girlfriend. I'm single now, for obvious reasons. I'm not a cry baby, I've had time to adjust." He said quickly, wiggling his eyebrows.

Della smiled kindly. "Let's focus on the problem at hand, shall we?" She asked. He nodded somewhat reluctantly; his face so red it matched the ketchup dripping off the fry he picked up. "What happened to her?"

"She was our director. She was awfully bossy when it came to filming, always wanted to be ahead. Was 'er 'ownfall." He said through a mouthful of fries, spraying Della in spit. "Duh police don't be'weive us."

Della wiped her nose, nodding, egging him to continue.

Wesley scratched his head. "I was messing around with the old video camera we were using, and I heard her scream. Me and *Isaac*," He spat, rolling his eyes. "Went to check it out. She was over by this pile of weird leather, or so we thought, but it moved. I don't know what it was but. . ." He stopped, staring at the ketchup on his fingers.

"It's okay; you don't have to say anything you don't want to," Della said in a motherly tone.

"No, it's okay. I'm a man now. I can admit when I pee myself from fright." Wesley assured her. He shrugged to himself, licking his fingers.

Della raised her eyebrows, looking over her shoulder to see Porter leaning against the doorway full of beads, looking smug. Della stuck her tongue out at him, turning back to Wesley.

"Is that your boyfriend?" He asked, staring Porter down like Della was a piece of meat they were fighting over.

"No." Della said a little too quickly.

Wesley smiled. "Okay, cool. Anyway, *Isaac* and I were all like 'Ah, what is that thing? Charity move!'" He said, faking a little scream, waving his hands around in the air. "But she didn't. She kinda like—" He lifted up his hand, slowly laying it on the table like a falling tree. "—fell over and then more of these weird little lizard-goat-things appeared, like I don't know, melted together and dragged her away." He explained.

"How many?" Della asked.

"Tenish." Wesley said, puffing out his chest. "The ones that didn't take her, I scared away." He said proudly.

Della stared at him, wondering how many of these Grunches there were and what their master wanted.

"I suppose wherever they took her, she isn't too upset about it. Can't be worse than what she dealt with at home." Wesley said quietly.

"What makes you say that?" Della asked.

"Promise not to tell anyone?" He asked. Della nodded. "Pinky promise?"

Della sighed as Wesley held up a finger covered in grease and ketchup. "I pinky promise." She said, begrudgingly wrapping her finger around his. Wesley smiled with delight, holding firmly onto her hand as she tried to make him let go.

"She lives with her grandma. Her parents died when she was little; they were druggies. The grandma was," Wesley lowered his voice. "*Abusive.*" He whispered. "I bet she is happy to get away from her. She always came to school with bruises on her wrists that she tried to hide."

Della thought for a moment, sitting back in her chair, finally free of Wesley's grip. An idea popped into her head, causing her to smile.

"Wesley, did you happen to run across a young girl named Anna Dixon?" She asked.

Wesley shrugged. "I knew Clara Dixon. She babysits me and my little brother." He choked on his hot cocoa. "Not that I need a babysitter, my parents just don't trust me. Not that I'm not trustworthy! I just—There was this incident last year with a bottle of fake spray tan and chicken wire and—"

"Right." Della said, rolling her eyes again. "Did—did Clara have bruises?" Della asked.

Wesley's eyes widened. He leaned forward, a look of awe on his face. "How did you know?" He breathed.

"Just a hunch. Did you ever overhear anything that might make you believe Clara's parents were abusive too?"

He thought for a moment. "You know what? I think I did. I heard her crying one night. Something about how she hated her life or whatever. *Drama.*" He sang. "I'm not really into that; I stay out of trouble." He said, leaning back in his chair and winking at her.

"I'm sure you do. . ." Della said slowly. This was the missing piece of the puzzle she had been looking for, something that connected all the victims. She stood, brushing off her jacket. "Thank you for your time, Wesley."

Wesley stood too, a look of disappointment on his face. "That's it?" He asked.

"I'm afraid so. I have to get back to work." Della said, faking a sad expression.

"Oh, yeah. Uh, me too. I help my dad out at the mechanic shop." He said, puffing out his chest again. Della smiled, turning to walk away. "Hey, wait!" He yelled. "There uh, there is this stupid dance at the school on Halloween. I—I have to bring a date. You know how it is." He made a show of rolling his eyes.

"Ah, gosh darn it. I already have plans." Della lied.

"Oh, yeah. Uh, do these plans require a plus one?" Wesley asked hopefully.

"Sorry, the RSVP closed yesterday. I don't have the power to fit another person onto the list." She smiled sadly.

Wesley scowled, finishing off his hot chocolate. "Fine. I'll see you around then." He sighed. "Oh, and don't forget to pay. Uncle Norman said it wouldn't be any trouble. I think it's like thirty bucks or whatever?" He said, gesturing to his food as he swept past her.

Della stared at the half-eaten sandwich and fries in disgust. A sniffling laugh came from behind her. Porter was standing, his hands in his pocket, a satisfied smile on his face, watching Wesley bounce his way back inside the restaurant.

"Looks like you have an admirer." He said slyly.

"Shut up," Della said, her face involuntarily burning red.

"All right," He said, walking with her back inside. "*Cougar.*" He whispered.

She elbowed him as she dug into her alien-head-shaped purse, grabbing her simple black wallet and pulling out a twenty and two fives.

"It wouldn't have worked with Wesley and me anyway." She laughed.

"How come?"

"As far as you are concerned," She said as she handed the old hillbilly her money. "I like my men like I like my rainy days, atrabilious." She smiled.

"Atrabil—What?" Porter smiled.

"Never you mind." Della smiled back.

Gil was smiling toothily again, handing her her change. As his fingers brushed against her palm, a pain erupted between her eyebrows. All the noise in the restaurant exploded in her ears, her vision blurring. Della dropped the coins onto the counter, her hand shooting up to her forehead as another wave of pain hit her. An image of a toothy grin filled her minds-eye, though it wasn't his. This one had sharp fangs. What scared her the most, was that somehow she knew that smile.

"You all right?" Porter asked.

All she could do was nod and pick up the change. She heard Porter swallow. Rubbing her forehead, she pushed away from the counter, wobbling back to their table. The boys stared at her as she plopped back down in her seat.

Perturbed to being coddled, Della told the boys what Wesley had said about Clara. Max sat quietly, rubbing his chin. Porter stared past Della and out the window, his eyes tracing the scenery.

"Doesn't she own a flower shop?" He asked.

Della nodded.

"She give you that flower?"

"Yeah, why?" She asked, reaching up to take the flower out from behind her ear. It was a miracle she hadn't lost it in the kerfuffle earlier.

Max rolled his eyes, snorting down laughter. "Yeah Porter, why?"

Porter scowled at him. "I grew up in a cemetery, in the boot. I know a thing or two about flowers." He grabbed the flower from her fingers, holding it up to the light. "This is Monkshood, Aconitum, or wolfs-bane. It means disdain or hatred. You don't give this to someone you like."

Della furrowed her eyebrows, squeezing the last little bit of pain out of the bridge of her nose. "But Clara likes me." She thought for a minute. "Wait, I saw this flower at the Dixon's. There were lilies and carnations with them."

"What color?"

"Uh, yellow and orange?"

Porter laughed darkly. "You'd have to have quite the animosity for someone to send them those."

"Do you think Clara knows?"

"She'd have tuh." Max said, wiping his fingers off on a

dirty napkin.

"Let's go pay Miss Clara a visit, shall we?" Porter smiled.

~CHAPTER FOURTEEN~

Euphoria

Rhapsody in Bloom was a quaint little shop in the outer circle of town. The old awning was fraying, and the pale green paint was chipping off the bricks, but it was an inviting place, nonetheless. Bouquet upon sweet-smelling bouquet lined the sidewalk, filling the dreary town with all the colors of the rainbow.

Porter pushed open the door, a tiny golden bell jingling in their ears. Clara sat at the front counter, trimming thorns off a yellow rose. She smiled, waving to Della.

"Hello!" She exclaimed, placing her clippers a few inches away. Her fingers rested near them oddly, almost as if she was waiting to see whether she'd have to use them in a very unorthodox way.

"Good afternoon, Ms. Dixon." Della smiled, taking in the tiny shop. It looked more like an ice cream shop, with its pinstriped pink and yellow walls and the black and white tiles. Refrigerated display cases showed off extravagant vases full of gorgeous flower arrangements and hanging baskets full of vines hung from the ceiling.

"How can I help you?" She asked.

"Mandatory questioning, ma'am." Porter smiled, reaching for his wallet and flashing his ID at her.

Reluctantly, she moved her hand away from the clippers, nodding. Her eyes lingered on Della, looking slightly betrayed. "What would you like to know, Officer?" She asked.

"Odd question, but my colleagues and I are just checking off a few boxes, do you know anything about the Language of Flowers?" Porter asked.

Della nodded at Max over her shoulder. He reached into his book-bag, hiding the EMF detector under the flap. He turned away from the counter, pretending to check out a vase of peonies, but in reality, he was checking for signs of spirits and demons.

"I dabble." Clara blushed.

Porter smiled kindly, slowly walking up to the counter. "Do you know what Monkshood, yellow carnations, and orange lilies mean?"

She looked away, nodding. "My parents didn't."

Della stepped forward, her arms crossed over her chest, lost in thought. "Clara, do you—would you ever want to *hurt* your parents because they hurt you?"

Clara paled, looking absolutely appalled. "How do you— why would—*I would never hurt them.*" She insisted, a stream of tears leaving her eyes.

Max cleared his throat. Della glanced at him. He shook his head, mouthing 'nothing.'

"What about your fiancé?"

"Arthur was in Maine when all of this happened." Clara spat, grabbing her clippers and pointing them at Della's chest. "I was good to you. How can you accuse me of such things? I would never want to hurt my parents. Yes, I sent them that bouquet, but it wasn't anything more than a little closure. I've never been able to say anything to them, and that was my way of doing so. I never knew they'd be dead a day after. I wouldn't have sent it to them if I did." She cried.

Porter nodded. "We are sorry to have bothered you." He assured her, pulling Max and Della out the door with him.

The three of them lingered outside his hearse, staring at each other.

"Ei think she's lying," Max said.

"She isn't." Porter and Della said in unison. They eyed each other, looking equally confused.

Della cleared her throat. "She would have been more fidgety, would've played with her hair, or twisted her engagement ring around." She sighed. "So much for a lead. . ."

~ ~ ~

Porter spent the weekend looking over the list of names and dates in MHPD's files, Della spoke with the parents and guardians of the other missing children—all of whom did not answer her question—and Max kept a watchful eye on Clara. Della was wary of him being out on his own, stalking her and her family, but Max assured her he wouldn't be seen.

Difficult as it was not having a lead, Della had other things on her plate. Her medication was on backorder, she was a hundred dollars short for rent, and she kept waking up in the middle of the night, her mind plagued with very real, very *morbid* dreams. In most of her dreams, Clara died. Others, all she saw was eight crows and a pile of bones.

Every day, twice a day, she took these little clear pills. Not once in her life had she gone this long without taking something for her massive migraines. How exactly her parents had gotten her on this medication, she couldn't quite remember. She was wondering if she was losing her mind without her medication. She kept thinking she was being followed, kept seeing things that weren't there, kept forgetting where she had left her bus pass. Stranger still, whenever she asked her mother if there was anything she could take instead, she skirted the question.

Della sighed, taking a few painkiller options off the shelf at the general store. The one in the blue bottle said it was long-lasting, but the orange one said it was stronger. The pink bottle said both, but it was extremely cheap compared to the things it promised.

"I recommend these ones." A familiar voice rang. Della turned to see Mavericks standing behind her, pointing at the orange bottle. His hair was pulled back into a ponytail, his glasses hung loosely around his neck, resting on his satin button up. He wore a pair of beaded sandals and bright purple Siam pants. Some days he looked like a second grader who tried to dress himself, other days he looked like a tourist. Today it was a combo.

Della smiled, replacing the other bottles and throwing his choice into her basket. Mavericks looked her over, his eyes lingering on her sweatshirt.

"Cold?" He asked.

That was another thing. Her skin was nearly as cold as ice. "Little bit."

Mavericks raised an eyebrow, nodding and shrugging to himself. "So, how are you this morning?"

"Uh, fine," Della lied. "How are you?" She asked, walking with him as they shopped.

"Horrible, really. I assume you are feeling the effects of the new moon in Virgo, too? I myself am feeling *awfully* flustered with the fact of how much work I have to get done this month." He said. The new moon was excellent for Della; productivity was her strong suit. "I have field agents in Toronto looking into a possible Yeti sighting. They haven't called in a couple of days. . . I'm sure they are just having a good time alone in a cabin in the woods, though I still worry."

Della snickered, opening her mouth to contradict.

"Not to mention Milliano has been absent. When I said I wanted you two to get along, I never meant for him to miss dinner." Mavericks shook his head as he smelled a cucumber. "Isn't this stuff good for digestion?"

He went to place the cucumber back where he got it from when the rest of the cucumbers toppled to the floor. As Della reached for some of the rolling cucumbers, they stopped, shaking for a minute before launching themselves into Della's hands. She stood, shaking violently.

Her eye twitched as she stared at Mavericks.

He gave a questioning look, placing his own cucumbers back on the shelf. "Are you all right, Delphee?"

"Did—Did you see that?" Della asked.

"See what?" Mavericks asked dumbly.

Della stared at the floor, then at her hands. "Nothing." She said, pushing the cucumbers into his hands. "Have a nice day. See you at work."

She high tailed it up to the register and quickly left the general store.

Yes. She was most definitely losing her mind.

~ ~ ~

Porter stared at the files that had popped up on the old laptop in front of him. The smoke from Cheif Eric Steiniger's cigar stung the inside of his nose as he looked up at him.

"How come these aren't in the news?" Porter asked,

pointing to the list of court visitations regarding abused children and their guardians.

"Bad for business." Steiniger said, blowing a smoke ring into the air. "Most of these people are 'upstanding citizens.' The public loves them." He shook his head angrily. Steiniger had never liked this town and the corruption in it. He'd put a lot of evil people away, but even then, there were things he couldn't do. He was human. Fully human.

Porter rolled his eyes, returning to stare at the computer screen. "That doesn't mean you have to comply with their bull—"

"Language, Porter." Steiniger said, though not unkindly. Eric Steiniger was more of a father to Porter than Jed or anyone else had ever been. There was many a night when he had let Porter crash at his house or picked him up from school. "I know you hate hearing about this kind of stuff, but there is little I can do for those poor kids. At least not until we find them. We get them; we can prove they've been neglected and abused." Steiniger explained, crossing his thick tattooed arms over his chest.

Porter nodded, simmering in his anger. He knew better than anyone what it felt like when people turned the other cheek at your problems. He was going to find these kids, help them no matter the cost. This was no longer about finding an excuse to hang around Della, or keeping an eye on Max, this was about justice.

Steiniger stared at him in the reflection of the screen for a while before finally smiling. "I heard you've been hanging out with Max McGregor-Mavericks again. What brought that on?"

Porter shrugged. "A girl."

Steiniger chuckled, blowing another smoke ring. "A pretty girl." He corrected.

Porter's face turned red. "She barely knows I exist. I'm just helping her do her job, you know?"

"Boyo, you're going to be stuck in this town for the rest of your life with a mindset like that. Get her before the kitty does." Steiniger smiled. "And would it kill you to erase a file or two? We don't need Jacobson freaking out again." He gestured with his cigar to the cameras.

"You know very well that wasn't my fault."

"Porter, you punched a table and it shattered." Steiniger said dryly.

Porter rolled his eyes, clicking on another domestic violence report. This one was rather recent. Some kid named Angus Cummings showed up to school with a black eye, his stepmom was seen yelling at him, and the school board reported it. A woman named Eloise Heiser was meant to testify on the kid's behalf this coming Thursday.

"Yeah, Ellie will be able to handle it." Steiniger said, leaning over Porter's shoulder to look at the report. An odd light flickered in his eyes, something Porter had never seen before.

"Mind if I print this out?" Porter asked.

"As long as it won't end up in the Tribune with my name, you can do whatever you please."

"Thanks." Porter said, gathering up his jacket, making for the door.

Steiniger put out his cigar on the table, adding to the burn marks that were already there. He gave Porter a knowing look, crossing his arms over his chest.

"I hear women like flowers." He began. "Chocolates would be a good option too. Maybe even dinner and a show?"

Porter thought for a moment. "How would you know?"

"I have a life, Porter. That's how."

~CHAPTER FIFTEEN~

The Other 'F' Word

With two sets of murders relating to two abused kids, Della and the boys thought the next place they should visit was pretty obvious. The place where all the sticky handed, black eyed, snot-nosed children spend their days.

"I have a bad feeling 'bout this," Max admitted as they stood outside the middle school, scanning the field. If she was being absolutely honest, Della had a horrible feeling too. Right in the pit of her stomach, like something was dead wrong. Nonetheless, she ignored it.

The middle school was a tiny little place, about half the size of even the Sycamore Heights elementary. Trees jutted out from the ground, cracking the pavement, and the schoolyard was littered with lunch tables piled high with textbooks and crumpled up pieces of paper. Laughing voices filled the air, setting Della on edge.

Porter was grinning widely, pointing out the firecracker that was Wesley to Della. "Go be sexy for that deranged thir-teen-year-old."

Della glared at him, the anger she felt hiding how em-barrassed she was to hear him call her sexy. "You both owe me." She said, taking a moment to arrange her face into a sweet little smile.

She stood, lazily leaning against the fence, her hand

resting on the charm on her necklace, staring wistfully at the teenage version of a playground.

"Hey!" She called, shaking the fence around the school. Porter snorted. "Hey! Hey, Wesley!" She screamed.

Wesley's head shot up as soon as he heard her voice. He was sitting under a tree, his face buried in a textbook, looking like he wished the world would end. As soon as he spotted her, his face broke into the biggest smile Della had ever seen. He threw his textbook to the side, rushing over to the fence.

"I don't know Della, he looks pretty—" Porter paused. "Atro—Atrabil—Atrabilious. . . to me." He finished, his words laced with some unknown accent.

Della glared at him. "You sure you are using that word, right?"

"Yes. I *Googled* it." Porter said, holding his head high.

"Get a room." Max breathed, more intrigued by a lady-bug flying around his head then their love lives.

"Hey, Della!" Wesley said as soon as he reached the fence. It seemed to him that the fence separating them was committing the worst crime imaginable.

"Hey Wes, can I call you Wes?" Della sang.

"This is a crap idea." Max yawned.

Porter glared at him.

"Sure," Wesley said. "You can call me anything." His puppy-dog eyes made Della want to gag.

Instead, she smiled, giggling a little. Her talents were lost on people like him. She should be in Hollywood right now, sipping on Shirley Temples as she prepared for a role in a blockbuster.

"Hey, so you know how you were talking about those *super* annoying classmates of yours?" Della asked, twirling her hair between her fingers.

"Yeah, what about them?" Wesley asked, eyeing Porter. He shifted uncomfortably under the kid's gaze, clearing his throat.

"Do you know an Angus Cummings?" Della asked, popping a piece of bubblegum into her mouth, winking at him as she chewed it.

"Are you kidding? Who doesn't? That little ass-hat is the reason we can't have our phones in class anymore." Wesley spat.

"What a *jerk*!" Della exclaimed, letting her mouth hang

open.

"Oh my gosh, right?"

Max audibly rolled his eyes. "Listen, kid, can ya get us a chat with him, or not?" He asked.

"I'm sorry, who are they, exactly?" Wesley asked.

"Just a few—" Della's eyelids flickered with frustration. "*Friends.*" The other 'f' word was hard to say.

"Right, okay. Well, any friend of Della's is a friend of mine." Wesley smiled tightly.

"Answer." Max demanded.

"Geez, lay off it. No, and even if I could, I wouldn't. That kid is trouble. With a capital everything."

Della frowned, her facade faltering. "Wes, please."

He shook his head.

Della looked away for a moment, mouthing several swear words. Regaining her composure, she turned back to him. "Thank you for your time, Wes." Della winked, blowing a bubblegum bubble.

"Anytime—Hey, are you free tomorrow night?"

Della smiled, shaking her head. "Yeah. . . no." She laughed, walking away with Porter and Max. The three of them ignored Wesley as he tried to call them back.

"Man, that kid is really carrying a torch for you," Porter said as soon as they were out of earshot. Was that *jealousy* in his voice?

Della spat her bubblegum on the pavement. "I feel like I need to bathe in hand-sanitizer, I feel dirty and—" She shook her head violently. That was a mistake. Her head rippled with pain. She winced, stumbling to a stop.

Porter turned on his heels, looking at her, his eyes wide. "You okay?"

She nodded, but her knees gave out. Stinging bolts of electricity erupted through her veins. Porter caught her as she slumped to the ground. She held her head in her hands, panting hard. The sounds from the school were burning like hot fire pokers in her ears, the smell 'of fresh air feeling more like a thick smog. In her mind's eye, playing out like a movie, eight crows flew off the hood of Porter's hearse. A flash of white filled her eyes, the scene changing to a building set ablaze.

She felt Porter shaking her, snapping her out of whatever had just happened. He had pulled her to his chest, his face stark white. His lips were moving, but they made no sound.

Max was next to her, blabbering on.

Everything went dark.

~ ~ ~

Della groaned, leaning up to pound on her alarm clock. She couldn't quite remember what happened after her chat with Wesley, but somehow, she had gotten all the way home and had passed out on her bed. Her skull was pounding. It sounded like an entire army of soldiers was marching around in her head. She fell back onto her pillow, wondering how she had gotten to sleep. It was not like her to stop in the middle of a project, especially for something as feeble as sleep. Her eyes felt heavy as she shut them, trying to gain a better grip on reality. Something told her she was dangerously close to being stuck inside her mind permanently.

All she saw when she closed her eyes were eight crows and burning white light. She rolled over, staring at the ceiling.

A noise came from the kitchen.

Something deep inside her made her shoot out of the warm covers on her bed and reach for the machete she had taped beneath it. She ripped it out from underneath the bed frame, rummaging around in her nightstand for her pepper spray—another small crash.

She stood, slowly slinking out of her bedroom and down the hallway. The machete slung over her shoulder, her finger on the trigger of her pepper spray, she looked over her shoulder, turning to open the bathroom door to make sure it was empty. As she closed the door, she heard the creak of floorboards behind her. Rounding on the intruder, she sprayed him right in the face. He had black hair, brown skin with patches of—

"MAXIMILIAN MCGREGOR HOW DARE YOU SNEAK UP ON ME LIKE THAT!" Della screamed, but she threw her arms around him, pulling him into a tight hug. Maybe the hug was unnecessary, but to her it felt right.

She let the machete and pepper spray fall from her hands and onto the floor as he tried to pull away.

"Della—Della, let go—DELLA MY EYES ARE BURNIN'!" He yelled, shoving her away and running into the kitchen where Porter was standing, pan hanging out of his hand, making breakfast.

"I hope—" He laughed, trying to pass it off as a cough, using his free hand to pat Max on the back as he rinsed his eyes out under the sink. "I hope you like eggs."

Della shrugged, feeling horribly bad that she had assaulted Max.

Usually, she could go a whole day without eating more than a bowl of cereal and a bowl of fruit, but as Porter cracked an egg on the skillet and it sizzled, she realized she was starving. He seemed to understand that since he pushed a bowl full of freshly cut apples and grapes in her general direction.

Max screamed in anguish, running to the bathroom.

"Eat, you will feel a lot better," Porter said quietly.

Della walked through her tiny living room and over to the breakfast bar, pulling up one of the bottle cap stools she had bought and greedily munched down on a piece of apple. Porter smiled to himself as she ate.

"How are you feeling?" He asked.

"Better." She said, pulling the whole bowl of fruit towards herself.

Porter nodded. "I'm glad." His voice was cold. "You scared us, you know."

"I'm fine," Della said truthfully.

"Now." Porter laughed darkly. "Love, you passed out in my arms. I mean, I know I'm a dashing young man with a great personality, but I don't do that to people. I'm far too full of myself." Della rolled her eyes. She knew his arrogance was only an act. "What happened?" He asked, or rather demanded. He seemed angry, though she didn't feel the anger was directed towards her.

"I stopped taking my meds," Della explained, popping a grape into her mouth.

Porter shook his head in confusion. "What meds?" He asked.

"My migraine medication, sumatriptan. I ran out." She replied. She hadn't realized grapes had tasted this good before.

Porter stopped cooking, turning to stare at her. "Are you going to be okay? Do you need me to call anyone? Dammit, I knew we should have sucked it up and took you to the hospital." He spat, turning around in the kitchen in a panicked little whirlpool.

"I'm fine, really. I have dealt with this my whole life; I can handle it." Della smiled reassuringly. Funny how people believe their own lies so easily.

"*You passed out, Della.*" Porter hissed, returning to the burning egg in the skillet. His face was full of dismay as he struggled with the pan, trying to scrape the egg onto a plate.

"Fine." Della snapped. "I've got new stuff coming next week. For now, we should return to our regularly scheduled program." She said.

"I think you should rest and eat, and then maybe, if you've been a *good* little reporter, we can get past this commercial break." He said, turning away from her with an air of superiority.

Della stared at his back in silence for quite some time, absentmindedly eating the fruit before her, until Max plopped down next to her. His eyes were bloodshot; his cheeks rubbed raw.

"Ei would ask where ya got a machete and pepper spray, but something tells me Ei don' want tuh know." He said sourly, stealing a grape right out of her fingers and popping it into his mouth, making sure to chew on it with his mouth open, so it sprayed her with juice.

"I got them from my grandpa." Della explained.

"Aye, because everyone gives their granddaughter a machete for her birthday." Max said, rolling his eyes. Sometimes, Della wondered just how much of his Irish heritage played into his sass.

Porter placed two plates in front of them. He had arranged Della's eggs, sausage, and hash browns into a regular smiley face, whereas Max's had cat ears.

"Casually." Della said, picking up one of the sausages that made his smiley faces cat ears. It was only fair, since he stole her grapes. "Thanks, Porter." She said.

The way he looked at her when he thought she wasn't paying attention made her uncomfortable. Max grunted his appreciation but didn't look up from his plate.

"You're welcome." Porter said, beginning to cook some breakfast for himself. Della noticed, though she couldn't tell if it was an ordinary thing or not that Porter cooked himself more food than both her and Max's plates combined.

It was a beautiful little scene. The early morning light shone through the shutters, showering them—except Porter—in golden light. The room was comfortably warm, and for once, Della didn't want to be alone. She didn't want them to leave.

"So, what's the plan for the day?" Max asked.

"You need to finish up testing those samples I gave you; I have to tie up some loose ends at work, and—I have a job for you, Mr. Garroway." She said, catching Porter by surprise.

"What do you need?" He asked skeptically.

"I need you to find someone to keep an eye on some of the kids. We don't know who the next target is, so better safe than sorry." She explained.

"When I said I had connections, I didn't mean—" He sighed. "Anything for you, Miss Coleman." He said slowly as if the weight of the world was suddenly on his shoulders.

"It's settled then." Della said, a sly smile on her face. "Pedal to the metal Mr. Garroway."

~ ~ ~

The boys had patiently waited out in the living room for Della to get ready, then Porter drove them into work. Max raced inside as soon as the hearse parked, leaving the others in his dust. Porter got out of the hearse and opened Della's door, holding out a hand for her. She smiled deviously, refusing his hand.

He frowned. "You sure you're up to this today?"

She nodded. "I'm fine, Porter, really." He stared at her with an odd look on his face. "And if you are wondering about how I felt seeing the Grunch," She said slowly, his face paling. "I've seen my fair share of strange in my time as a—"

"As a reporter." He went stiff and pointed up to the sign above them. "P.J. Mavericks Law? Really? *The Utopian Courier*?"

She held her head high, raising an eyebrow. "Yes. You have a problem with that?"

"Listen, Coleman, I meant what I said. If Max is around, that means trouble. Trouble you shouldn't be dealing with. I don't know who you are or why you are in cahoots with the geek and his Master Weirdo, and honestly, I don't think I want to know, but I advise you to think before you jump. And for the love of God, please don't do anything stupid." He stepped closer to her, lowering his voice. "If you ever need to talk about anything, you know where to find me."

She glowered at him, sticking her hands in her pockets. Their faces were inches away, him slouching down so he could look her directly in the eyes. It was the stance of someone who wanted to kiss you goodbye for fear they'd never see you again.

"Listen, *Garroway*," She began, fully tempted to place the heel of her platform boots on his toes. "I can handle myself."

"Oh yes, that was pretty obvious. You haven't crossed the street and nearly died, walked into a gate, or locked yourself in a freezer recently. Or passed out. No, only crazy people do that." Porter said snidely.

"I didn't lock myself in there. It closed, and I heard someone lock the door. How do I know you weren't the one to do it? I know nothing about you. You could be some psycho murderer for all I know." Della hissed.

"Well, maybe you should get to know me," Porter mumbled, staring at her lips with a sad yearning in his eyes.

Why must he do that? It was like he wanted her to get mad at him. Della opened her mouth to contradict, utterly flustered when Max came running out of the tiny law firm.

"Mavericks wants tuh see us." He said, he seemed like he wanted to say something else, but instead, he just stared at Porter and Della with a confused little smile on his face. "Am Ei interruptin' somethin'?" He asked, his vocal cords playing a sweet little tune.

"Not at all," Porter said, slowly straightening back up to his full height, his eyes still on Della.

Max made a clicking noise with his tongue, pulling Della out of the street by her arm. When they heard Porter close his door, he smiled at her.

"What?" Della asked.

"The eejit does have a certain appeal tuh him, Ei must admit. Just don' get hurt. Ya don' know the full story." Max said.

"Maybe that's because you won't tell me." Della proposed, linking arms with him.

"Ei played a part in writin' said book, but it is not my story tuh tell. Ya should know, Delphee. Copyright infringement is a serious crime." Max chimed. "What has gotten intuh ya today, ya seem. . . not. . . not like a jack—"

Della scowled, sticking her nose up into the air. "Finish that sentence; I dare you."

"Ah, there it is." Max smiled. "The Della Porter loves." He put his fingers together like his hands were kissing.

Her face reddened. "What does Mavericks want?" Della asked, realizing that she would get nowhere by bugging him. Or at least that's what the mind readers would think. In reality, she just wanted to change the subject, so Porter's beautiful face wouldn't be burned into her eyes anymore.

Max opened the front door for her, bowing slightly. "He wants tuh see the pictures ya took, my blood samples, and he has a stack of insurance papers for ya tuh look over. Says he doesn' want ya tuh end up in the hospital without insurance."

Della rolled her eyes as they made their way down to his office. The door was already open; Mavericks was scolding the reptilian chair, which was moving and crying. Like an actual, live animal. Near the left wall of the office, a stuffed duck was torn to shreds.

"I love how this is the new normal. I'm currently researching an actual, real cryptid, I work for a conspiracy newspaper, my boss refuses to wear shoes, werewolves run restaurants, and inanimate objects eat taxidermy." Della whispered wistfully. Any sane person would hightail it out of this idiosyncratic town.

Apparently, that meant Della wasn't sane.

How wonderful, she thought, *sarcasm intended.*

"Oh dear, that isn' even the half of it." Max smiled. There was a strange glint to his dull amber eyes. Like a certain kind of magic was swimming deep beneath their surface.

Mavericks looked up, waving them over, patting the chair and sending it over to the corner to think about what it had done. The duck had been one of the last of its kind. Something similar to a jackalope.

But poultry.

"The adventurers of the hour have returned!" Mavericks exclaimed. "What have you got for me?"

Della handed over her phone, Max the samples. Mavericks examined both in silence; his thick eyebrows raised so high they touched his receding hairline.

"I would suggest keeping your little endeavor under lock and key for the time being."

Della sat down in the patchwork chair, exchanging a look with Max.

"We saw it. The thing." Max said, leaning against her chair.

"Go on." Mavericks said, sitting down in the other chair.

The adventurers related their expedition to him in as much detail as they could muster. They hadn't had a chance to talk to him all weekend, and it seemed they all wanted a chance to share their findings. Mavericks' face was set in a stone-cold stare as they spoke, looking at everything and nothing at the same time.

"That's a new one." Mavericks said. "I've never heard of a Grunch stealing children before." He said mysteriously. The thing that worried Della, was that he implied he had seen one before.

"We're thinking that maybe the legends are true, and someone is controlling the Grunch. That maybe it is a demon spawn. I mean, come on, there is so much lore about rituals requiring human sacrifice, or children in witch lore, it would make your head spin." Della explained, gesturing wildly.

Max and Mavericks looked at her with a very offended look. "We know." They said in unison.

"I just meant that. . . You know what, never mind." Della said, pinching her nose and shaking her head.

"Ya okay?" Max immediately asked.

She looked up at him, letting her arm flop down onto the armrest of the chair. "Yes, Max. I'm fine." She said sternly. That was the truth; she just wished he believed it.

Mavericks cleared his throat. "We have a vast population of Wiccans, Pagans, and natural-born witches in the area. The frauds are always looking for the real deal. Someone might have stumbled across a real spell book, not knowing what they were meant to do with it. It's always best to read the small print." Mavericks winked. "Did you figure out my little clue, Miss Coleman?"

Della nodded. "A friend of ours solved your puzzle." She smiled. That was twice in two days she used that word.

Mavericks furrowed his eyebrows. "Who?" Danger flared up in his gray eyes. Della watched him with growing suspicion. Some days, she did not know whether she could trust Percival James Mavericks.

"Just a friend," Max said quickly. "Norman hooked us up." He shot Della a warning look as she opened her mouth to contradict.

"Hmm. . ." Mavericks said.

Mavericks' demeanor had changed instantly. He no longer looked like the cheerful old man the two of them were used to. He looked almost sinister like a deeply rooted evil had surfaced. It was beyond that of a caring father who knew you were lying. It was like a mob boss who knew who the mole was.

"Very well." He sighed. "Della, talk to the local covens, Max, use your. . ." He paused, eyeing Della. "Use your resources." He chose to say.

Max nodded. "Ei'll get on that." He left, patting Della's shoulder lightly.

"How are you feeling?" Mavericks asked before Della had time to move. "And before you say 'fine,' know that this is a safe place, and I will not tell the boys."

Slowly, Della turned back around to look at him. "So, you know about Porter?" She asked, changing the subject.

Mavericks shrugged. "In a town like this, do you really think my son isn't watched twenty-four-seven? I have done background checks on every person he even looks at. I have people watching over him every minute of every day. You are a fool to think I don't know about Porter Garroway, the boy with anger issues, four DUIs, and a bad habit of killing people. And so is Max." There was fiery anger in his words.

Della inhaled sharply at this newfound information. This seemed to calm Mavericks. He smiled, adjusting his glasses, a look of sympathy on his face.

"I thought you knew, my dear." He said.

"Doesn't matter." Della decided. "I'm sure he had a good reason for whatever he did." She smiled. Not once in her life had she ever wanted to be lied to before, but boy did she hope he was lying.

Mavericks kicked his feet up onto the table, yawning. "Yes, I'm sure he did."

Della squinted at him. He thought he had so much power when really, all he was was a washed-up old fraud who made money on other people's creativity. Hatred was beginning to grow inside Della's chest like the roses Clara Dixon grew, its thorns wrapping around Della's heart.

Max was her friend. There, she said it, she finally admitted it. However, so was Porter. Furthermore, *Mavericks* was a fool if he thought he could convince her of any difference. When Delphee Chrysanthemum Coleman got her hooks into someone, they couldn't wiggle off the hook that easily. Especially when she took the time to give a crap about them.

~CHAPTER SIXTEEN~

The Covens of Moss Hollow

"Don' touch anythin', and please, don' speak about their religion sarcastically." Max pleaded as he opened the door of *Weeping Crow Occult Shoppe.* He seemed to be speaking out of experience.

They had 'borrowed' Mavericks' yellow convertible to drive through the town. It had been Della's idea. A small price to pay for the things Mavericks had said. She totally hadn't been hoping that fate would have pity on her and have someone chip the paint on his perfect little car. She wasn't disappointed that hadn't happened.

Not one bit.

Moreover, Della hadn't assured Max that he could leave the keys in the car, that no one would steal his father's precious relic. She wasn't hoping that she would be wrong.

Nope. Della was trustworthy.

"I won't, trust me," Della assured him, smiling to herself.

Max sighed heavily, whisking her inside. She found joy in the fact that he was uncomfortable here.

The shop was full of hanging shrunken heads, burning incense, crystals, cauldrons, tarot cards, crystal balls, and every other witchy thing you could think of. The walls were covered in peeling purple velvet filigree wallpaper, and black candles were burning on almost every table. Della smiled widely, beelining to a display full of crystals with protective powers. Greedily, she grabbed a black mesh sachet and started shoving crystals into it.

"Ei told ya not tuh touch anythin'!" Max hissed.

Della smiled at him over her shoulder. "You cannot expect them to talk to us without a little compensation." She said, shaking her bag of crystals in his face.

He groaned, following her around the little shop.

Places like this were her happy place. Everything around her made her feel normal, accepted, and happy.

So why was she so afraid of things she was seeing deep in her brain?

Why was she scanning the shelves around her for something to block them out? Of course, even people who believe in God get scared of miracles.

"Can we hurry this long?" Max asked.

"Why? Are you scared?" Della asked, tapping a shrunken head so it swung into his face, dreadlocks, dried skin, and all.

He shriveled up his nose, shaking all over. "No." He said sternly.

Della laughed, shaking her head. "Come on." She said over her shoulder, slowly making her way to the front counter.

The counter was a glass case full of odd jewelry and magical looking books. Della knelt to look at them all, her smile widening as she tried to read all the titles. Some were in languages she could not understand, others in languages she was pretty sure didn't exist. At least not in this day and age.

"Fingers off the glass, please." A voice rang.

"Ei *told* ya." Max hissed.

Della stood; a tall, curvy African American lady was standing in a doorway behind the counter. She smiled wistfully at them, her eyes glazing over for a moment.

"We weren't expecting you until tomorrow." She mused. She had a thick, stereotypical bayou voice. Her tone harsh, yet flowery. "Names Nicoletta, I'm the eldest daughter of the coven that calls this shop it's home." She explained, holding out her hands for them to shake.

"Nice to meet you." Della smiled.

Nicoletta dressed in long, stereotypical tie-dye dresses and jewelry of every color, shape, and size. The largest, being the pentacle hoop earrings that hung from her ears.

"You too, mademoiselle. Not every day we get one of you showing up." Nicoletta said, her eyes staring deep into Della's soul. There was an odd sparkle in her eyes.

Max cleared his throat. "We have some questions." He said.

Nicoletta scowled at him, though Della could tell from her eyes that she found him amusing. "Boy, don't you think I know that already? Where exactly do you think you are shopping?" She asked.

Max straightened, scowling so deeply at Nicoletta that Della was sure his face wasn't going to be able to return to its resting position. Which honestly was not that far away from a scowl, but compared to this, it was a cheerful little grin.

Nicoletta rolled her eyes, turning back to Della. She smiled widely, forcefully linking arms with her and leading her through the doorway she had come from. Della looked over her shoulder to find Max reluctantly following, mocking Nicoletta with his eyes crossed.

Nicoletta leaned down to Della, her jewelry jingling like bells, lowering her voice. "Men. I swear, they think they know everything."

"Amen to that, sister," Della replied.

Nicoletta smiled. "I see you picked up some protection stones. Everything all right?" She asked.

"Hopefully." Della shrugged. "I have some back at my apartment, but they don't exactly fit in my handbag."

"I could make you a necklace out of a couple of them?" Nicoletta said as they ascended a flight of stairs.

The smell of lavender and cinnamon filled Della's nostrils. She smiled. "I'd like that."

Nicoletta snapped her fingers a couple of times, holding out her hand for Della's bag of goodies. "I will get right on it as soon as you and the beastie leave."

"Uh, do you mind making one for the beastie and—"

"And the monster?" Nicoletta asked.

Della sighed. "He's not a monster." *Why does everyone in this damn town think of Porter and Max as something less than the rest of them?* Della thought. *Don't they know that we are the good guys?*

"Maybe not. . . Yes, I will. I admire how much you care about them, even though they do not know it." Nicoletta said as they came to a door at the top of the stairs. "Ask, and you shall receive, mi amor."

She pushed open the door to reveal a room with a bar in one corner and ottoman poufs in the other. The room was full of colorful characters, all ranging in styles from boho chic to full-on heavy metal goth. As soon as Della's foot crossed over the threshold, she felt at home. Far more at home than she had ever felt anywhere ever before. Including *The Utopian Courier* and her parents tawny-colored colonial back in Sycamore Heights.

The walls in this magical place were adorned with old pieces of parchment in picture frames that listed every magical symbol and what it was used for and why, beautiful tapestries and hanging jars filled to the bursting point with herbs.

"This is our little hotspot," Nicoletta explained. "We cast our spells in private here, safe and away from the public eye. You can always join us. There is always room for one more."

"Don' ya mean two?" Max asked, making his way over to the bar.

"I meant what I meant, beastie." Nicoletta scowled. She lowered her voice again. "If you only knew the truth, you would understand." She said, warming Della's ear with her breath full of incense.

Della stared at Max in wonder as he ordered himself a club soda, sitting heavily on the sequin-covered bar stools, chatting up the bartender like they were old friends. She suddenly realized she knew just about as much of him as she did of Porter. Nothing.

Nicoletta pulled her away from him and to the other corner, sitting her down on a purple pouf. An assortment of witches crowded around her, expectantly waiting for Nicoletta's command.

"You may sit." She said kindly, waiting until everyone was seated to sit down herself.

These people seemed to have the utmost respect for Nicoletta, and she seemed to feel the same way about them. It was like she was the captain of a pirate ship, keeping her crewmates in line, but still respecting them as her equals.

"These are my closest friends and the most skilled and knowledgeable of our coven. Ask us anything, and we will give you as many answers as we have." Nicoletta explained as Max came to sit on the floor next to Della, splashing his club soda onto the floor. Some wrinkled their noses at him in disgust, others laughed, offering him a handkerchief to clean up the mess.

"Max and I work for *The Utopian Courier*," Della began, causing Max to spray club soda out of his nose. Even the witches who seemed to know this already looked extremely excited, each and every one of them leaning in closer to get a better look at Della. "We are doing some research on the odd events that have taken place here in town—my article will be out the week of October thirty-first." She explained. "We have a lead, but we don't know how to fit all the pieces together, so we were hoping you could help us."

Several of the witches nodded, showing that they would help.

"Without spoiling my work, we have realized that someone is summoning a Grunch," Della said.

Some of the witches looked satisfied; others looked gravely concerned.

"You'd be a damn fool to mess with that kind of magic." An older African American man with dreadlocks said.

Nicoletta nodded, a dark look on her face.

Della, Max, and the rest of the witches were silent for a while, everyone lost in thought.

"Do you know how to kill a Grunch?" Della asked them.

Nicoletta thought for a minute, crossing and uncrossing her legs a couple of times. "I suppose you would have to break the sigil that summoned it, or kill whoever had the nerve to summon one, to begin with. They're demon spawn, you know. It is people who mess around with things like that, that give us a bad name. Iron and salt might work. . ."

The group nodded its collective head.

"What would we need to break the sigil?" Della and Max asked at the same time.

"It depends on the witch. Some of us like to draw summoning sigils on our bodies, so you'd have to kill us to break it. Some find the sacred parts of the woods and draw them on rocks." Nicoletta explained. She stared out into space, shaking her head. "I do not understand why we haven't caught this. None of us would be stupid enough to mess with that kind of—" She gasped. "Caroline, didn't you say that a book was stolen a couple of nights ago?"

A woman with short, bright pink hair nodded. "It was the only thing missing. Very dark stuff inside it. It was an ancient tome."

"A spellbook?" Della asked, trying to hide the disbelief in her tone.

Caroline nodded again. "Sad that someone would steal such a thing. . ."

"Do you know of anyone who would be in the market for such a spell book?" Della asked.

The witches eyed the magical patrons around them, beginning to look suspicious. They whispered in their neighbors' ears, the tension growing. Someone in the back pushed their way to the front, whispering in Nicoletta's ears.

Her eyes widened. "Potentially." She said, looking very angry.

Max rolled his eyes, finishing off his club soda and standing. "Well, you have been a royal pain in our rear." He said, saluting them all. "Come on, Della, let's go."

Della didn't move. She bit her lower lip, glancing at Max. "Nicoletta?" She asked nervously.

The beautiful coven elder nodded.

Della opened and closed her mouth several times, pulling at her fingernails. She had so many questions burning inside her head, and Nicoletta may have been to only one that would answer truthfully. Sadly, she shut her eyes tightly, deciding now was not the time to talk about herself. Well, it never was, but now more than ever. She smiled weakly, shaking her head.

"Never mind."

Nicoletta frowned, a hand resting on her chest, looking gravely concerned. "If you ever need to talk, I am here."

Many people kept telling her that. Even Lenora. So why on earth wouldn't she take them up on their offer? Hadn't that been what she wanted her entire life?

~CHAPTER SEVENTEEN~

The Man in The Mirror

Porter sat in his rusted old hearse outside the Cummings's house, observing the windows. He heard no screams, no crying, nothing. The boy he presumed to be Angus was lying lazily in a hammock, typing away on his phone.

Oh, to be young. To not have a care in the world. To be able to sit outside in the fading sunlight, watching the world go by.

Porter forced himself to look away. Instinctively he rubbed his wrists, staring down at his veins, watching them pump his blood throughout his body. How easy it would be to stop the flow. . . Looking up at his reflection in the rearview mirror, he hated what he saw. He wished he could go back in time and revel in being a child. No matter how crappy his life was back then, it had to be better than what he had to deal with now. Back then, at least he was innocent, at least he didn't know the things he knew now.

His phone rang next to him, startling him out of his morbid little thoughts. He reached for it, seeing that name 'Eric' flashing on the screen, his fingers grazing the cold glass. Out of the corner of his eye, he saw that Angus had disappeared. The hammock was swinging violently back and forth, and the front door was now open.

A sinking feeling erupted in Porter's chest. Something

was telling him that whatever Eric needed could wait. He tossed his phone aside leaving the safe confines of his hearse and making his way to the house across the street.

Slowly, he pulled his gun out of his pocket—an old Colt Single Action Army that had belonged to Steiniger's father. He checked how many silver rounds were inside, disappointed only to see three. Good thing he never missed.

"Mrs. Cummings?" He called through the doorway.

His ears were greeted with nothing but silence and the buzz of mosquitoes.

He looked over his shoulder, his foot crossing over the threshold, closing the door behind him. A vase of flowers sat on a bench near the door. A vase full of Monkshood.

"Hello?" Porter called. "My name is Porter Garroway; I work with the Moss Hollow police."

No answer.

He continued through the house; the soles of his muddy combat boots were silent as he walked across the carpet. A door behind him opened seemingly without cause. He turned on his heels, his gun pointed, ready to shoot anything that moved.

A scream floated through the house from the backyard. Porter raced outside, scratch marks on the walls whizzed by his eyes as he burst out the back door.

Lying on the back porch was a woman with bleeding, five-inch wounds. She was screaming in pain, looking at Porter with a dazed sort of fear. He knelt next to her, trying to help her off the floor, but she struggled against him, confused. Angus was nowhere to be seen. The woman, Mrs. Cummings, clung to him for dear life as soon as she got to her feet. Her face was tear stricken; her shirt torn to shreds.

Porter opened his mouth to speak when he heard a growl, fear erupting in his chest like a geyser. He pushed Mrs. Cummings away as a lumbering green figure crashed into him. The Grunch tore its teeth into his arm, stopping him from shooting it, his blood spattering him in the face. Porter struggled, trying to push the thing off him. It reached down with one of its hands, clamping its claws around his neck. Instantly, he felt his breath leave him. Porter switched his gun from one hand to the other, shooting all three silver bullets into the Grunches chest.

It screeched in pain before slumping to the side, bursting into blue flames and disappearing.

Gasping for air, Porter turned to Mrs. Cummings, who was staring at him in horrified disbelief. How come he always got stuck with the ones that knew nothing about magic?

His arm was searing with pain as he reached out to help her off the ground again. "Sorry for knocking you down." He said casually.

She pointed dumbly at the burnt porch, tears filling up in her eyes. "W—Where is my son? Where is Angus?" She demanded accusingly.

Porter squeezed the bite marks on his arm, trying to staunch the bleeding. "Don't know." He choked out. The edges of his vision were blurring as white-hot pain traveled through his arm.

"We have to find him!" Mrs. Cummings screamed, looking around wildly. She called Angus's name over and over but to no avail.

Porter rolled his eyes. "He's gone." He said weakly, leaning against the wall behind him. The cuts on his arm were bubbling with white foam.

Mrs. Cummings turned to look at him as his eyes closed.

~ ~ ~

"Ei coulda sworn Ei told ya tuh remove me as yer emergency contact," Max said sourly, poking at the bandages on Porter's arm as he looked over a stapled stack of papers.

Porter smiled. He was sweaty and pale, and his eyelids were heavy, adorned with dark circles. "I'd rather it be you then my parents." He laughed, glancing at Della, who was staring at him, her eye twitching madly.

Max flicked the side of his head, scowling. "Eejit."

"Takes one to know one," Porter said, flexing his arm. It was swollen, the bandages cutting off his circulation. He had passed out before the Cheif Steiniger, and the rest of his colleagues got there.

"Viva la, screw *you*." Max said casually, his Irish accent tainted with American sass, as he plopped himself down in a chair near the hospital bed. He tossed the stack of papers aside, grabbing a magazine off the side table instead.

"Ha-ha." Porter yawned. "You good, Coleman?"

She nodded slowly, forcing herself to look at something other than him. Other than the bruises around his neck and the state he was in. Seeing him like this broke her heart. He could have died, trying to save that woman. Anger pumped through her veins.

"I'm good; you?" She asked her voice nothing but a squeak.

Porter eyed her carefully, looking over his shoulder at Max. "Only a flesh wound, my love."

Della rolled her eyes, propping her foot on the wall, crossing her arms and staring at him.

Porter raised an eyebrow at her, searching her face. Eventually, he shook his head angrily, rubbing the back of his neck. "Mrs. Cummings is in witness protection, don't worry. We got her talking about Angus, her husband was abusive, she wasn't that great of a parent either. Oh, and there was a vase of monkshood in her house. She doesn't know who sent it. I asked."

Della stared at him, confused. His tone was all over the place, partially angry, partially sad, partially dry. The way he was looking at her saddened every bone in her body.

"So, what did the witches say?" He asked with a yawn.

"A lot of death and destruction bullshit," Max said, echoing his tone.

"Sweet of you to think I was addressing you," Porter grumbled.

Della rolled her eyes. "A spell book was stolen, and we have to break a sigil to stop the summoning. Or you know, kill some monsters."

Porter nodded to himself, scratching his chin. "Silver seems to do it. Do we know who stole the spell book?"

"Do ya think we would be here if we did?" Max asked.

Porter whipped his head around to look at him, scowling. Della cut him off before either of them could say anything else.

"All right, that's enough." She hissed, pushing away from the wall. "Stow your crap, and get it together, you viperous maggots. We have a fallen soldier and work to get done."

The boys stared at her, their mouths hanging open.

"I am not a fallen soldier," Porter said dumbly.

"I beg to differ. We have no idea how much of this legend is true, right? Well, legend says if you get bit, you start turning into a Grunch. You are down for the count until we know you're not some brainwashed inside man." Della explained.

Porter shook his head. "Wow, you're paranoid."

"*I'm not paranoid!*" Della hissed.

The boys raised their eyebrows. Max stifled a laugh, shaking out his magazine.

"Just—" Della growled.

Porter began to smile a cheeky little smile. "You're worried about me? How cute."

"Shut up."

"Love," He began, standing. "I have been fighting off collapsed lungs, burst arteries, and broken bones since the day I was born. If you think either of you are gonna do this alone—"

Della took two swift steps towards him, their faces merely inches apart. "Cut the bad-boy act," she demanded, letting the tip of her purple velvet heels rest on the top of his foot. Butterflies danced in her stomach as she did. They were so close. Too close. "I know fear when I see it. You are scared—"

"I am not."

"Yes, you are. You are scared something horrible happened to Angus, and you are scared something is going to happen to Max and me."

Max angrily flipped a page in his magazine.

"That's ridiculous. You think I care about you and the runt?" Porter laughed, scratching the back of his neck nervously.

That should not have hurt her as much as it did. Damn this town. Damn these people who made her feel something. She looked away as tears stung her eyes.

"You cannot lie to a liar. I know your tells." She said, stepping hard on his toes as she turned away. Her hair smacked him in the face again.

She felt his eyes bore into her back as he rubbed his nose. "Fine." He said. "But I won't be watching TV; I'll be reading a book. You do know what a book is, right, D?" He asked, sitting back down on the hospital bed.

If he ever called her that again, she'd kill him.

~CHAPTER EIGHTEEN~

Della paced back and forth in front of her evidence board, staring at the names of abused children. They lost one. The whole reason Porter was supposed to be watching over them was, so they didn't lose another one. She chewed on her lip. Now he was hurt too. It made her blood boil, filling her with an anger she had never experienced. All she wanted to do was break something.

As if on cue, a light bulb shattered.

Della let go of a breath she hadn't realized she had been holding, a sense of relief flooding through her. She wobbled on the spot, a trickle of blood flowing out of her nose. The colors around her were screaming at her, every noise feeling like missiles in her ears. The door squeaked open, causing her to turn.

Max stood there, eyeing her suspiciously. Della panicked, turning away, stumbling over to her desk and grabbing a tissue to dab the blood away.

Max made a small noise but didn't say anything.

"What's up, Max?" Della asked, thanking the Lord above that her voice sounded steady.

". . . Just comin' tuh check on ya," Max assured her, his footsteps echoing in her ears painfully.

She turned back to him, rubbing her temples. He stared at her, wondering whether he should say something. He shook his head, putting on a smile.

"Heard some police chatter earlier. No one has seen Angus. Mavericks said ya should ask Norman for one his extra scanners or whatever." He said slowly.

Della nodded, one hand on her hip, the other gripping the edge of her desk for dear life. Her head was so hot it was like her brain was in a frying pan.

"Cool, I will get on that." She said, gesturing at the light switch near Max at a loss for words. "Uh—" She pinched her nose with one hand, pointing rapidly with the other.

"Fan?" Max asked.

"*Yes, please,*" Della begged.

He furrowed his eyebrows, flipping on the switch to the dusty fan above them lazily. The cool breeze that soon followed brought immense joy to Della.

"Ya aren' dyin', are ya?" Max asked dryly.

Slowly, Della sat on the edge of her desk, crossing her arms. She frowned, shaking her head. "Whatever would make you think that?" She asked unconvincingly.

Max raised an eyebrow. "Ya look worse than Porter."

Della rolled her eyes. "Speaking of the Devil himself, have you heard from him this afternoon?"

"Not yet, but Ei am sure Ei will." He said. The way he was staring at her like a parent who knew you were lying to them made her uncomfortable.

"Are you here to bother me or. . .?"

He paused at the doorway, tapping the doorframe. "Once a month, Mavericks drives into New Orleans tuh get gumbo from a friend. Yer welcome to come have some." He said quietly.

Not what she was expecting by any means. Honestly, she thought she was going to be lectured.

"I—" Della began, watching as Max's face fell. Della shook her head.

"When was the last time ya ate somethin' other than ramen or toaster strudels? And ya wonder why ya passed out." Max said accusingly.

She opened and closed her mouth a couple of times, standing.

Della had no intention of spending what could have been her only free night sitting at a dinner table with Mavericks, but then again, to decline Max would be so much more of a crime than anything Mavericks had said or done.

"I—I would love to come Max. Do you mind picking me up?" She asked.

Max smiled. She had never seen him this happy. "Sure thing. See ya around seven?" He asked excitedly.

Della nodded, though there was no use trying to hide the reluctance on her face. She had a horrible feeling about tonight.

~ ~ ~

Della's mouth dropped open when she saw where Mavericks and Max lived. They lived in a mansion. An actual mansion that looked like it belonged to some Duke from Austria. The lawns were manicured, cut into animal shaped hedges, there was a fountain with marble statues and a glistening path lead to the front doors. Max smirked, leading her inside. The wallpaper was made of velvet, the dark floor marble.

"It's all right, Ei guess. Lots of space tuh stretch my legs." Max smiled. "Ei have a whole wing to myself." Della stared at him. "And we have two pools, a golf course and a—"

"No one likes a bragger, Milliano." Mavericks' voice rang. For once, he was wearing shoes. And a tuxedo. He locked eyes with Della, once again putting on that terrifying air he had had back in his office. He nodded once in her general direction, sweeping past her to look at Max. Della scowled at his back when they were not looking.

Max rolled his eyes. "Can Ei show Della my room?" He asked, reminding Della of her little brother.

A sudden sadness washed over her as she once again mulled over Max's words. Before she could stop it, the burning question at the back of her mind bubbled to the surface; had her parents really sent her away? She shook her head slightly to clear her mind, smiling.

"I suppose, keep the door open." Mavericks smiled.

"Ew. That's just—*wow*." Max frowned, gagging as he led Della up the magnificent stairs and through a few long hallways.

Funny, Della thought, *I always thought he had a little bit of a thing for me.* She smiled to herself, shaking her head when he gave her a questioning look.

After a while of traversing through their lavish house,

Max pushed open a door covered in caution tape, making a show of waving his hands. In contrast to the rest of the house, which looked like it could have stepped out of some old black and white film, his room was decorated like a mad scientist's evil lair. It was dimly lit, the only light coming from the blue and green light bulbs in lamps that were shaped like beakers. His bedspread depicted the periodic table, framed quotes hung on the walls, and there was a fog machine in the corner.

"Like?" Max asked.

She nodded, taking a seat on his bed and examining the town map he had on his wall. There were different colored pushpins tacked in to it, each connected by a corresponding thread.

"Ei've been keepin' tabs on all the projects this year. The green ones are for ours." Max explained, following her gaze. The butcher shop and the cemetery were marked, as well as the Dixon's household. Max smiled at his handiwork, plopping down on the bed next to her.

They sat awkwardly for a moment, both examining their surroundings with equal curiosity. Della let her leg bounce up and down nervously, not knowing what to talk about. She could always tell him about what she saw when she passed out the other day. That might be a good conversation starter. However, she would not even entertain the thought of talking about it. What would he do—what would *Porter* do—if they knew she was having weird visions about fires and crows?

Max cleared his throat. "So, did ya see the game?"

Della shook her head in surprise. "Did you?"

"What are ya talkin' about? Ei love sports!" He said with no shame whatsoever.

"Really? Name one sport."

"Soccer, football, basketball, baseball, lacrosse—"

"I said one."

Max smiled to himself. "Ei have trophies in the lounge. Ei used to play rugby at school." He cracked his knuckles as if that was supposed to impress her.

"Nice. I won a debate meet last semester." Della smiled.

"Nerd." Max breathed.

"Are you serious? Have you seen your bedroom?" Della laughed.

"Have ya seen *yerself?*" Max joked.

Della raised an eyebrow, pulling out her phone. "Who

won last year's football season?"

"That is not how ya say that," Max said matter-of-factly, refusing to answer. "Mavericks took me tuh the winnin' game though."

Della squinted suspiciously. Not fair. *Her* father hadn't even taken her out for ice-cream. "Okay, who won the two-thousand-and-three world series poker match?"

Max shut his eyes for a minute. "Poker isn' a sport."

"If you can cheat your way to victory, it is to me."

Max looked startled at that.

"I'm quite good at it." Della yawned, leaning back on her elbows.

He rolled his eyes and scratched his chin, staring at his feet. His face was screwed up in an expression of worry. Slowly, he turned to her, searching her face.

"What?" Della asked an air of worry in her voice.

"Ya know how Nicoletta called me beastie?" He asked.

Della nodded.

"Ei—" Max fought himself for a moment.

"Oh dear, you and Porter don't have a *thing*, do you?" Della quipped.

Max's face turned bright maroon. "No—Why would—Are ya—" He coughed a couple of times, pulling his shirt away from his throat.

Della chuckled, falling back onto his bed, staring up at the ceiling. "Continue."

Max took a minute to regain his composure, scowling at her. He laid down beside her, his arms crossed tightly over his chest.

"Ei'm a witch." He said, acting as if saying it was the end of the world.

"Okay." Della yawned. "I kind of already figured that out." That was a lie, but in her mind, the possibility of her new 'friends' being anything but normal was, well, normal.

Max groaned. "Okay fine, so ya know what happened to the cat?"

Della shot upright. "If you say you used it in a ritual, I will kill you."

Max's expression went sour. "No, ya eejit, Ei am the cat."

"Ew." Della gagged. "You sat on my lap, I held you to my chest, I friggin—"

"Not the reaction Ei was expectin'," Max said, sitting up.

"You disgust me."

"Ei just told ya my biggest secret, and that's all ya have tuh say?" Max asked.

"What were you expecting?" Della asked. "Oh, my! My best friend is a cat! Call the police!" She said in a high-pitched voice.

Max smiled. "Best. . . friend?"

"Don't tell Porter," Della commanded, her face burning red.

"Wouldn' dream of it." Max promised, drawing an 'X' over his heart.

"Okay, so let me get this straight. You are what, a shapeshifter—"

"Familiar." Max corrected, though he nodded.

"But familiars are animals." Della said, confused.

Max nodded. "Most are. Some are humans, some can pass between. Ei was born human, if that's what yer asking."

"Right, and Nicoletta is a witch, and—and what is Mavericks? A vampire?" Della asked.

"No, but Lenora and the rest of the Ambrose's are. Every town has a mob." Max stared off into the distance for a second, then shook his head. "Mavericks is an immortal demon who worked under *Nicolas Flamel*."

"Are you serious?" Della asked in amazement. That would explain so much.

"Half. He is immortal." He snickered.

". . . Immortal wasn't the half I thought was right. . ." Della mumbled under her breath as she scratched her nose, shaking her head. "Is that one bookstore run by werewolves? I never got a chance to ask Bayou Gil and Cheryl." Was all she could muster up.

Max nodded. "Rival gang to the Ambrose's. The wolf packs don' exactly get along, so it's probably best ya didn' ask."

"Wow."

"Yeah."

"Cool," Della said dryly.

"Most people would have had a heart-attack by now, what's yer deal?" Max asked.

She shrugged. She wasn't surprised that any of the things she believed in existed, she was more afraid of waking up and realizing all of this was just some crazy dream. Perhaps

Porter *hadn't* saved her before that car plowed into her.

"I'm not in a coma, am I?" Della blurted out.

Max furrowed his eyebrows in surprise. "No. . .?" He said, sounding unsure of himself.

Della nodded, a twitching grin appearing on her lips. "I love this town."

He eyed her for a moment, his cheeks turning a lovely shade of vermilion. "Hey, thanks for nippin' over tonight." He said quietly.

Della shrugged. "I'm broke and have an empty fridge." She laughed at her half truth. Part of her was here because she didn't want to be alone.

"Well, whatever made ya come over, Ei am hopin' it sticks around for a little bit. Ei like it when ya smile. When ya aren' broodin'." Max admitted.

"I do not 'brood'. . ." Della scoffed. "I think deeply about subjects that make me unhappy. There is a difference."

"Yes. One is the word; the other is the definition." Max chortled.

Della rolled her eyes. "So, when's dinner?"

~ ~ ~

Steiniger watched him from across his office, his thick white eyebrows raised as Porter shoved another one of the chocolates he'd given him into his mouth. It was supposed to last him a couple days, but Porter Garroway loved to stress eat.

"Don't beat yourself up about the kid, all right?" Steiniger said once Porter was done telling him about everything that had happened unfiltered.

"I could've saved him," Porter whispered, shoving what he thought was a caramel into his mouth. He gagged, spitting it out, his tongue covered in coconut.

Steiniger chuckled to himself, coming over to sit on the couch next to Porter. He hadn't wanted to go home just quite yet, so instead, he was spending a couple hours at the station, doing whatever he could to distract himself.

"I'm proud of you." Steiniger smiled, nudging him, stealing a chocolate covered in red sprinkles from the box.

"I don't feel like you should be, I feel like I failed." Porter sighed, refusing to meet his eyes, instead looking over the empty office they were sitting in. Pictures of the missing kids were pinned to the wall, their judgmental smiles staring him down.

"Don't beat yourself up about it," Steiniger repeated. "It's out of your control."

Porter sighed heavily, handing over the rest of the chocolates, standing. He couldn't sit here any longer. He was exhausted, all he wanted to do was sleep.

"You need a ride?"

"Naw, I feel like walking."

Steiniger rolled his eyes. "I didn't pay to fix up that hearse for you to walk everywhere."

"Thank you for thinking about my health, Eric. You know, I wouldn't want to be stuck with arthritis because I walk too much. No, I want to be in a wheelchair because my legs gave out from years of misuse." Porter quipped, pulling the burly Cheif into a hug.

"You know me, always looking out for you." He said, lingering in the embrace a little too long for Porter's liking. "I'll see ya tomorrow, kid." He whispered.

"You too, old man." Porter winked.

~ ~ ~

It was evident that Max and Mavericks did not get many visitors. They talked Della's ear off, not letting her get a word in edgewise. Max had even given her an extensive tour of the house, complete with him showing her how to use the industrial washer and dryers. She would have never expected them to live here. They were so humble. Della had often thought that they lived in the basement of the law firm.

All that aside, the happiness Max had thought he observed, was fake. Sitting here, having to act as though everything was fine, in a house where a happy family lived, seeing Max and Mavericks chat blithely about their lives—it made her realize something; she was fatally homesick.

Della, though her brain sometimes scared her, liked being alone with her thoughts. She was able to think things over and get a better grip on the reality she hated so much. So, much to her hosts' chagrin, she had insisted that she take the bus home.

Walking to the bus stop, tears welling up in her eyes, she felt like someone was staring at her. She reached for her phone, shooting her mother an unexpected 'I love you' text.

~ ~ ~

Porter watched her as she sat at the bus stop. He was pretty sure she was not shaking from the cold. He noticed with grave concern, that she looked like an absolute wreck. Her hair was flat, her mascara was smeared down the side of her face, and her cracked glasses were crooked. He desperately wanted to help her, but he didn't know how. He had always been the one people tried to help, even now. It was not in his DNA to try and help them back.

So instead, he stayed back, waiting for her to turn around and look at him with her beautiful brown eyes. He hated seeing her like this, and he knew he wasn't supposed to. He was pretty sure no one was ever meant to see her like this.

That is what saddened him the most.

He kept coming back to her because she was the embodiment of the stability he so wished he had in his life. Seeing her in such a state like this, made him question society. Who would have the power to break her like this? Surely, she wasn't as self-destructive as he was? Surely this was just a fluke. Maybe she had walked through a sprinkler? Perhaps that's why she looked like this. . .

He had to hold on to that.

If she wasn't as strong as he thought she was, then that meant there was no hope for him or anyone else. He would be stuck with his mother and Jed for the rest of his life.

His thoughts traveled back to the 'lovely' events that had happened when he returned home from the police station.

He had never understood why doing the right thing got you in trouble. Never understood why Jed saw him in the light that he did.

Maybe that's why he was out in the cold again tonight.

If he was honest, he was a good kid. He did everything his mother asked of him, and then some. He volunteered at the food bank, he got up on Sunday mornings and went to Church. He did everything he could to be better than the person he was when he was younger.

Other than Steiniger, Jed had been the only fatherly influence in his life, and he was very far from being a good one. Each night he came home from work, he would return drunk and angry. And Porter was a huge stress ball. Tonight had been nothing out of the norm. Porter was cleaning up after dinner when he bumped into Jed. In reality, it had been the fault of the old drunk, not his, but that didn't seem to matter in Jed's mind.

Of course, his mother was nowhere to be seen as Jed threw a wine glass, showering her son in the deadly glass. She never was. She had no idea what went on when she left the room, all she knew is that every once in awhile, Porter had odd bruises or cuts on him.

His mother had never been the cream of the crop, but Porter would have thought that after thirteen years, she would have caught on to her boyfriend's bad habits. Maybe she did. He honestly didn't know. It wasn't like they were close or anything. She was his boss, not his mother.

Porter sighed heavily, snapping himself out of the death trap that was the depths of his mind, still staring at Della. She never turned to grace him with the sight of her eyes, so he edged ever so closer to her, reaching into his pocket for some loose change so he could pay for her bus fare.

~ ~ ~

Never in her life had Della seen an ad on a bus and had wanted to cry. Nevertheless, here she was, staring at the side of a bus with an advertisement for a home loan that depicted a happy family smiling in front of a new house.

Apparently, there was a first time for everything.

As Della stood, staring at the bus, the driver honking at her, asking her whether she wanted a ride, the tears she had been choking down finally spilled forth from her eyes. She nodded dazedly, but just stood there.

"I've got it." A voice rang. Someone pushed past her as she stared at the ad. Someone had paid for her bus ride home.

She thanked the person, not bothering to look at them as she walked up the steps. She took a seat at the back, pulling the hood of her tie-dyed purple jacket over her face and staring out the window.

"You okay?" Porter's voice rang. Della turned to see Porter had slid onto the seat next to her, his handsome face cracking into a smile. He held a couple of loose coins in his hand, trying to hide them from her.

He was the one that had paid for her bus ride.

Damn him, she thought.

She nodded.

"Are you sure?" He asked.

She nodded again and turned away from him, tapping her foot on the floor to distract herself from him, wiping away her tears.

"That's sad." Porter frowned. He grabbed her chin, pulling her face away from the window so he could examine her.

"What is?" She snapped, searching his eyes. She wanted nothing more than to take all her anger and sadness out on him.

"That you think to be strong, you cannot talk about your problems." He said softly.

"I thought you said you didn't care." She snapped.

"Honey, if I didn't care, do you think I'd be sitting here? I'm supposed to be home." He smiled sympathetically.

"Stop doing that." She said before she could stop herself.

"Doing what?" Porter asked, his emerald eyes darkened, no longer reflecting the beautiful golden sparkles Della had once noticed.

Flustered, her lips started moving without her consent. "Being so charming, caring, and—STOP LAUGHING!" Her face flushed red. Her chest tightened as the room began to spin.

Porter stared open-mouthed at her for a moment, then grabbed her hand, trying to comfort her, but she ripped it away. Softly, he reached up and gently wiped away one of her tears.

"I'm not a child." She hissed, slapping his hand away.

"I know."

"Then why are you treating me like one?" She snapped, finally turning to look at him.

He shrugged. "I don't mean to." He said sincerely.

She stamped her foot down on the floor in frustration. He raised an eyebrow. They both knew that was a childish move, but he didn't bring it to her attention like she thought he would've.

"Why do you care so much, anyway?" She asked, sitting back down on that ripped up old bus seat so hard that he bounced a couple of centimeters up into the air.

"Because I did not save your life to have you turn around and waste it." He said simply, staring blankly in front of him.

"I'm not wasting my life."

"Not yet." He said. He was once again as stiff as a board. "You have caught my eye, Miss Delphee Coleman, who *doesn't* work for the local paper."

"I'm not an object. I do not sparkle like a diamond, so therefore I cannot catch your eye." She hissed.

"Oh, trust me, you sparkle. You shine. You glow." Porter smiled, still not looking at her.

"No, I don't."

"You *are* blind, aren't you?" He asked, finally turning to look at her.

"At least I have an excuse. You have got twenty-twenty vision, and you cannot seem to take a hint. I'm not interested." Della said, subconsciously adjusting her glasses. The golden flecks had returned to his eyes.

"Tell you what. If you really are bothered by me, if you think I'm so *annoyingly* charming, I will leave you alone. If you need help with your weird research, come find me, but other than that, you can pretend I don't exist." He said, daring her with his melancholy smile.

She stared at him for a long while, her mind racing. For every lousy trait he had, there were thousands of good ones. For every tiny little thing that annoyed her about him, there was something else that made her smile.

"I never said your charm was annoying." Della reluctantly admitted.

Porter laughed, looking back down the row of seats on the bus. His ears were glowing red. He was embarrassed. Della stared forward, too, not wanting to give him the satisfaction of her eyes lingering on his perfect cheekbones.

"So," He said after a while. ". . . No deal, then?"

"No deal. As much as I hate to admit it, I need you—and Max, of course." She added quickly. "You are my. . ." The word tasted sour on her lips. "You are my *friends*." She said with some difficulty.

"I'm honored." His tone wasn't sarcastic, it was the sincerest thing she had ever heard. "You know I have sat here and watched you—"

Della's brain shut off at that word. Her eyes widened. "The watch." She breathed.

Porter stopped midway through his sentence. "—the way you. . . I'm sorry, what?"

Della dug into her bag. "The watch." She had completely forgotten about it. Honestly, she was kind of angry with herself for that. No matter how insignificant a piece of information was, she never forgot about it. Somehow, she always needed every clue, even if it seemed irrelevant.

"What watch?" Porter insisted.

"This watch." Della said, pushing up her glasses and holding the dirty little thing up to the light.

"You stole a watch?" Porter asked jokingly. She couldn't tell if he would have been disappointed or impressed if she had.

"No, I found it in the butcher's shop. In the freezer. Right before I slipped and hit the door. . ." Della said. Porter laughed, reaching out for the watch. "You aren't a klepto, are you?" She asked, pulling it away from him.

Porter leaned forward and gently took it from her hands. "I thought you said I was a psycho murderer."

"Is that a confession?"

"Yes. Ask Max, he will tell you just how many strapping young ladies I have totally *annihilated* during my twenty years on this earth." He said through tight lips, examining the watch. "Hey, there's a name." He rubbed away the grime on the watch with his shirt, leaning closer to her. "Does the name Theodore Heiser ring any bells?"

Ignoring the previous comment about his love life, Della shook her head. "I know Jimmie Heiser. He's the one who sent me the horn sample. He said it was a gift from his brother. . . and I think I know his wife too. Eloise."

"That's not what I meant," Porter said, smiling glumly. "Back in the eighties, our town was plagued by mysterious disappearances and deaths—sort of like what has been going on now. Anyway, after a year of searching, the police caught a guy named Theodore Heiser. He admitted to committing the crimes and was sentenced to life. The thing is, the only evidence against him was a letter with his fingerprints on it addressed to one of the victims." Porter shook his head. "He was a cop. Used to work with the Cheif."

"Is he alive?" Della asked.

Porter nodded. "Yup, he is rotting away in prison as we speak."

"I think I should pay Mr. Heiser a visit." Della smiled, grabbing the watch back from him.

"He was said to be violent and insane, Della. You aren't going in there. You could get seriously hurt. And don't even get me started on all the other sadistic lunatics that call prison their home sweet home."

"But what if he was framed? Come on, Porter," Della said as the bus pulled up to her apartment building. "The same events are happening all over again. What if the police got the wrong guy? What if he knows something? Don't you think that if he could control demon-things, he would have broken himself out of prison a long, *long*, time ago?"

"Concrete is too thick," Porter said quietly. They stared each other down, lost in thought. With growing worry, she remembered there was still so much she didn't know about the pretty face before her. "Say that you do go visit him, what would you say? 'Hi, I am Delphee Coleman. Oh, where do I work, Mr. Scary-Police-Officer-Man? Oh, I can't tell you that.'" He said mockingly in a nasally voice. "I trust you; they won't."

"I'll figure it out. I still have my fake Moss Hollow Tribune badge." Della explained.

"I'm going to pretend I didn't hear that," Porter said, wrinkling his nose.

"That's probably for the best," Della admitted. She stood, making her way to the front of the bus, Porter on her heels.

"Della, you can't." He grabbed her by her hand, spinning her around to look at him. "I won't allow it."

"Too bad you don't have any say over anything I do," Della smirked.

"That may be true, but I just so happen to know others who do. Both of which wouldn't approve of your plan." He let go of her hand, crossing his thick arms over his chest.

"Are you threatening me with Max and Mavericks?" She asked. He nodded. "That's a feeble threat. What are they supposed to do? Tie me to a chair and lecture me? With science, maybe? News flash, I spent all of last Summer looking up escape tactics because I don't trust people."

He rolled his eyes. "Don't underestimate Maximilian McGregor-Mavericks, Della. It would be your downfall." Porter said, staying at the top of the steps as Della hopped down.

"You know, people keep saying that, but it looks like I'm still standing." She smiled.

"You know what," Porter began, a dangerous look in his eyes that dared her to get back on the bus and follow him home. "All this witty banter has made me hungry. I'll expect you to buy me breakfast in the morning. You know, because I saved your life. Twice now." He waved to her, disappearing back inside the bus.

~CHAPTER NINETEEN~

Theodore Heiser

She had sincerely thought he had been joking. Maybe even bluffing. But here he was, standing outside the big glass double doors that led into the apartment building, thoroughly drenched form the first rain of fall. He was wearing a faux leather jacket over his gray sweatshirt, his hood was up, a thick knitted beanie over top it—one with a rather ugly bobble that blew back and forth in the wind.

"What are you doing?" Della asked, opening the doors, the cold misty breeze ruffling her hair. She, too, was wearing a beanie, but hers was much more tasteful. It had a tie-dye patch on the front that read 'T.U.C.' The unofficial abbreviation of *The Utopian Courier.*

"I was cold this morning. And now I'm wet." Porter smiled, wringing out one of his sleeves on the pavement.

She rolled her eyes, beckoning him inside. "You could have just worn the hat. Then you wouldn't have looked so stupid."

"But my neck would be wet."

"Wear a scarf."

"I don't have a scarf. They are itchy." He said simply, looking at her as if she had just propositioned him to commit some heinous crime. You know, other than faking her identity to talk to a supposed serial killer. "So, where are you taking me to go get breakfast?"

"We can have *lunch* after we go talk to Theodore Heiser." She said sternly, though her voice was sweet.

He rolled his eyes. "I should have learned my lesson the first time that you refused to take 'no' for an answer."

"Honestly, you learned that quicker than my parents did, so props to you." Della smiled, reaching down to tie the laces on her teal rubber combat boots.

"Come on, let's get going." Porter laughed, rolling his eyes, holding the door open for her. His eyes lingered on her shoes, an odd little smile playing across his face. "Those are cute." He said.

"Porter, you are hurt." Della said, crossing her arms. She cursed the fact that he made her blush so much.

"As long as I can still breathe, I don't see an issue." He said, copying her pose. She could see the bulges of his bandages even under his clothes. "Plus, so are you."

"I am not."

Porter blinked slowly.

She swept past him, reveling in the crisp September air. It was crazy to think she had barely been here a month. It felt like just yesterday the weather was still pleasant enough to wear shorts. She smiled. The wind had died down, but the rain was still pounding on their heads. Della looked around the parking lot for Porter's rusty hearse, leading the way much to Porter's disdain. She tapped the Jesus bobblehead as soon as she slid into the passenger seat. Was it just her, or was the tiny figure giving her a judgmental look? She shrugged it off. Probably nothing. Just like how she thought the eyes on one of the paintings at the law firm had followed her.

"I could drive you in the opposite direction." Porter said as he pulled out of the parking lot, snapping her out of her thoughts.

"You could, but you wouldn't. You want to figure this out as much as I do, though I have no idea why. We don't exactly talk to each other." Della said.

"What do you call words then?" Porter asked, messing with the radio. Della's ears filled with post-modern punk music as Porter began bobbing his head.

"I call that communication. We don't have normal conversations."

"Ask me something then," Porter said.

"So, have you heard anything about Angus?" Della asked.

Porter's eyes lit up with recognition. He nodded. "Nothing yet. His grandparents have not seen him, hasn't shown up at school either."

They were silent for a long minute, lost in thought.

Porter cleared his throat, messing with the radio again. "You know, I meant that you could ask me something about my life. Not something work-related."

"Oh. . ." Della thought for a moment. "Uh. . . Did you grow up here?" She asked awkwardly.

He nodded. "Born and raised in that mortuary. Literally. My mom couldn't make it to the hospital in time."

Della rolled her eyes. "Is it just you, your mom, and grandpa?"

He glanced at her. "And my mom's boyfriend, Jedidiah." He fell silent for a moment, gripping the steering wheel tightly. "My dad died when I was little. He's buried out back."

"What happened?" Della asked before she could stop herself.

Porter laughed grimly. "Car accident. Went up in flames. Not much of him was left." He scratched the back of his neck. "He died when I was seven, but I don't remember him much, but I know he was a good man. He taught me everything I know about my Portuguese heritage. Taught me the language, taught me the proverbs. . ." A heavy sadness fell onto them.

Della cleared her throat awkwardly. "Are you and Jedidiah close?" She asked, trying to move the conversation away from the inevitability of life.

Porter shook his head, clutching the steering wheel with all his might.

Della nodded slowly, thinking of another question. "Would you ever leave this place?"

"This is home, and there are parts about it that I love, but most of the time, I hate it here. I only stay because I don't have the means to leave. Plus, Pops is sick. When he kicks the bucket, we won't get his social security checks. I have to stay until my mom sells the whole place, or she finds another job." His eyes were dark.

"I'm sorry." Della sighed. Her heart ached for him. He nodded sadly, staring straight ahead. Della thought of another question, something a little lighter. "How many girls have you dated?" She asked smirking.

"Blunt, but okay. Four." He said, smiling a little, loosening his grip on the steering wheel.

"Four? Seriously?" Della questioned. That had to be a lie.

"Would you prefer more, my love?" He asked, turning towards her, a playful look on his face.

Della's face turned burgundy almost instantly.

"I'll say that's a no. . . If you must know, there was one in elementary school, but I guess that's not a real relationship, two in middle school, and one in ninth grade before I dropped out. I only kissed the one in ninth grade, the others I only held hands." He smiled, reminiscing about a past love.

Dear Lord, he was so wholesome. Della thought.

"You dropped out?"

He nodded energetically. "Best decision of my life. The government corrupts bright minds. I broke free from my cell just in time."

Looks were nothing. Or at least, they didn't matter as much as him saying that simple little phrase. She smiled widely, making a mental note.

But that admiration quickly faded. Her mind flashed back to what Mavericks had said about his criminal record. "Do you have DUIs?" She asked quietly.

He turned to her, a look of knowing on his face. "Also, four. I used to get really drunk when Jed—" He paused, shaking his head, clenching his fingers around the steering wheel again. "All right, it's my turn. Where did you grow up?" He asked as he turned down a busy side street.

Taking the hint that he would not talk about himself anymore, she answered his little question. "This little place in Washington called Sycamore Heights."

"Wow, that is pretty far. Do you miss it?"

She shrugged. This was a subject she would rather not talk about. Admitting to herself that she was missing the town she hated so much was more painful than any migraine she had ever experienced.

"I guess I miss my family, my mom and my siblings especially, but not the place." She half lied. "It was so boring there. We had literal white picket fences, and half of the houses were beige."

"No wonder you left. That place could not hold all of—"

He waved his hand around her face. "—this."

She smiled.

Porter thought for a minute. "Y'know, we never really talked about how far you've gone."

"Excuse me?" Della asked, horrified.

"Like, I don't know, are you a 'the moon landing is fake' kinda girl or are you a '*JFK Jr* is still alive' kinda girl?" He asked, his tone serious.

"Bold of you to assume I believe in the moon at all." Della said lazily. Porter smirked. "If you are truly interested, I have a blog." She explained, her cheeks red.

"Oh, really?" He asked, staring at the road, mischief in his eyes.

She nodded. "*Yours Truly, Della Coleman.*"

Porter smiled to himself. Part of her thought he already knew this. "So," he said after a while. "You've got some siblings? How many?"

"Twins. Leonel and Cassandra." Della smiled.

Porter smiled widely. "Are they annoying?"

"They're eight." Della laughed. Then she scowled. "I have an older brother too. . . My parents don't talk about him much. He ran away at sixteen. We used to be super close, and he always came around for Christmas, but no one has heard from him in five years. Last I heard, he was pursuing a career in music." Della stared at the road, blocking all the pent up rage she felt about her family.

Porter glanced at her, then nodded to himself. "H—How many guys have you dated?" He stammered, a cheeky expression hiding beneath his blank stare. She had a feeling he knew the pain she was feeling.

Della cleared her throat, glad to change the subject. "I went on one date with an acquaintance. Worst experience of my life." She laughed.

"Yikes, what happened?"

"He took me to a poetry bar." Della started. "We hung out for a while, but uh, apparently, I am allergic to tomatoes." She laughed. "I had to go to the ER because my windpipes closed up. I swear, I thought I was going to die." She thought back with a smile on her face, seeing a panicked Sebastian running around in her head. "He fell down a flight of stairs trying to bring me flowers."

Porter stared at her. "Your life is like a bad rom-com."

"Yes. A medieval rom-com. You have no idea. . ."

"You're the main character, a princess, maybe. Max is the court physician, and. . . Hmm? Where does that leave me, Miss Coleman?" Porter smiled.

"Don't flatter yourself." Della smiled. "You are the stable boy."

"I'm a stable boy?!" Porter scoffed. "I'm very far from stable. I was thinking I was the knight in shining armor. I'll have to talk to my manager."

"There is no room for a knight in my story. He's too noble. Too proper. I would much prefer a buccaneer of sorts. Someone who rebels." Della looked at him with a knowing look.

"Oh right, right, I must have read the script wrong."

Della laughed. "Okay, ask me another question."

He stared out at the road, fiddling with the collar of his shirt. "If you had a secret, and you knew that sharing it would make others look at you differently, but the knowledge you had would save lives, would you tell someone?" He asked.

"Odd question, but yes. The needs of the many outweigh the needs of the few. Look at me; I'm as weird as I can get. I am pretty sure that the world could handle whatever secret I had." Della mused.

He turned to look at her, his eyes widening in surprise. "Sometimes, I forget your hair is green. Yeah, I guess that's pretty weird."

"Ha-ha, very funny."

"No, I am serious," Porter said. "For some reason, it just doesn't stand out anymore."

She raised an eyebrow. "That is usually the first thing people point out."

"Your eyes stood out to me." He blushed.

"Why? They are only brown. They're boring."

"Your eyes," He began as he parked in front of the jail. "Are like wet tree bark."

"Thanks. . . I guess."

Porter laughed. "It's true! They are beautiful, Della; I don't know why you cannot see that. Why can't you see how amazing you are?" He asked. His voice was nothing but a whisper.

"Because I don't pay attention to that. I am the one thing I forget to observe. I can tell you the license plate number of the guy in the red *Yaris* we followed halfway here, but if you asked me what my face looked like, I would draw a blank." Della said seriously, her tone hysterical. She honestly didn't understand what he saw in her.

Porter leaned over and pulled down the mirror above her head. "Well," He began pointing in the mirror. "I see perfect cheekbones, plump little lips, dazzling brown eyes, and a cute little nose that reminds me of a deer. You are the embodiment of my favorite place on Earth: the forest. Your hair is the color of dirt and moss, and your complexion reminds me of the moon. When you are angry, your face turns as red as a rose, when I make you blush like I am right now, you go the color of peonies. Which just so happens to be my favorite flower."

She stared at her reflection. "Flattery will get you nowhere." She lied; her voice small.

"Fine, do me now." He closed the mirror and turned her face to his.

She thought for a moment, watching him stare at her. "I see a face that has been chiseled from the purest marble. You have thin little lips that change color with your mood. Your eyes are like jewels, like a broken piece of peridot that is held up to the light. Your nose is pointy, and that is the only place on your face where you have freckles. Your hair sucks the light out of the room. When you blush, it's barely noticeable unless you look at your ears. Which are pointy like an elves." She smiled, watching him stare at her in awe.

He sniffed a couple of times as he stared at her lips, leaning in closer. They held each other's gaze for a minute, before he pulled away quickly, once again as stiff as a board. He rubbed his nose, unlocking the truck.

"Y—You should go inside." He stammered. "I don't know when visiting hours end." He added, an odd little smile making his lips twitch. He squinted at the road, shaking his head in inward anger.

She got out of the truck quickly, feeling the tension flowing out of him with every breath. She walked away without looking back, staring at her feet. She felt like a fool. She felt so stupid for getting attached.

But it was Porter Garroway.

He was irresistible.

~ ~ ~

"Theo, you have a visitor." The warden said as he opened the door and let Della in. "Knock on the door if you want out. You have half an hour." He explained. He had been an awfully chatty guard. He would not shut up about the weirdest crimes that had landed the people he watched over in there cells.

Della nodded, thanking the kind old police officer, nonetheless. The man before her looked nothing like a violent murderer. Though his face was sagging with old age, you could still make out that he had been quite handsome. He smiled kindly at her, gesturing for her to sit despite being shackled to a table.

"To whom do I owe the pleasure?" He asked. His voice was hoarse like he had not talked in a while.

"I'm Della Coleman; I think your brother told you about me?" She smiled.

His eyes lit up with recognition. "Ah, yes, the girl from the paper. Excuse my manners, but I was expecting someone a little older." His eyes told her that indeed he had been expecting someone.

"You're fine." Della smiled. "I don't have long, but I have a couple of questions for you—and this." She reached into her pocket and pulled out his watch, sliding it across the table to him. She had spent the evening cleaning it up, thinking she would have to use it as leverage.

"W—Where did you find this? It has been missing for years." He said, running a finger over the cold metal. "My best friend was the last to see it."

"My friends and I were doing some research for an article about what your brother and his friends saw. We were led to an old butcher's shop, I found it in a freezer."

"Oh, dear." He whispered. His eyes had gone cold, he stared at the watch, his breathing erratic. "I haven't been out there for years. . . Thank you for returning it."

"Of course! Can I ask you about the crimes that landed you here?" Della asked.

He thought for a moment then nodded sadly. "What would you like to know?"

"Mr. Heiser, it is my understanding that you turned yourself in, but the only evidence against you wasn't enough to land you a death sentence. Pardon my confusion, but why would you do that? You were a cop. A *good* cop, in line to take over for the Cheif at the time. Why would you do that?" Della asked. She'd done a bit of research early this morning at the law firm. Filed away in her cabinets were reports of his crimes, as well as a description of him. She had a feeling that report was wrong. *Really* wrong.

He sighed slowly, his eyelids flickering in frustration. "Because I had too. I was tired of running." There was no emotion in his voice.

Della stared at him, her brain working overtime, trying to figure him out. She did not get the same odd vibe from him that she got from Mavericks, but she did not feel as safe with him as she felt with Nicoletta. She squinted at him, leaning back in her chair.

"Was there a certain flavor to the victims?" She asked.

He shrugged. "There is a difference between *cereal* and serial, Miss Coleman." He smirked a little.

Della nodded. "What was in the letter the cops used as evidence against you?" She asked.

"It was a note to my wife." He began. Della furrowed her eyebrows. That's not what the police report said. "I was telling her I was sorry and that I loved her. We were newlyweds, and seeing as I was stuck here, I was apologizing for not helping her bear children and make a life for ourselves like I promised I would." He said sadly. His eyes were an ocean of remorse and regret.

Della dropped her voice, leaning closer to him. "Were you being blackmailed back then?"

He paled, glancing at the camera above her head. "No." He said simply. He swallowed hard, his fingers twitching his eyes widening ever so slightly. He was scared.

"Mr. Heiser, did you really commit those crimes?"

Theodore stared at her. He made a conscious decision to cover his mouth, staring at her without blinking. He gave her a questioning look as if trying to see if she was catching on to his body language. She nodded.

"Yes, I did commit all those crimes on the seventeenth of November, nineteen-eighty-eight. I was twenty-four." He nodded quickly, looking back and forth between her and the camera.

People who lie tend to over share, nervously cover vulnerable parts of themselves, or go as stiff as possible. Finding a liar was easy, as long as you knew where to look, and for someone with as many trust issues as Della had, she knew all the tells.

"Was it. . . Was it a normal crime?" She asked.

He returned to having his hands on the table, acting normally. "No, indeed, it wasn't."

"Have you ever seen anything strange?" Della asked, raising an eyebrow.

He nodded, though the motion was minuscule. "There are things in this town, things that would make your skin crawl. Things Miss Coleman, that a girl like you should not be messing around with."

"Are these things human?" She asked, already knowing too much of the truth.

He leaned in close. His breath smelled like old beer. "That my friend is a moral conundrum. Are criminals still human after they commit heinous crimes? Is a monster really a monster when they think they are doing the right thing?"

The two stared at each other, expecting each other to say something that proved their suspicions.

"Have you ever participated in witchcraft?" Della asked.

"Are you crazy?" Theodore scoffed, catching her by surprise. "Sure, Ellie and I could have used the extra money, but I wanted to earn it. We were honest folk, we minded our own business, and we made the best of what we had." Odd answer.

Della inhaled sharply. "Do you have any enemies?" She asked.

Theodore shook his head. "Of course, I do. I killed five people, Miss Coleman. I am being transferred out of here pretty soon since ten people have tried to assassinate me."

"Does anyone know, other than you, what really happened?" Della asked.

"My brother, Jimmie," Theodore said. "I suppose he told my Eloise. . . They have become close given my position. Ellie always did like him." He said sourly. "Maybe Steiniger. He was my closest friend."

Della made a mental note of that, watching Theodore scowl at his watch. "Wasn't Eric Steiniger the one who took you in?" Della asked. He nodded. "Do you think he or Jimmie dabble in the arcane?" She asked.

"Eric is a hard-nose, but Jimmie did when we were younger, but he swore to me that he had stopped." He sighed.

"Did he ever summon anything?"

He shook his head, smiling a little. "We Heiser's were not known for our brains, but he wasn't that stupid. He was into the little parlor tricks, y' know? Changing a penny into gold, levitating water out of a glass, just the little things. He wasn't into all the mind reading and tarot cards like others." A flicker of life danced behind his eyes.

"Did he hang out at a voodoo shop in town? The one the local covens hang out at?" Della asked.

"He and Nicoletta Francis had a spring fling." He laughed. "He was in a couple weeks ago saying that he was finally going to donate all his old magic stuff to her shop."

Della's eyes widened. "Did he have a book?"

Theodore inhaled sharply. "As far as I know, he only had one; this big one we found while we rummaged through our grandmother's house. I doubt the old hag ever knew we took it." He sighed, eyeing the camera again.

"Were there summoning spells in that book? Did anyone else know about it? Did Eloise?"

Theodore rolled his eyes. "For the love of—no, okay?" He spat. "It was just Jimmie and me."

"I'm sorry Mr—"

"Listen, kid," He interjected, leaning as close to her as his shackles would allow him to. "Stay out of the trouble this town likes to call formality. The look in your eyes tells me you didn't grow up here, which means you are observing the town through the eyes of a tourist. No matter what you believe, this town will challenge it." He said sharply. "Stay out of this. You shouldn't even be here."

"No, you listen," Della said, lowering her voice to an angry whisper. "The answers are out there and I—"

"You were not supposed to ask those questions to begin with." Theodore spat, echoing her tone.

"I question everything, Mr. Heiser," Della said, sitting back in her chair and crossing her legs.

Theodore watched her, his face darkening. "I think we are done here." He called to the guards. He smiled like she usually did when she had the upper hand over Ms. Durnell.

There was a tiny buzzing sound from behind her, which made her jump slightly. The door opened, and the warden came in, holding onto his belt and glaring at Theodore. Reluctantly, Della stood, glaring at Theodore for doubting her. As she turned to follow the guard, he cleared his throat. She looked over her shoulder at him, seeing that he had somehow managed to get his watch on under the handcuffs.

"One more thing, Miss Coleman." He began. "Trust your gut. Trust your mind." He said, eyeing the guard. "You stink like pain medication. Lay off it; you'll be surprised to see what happens when you do."

Della stared at him, utterly perturbed and confused.

"Move it." The guard next to her said sternly.

Della shook herself away from Theodore's gaze. Something deep down inside her told her to trust him, and to her, that was the scariest part. He smiled kindly at her. There was something about him. Something that reminded her of herself.

"I am going to figure this out, Mr. Heiser," Della whispered. She was dead set on that promise. Even if the rest of the world didn't believe it, she would find out the truth.

~CHAPTER TWENTY~

Well, That Escalated Quickly

When Della finally got back into Porter's rusty hearse, she did not say anything. She just sat there, staring at the world in front of her, pretending like she could not feel the weight of it on her shaking shoulders. She rubbed her temples, closing her eyes softly, feeling her thick eyelashes resting on her cheeks.

"You okay?" Porter asked.

"I really wish you guys would quit asking me that," Della said, her voice small.

Porter was quiet. He did not start the car; he did not move; he barely even breathed. "Sorry." He said softly.

Della just sat there, eyes shut against the pain in her skull, mulling over every word Theodore had said. It was all so confusing. It seemed like every time she found a piece to this crazy puzzle, she found out it did not fit properly.

"Listen, if you—"

"Can we just go get lunch or something?" Della asked, cutting him off, her voice a little too harsh. She turned to look at Porter, who was staring at her with a concerned expression.

He opened and closed his mouth a couple of times before nodding, reaching down, and starting the car. "Yeah, yeah, let's go get lunch." He said quietly.

"Thank you," Della whispered, leaning forward to flick

the head of the Jesus bobblehead.

"Welcome," Porter whispered back.

~ ~ ~

Much to Della's disdain, Porter had chosen their restaurant.

Bayou Gil's Crab Emporium.

Again.

She sighed as she followed him along the boardwalk in silence, her ears picking up on every little noise around her. There was an odd air to the place now. Maybe it was the fact that Della had just spoken with a supposed criminal, or maybe because she now knew everything the world didn't want her too, but the swamp and the shack looked even more foreboding. A frog hopped across the path in front of her, sending shivers down her spine. She swallowed hard, forcing a smile as Porter opened the door for her, trying to find something else to dwell on to distract herself.

Della watched Porter as he said hello to a few patrons, chatting with no real reason behind his words, as he led her to a table in the back. He was so strange sometimes. The way he carried himself alone was enough to make her head spin. Sadly, it seemed no one else could pick up on it. She alone could tell he was broken. She had known that far before Mavericks had ever toyed with the idea. In her eyes, she had seen him in the shadow of someone who had been beaten down by the universe time after time. See, Della, unlike the rest of these isolated, computer dwelling, self-centered people, saw not only what was on his face, but what was on his heart. Although Mr. Porter Garroway tried so hard to act as if he had never felt pain, when you looked closer, you could see every cut, bruise, and broken bone he had ever endured.

After all, it takes someone with your same shoe size to walk a day in your pumped-up kicks. At least her shoes could be cleaned now and again; it seemed his were caked in so much mud, he didn't even know what color they were.

"I don't get it." She said, cursing herself at the words she was going to say.

He glanced over his shoulder, kicking a few peanut shells away. "What don't you get?"

"You." She replied.

Porter stopped dead in his tracks, slowly turning around

to look at her. ". . . Why?" He asked.

"You are like a thousand different people all the time." She said. "One minute you are the sweet little boy who reads too many romance novels, the next you are the bad boy, then it is like you flick a switch and you're a giant goofball, then back to being starry-eyed. I am just trying to figure out why."

Porter smiled, crossing his arms over his chest, shifting his weight from one side to the other. "I guess that's just who I am." He laughed, shrugging.

"Nothing we say or do is without purpose. Every emotion has a cause. Every time we wiggle our fingers, there is a reason. Each time you stop looking directly into my eyes, there is a subliminal message." She began, brushing past him. "You said something earlier that got me thinking; why do you act the way you do." Of course, she was talking about what he said about being drunk. "Given the recent string of events, I'm not going to take any chances. I think you can sympathize with the kidnapping victims."

"Why would I—" He pounded on his chest. "—sympathize with abused, kidnapped, children?" He asked nervously.

"Because you have been ab—" She began to say over her shoulder.

Quickly, Porter pulled her around by her back pocket so that they were barely centimeters apart. "I could kiss you right now. In front of all these people. Just to see how they would react." He whispered. He reached up and ran a thumb over her cheekbone.

She looked back and forth between his eyes. Danger was written all over his irises. He was scared, terrified even, of the words she had meant to say. Luckily for him, he had left her breathless. Wordless even.

"To see how *you* would react." He finished, letting go of her. She hadn't realized he had had such a firm grip on her waist.

He walked away, taking her by the hand until he had chosen a sufficient table.

"Nepenthe whiffler." She said finally, sitting across from him at a table in the corner. The colors in her face were fighting for attention. On one hand, she was white with fear at the notion of his lips on hers; on the other, she was so embarrassed and excited her cheeks were burning hot pink.

"What?" He asked breathlessly, acting as if that had

been an insult.

He didn't need to know that those words were actually somewhat of a compliment. It would inflate his big head so much that he would burst through the roof of this dingy place. Nepenthe meant something that could take away grief, pain, or sorrow, and whiffler meant someone who changed their ideology rather quickly. She knew he had wanted to kiss her back at the jail, so why hadn't he? Why was kissing her right now, his defense mechanism?

"Nothing." She said, stealing a smile behind his back as he looked through the free papers resting behind the napkin dispenser.

"All right. . ." He said, glancing at her.

He flipped through the paper, absentmindedly checking his phone. He had one of those cases that doubled as a wallet. He frowned and rolled his eyes at the text message Della caught a glimpse of on his screen.

"Why did you do that?" She asked, biting her lower lip.

"What do you mean? The Cheif is over protective, he always checks up on me at the worst of times. Especially lately." Porter said, somewhat absentmindedly, referring to the text.

"That's not what I meant."

"I would have thought you wanted to skirt the subject."

She shook her head violently. "You cannot say something like that and not expect me to wonder."

"That was the only thing I knew that would shut you up. At least for a second." He said blankly.

"But did you mean it?" She asked, stopping herself from asking the real question floating around in her head; *what are you afraid of?*

Part of her wanted him to say no. It would be easier that way, to have him walk away, to let him play the role of a jerk, or better yet, a player. However, that wasn't who he was. He was sweet and lovable, and an all-around good guy. Just annoying. *Very* annoying.

"What do you think, Coleman? Why would I do that?" He asked quizzically, setting the paper down between them.

"Why does anyone do anything?" Della asked, thinking she had beat him at his own game.

"Because they can," Porter said, craning his neck to look at her upside down. "Because I could. Max wasn't there, so I could say whatever the Hell I wanted too. It has been on my mind for quite some time. I am just good at hiding it."

"No, actually, you aren't," Della said, looking out the window.

He took off her beanie, putting it in his pocket and ruffling her hair. "Well, maybe it's obvious to you, but Max is clueless." She could see her reflection in the glass before, her scowl illuminated by candlelight. She smoothed down the hair that was sticking up, fiddling with a loose strand around her face.

"He is a scientist. Social cues aren't really his thing." Della said, turning around to scowl at him.

He smiled at her.

"Stop it." She hissed, trying not to smile back.

"Stop what?" He asked wistfully, his eyes wide.

"Stop smirking, you absolute idiot." That only made him snicker. "Stop. Laughing."

"I'm not." He said, holding up his hands in defense.

"What do you call it then?" Della asked.

He thought for a moment, staring out the window, the sunlight making the gold specks in his eyes look like the sparkling mirrors on a disco ball.

He cleared his throat, his lips twitching. "I call this my cock-a-hoop disposition. I find it quite—"

"You're still laughing at me." Della cut in, an irritated look on her face. "Stop it."

"Anything for you, Miss Delphee Coleman, not from the paper." He said, standing. "Don't go anywhere; I am going to get Cheryl to come give us our menus."

She nodded, sinking into her seat, left to wallow for what felt like days. He returned moments later with Cheryl in tow—she looked immensely amused to see Della back in her little shack. Again. They ordered quickly, both starved; he chose a bowl of clam chowder, her a cheeseburger with a fried patty, and a chocolate milkshake. Being off her medication for a week had given Della a monstrous appetite, and when the food arrived, she could not help but devour it like a wild animal.

Seeing as her stomach was full, and he seemed distracted, Della took this moment to pry more information out of him. She shoved a fry in her mouth before wiping her hands on a napkin and observing her next delicious meal.

Nothing was more filling than knowledge.

"So, as you were saying in the car, why do you get

drunk? Why do you have DUIs?" She asked.

Porter froze, his spoon full of soup hanging out of his mouth. "Drop it." He said, trying his best to smile.

Della pushed up her glasses. "You do realize I am trying to help you, don't you?" She asked.

He nodded. "I do, but that does not mean I want your help." He admitted.

"Liar." Della scoffed. "Everyone wants my help."

"No, Della, I don't," Porter said, a sadness swimming in his eyes.

She inhaled sharply, ignoring his little 'Della, stop.' "Whatever you think will happen when you admit that you have been abused, will not happen. I won't let it. I swear to you that—"

He leaned across the table so quickly, he knocked his bowl of soup over, its contents spilling onto his lap. He reached out and wrapped his fingers around the lapels of her jacket, pulling her to him, pressing his lips against her own. He lingered for a moment, his heavy eyes taking in hers, then quickly pulled away, his face the color of the red basket of fries in front of them.

"I hate you so much right now." She whispered, her heart feeling as if it were going to beat right out of her chest.

"I hate me too." He whispered back. She opened her mouth, but he silenced her, holding up a trembling finger. "That was a mistake." He said, tears welling up in his eyes, looking away. "We will *never* talk about this ever again; do you understand me? We—" He pointed between them, jabbering, his face going through a multitude of expressions. "—cannot happen. We will *never* happen. I'm not good for you, I'm too dark." He said, more to himself than to her, his breathing as fast as her heart rate. "I should not have gotten involved; I shouldn't have even saved—" He stopped, biting his lip, staring down at his hands. He had not meant to say that.

"No, please, continue," Della said, tears welling up in her own eyes.

"I didn't mean that," Porter said sternly.

"Oh, don't pull that *bullshit* on me!" She said, standing. "Of course, you meant it! I am so sorry I am that much of a burden that you wish you wouldn't have saved my life." She snarled as she walked away.

He grabbed her hand, trying to make her sit back down,

which was the biggest mistake of his life. She spun around, grabbed her milkshake, and poured it on his head. The restaurant fell silent. She had seen that move done in so many movies, and never thought she would have the guts to copy it. Nevertheless, it felt terrific to do that to him, no matter how insignificant it might have seemed. Porter let go of her hand, wiping the milkshake out his eyes—which turned an eerie shade of bright, fiery gold for a split second—and gesturing for her to leave.

The thing that hurt the most was that he did not try to come after her again. Perhaps if he had, she would have stayed. But no, he let her walk away. He let her stand out in the cold, bawling her eyes out until a bus finally came to take her home.

No one let Della do anything on her own accord.

He was the first of many things, but he was the last person she would ever pretend to love.

~CHAPTER TWENTY-ONE~

Castle Walls

Della ended up doing what she did best over the next few days, ignoring her problems until they were unbearable. She did not tell Max what Porter had said, she didn't even write what she saw his eyes do in her notes like she would have, she didn't try to call him—honestly, she didn't do much of anything. She was so angry with Porter for saying what he had said that it consumed her. She had just begun to trust him, began to open up, but he ruined that. Forever. She tried not to take it out on Max, instead, locking herself up in her office, ignoring the little knocks and whispers that came from the door.

The new bottle of migraine medication she had asked her mother to order sat on her desk, completely untouched, though her head was pounding like someone was in there knocking on the walls of her skull. Drowning her sorrows in heaping handfuls of junk food was the only thing that was keeping her going right now. If she stopped for even one second to look around, her scratchy, puffy, red eyes would well up with tears, and scary thoughts would take over her feeble brain. All she wanted to do was distract herself, and even that wasn't working.

Whenever she closed her eyes, she saw *his* eyes glowing in her head. They reminded her of a bat's eyes, bland and lifeless. Della knew that Porter had not committed those crimes.

He did not have the capacity to do so, and she had already seen the thing that had, but she couldn't shake the feeling that he had done something he should not have. Mavericks had practically told her he did.

She rubbed her arm up and down, making her itchy sweater turn her skin red as she stared at her computer screen. She just wanted it all to go away. All the pain that people brought her because she got too attached.

A flicker of a memory crossed her mind before she could stop it. A very, very, *very*, bad memory she had tried to repress for years upon dreadful years.

There had been a time in her life when her parents were not happy, and ironically, a lot of that unhappiness came from Della's existence.

Della was weird.

Della wasn't normal.

Della was strange.

Those were the topics she heard her parents arguing about when they thought she could not hear. Her mother embraced every part of her, her father told her everything she loved was useless and that she needed to grow up. It wasn't until one night that her dad left out of the blue. He returned in a couple of weeks, but it was not without him sitting down to tell her exactly what he thought of her. He thought highly of her intelligence, but that was about it. Her father never understood the way she was. Never understood that her strange little ways were the only way she knew how to cope. They were never close after that, and it caused a rift with her siblings and her mom too.

Abandonment issues became her reality.

She stopped letting people in because she didn't want to get hurt, and in reality, who ever does?

It's not like she hated this kingdom of solitude she had been forced to build around her heart, it protected her. It kept her from all the things that the rest of the world left, cheated, ran, and fought over. She wasn't sad. She was not necessarily happy. She was just there, and here, and she was. Nothing more, nothing less. She lived without truly being alive.

When she had met Sebastian, he was in the same boat. He had been raised in the foster care system all his life and had felt his fair share of sorrow. The sad part was that they could've been soulmates. They could have helped each other so much. But Della's walls were not the kind a single cannon could break, let alone put a dent in. Furthermore, Sebastian did not know how to talk to her, to at least try to chip away at the castle walls.

It wasn't like she didn't have people skills either. In fact, most of the school knew her as the 'therapist' because she could help everyone with everything. She had so much sympathy for the broken, the lost, and the forgotten, that they knew she could help them. Della stood waiting for them with open arms, to embrace them and all their flaws.

But they could never love the way she did.

They could never stand for hours, letting everyone trade their darkness for her light like she could. They would break. Crumble. Fall to thousands of pieces. They couldn't even put themselves back together, so how were they supposed to help others?

Della believed in the universe, in God and a higher power. She had a Bible; she had tarot cards; she had a star chart. She had placed all her faith in those things, patiently waiting for the day when all the good she had done would be returned to her seven-fold.

Sometimes she felt so trapped in this imperfect world.

She sighed heavily as a tear fell down her cheek. Her head buzzed like someone had zapped her with lightning and rubbing her temples only made it worse. She shut her eyes tightly, shutting her computer angrily.

Staying in this office any longer was going to drive her insane if she was not already. She stood, gathering a couple of pens and her *Smash Mouth* notebook. Briskly, she made her way through the old law firm, and out into the cold.

Thanks to Theodore, she had a lead.

Hopefully, Jimmie was still as nice as he had been back with the rest of the bird watchers. . .

~ ~ ~

Della knocked on Jimmie Heiser's front door, rocking back and forth on her heels. Ironically, he lived a couple of houses down from the Dixon's. You would think that someone would have heard their screams and gone to check on them. Unless, of course, they had been too scared to even move, let alone scream.

Chapter Twenty-One

Jimmie answered, looking oddly happy to see her.

"Ah! Miss Coleman! How are you, dear?" He asked. It was apparent that Jimmie was the older brother. At least by half a decade. His hair was much whiter, and his skin full of wrinkles, but the resemblance was uncanny now that she knew.

"The case I am working on led me to speak with your brother, Theodore. I have a couple of questions for you." Della said sweetly, smiling through the pain in her head.

Jimmie nodded sadly, but there was animosity in his eyes. "Theo and I talked last night. We chat a couple of times a month. Find anything out?" He asked, opening the door for Della and sweeping her inside. When the door was closed, he looked out the window next to the door, looking slightly worried.

Della shook her head, acting as if she hadn't seen his odd look. Jimmie smiled, whisking her into the living room and shutting the blinds. He sat down in a fraying old armchair, gesturing for her to sit on the couch across from him. Della sat, pulling out her notebook and pens.

"Theodore said you had a spell book, that you used to mess around with some. . . lesser witchcraft?" Della asked.

Jimmie's eyes lit up. "Oh, yes. Better than him, I might add, though I bet he assured you he never used that old book." He chuckled.

Della raised an eyebrow. "He said he and his wife were strictly against it."

"Theodore spooked himself when we were little. He didn't really believe in all that until he moved his derby car halfway across his bedroom. He was much more powerful than me. He could read minds, could figure out the spells, teach himself to create new ones." Jimmie smiled even wider, enjoying reliving that old memory.

Della smiled kindly. "I'm sure you had a great time back then." Jimmie nodded excitedly. "So, do you still have the spell book?"

"Which one?" Jimmie asked, but it was almost as if he hadn't meant to say that. He bit his lower lip. Della could see the wheels in his head turning, wondering what on earth he was thinking.

"The one you and Theodore used to use." She explained.

Jimmie shook his head. "I passed all that on to an old

flame. I had a bunch of crystals and some tarot cards, oh! And this weird little spiny thing that had something to do with the moon!" He explained, spinning the golden band he wore on his finger around a couple of times. He seemed to think he had skirted the question of how many spell books he truly had. Luckily for him, Della was satisfied with his answer.

For now, at least.

"I did not know you were married, Mr. Heiser." Della smiled.

"I was; we split a couple of years back. I still wear the ring. It helps me keep the good parts fresh in my mind." He said.

"That sounds lovely," Della admitted. She looked down at her own fingers, accidentally allowing herself to think of Porter. She cleared her throat, writing a couple things down in her notebook. "Are you close with Eloise, that is Theodore's wife, right? I think I met her when we first met. What about Eric Steiniger?"

Jimmie's face fell, though he tried to hide it. "We talk." He said, his voice small.

Della eyed him. Like his brother, he was hard to read. At least Theodore seemed to wear his heart on his sleeve, Jimmie, on the other hand, seemed like he was doing everything he possibly could to keep from spilling his guts. Della never trusted people like him.

She moved her attention to his house, which seemed to be decorated a little too nicely for a grizzled man who lived alone. To each their own, but she was pretty sure old birdwatchers do not tend to have lace doilies on their tables or pink cushions on their couch.

"Did you ever talk to them about the spell book?" She asked after a while.

"Why do you ask?" Jimmie questioned, furrowing his thick gray eyebrows.

"I spoke with Nicoletta; she said a spell book was stolen from her shop not too long ago, one that had some mighty spells in it," Della explained.

"What does that have to do with the Dixon's death?" Jimmie asked, wringing his hands. He was hiding something. He was scared to say the thing he wanted to say most.

As he wrung his hands, his sleeve moved, revealing part of a tattoo. Before Della could make it out, Jimmie pulled his sleeve down, rubbing his wrist instinctively.

"I'm just checking off all the boxes, trying to figure out what is going on." Della assured him.

"I—I don't know anything, Miss." He said.

Della nodded understandingly. This poor man was scared to speak freely in his own home. Della glanced at the closed blinds behind her.

"Do you have sensitive eyes?" Della asked.

"Hmm?"

"I have extremely sensitive eyes," Della began, pointing to her glasses. "I keep my lights dimmed in my apartment; it helps. I don't have blinds like you do." She smiled.

"Oh. . . Well yes, very—very observant of you. I have got old eyes, y'know." He said nervously, looking around the room awkwardly.

Della nodded to herself, digging into her purse for one of the business cards she used to hand out back in Sycamore Heights. She had designed the bright purple cards herself, and she was still delighted with the design, though they were slightly outdated. She leaned forward, sliding one of the cards onto Jimmie's coffee table as she stood.

"If you need anything, whether it be something related to the case, or anything else, you call me, okay?"

Jimmie took the card graciously, nodding several times. He stood and shook her hand, looking a little less scared of the world around him. "Thank you, Miss Coleman."

"You are very welcome, Mr. Heiser," Della said sincerely.

He hobbled her over to the door, once again thanking her for coming and for the business card.

As she walked through the cul de sac, she had the feeling she was being watched. Looking over her shoulder, she saw someone looking at her through their window from across the street. Before Della could take in the figure's features, it disappeared out of sight, pulling the curtains shut. Picking up the pace, she reached for her phone. She'd copied a certain phone number off a certain flower shop's door.

"Hey, Clara?" Della asked. "This is Delphee Coleman, I was wondering if you needed any housework done?"

~ ~ ~

Della and Clara sat outside on the back deck, sipping out of mason jars, sweet tea stinging the back of their throats. The chairs were awfully uncomfortable, but Della wasn't going to complain. This was the first time in a long time she had gotten to sit and just breathe. Plus, she was in no mood to ruin Clara's little smile as she sat watching Arthur play with Everett in an old kiddie pool. She had made a point to put on her makeup and put her hair in a neat ponytail. She looked pretty today. She looked happy.

"So, how are things?" Clara asked.

Della squeezed a lemon into her drink, then rested the cup on her forehead. There was no winning. She was either way too hot or way too cold, no in-between. "Been better, how are you guys?"

"I'm sorry to hear that. We've been good." Clara said unapologetically. Della smiled. "So, what do you need?"

"What do you know about the Heiser's?" Della asked.

"Oh, uh, Jimmie and Eloise are nice people. Eloise used to come over a lot. I think she was a counselor at the old elementary school, but my parents never let me speak with her." Clara said, taking a sip of her tea.

"Ever notice anything off about them?" Della asked groggily, letting her eyes close a little.

"Not that I can think of, they sure did love birds though. Especially Jimmie." She shivered, laughing a little.

"What about Eric Steiniger?"

"He's the Police Chief here in town. I don't know him personally, but I've heard he's a good man. Why do you ask?"

"Loose ends." Della sighed, removing the freezing glass from her forehead and rubbing her temples.

"Can't you ask your hunky little cop friend Porter?" Clara asked, smiling at her.

Della glared at her. "Not exactly in a position to ask for his help." She explained.

"Too bad," Clara said. "I saw the way he looked at you, you know. I don't think he is just helping you because you guys are working the same case."

Della nodded, raising her glass sarcastically. They sat there for a moment, listening to the sounds of croaking frogs and buzzing mosquitoes. This was the kind of life Della craved. Sitting here, in good company, not having to care too much about anyone or anything.

"You okay?" Clara asked. "Need an Advil?"

Della laughed darkly. "Thanks, but no thanks. I'm fine, I just need some rest."

Clara nodded her agreement. "Stay as long as you like. We have a spare mattress." Della couldn't tell if she was serious or not.

She took one last swig of her tea, then set it aside on the rusty side table. "Thank you, but you have things to do, and I have work to get done. I'll see you around."

~CHAPTER TWENTY-TWO~

Mind Over Matter

Della spent the rest of the day locked in her office, mulling over old police reports and calling the family members of both the missing kids and the people Theodore had 'killed.' None of them were much help, although one girl said she had never seen Theodore Heiser in her life. She did know of Eric Steiniger, though. Not much was known about the mysterious Chief, and he sure as Hell didn't seem to have time to answer any of Della's calls.

She sighed, feeling a wave of exhaustion pour over her. She was so tired. So *very* tired. Slowly, she sat back in her chair, letting her eyes close for just a minute, hoping to rest her weary eyes for a while. Before she knew it, she was fast asleep, a thin line of sweat beading on her forehead. Her body twitched, her chest rising and falling weakly.

In Della's dreams, she dreamt she was being chased by something she could not quite see. She was running through a forest full of decaying, black trees, the ground beneath her covered in thick moss, ivy, and thorny vines that tried to reach out and grab her. She stumbled to the ground as she ran, a vine ensnaring her by her ankle.

Lying next to her was Theodore Heiser, his eyes white, staring at her with a pained, lifeless expression.

The thing that had been chasing her now had her

pinned down, thick, stinking drool dripping onto her face.

The Grunch. However, it was not the only Grunch; there were several of them, all hissing at her, their high-pitched clicking noises sounding eerily like words.

"Oh, how I wish I could kill you." They whispered. "But you've been marked for a different fate."

It leaped from her, plunging its claws into Theodore's body.

A bright white light flashed in her eyes, and suddenly she was sitting in the passenger seat of Porter's hearse. Her favorite song was playing on the radio, a warm breeze flowing through the cracked windows, as they drove through the woods. Della looked to her left. Porter sat gripping the steering wheel, his face was pale, his eyes the same lifeless white Theodore's had been.

Slowly, his head turned to Della.

The scene flashed. The radio buzzed with static, the cabin of the hearse now covered in cobwebs, the breeze cold, the forest full of decaying oaks.

"Help. . . us. . ." Porter whispered. His voice was distant and dry, like a zombie.

Della scooted away from him, catching a glimpse of more ghastly faces in the rearview mirror. The backseat of the hearse stretched on for miles, seat upon seat full of children whose faces matched Porter's.

"Help. . . us. . . please. . ." They whispered in that same voice.

Suddenly, the hearse crashed.

~ ~ ~

Della screamed, jumping out of her chair, her head aching. She fell to the floor, holding her head in her hands. That dream had seemed so real. She could still smell the Grunches breath. Her breathing was erratic as she sat there on the floor, her hands clamped around her ears. All she could hear was a dull ringing. All her senses were screaming at her, making the room swirl like the contents of a blender. She shivered, soaked in a cold sweat.

Someone placed a hand on her shoulder. She turned, startled, grabbing the person's hand. Her vision swam. Four different Max's were fading in and out of her sight. She let go of his hand as he knelt next to her, his face full of worry.

". . . Ya all right. . . ?" His voice rang in her ears.

She nodded, a wave of pain erupting in her head. She groaned, grabbing the back of her office chair and Max's hand as she pushed herself off the floor, the dizzying feeling she felt only worsening.

He placed his palm onto her forehead, frowning. "Yer burnin' up."

She ignored his statement, wiping the sweat off her lip. "How did you get in?" She asked, her voice shaking.

"Mavericks has a master key tuh all the rooms. Ei was worried about ya." He said, letting her steady herself against him.

She looked around, partially unaware of her surroundings. She yawned. As she rubbed her eyes, wiping the sweat from her forehead, she wondered if she *had* been asleep for a week.

"Ya all right?" Max repeated, sitting her back down in her chair.

"Mmhmm." She grumbled.

Max rolled his eyes, forcefully placing a hand on her forehead again. He shook his head, muttering to himself incomprehensibly. He sat down on her desk, eyeing her suspiciously. "Ya look like death, Della."

"Thanks." Della said, rubbing her temples.

Max was quiet for a minute, sitting there watching her. "Wanna talk 'bout it?"

She ignored him, noticing the pit in her stomach. Her body was tense, her veins feeling like sandpaper. Her brain was buzzing, flashes of her vision appearing behind her eyes.

"We have to go." She said suddenly, beginning to gather her things, Hell-bent on making sure Theodore was okay. If she had been filled with any doubt that he was innocent, her dream had scared those thoughts away. He was a victim, just like the murdered parents and the missing kids.

"Della." Max said sternly, grabbing her notebook out of her shaking hands.

"What?" She asked dumbly, snapping out of her thoughts.

He stared at her, his eyes wide with concern. "Ei found ya passed out in yer office, drippin' with sweat, screamin' yer lungs off! Ei have every right mind to lock ya in yer apartment!

Chapter Twenty-Two

Ya look like *shit*."

Della reached into her desk drawer for a scrunchie patterned in holographic aliens, pulling her hair into a ponytail. "I'm fine." She said, rolling up the sleeves of her lilac cardigan.

"Della."

"Max."

"*Della!*" Max said loudly, throwing his hands into the air. For a second, his eyes looked more animal than human, causing Della to recoil.

"I'm not going to sit here and banter back and forth. I'm okay! I just had a bad dream or whatever." She hissed, eyeing him cautiously. If only it was that simple.

Max bit his lip so hard it started to bleed. Probably because his teeth were sharper than any humans should have been. Once you know something about someone, you start picking up on little things. Like how Max got easily distracted by flying bugs, or always made a point to knock over her cup of pens, or how he lounged lazily on the couch whenever he could. Just like a cat. He shook his head, running a hand through his dark curls, the tan patches on his skin glowing bright red.

"Ei have tuh make a stop somewhere." He grumbled, then swept out of her office.

~ ~ ~

The cat jumped up onto one of the mausoleums, watching the boy work. He dug a grave, wiping the sweat off his brow, grumbling along to a song in his headphones. He tapped his foot on the shovel, lip-syncing like an idiot. The cat stretched, slowly turning into a human. Max yawned, brushing some moss off his favorite teal and orange sweater.

Porter danced around. His eyes traveled over Max without really seeing him as he used his shovel as a microphone.

"Whatcha listenin' tuh?" Max sang loudly.

Porter jumped a foot into the air, dropping the shovel on his toe. He swore several times, hopping around. "*Max!*" He screeched.

Max smiled to himself, satisfied.

"What are you doing up there?" Porter asked, snatching the shovel off the ground and stabbing it into the pile of dirt he had made. Max was pretty sure Porter imagined it as plunging a dagger into Max's chest.

"Observin' things," Max sang, stretching out his arms.

Porter put his hands on his hips, squinting up at him. "Why?"

"When Ei get free tickets tuh a freak show, Ei use 'em," Max said with a sweet little smile.

Porter blushed. Max loved making the pretty boy feel like an idiot. After all, that's all he was. He wasn't smart like Della, or clever like Max, he was just a bumbling fool who happened to be blessed with a perfect skin tone and nice hair.

Max hopped off the mausoleum, flicking a spider off his shoulder. "Ei found her passed out in her office this mornin'." He said quietly, walking over to peer over the edge of the hole Porter had dug.

"Is she okay?" Porter said, trying his best to sound uninterested.

Max nodded. "Awfully pale, but Ei think she'll live."

"*Think?*" Porter asked defensively.

"Dude, Ei ain' a doctor! Not like Ei can look at her and tell ya if she is gonna die tomorrow!" Max said, throwing his hands up into the air.

Porter crossed his arms, turning to look at the hole. "Don't call me 'dude.'"

They stood there for a moment in silence, letting the gray sky bathe them in gloom. Soon the clouds began to weep, their cold tears dripping on to the back of their necks. Porter shivered, popping the collar of his zip-up sweatshirt.

"Who died?" Max finally asked.

"My sanity." Porter breathed.

Max smirked. "The funeral is a couple of years late, doncha think?"

Porter nodded, his face set in sorrow. "Another one of the missing kid's parents died. This makes five."

"Ya goin' tuh go check it out?" Max asked, a shiver running up his side.

"No, Eric has it all locked down. Won't even let me in. I looked over the reports, they're calling it an animal attack, but we know better. Tell *Della* they found more monkshood. Found at every crime scene." Porter explained, his words mumbled and dry. The way his voice ached when he said her name made Max sick.

"Ya guys need tuh kiss and make up; Ei cannot be the

mediator," He said sternly.

"See that is the whole problem, I kissed her," Porter said unenthusiastically.

"Shit," Max said, leaning over to look into Porter's eyes. "Are ya serious? Like for real?"

"No, *dude*, I am trying to make you jealous," Porter said sarcastically.

Max's mouth hung open in disbelief. "And Ei missed it?"

Porter rolled his eyes, turning to walk away. "Careful, or a mosquito might just fly into your mouth." He said dryly.

Max's footsteps followed him up to the porch of the mortuary, stopping on one of the steps. Not once had Porter ever let him come over. He always insisted that they spend their days at the Mavericks' Mansion.

"Watch over her, okay?" Porter pleaded.

"Always." Max sighed.

They locked eyes, equally worried about the only person who had ever been able to get them back together. If something happened to Della, Max was pretty sure they would tear each other's throats out. She seemed to be the only thing keeping Porter alive and Max. . . Max was fine either way, but he did care about that annoying little cryptozoologist.

"PORTER!" A voice screamed, causing Porter to recoil.

Max furrowed his eyebrows. "Was that Jed?" He asked.

Porter nodded. "He got laid off." Some sort of emotion was floating behind his peridot eyes, but Max could not make out what it was.

"Tell yer mum hi for me," Max said, moving his feet away from the step.

Porter tensed, looking like he wanted to say something but was forced to think otherwise by the fact the front door opened behind him. Jed stood there, his eyes glazed over, his face red.

"See you around, Miliano." Porter smiled, shoving Jed inside.

"Yeah, see ya," Max called as the front door closed.

That was odd.

~CHAPTER TWENTY-THREE~

Chatter From The Cellblock

"Are you all right?" Theodore asked, eyeing her with grow-ing concern.

Della had thought to return to the jail rather than try to explain what she had witnessed this morning. After all, it was apparent Theodore—and Jimmie for that matter—knew far more than what he was letting on. Why he wasn't telling her, well, that was to be determined. Much to her chagrin, Maver-icks had paid one of the less trust-worthy wardens to let her be inside his cell where they could talk freely.

He was referring to her complexion. She was completely white. "I'm fine." She said, though, he did not believe her. Hon-estly, she didn't even believe herself anymore.

He nodded. "How can I help you?" Theodore yawned, watching her from his position on his cot, staring at her as she tapped her foot nervously, standing to try and block the sight of a nearby camera.

"I was actually here to ask you that same question." She said simply, her eyes carefully tracing him. He looked fine. Better than her, she might add, but still, the pit in her stomach wouldn't go away. Her eyes danced across his cell. Numbers were scratched into the walls, posters hung from dirty old tape, and a plastic vase full of flowers sat on the back of his toilet.

He looked confused but nodded. "I would kill for some pudding."

Della rolled her eyes. "Not what I meant."

He nodded, looking away, pulling a copy of the Moss Hollow Tribune out from under the cot. He popped it open, tapping the front page. "Have you seen this?" A smiling man was printed on the newspaper, the caption 'local realtor found dead' floating above his head. He was the father of Angus Cummings.

Della nodded. "I saw. My associate and I—"

"Associate? I thought you said you were working with friends." He smiled softly, laying down on the cot as he tossed the newspaper aside, instead reaching for an old bouncy ball.

"Things change," Della said simply.

"I know that better than anyone," Theodore said, tossing the ball between his hands.

"Nice flowers," Della said. Once again, the vase was full of monkshood.

"Thanks, my Ellie got them for me." He smiled widely.

Della raised an eyebrow. She'd have to pay a visit to this mysterious Eloise Heiser.

Theodore eyed her; his eyebrows furrowed deeply over his eyes. "Find out anything?"

"Nothing related to the case."

He smiled. "How's your head?"

She scowled.

"You know, the Weeping Crow could help you out. Cast a little spell, give you a shove in the right direction."

Della nodded. "My next stop is Nicoletta's; I have to pick up a thing or two."

"Didn't you say a book was stolen from her?"

"Yup, one of the ones Jimmie gave her. Supposedly the one you guys used to use. The police can't do anything about it, no cameras."

Theodore stared at the floor. "Eric still in charge down there?" He asked absentmindedly.

She nodded. "I haven't had the pleasure of meeting him yet, but I've heard he is a good man."

"And I'm an arson." Theodore whispered.

Della gave him a questioning look, which he returned with a shake of the head.

"You don't trust him, do you?" She asked without thinking.

"He locked me up, Miss Coleman. Would you?"

She shrugged, looking away. "I spoke to your brother," Della said, telling him all about the way Jimmie had acted, and how she felt she had been watched.

"That's not like him," Theodore said, wiggling around on his cot.

"That's what I thought. When I had spoken with him before, he had seemed so cheerful and confident." Della explained, shaking her head a little.

"Maybe whoever was watching took the book? Jimmie isn't the most. . . *secretive* person in the world." Theodore proposed.

Della nodded. "Have any new information for me?"

"No." He said. It was almost like it was a struggle for him to say that. Like he hated the fact he had to let her down.

"Know anyone who would?" Della asked.

"It's good you are going back to Nicoletta, I think she is the only one who would be of any use to you," Theodore said, holding the bouncy ball up to the light. One of those transparent ones with glitter in them. "Plus," He began, throwing the bouncy ball so it ricocheted off the wall and back into his hands. "They might be able to help you with some of your other problems too." He finished with a wink.

"I don't need help," Della said, rolling her eyes.

Theodore smiled. "We never do." There was a glimmer in his eyes that made him look younger than he was.

Della crossed her arms. "You'd think with all the things I've seen in this town; I would trust you people a little more." She scoffed.

"I'm glad you don't, it will help you stay alive." He admitted.

Della rolled her eyes again, smiling a little. "You going to tell me I'm special?"

"Would you believe me?" Theodore joked.

"Why would I?" Della asked in disgust, but deep down, she knew she was.

Theodore looked her up and down. "Because even the smartest scientist still does not know everything. He chooses to believe what he wants. The most intelligent Preacher, one who knows the Bible cover to cover, still will believe exactly what he wants." He said.

Della's eyes widened, she stepped forward, pointing an

accusing finger at him. "That's my paper—how did you—where did you—"

He shook his head. "I can *read*, Miss Coleman."

She shivered, thinking back on what Jimmie had said. Theodore could read minds. She scowled at him, turning away and pacing back and forth. She opened and closed her mouth a couple of times before stopping and staring at him in disbelief.

"I'm not going to answer your questions, so I wouldn't ask them." He scowled.

Della clenched her fists, inhaling sharply. "Fine."

Theodore chuckled, squeezing the bridge of his nose.

"What?" Della snapped.

"That was a test, Miss Coleman." He smiled. "One that I can't tell if you failed or passed."

Della gave him a quizzical look, tapping her foot on the ground and scowling. "What kind of test?"

"I have a feeling the rules do not apply to you, so why do you follow them?" Was his answer.

Della looked over her shoulder. "Because I don't want to end up here." She said, though not unkindly.

Theodore smiled widely. "Prison isn't for everyone."

She smiled, taking a step closer to him, her chunky velvet heels clicking on the floor. She was wasting time entertaining his odd fantasies. She hadn't come here to find out the secrets of the universe; she had come here to solve a mystery.

"Back in the eighties, prior to your arrest, you had a clean record. Not even a parking ticket. I know you didn't do this, so who did?" She began.

He shrugged. "I wish I could tell you that, Delphee."

Della sighed. "Did you have any hunches? Any leads at all?"

"Delphee." Theodore said, smiling weakly. "I gave up long ago. Hell girl, I think I've begun to believe that maybe I did kill all those people." The fact that he was blatantly lying made her want to scream.

"You are just saying that because you are scared of what someone will do to you if you don't." Della snapped.

Theodore sat up, staring at his feet. "Maybe I am."

"I know I already asked, but back then, was there a connection between the victims?" She asked, fiddling with a loose thread deep inside the pocket of her jacket. "Were they abusive to their children?"

Theodore shook his head in confusion. "No, they were all on the city council. They all were upstanding citizens. Except for one tiny detail. Everyone has their vices. These people loved money, so they took it any way they could. And no one ever knew." He explained. "One of them even tried to take Jimmie's house out from under him."

Della furrowed her eyebrows. "This doesn't make any sense." She whispered.

"It won't until you stop looking at this like you are going to be able to fix it with your wits alone. There is a lot of culture swimming down in the swamp. A lot of bad mojo. You'd be surprised what people will get themselves into when someone wrongs them."

They locked eyes for a moment. They were kindred souls. Della trusted him. Nevertheless, that didn't mean she wasn't annoyed with him for speaking in riddles.

She nodded. "I guess I better go." She said, turning away.

He winked at her. "Sounds about right. Can you ask them to bring me some paper on your way out? I need to write something down before it's too late."

She turned back. "What do you mean?" She asked, the memory of her nightmare this morning filling her with a sudden dread.

"Inevitability." He said simply. "Don't stay out too late. Don't look back. And remember, it usually isn't the wind that howls. This really isn't your fight, Delphee. You're only human. Don't—" He stopped, staring at her with a rather odd look as he rubbed his forehead. He seemed to be processing something deep inside his brain. "Thank you for trying to clear my name. Thank you for giving me a little hope." He said finally.

She stared at him, her hand resting on the bars of the cell. "Did you see what I saw this morning?" She asked, a shiver running down her spine.

He turned his head quickly as he lay back down on the cot. "No, Miss Coleman." He said simply, dismissing her with a curt nod.

A warden unlocked the cell door for her, beginning to lead her away. Lost in thought, she followed him through the prison. Theodore knew more than she had perceived. She looked at the back of the warden, wondering if she could make a run for it and break him out of this desolate, dreary place. The warden stopped abruptly, turning to look at her. He eyed her curiously, then continued walking.

Max was waiting for her in the tiny waiting area, looking agitated. He waved at her, relief flooding his face, running over to her and the warden.

"Thank you." Della said to the warden.

He nodded, smiling, beginning to walk away.

"Hey," She began, he turned. "Can you bring him some paper and a pen? He needed to write something down."

The warden nodded again, then walked away.

"So, what did he say?" Max asked as they walked out into the freezing cold. They had taken Mavericks' car again and still couldn't figure out how to put the canopy up. It had been a rather cold drive.

"Nothing much." Della lied. She didn't know why she was lying to him. "He did not really want to talk." She said blankly.

"Ei guess we are back tuh square one then, huh?" Max asked.

Della nodded, brushing past him. She really wished they were. "Let's go chat with the coven again."

~CHAPTER TWENTY-FOUR~

Blunders Of A Magical Dropout

Steiniger was staring at him oddly. Well, to be honest, Steiniger *always* stared at Porter. But today, it felt different. His expression was blank, his hand clenching the table. Porter smiled widely at him. All he got back was a couple blinks.

"Eric, are you okay?" Porter asked.

Steiniger shook himself out of whatever funk he was in, nodding. He forced a smile, removing his fingers from his desk. They were sitting in his office, overlooking the reports of the missing kids.

"I'm fine, just a lot on my mind, y'know?"

Porter nodded slowly, kicking his feet up onto the tiny desk he called his own. He had always loved Steiniger's office. Sunlight always streamed through the blinds in just the right way, the coffee machine was always on, just like the radio. He knew where everything was; the refills for the staplers were in that old filing cabinet, the handcuffs were in the bottom left drawer of his mentors' desk, and the *Cosmopolitan* magazines were hidden under the newspapers. He smiled to himself. This was more of a home to him than anywhere else.

Steiniger raised an eyebrow. "What?"

"Nothing." Porter quipped.

Steiniger rolled his eyes. "Been drinking again?" He asked.

Porter paled. "No." He lied. Jed had bought a case of beer, who was he to refuse?

"Right, and I don't roll cigars on my lunch break."

"You know, that is extremely unhealthy. At least I actually eat breakfast, lunch, and dinner." Porter scolded.

Steiniger lifted his coffee cup in solidarity. "How's the old man?"

Porter scowled, rubbing his wrists. "Everything is great. I broke a vase, and he didn't even try to hit me." He said darkly.

Steiniger stood, briskly walking over to his favorite not-so-human being. He gave him a questioning look, forcing Porter to hold out his wrists. Steiniger set his coffee cup aside, rolling up Porter's sleeves. No marks. He was clean.

"What have you been doing to pass the time?" Steiniger said, reaching over to push Porter's head back and look up his nose. Porter blew in his face. No smell.

"I made brownies."

"*Good* brownies?"

"Double chocolate," Porter said with a roll of his eyes.

Steiniger pulled his shirt away from his neck, looking impressed. "What about that girl? You go on a date?" He asked.

"I kind of screwed that all up," Porter said, taking a minute to roll up his sleeves and show that his arms weren't bruised, and his veins weren't bulging.

"Feet." Steiniger sighed, sitting down on Porter's desk. The wood creaked under his weight as Porter pulled off his muddy boots and dragon socks, tossing them aside. "You were never a lady's man." He said distractedly, checking Porter's toes. "Alright, you're clean."

Porter smiled, putting his socks back on. "Your niece didn't think so." He laughed.

"Watch your tongue," Steiniger said sternly, lightly smacking him up alongside the head.

For years now, Steiniger had been doing these little checks on him. Making sure he wasn't doing drugs or cutting himself. When things were getting bad again, Steiniger promised little things for being clean. One month of no alcohol meant a prepaid movie night. This town had lost a lot of young minds, and Porter had been extremely close to being added to that long list. Steiniger had found him one night, bawling his eyes out, set on doing something unimaginable, behind the police department. The consequence was a night in jail, far away from anything that could harm him. After Steiniger had talked him off a cliff, he showed Porter what he had to live for, and took him to Church.

"So, how do you think you are going to fix this?" Steiniger asked, tying Porter's shoes for him.

"What part? The missing kids or my love life?"

"All of the above?" Steiniger proposed.

"Jacobson and Nickels are watching the kids that are left. That's about the best I can think of without drawing pentacles and surrounding houses with salt. We talked to Theodore Heiser up at the county jail, he has been quite the help." Steiniger paled at that. "As for Della, I don't know." Porter sighed.

"Well, what did you say?" Steiniger chose to say. He seemed like he wanted to say something else but bit his tongue.

"I may have accidentally, sort of, maybe. . . *told her I shouldn't have saved her life.*" Porter said in one high pitched breath.

Steiniger's eyes widened. "Wow, when you do something, you sure as Hell don't do it half-assed."

"I try." Porter laughed, reaching into the drawer in his desk and pulling out a bag of lemon candies. He popped a few into his mouth, sighing heavily. "That girl. . . She's up, she's down, she's up again, she wants to kill me, she wants to take me out for lunch. . . I just don't get it."

"She is a *she*. We aren't meant to understand them, we are meant to try and convince them we aren't punching bags." Steiniger smiled.

Porter nodded.

"Like I said, flowers are nice. So are chocolate, or a dinner date."

"Maybe."

~ ~ ~

"Good afternoon, Della, beastie," Nicoletta said, nodding from behind the counter.

The *Weeping Crow* was just as depleted of customers as it had been the first time Della and Max had come in, but today it seemed even more empty.

"Hey, Nicoletta!" Della said, waltzing up to the front counter, ignoring Max, who was distracted by an old telescope in the corner.

"What can I help you with on this beautifully blustery day?" Nicoletta asked. All Della could do was smile sympathetically. Nicoletta sighed. "And here I thought you two were interested in my little shop. . ."

Max pointed at the telescope, unaware of what Nicoletta had said, as he walked up to the counter. "Hey, how much for *Hubble* over there?"

Nicoletta scowled at him. "More than your worth, beastie." She said, her thick accent tainted with salt. Max frowned, looking quite hurt.

Della cleared her throat. "Did you finish those necklaces?"

Nicoletta nodded, turning away from them and digging into the cabinet behind her. "Things getting worse?" She asked as she pulled out one of the black sachets, placing it on the counter. Inside were three necklaces made of fluorite and black tourmaline. The gems were strung on a brown hempen cord and were almost identical.

"Just precaution." Della lied.

Nicoletta smirked, handing over the necklaces. "Here you are, my dear." She said, glaring at Max.

"Thanks," Della said, putting on one of the necklaces and giving one of the others to Max. Instead of wearing it as a necklace, Max wrapped the necklace around his wrist like a bracelet, smiling like a little kid. It pained her to think the other was for Porter.

"I have another gift for you," Nicoletta said, leaning down and looking inside the glass display case Della and Max were leaning on. She pulled one of the spell books—one whose cover was made of scuffed up green leather—out of the cabinet and handed it to Max. "Just because my shop is empty, it does not mean I have all the time in the world. If you need magical help, you'll have to figure it out on your own." She looked directly into Max's eyes. He cowered under her gaze, looking to Della for help.

All Della did was shrug and reach into her pocket for her wallet. "How much do we owe you?"

Nicoletta shook her head. "You can repay me by stopping whoever is taking kids and killing people."

Max rolled his eyes, taking the book roughly as he walked towards the door. "Come on, Della."

"Yeah, hang on," Della said, turning back to Nicoletta. She heard the door close behind them, nervously smiling.

"Everything all right, Delphee?" Nicoletta asked. The look on her face told Della she already knew the answer.

"Far from it, actually," Della admitted.

"How can I help?" Nicoletta asked, leaning forward on her arms, smiling widely.

"I keep having these weird dreams, and I think I moved something with my mind." She explained, relating every weird little thing she had experienced in her time here.

Nicoletta laughed, turning away from Della and searching through the cabinet behind her. "How are you feeling? Break anything yet?"

Della laughed darkly. "We talking physical or something like trust?"

"Both," Nicoletta said after a while of being lost in thought.

Della swallowed hard, sighing heavily, talking about everything that had gone on recently. Everything from her suspicions about Porter to the fact that she felt like she was losing her mind. When she was done spilling her guts, all Nicoletta could do was smile.

"You should get used to feeling like an outcast; it's only going to get worse from here," Nicoletta said. The truth was harsh, but Della was glad she didn't try to sugar coat anything. "And you are far from going crazy. You may be the sanest out of all of us."

Della smiled weakly, watching Nicoletta. "What exactly am I?" She asked as Nicoletta poured a mixture of herbs into a sizable maroon sachet, writing down each of the names as she did.

"Child, if I told you all the secrets the universe had, you would be very bored with the rest of your existence." The old witch said.

Della playfully rolled her eyes. "Am I a witch?"

Nicoletta nodded. "Human, witch, daughter, friend." She said, looking up at her over the note she was writing with a small smile. "You are many things. Maybe most importantly, is the thing I should keep from you."

Della watched her with growing curiosity. "But you're

going to tell me, anyway, aren't you?"

Nicoletta nodded, waving her hand over the sachet of herbs. Her fingers sparked with electricity that illuminated her old eyes with joy.

"You, my dear, are telekinetic." She said, handing over the sachet and note. "On top of that, you are something that I do not have a name for. The closest thing I know would be a Seer, but I do not believe your powers stop with mere visions. Try not to worry too much about it now, everything will be revealed in due time."

Della sighed heavily. "Well, that's just peachy."

Nicoletta smirked. "You might actually believe that in the future." She said, watching Della with keen perplexity. "I am putting my faith in you." She said after a minute, her voice brittle. "I am believing in you when others will not. I can't vouch for you for the rest of your life; I'm not going to be around forever. This town—this *world*—is never going to be the same when you find the person who summoned the Grunches."

"This whole thing is going to be the least of my worries, isn't it?" Della asked.

This town kept throwing curveballs at her. Right when she thought she had met the quota for all the weird and wonderful, she found out that something akin to pigs flying truly did exist.

"This will look like nothing but a poorly written line in your story compared to the horror novel the world is writing for you." Nicoletta agreed. "And your friends," She added sadly.

"Thank you," Della said, offering her hand for Nicoletta to shake.

Nicoletta ignored it, leaning as close as she could to her. "There will be two paths before you. Both have consequences, my dear. Choose wisely." She whispered.

Della swallowed hard, letting her hand drop on top of the counter. "Well, I should get back to the beastie," She said shakily, looking over her shoulder and out the window of the shop. "Thanks for the tea."

"You are very welcome, dear. A glass of that tea a day will do you good; it will help clear your head, make it easier for you to tap into your powers." Nicoletta smiled. "Enjoy tonight. Live it like it is going to be your last because, in this town, it just might be."

~ ~ ~

"Not that I'm jealous or anything," Della began as she and Max flipped through the encyclopedia of spells Nicoletta had given them. "But why exactly did she give you of all people that thing?"

If Della was being honest, she was *very* jealous of the fact that Max was the one with the spell book and not her. Especially since he and Nicoletta had such a strained relationship. Of course, it wouldn't do anyone any good to pout, so she was trying to be supportive.

Like always.

Max sighed heavily. "Swear on yer feeble little life ya won' tell anyone." He said with some difficulty.

She took a sip of her tea, the smell of oolong, and pure cocoa powder warming her nose as she sat next to Max on the couch in her office.

"Cross my heart," Della said, scooting closer to him to better read the instructions on a spell.

Max handed her the book. "Dad always said that tuh get anywhere in this town, that Ei would need a special set of skills. He used tuh pay Nicoletta tuh tutor me in the arcane arts. She knows all about my powers and how Ei can turn intuh a cat." Max crossed his arms over his chest. "Im special. Not all familiars can cast spells. That's why she calls me beastie. But. . . uh. . . Ei used tuh use my gifts tuh. . . *acquire* things around town."

"I don't doubt it one bit," Della said, flipping through the spell book, looking for something that might help them. If only they had something left behind by the perp, they'd be able to use a locator spell.

Max rolled his eyes.

Della looked at him. "Wait, is that what Mavericks meant by 'use your resources?'" She asked.

He would not meet her eyes. "Ei—Partially. But Ei didn' do anything. Honestly, I don' know what he meant by that. . ."

"Damn, you must be quite the thief," Della smiled, oddly impressed.

"Ei'm not a thief! Ei just know. . . how tuh obtain. . . objects that don' belong tuh me." He said defensively.

"Right. . ." Della smiled.

Max was quiet for a minute. He cleared his throat, looking around the room nervously. "Ei spoke with Porter and—"
Della rolled her eyes. "—he said there's another body. More monkshood."

Della sighed heavily. "Sometimes when people summon demons, they need a binding agent, something to draw the demon towards a target and not just a random person. Maybe that's what the monkshood is?"

"But Clara doesn' seem like the kind of person that would summon a demon. She said it herself, she wouldn' have sent those flowers if she knew what was gonna happen." Max said defensively.

"Maybe she isn't the one who grows the flowers." Della proposed.

Max shrugged, rubbing his eyes. "Y'know, Ei should be tryin' tuh make Halloween plans right now. Comin' up with a costume, tryin' tuh convince Lenora and Richie tuh not scare the children. . ."

Della laughed. "If it's spooky you want, than spooky you shall get. Think you can do this spell?" She asked, handing him over the book. She had it opened to a page full of practical spells, her finger pointing to one that was meant to heat food or water.

"It has been years, but Ei can try," Max said. "Grab me my coffee out of the fridge, will ya?" He asked.

Della raced out of her office and into the community kitchen, returning moments later with a cold cup of decaf. She set it on the table in front of Max, expectantly waiting for him to make it start bubbling. Max sighed, placing the book in Della's hands. He hovered his palm over the cup, closing his eyes.

"*Varmet.*" He whispered.

The coffee began to steam, the smell of fresh brew stinging Della's nose. She smiled widely, glancing at Max, who was lost in concentration. He furrowed his eyebrows, his hand beginning to shake. The cup began to shake slightly, the coffee beginning to boil.

"All right, show off; you can stop." Della laughed.

Max didn't seem to hear her. His face was scrunched up in pain, a tiny trickle of blood escaping his nose.

"Max," Della said sternly.

The outside of the white paper coffee cup began to brown, small embers glowing around the lip of the cup.

"Max, stop." Della hissed.

Max opened his eyes, looking utterly exhausted. The coffee stopped boiling, the embers flickering out. Max wiped the blood from his upper lip, looking like he was going to pass out.

"You okay?" Della asked, shoving a tissue into his hand.

He nodded weakly. He opened his mouth to say something when the coffee cup burst into flames, showering them in tiny sparks and drops of searing hot coffee. The coffee table soon caught on fire, but neither of them made to move until the flames reached a stack of magazines near Della.

"Holy shit, Max," Della said, rushing out into the hallway to grab the fire extinguisher. She sprayed the coffee table, shaking her head in amazement.

Max held his head in his hands, glancing at her. He squinted at something on her shirt, his eyes widening. "Yer shirt." He said weakly, sitting up.

"What?" Della asked, pausing her stream of CO-2 aimed at the coffee table.

"Yer shirt is on fire," Max said calmly, pointing at her chest with a shaking finger.

Della looked down to see that a spark had hit her shirt, setting it ablaze. Panicking, she dropped the fire extinguisher, madly patting at her shirt to try to stop the flames from reaching her hair. Max just sat there staring, a cheeky smile on his face.

"MAX!" Della screeched, pointing to the coffee table as the flames on her shirt began burning her hands, part of her shirt—her favorite shirt, one with *Casper The Friendly Ghost* on it—burning out of existence.

"Oh, uh, right," Max said, reaching for his spell book. He riffled through the pages for a moment before landing on a page. He held out his hand, pointing it at Della, focusing all his energy on her. His fingertips glowed blue as he spoke. "*Nemmortis.*"

For a moment, nothing happened. Della was about ready to start screaming at him when a jet of ice-cold water erupted from his palm, striking her so hard, it knocked her to the floor. Max shot up out of his seat, leaning over the now extinguished coffee table to look at her.

"Uh, ya, good?" He asked, looking a bit better than he had a few minutes ago.

She glared at him. "You are just lucky I am not on fire

anymore." She hissed as he helped her off the floor.

She was soaking wet, and she had lost two of her copies of her favorite magazines, but at least they had a new edge against the Grunches; one Maximilian McGregor-Mavericks.

~CHAPTER TWENTY-FIVE~

Dark Side of Venus

Porter sat at the kitchen table, going over a stack of reports on the newest body he was meant to embalm. Della would be excited to hear about this one; an animal had attacked the poor girl. Or at least that is what the papers would say. A wave of sadness washed over him. He kept forgetting that she was not speaking to him, no matter how many times he called her. He sighed heavily, returning his attention to the papers in front of him.

Maybe the lavender-scented embalming liquids would be better than the orange ones this evening. . . He wondered.

Just as he was about to go downstairs and start his work, a pair of heavy boots came up the stairs. The ugly face that followed those boots eyed him with the strongest disdain anyone in this world could ever muster.

"What are you doing? You have work to do." Jed said, his gruff voice echoing throughout the kitchen, bouncing off every surface and ringing into Porter's ears. Why his mother had chosen Jed over all the other suitable men in this town was beyond Porter. He was ugly, there was far too much skin on his bones, and his hairline was nonexistent.

"Sorry, sir, I was looking over the coroner's report. I was just about to go downstairs and start." Porter said, standing and bowing.

Jed walked up to him, their noses touching. Jed reached past him, grabbing something off the counter. He shoved a bowl of chips into Porter's hands, which he nearly dropped, half of the contents falling onto the floor.

"You lazy piece of—" Jed began.

"I am sorry, sir, I swear I was going down there right as you—" Porter interrupted, swallowing hard. He should not have done that.

"DON'T INTERRUPT ME!" Jed screamed, hammering his fist down on the table. "Don't lie to me!" Jed said, grabbing him by the collar of his shirt.

Porter looked away, cowering even though he was two full heads taller than Jedidiah.

"Where is your mother, does she know you have been slacking off?" Jed muttered, shaking him a little.

"No, sir, she does not," Porter whispered.

"What did you say?" Jed asked gruffly.

"I said she does not know, sir," Porter said.

"Are you sassing me, boy?" Jed threatened, pushing Porter away from him so hard he toppled back into his chair.

"N—No sir." Porter stammered.

Jed shook his head, sitting roughly down next to him. "Get me a beer out of the fridge." He ordered.

Porter practically ran to the fridge, daring a look over his shoulder. Jed had the coroner's report in his hand, his scowl deepening. Porter searched inside the fridge for as long as he dared for a beer, ale, or draught of any kind, but it seemed they were out.

"We're out." He said. Jed eyed him, rubbing his temples.

"What do you mean, 'we're out?' I have been gone all week trying to find a job! No one here drinks my beer, not your mother, not your damn grandfather." Jed said, raising his voice with every word.

"I—I can g—go get some. *The Burning Tankard* will be open, I'm sure of it, I can go—"

Jed stood out of his chair so fast it toppled over. "You think that you can take what isn't yours and get away with it?" He asked, slowly walking over to Porter, pinning him in the corner. "Your mother gives you too much free reign, you sorry excuse for a son." He snapped, brandishing his fist.

Porter closed his eyes as Jed's fist made contact with his face. There was no use trying to duck out of the way or reason with him, that only made things worse. Porter had learned that long ago. So instead, he stood there and took the pain. Jed wound up to hit him again when a new pair of footsteps echoed up the stairs.

Crystal Garroway stood at the top of the stairs, watching her son and the love of her life, an odd look on her face. She pushed a lock of her curly black hair out of her face, smiling.

"If you ask me," Jed began, his demeanor softening now that Crystal was in the room. "The Chief should quit putting you on drug duty. Damn tweakers." He said, smiling at Porter and patting his shoulder. Porter involuntarily winced, earning himself a scowl.

"Porter, I didn't know you were home." His mother smiled as she opened the fridge and pulled out a Ziploc bag full of marinating chicken. "Did you get into another fight?" Crystal asked as she grabbed a pan and turned on the oven.

Porter nodded but said nothing. He had tried speaking up in the past, it never worked. Jed was a great liar, and Porter was 'a scared little kid.' Crystal took Jed's word over his every time. There was no use getting Steiniger involved, he almost lost his job the last time he tried to smooth things over with Porter's parents.

"Poor boy got into it with the druggies again," Jed explained for him, kicking his foot a little, glaring at him.

"Yeah," Porter said, rubbing his nose. "The guy was so intoxicated; I don't think he even knew what he was doing."

Crystal shook her head. "Things keep getting worse around here, don't they? Did you hear about all the disappearances that have happened recently?"

Jed nodded, walking over to the kitchen table and sitting down. Porter followed, lingering near his mother.

"Do you need help with anything, mom?" Porter asked, not wanting to be stuck next to Jedidiah for longer than he had to.

"No, honey, why don't you sit down?" Crystal said, gesturing at the table.

Jed was smiling at him toothily, like a hunter waiting for a deer to come walking into his trap. He patted a seat next to him, nodding.

Porter inhaled sharply, shaking his head. "I am going out, Jed said he needed something from town," Porter said quietly.

Chapter Twenty-Five

"All right, don't stay out too long." Crystal said.

"Be back soon," Jed called to him as Porter descended the stairs.

As soon as he knew he was out of sight, Porter let two hot tears fall from his eyes, wiping them away angrily. Pops eyed him wearily, but Porter shook his head when he made to ask what was wrong.

He was so sick and tired of the way Jed treated him.

Sure, he was going to buy some beers, but they sure as Hell were not going to be for Jedidiah Oye.

~ ~ ~

Max and Della spent the rest of the day looking through archived records at the old library near the middle of town, trying to dig up all they could about spells, summoning things, similar strings of events, and whatever else she and Max deemed useful. Della suddenly realized she had been missing out on many glorious things such as paper cuts, dust, and cranky librarians in the time she had spent doing her research on her computer.

What a shame.

How *dreadfully* disappointing.

There were countless other things Della and Max needed to figure out, but it would take them hours to do so. Della was exhausted. Her bones were aching, her head was pounding, and her eyes felt like they were going to pop forth from her head. All she wanted to do was fall asleep on the couch in the confines of her home. The only thing that was helping her get through today was the tea Nicoletta had given her. It calmed her mind and soul, filling her with a sense of restful relaxation.

Max, though he seemed to be feeling a little bit better, agreed with her when she said they would have to regroup tomorrow. He had barely been able to keep his eyes open the past hour, snoring loudly occasionally.

As she climbed the stairs to her apartment, ignoring catcalls from Richie, she saw a shadow in the hallway. She slowly ascended the last three steps, peering around the corner. After everything that had happened today, she had been on high alert. The lights were flickering in the hallway, shrouding a figure in shadow. Out of pure paranoia, Della reached into her pocket, placing her keys between her fingers like a cheap pair of brass knuckles. Her footsteps were quiet as she snuck up on—

"What are you doing here?" She snapped as she took in the tall, broad-shouldered being before her.

Not that she wanted to talk to him, but she was a tad bit happy to see that he was alive and breathing. She could not help but worry about him. What if he was the next of the Grunches victims?

The lights stopped flickering as Porter turned to face her. "I was worried about you." He said. He didn't smile. His tone was sharp, his eyes cold, making him look like a psychopath. There was even a yellowing bruise stretching over his nose, and on top of it all, he stunk of alcohol.

"You don't get to worry about me." She hissed, still clutching her keys in her hand.

His eyes slowly softened as he took in the sight of her. It had been raining, so she was once again soaked, her hair sticking to the melting foundation on her face. He stepped back a little as he examined the keys in her hand.

"You're absolutely, undeniably, without a shadow of a doubt, crazy." He whispered, recoiling just a bit. It was *his* turn to be afraid, and she was enjoying it. Whether that fear came from the assumed immense amount of alcohol he had consumed, well, she decided she would take whatever she could get.

"I prefer the term creative." She said, smiling darkly. He looked very alarmed by that statement, staying out of her way as she unlocked her door. "What do you want?" She asked, eyeing him over her shoulder.

"As I said, I was worried." He said, smirking, though there was a heaviness to his words. His eyelids were very heavy, and it seemed like it was all he could do to stay upright.

"How long have you been standing here?" She asked, pushing her door open and leaning on the doorframe. Her apartment smelled like sweet lemon candies.

"Longer than you would like." Porter sighed, inhaling the smell. He shut his eyes softly, rubbing his nose. ·

Della rolled her eyes. "What happened to your face?" She asked. It was in her nature to care, even when she was angry with someone.

"Oh," Porter said, sounding confused. His fingers traveled away from his nose and to his eye, causing him to wince slightly. "My mom's boyfriend has a temper." He said, a dumb, drunken smile stretching across his face.

Della's eyes widened. Just as she had suspected. Her back still to him, she bit her lower lip in concern. "What happened?" She asked.

"Nothing you can fix," Porter said. "Do you mind if I crash here? I don't want to go back home." He paused, his head lolling to the side. "I shouldn't be driving either. I honestly don't know how I got here in one piece. . . I be drunker than a ship captain, me hearty." He snorted a couple of laughs.

She turned around slowly so she could stare blankly at him. His eye was drooping closed; his nose looked crooked, and an inflamed vein was popping forth from his forehead; he looked like a street rat the cops had had a run-in with on Bourbon Street. Trying to act like she did not care, she turned away and walked inside her little apartment, testing whether he would follow.

He didn't.

He instead stood, both hands on the doorway, leaning his head in to watch her take off her shoes and jacket and toss them to the floor.

"Listen, I know you are upset with me, but I don't have anywhere else to go right now." He said, a pleading tone to his voice.

"If I was only upset, I would still be talking to you, Porter. You said you shouldn't have saved me, you've played with my emotions, and you just so happen to be a—a—a *something*. Don't try to lie to me. I have seen it all. I saw your eyes the other day. I don't know if I should be scared of you, insanely attracted to you, or if I should shove you off a friggin bridge!" Della said, cackling menacingly, listing everything on her fingers.

"All good options, but can I choose? Please?" Porter asked, his glossy eyes daring her to respond.

"Ugh." She said, rolling her eyes.

"Can I come in?" He asked softly.

She nodded reluctantly, sweeping her hand around her home. "Make yourself at home." She said sarcastically.

He hesitated, then skipped through the doorway, shutting the door behind him. "Thank you."

"Anytime." She groaned. "I guess." She added, turning away to hide the smile that was creeping across her face, filling her cold, damp body with warmth.

When she turned back around to give him a set of irrational rules about sleeping on the couch, she was dumbfounded by the sight that greeted her. He was picking up her discarded shoes and straightening them along the wall with her other eccentric pairs and placing her jacket on an empty coat hanger. She stared at him, mouth hanging open. Her coat fell about five times, each time he tried to get it to stay put. When he finally got it to listen to him, he turned back to look at her.

"What?" He asked, looking confused.

"Do you do that just to be charming and cute, or are you trying to be annoying?" She asked.

He shrugged. "I don't know. I guess I feel I have to prove myself." He said quietly, staring at the jacket.

The light pink corduroy one she had worn when she went to investigate the markings at the cemetery. Why she remembered that little detail, she did not know.

"You don't have to prove yourself to me," Della said sternly.

That was the truth. She knew who Porter was. There was nothing he could say or do that would change her opinion of him. He did not have to try so hard around her.

He arched back, laughing. "Of course, I do. Did you forget why you are mad at me? I shouldn't have said those things. I never meant them." He said, his eyebrows furrowed over his bright green eyes. He sighed. "I will always try to prove myself to you." He whispered.

"That's just stupid," Della said, turning away and walking into the living room, taking off her socks and throwing them at him as she went.

She glanced back. He was stuffing them in her shoes so that way they wouldn't be on the floor. She smiled, plopping down on her couch and staring at him. He made to move towards her when the jacket fell again.

"Leave it." She said as he bent down to pick it up.

He struggled for a moment, then stood back up, awkwardly rocking back and forth on his heels.

"So, how was your day?" He asked.

She shrugged. "My day seems insignificant to yours." She said, pointing at his face.

"But my day was the same old same old. Was yours?" He asked. The light in his eyes broke her heart. He was trying so hard to cling to something happy, something that could distract himself from his life.

She shook her head. "Well, I had a *bizarre* dream, not only are we looking for whoever summoned the Grunches, but now I'm trying to help Max with his spell work, and trying to figure out Theodore's cryptic warnings." Della yawned. "I think that's pretty normal."

"Cool." He said, staring out her shutters with a stupid little grin on his face. "What was your dream?" He asked as he came over to sit next to her.

She hesitated. "I was running through a forest, and something was chasing me. It was the Grunch, but it spoke to me. And Theodore was there. And he was dead." Della shivered.

"Wow. I had that exact same dream." Porter said, his eyes wide.

Della straightened. "Really?"

"Of course not." He laughed.

She slapped him hard on the arm. He made a show of wincing, raising the eyebrow that wasn't swollen, smiling widely. "You are *such* a *jerk* sometimes." She laughed, letting herself lower the drawbridge of her mental castle as she stepped over him to get to the kitchen. "So, your mom's boyfriend is obviously an ass." She said over her shoulder.

He grunted his approval, slinking down into the cushions on the couch, closing his eyes and leaning his head back.

"He doesn't like me much." He said groggily, rubbing his eyes, wincing. "He never wanted kids, just wanted my mom."

Della let the water in the sink run until it was warm, rummaging through her spice and herb cupboards. She suddenly realized how sad it was that she had two cabinets filled to the brim with herbs, spices, essential oils, and vitamins and only had a fridge half-full of food.

She grabbed bottles of dried calendula, arnica, witch hazel, and a mortar and pestle, emptied half of the bottles into the mortar, added a splash of orange juice from the fridge, and some hot water from the sink, inhaling the odd smell. She stood at the kitchen counter, Porter watching her out of the corner of his eye, as she ground all the ingredients together. When it finally combined into a thick paste, she placed the pestle in the sink and sat back down next to him, scooping some of the paste onto her thin finger.

Porter moved away from her slightly. "What's that?" He asked, wrinkling his nose in disgust. There was no hiding how bad this little remedy smelled.

She sighed, leaning forward as he tried to scooch away until he was pinned between her and the cushions. She gently smeared the paste over his swollen black eye.

"I read it in a book. It'll help your eye." She said, squinting in concentration, trying not to press too hard on his cheek. She realized now just how witchy she was. When this was all said and done, she would have to take Nicoletta up on her offer and join the coven for a spell.

"It smells like crap." He laughed.

She rolled her eyes. "Hold still." She said through gritted teeth.

He took a deep breath in, then sat as stiff as a board, not even breathing. She quickly finished smearing the paste all over his face, then sat back, placing the mortar on her chintzy coffee table.

"Don't touch it. Just let it soak into your skin and then you can wash it off with a hot washcloth." She explained, eyeing him as she began to scroll through the channels on her old television.

"Okay m—"

"If you call me mom, you can go and sleep out on the road," Della said lazily.

"I was going to say, 'Miss Della Coleman.'" Porter laughed, making himself quite comfortable on the couch, using the coffee table as a footrest.

They sat quietly, watching the local news for some time.

"Hey, is my eye supposed to tingle?" Porter asked during a commercial for Bayou Gil's. Why did she get the feeling she was never truly going to escape that horrible shack?

"No, why? Is it tingling?" She asked, looking at his cheek with great concern.

"Not yet."

"*Yet?*"

"*You're* paranoid, I would have thought you would understand my concern." Porter smiled widely.

Della glared at the TV, squeezing herself into a tight little ball on the couch, trying her best to be as far away from him as possible.

"I'm not paranoid." She said after a while of staring at the news in silence.

Porter scoffed. "You have a machete taped under your bed."

"Touché," Della said.

Porter smiled widely. "Can I help with anything? Like interrogating people, or laundry, or something?"

She shrugged. "It's seven-thirty, if you feel up to anything, you can cook me dinner." Her cheeks flushed as soon as those words left her mouth. She hadn't meant for that to sound the way it did.

He smiled, waltzing into the kitchen with a satisfied little grin. He opened her cupboards, staring in disbelief at the amount of food she had. Or lack there of.

Della thought for a moment, swallowing hard. "And as you cook, you can tell me what you are."

Porter froze. "You don't need to know that." He hissed. His eyes glazed over, and not because he was drunk. He shook his head, shutting his eyes for a moment, then smiled. "What do you want for dinner?"

"There's a pizza in the freezer." She said calmly, watching as he turned his back.

She remembered watching his back muscles ripple under his shirt. She smiled slyly. "Are you a demon?" She asked.

Porter turned around slowly, ripping open the pizza box a little too hard. "Potentially." He said through tight lips, the pizza box now in half.

Della crawled across the couch, laying on her stomach and kicking her feet in the air as she stared at him. "Do you have wings?"

Though he turned, she saw him smile as he stared up at the ceiling. "Maybe I do."

"You know I can see right through you, right?" She asked.

He nodded. "Any other questions?"

"Did saving me have something to do with your powers?" She questioned. He stopped, halfway through putting the pizza in the oven. Della gasped. "It does, doesn't it?" She asked excitedly, vaulting off the couch, and leaning over the breakfast bar.

He stood up, scowling at her, slamming the oven shut. "Stop." He demanded.

"I was supposed to die, but you stopped it." Della smiled.

"Della, stop."

"And now something is happening to make you regret it." She stepped around the counter, watching as he gripped the knob on the door that held all her cutlery. "Are you an angel? That would make sense—"

"*Della, please stop talking.*" He pleaded, his hands shaking.

"—because your shoulder blades do this weird thing when you're angry, that's why I asked if you had wings. But then again, angels don't look like you, at least that's what I think. Are you a fallen angel? Are you half? Are you a guardian angel? Are you—"

He spun around, placing his hands on his hips, his beady little eyes staring into her soul.

"I'm no angel." He whispered. "I'm not a demon either, but trust me, I'm blacker than the night sky, and you should fear me. I *choose* for you to fear me." He said.

"Shellfish are scary." Della began, yawning. "You are not. You are a cute little puppy dog who won't go back home. Soft, cuddly, thinks he is fierce when really he is—"

He took several steps closer, holding her in a firm gaze that made her cheeks begin to glow. Their noses were touching now, his eyes were bright gold, illuminated slightly by the light that reflected off her glasses. He smelled strongly, almost intoxicatingly sweet. Like orange slices and lavender.

But there was a dark undertone to that sweet smell.

"No, my powers don't have anything to do with me saving you. I've just come to realize that people who aren't meant to be in this town have a tendency of dropping dead, so I made sure you didn't." He said, his voice was soft, not angry like she thought it was going to be. "But now, I don't know, Della! Have I damned you to this town? No one leaves this place, not unless they are in a casket. If something happens to you, you know that's on me, right? My ignorance? My selfishness?"

"No, it's not," Della said stubbornly. He squeezed his eyes tightly. "What are you then? What kind of powers do you possess?" She asked, snapping into 'interrogation mode.'

Porter raised an eyebrow at her tone, looking a little less friendly. "This isn't going to go on your blog, is it?"

"You read my blog?" Della asked, the heat from her cheeks was practically fogging up her glasses.

He nodded. "I like your take on Nessie. Interdimensional portals, very interesting."

Della brushed a hair behind her ear, looking everywhere but at his eyes. She'd drown in them if she did.

He smiled, sniffing a couple times. "What do you want with your vegan, low-fat, gluten-free pizza?" He asked, flashing the box at her.

She shrugged, just watching him. "So, I'm guessing you don't have wings, then?"

Porter whipped his head around to look at her. If looks could kill, Della would be spasming on the floor.

"You just don't get it, do you?" He asked, his voice barely a whisper, his ears pulled back like a scared animal. "You are human, do you hear me, human. I'm trying to protect you from this town, to keep from you all the dark parts, because trust me, they are dark."

She wasn't exactly listening to his words; her mind was too focused on her little observations. *An animal*, Della thought. An idea had struck her mind.

"Are you a cryptid?" She asked, walking over to him. "Are you a werewolf?"

His cold eyes were full of passion. "If I was anyone else, you'd be dead right now. I don't say that to scare you, I'm saying that so that you get it into your thick skull—"

"Shut up." Della cut in, surprising herself—and him—with the anger in her voice. "I get it, okay? I put the 'cry' in cryptozoologist. I know I'm the weaker link, and I guess now I realize I'm not even meant to be here, but without me, you and Max wouldn't even know what you're up against. Hell, you wouldn't even be close! Don't baby me, Garroway. I've had to deal with my fair share of troubles. Sure, you may be riddled with darkness, but I've got twenty flashlights that are just waiting to be switched on."

A wave of anger flashed through him. He shook, his fluffy hair moving like ocean waves. He shut his eyes tightly, clenching his fists as tight as he could.

Porter shook his head. "I just don't know—" He began, inhaling sharply. "I should go, I can find somewhere else to stay for the night."

Della looked around, sticking her hands in the back pockets of her jeans, looking at him like a disappointed mother. Porter furrowed his eyebrows at her, looking scared. Her face softened.

"I'm not letting you leave. I can't help you if you won't let me in." She said, blocking his path to the door. She knew the emotions he was feeling right now. He was scared, he was alone, he felt worthless. Della had been there before, and she knew it was a very dangerous place.

Even here. Even in Moss Hollow, she was always the one to fix other people's problems. She was pretty sure she was going to fix the whole town by the time she was done. But secretly, she had hoped that maybe, just maybe, she would be the one to be fixed this time.

"But you have to be straight with me. There is so much crazy *shit* happening outside that door that I need to know who and *what* I can trust. You, me, Max," She said, waving her hand through the air. "We are in this together. He's going to find out sooner or later what you are too, I want to know that I'm going to be rightfully standing up for you." Della said sternly.

Porter leaned against the counter, looking like the weight of the entire solar system was now on his shoulders, and honestly, it just might be.

"He already knows." He said, clenching onto the counter, his knuckles white. "I don't want you," He began shakily. "To see me differently." He said tearfully, fiddling with the strings on his sweatshirt.

"I won't," Della said softly, moving towards him slowly. He shook his head, running a hand through his thick black hair. Their eyes met; hers full of compassion, his full of regret.

He nodded reluctantly, gesturing for her to ask anything she wanted.

"Your eyes," She began. He glared at her but didn't move. "They reminded me of a bat—dammit! I should've figured it out before." She said, smiling. The bat, the cat, and the rat. Had a nice ring to it.

He began looking around the room with just as much terror on his face as she felt inside. He tried to talk, but the words were caught short. He clenched and unclenched his fists several times before finally meeting her eyes.

"You're an Ahool, aren't you?" Della asked.

"In the flesh." He said with very little emotion.

"Porter—" She began, reaching out to touch him.

He recoiled. "Don't." He snarled, moving farther away. "Don't touch me. Please."

"Okay, I won't." She promised.

He nodded, wiping away his tears. "I'm not lucky like the witches, or powerful like others like me. Everyone sees me as an abomination. My dad, as far as I know, was an Ahool. His family came over here from Portugal back in the twenties. The bloodline never died; it just weakened a little. I've got the eyes, I've got the strength, and I've got back pain like no other, but I'm still just—" He patted his chest. "—just me. Just Porter."

"So, you can't turn into a giant bat?" Della asked.

He nodded, biting his lower lip. "There are others like me out in the world, we keep in touch. Some other creatures in town feel the same way I do, but there's always trouble when we meet up." He looked up at her, a tear rolling down his cheek. "I think that you are the only person who would even remotely understand. I mean, Max used too, but that's a can of worms I'd rather not touch." He shook his head quickly, putting up his hands.

Della leaned against the counter behind her, reflecting on her day.

"This town, it has more secrets than I ever could have imagined." She said. She couldn't figure out her own tone, it was somewhere between disgust and wonder, and she didn't like it.

Porter nodded in agreement, wiping the tears off his face with the back of his hand.

"I really wanted to die young." Porter said after a while. "I'm not suicidal or whatever, not anymore, trust me. I have healthy outlets. Well. . . I mean, getting drunk isn't healthy, per se, but I like cooking, and I like working on cars, and I like reading, and it helps, but I never wanted to stay on this earth for more than twenty years." He smiled darkly, glancing at Della, who was still staring ahead. "Then, one day, this girl showed me a simple act of kindness, and I thought that maybe, I could find something to stay alive for. She gave me hope." He said.

Della blinked back tears of her own, reaching down and interlocking her fingers with his.

"I hate my life." Porter whispered. "Max may hate his powers because he is scared, but I hate mine because of who it made me. I hate everything about it. I hate Jed, I hate where I work, I hate my house. . . I'm pretty sure I have developed a certain kind of hatred towards my dad and my mom for even conceiving me." He laughed darkly. "I think the only things I have ever loved in this world, are you and Max. You and Max mean the world to me, you know that right? I screwed up everything with Max a long time ago, but I want you to know how much I appreciate you trying to mend things." He said. Della gave him a questioning look. He hesitated before continuing anymore. "I did something really bad the year I dropped out of school." He said, his eyes welling up with tears again.

"Oh Porter. . ." Della said shakily. Here it was, here was the thing she was afraid of learning about him.

"I was a nerdy kid with thick glasses who wore tweed, and Max was the freak of nature who got adopted by one of the weirdest guys in town. We looked out for each other since day one, always getting in over our heads when the other got hurt, or bullied, or yelled at. Man, we were *inseparable* back then." He smiled.

"Must've been nice to have someone to watch out for you." Della said, thinking of Sebastian. She was such a terrible friend.

Porter scratched his chin. "Can you imagine a fourteen-year-old with the strength of an ox who got bullied all the time?" He asked, not really looking for an answer. "There was this one kid—really chubby, thought he had everything—that tortured Max and me. I'm not even being dramatic; he took Max down to the bayou and held him under the water while he screamed. That kid was the Devil incarnate. . ."

He looked at Della, almost to make sure it was okay to tell her all of this. She swallowed hard but nodded. "I killed that boy." He said simply, though it wasn't without emotion. "I got carried away, and I killed him. I punched that little shit until there was nothing left, and I didn't even realize it. It was deemed self defense because he surely would have drowned Max, and Eric vouched for me but. . ." He shook his head angrily, shifting his weight from one leg to the other. "If I could change anything, if I could go back in time, I would stop myself from doing that. Max never forgave me. I never forgave myself either. For me to do that—I'm a monster, Della. I always have been, and I always will be. I think that's why I'm so attracted to you."

Della furrowed her eyebrows. "What do you mean?"

He shrugged, staring ahead. "The monsters have never frightened you; you've always felt at home among them. And I speak for all of us when I say that we feel the same."

Della finally turned to look at him, not knowing what exactly to say. It had taken all of Porter's strength for him to finally get all of that off his chest, and she doubted that there was someone else that truly knew what he felt deep down inside. Not once in her life had she felt good after hearing about the deepest, darkest secret in someone's life until him. That right there, was the thing that she truly loved about him.

They stood in the kitchen for a while, listening to the rain that was blowing in through the shutters. All their walls were down. They had both been waiting for years to find someone they could be this vulnerable with. Someone that understood.

Porter sniffed, gripping Della's hand so tightly that it hurt, but she didn't dare to move. No, she didn't *want* to move.

"Do—Do you think I'm broken?" He asked, swallowing hard.

Tears overflowed from her eyes, dripping onto their hands like warm summer rain. She hesitated before pulling him into a giant hug, forcing him to slouch and rest his head on her shoulder. He was the most broken, shattered object she had ever come across. Of course, that's what she thought. She was pretty sure that was what everyone thought of him.

Perpetually cracked.

Beyond repair.

But Della was cosmic glue. She had always been the glue, the tape, the repairman. She had never met a fragile object she couldn't put back together, and Porter wasn't going to be an exception.

She shook her head, squeezing him tightly. "No, Porter. I think you are just a little bent."

~CHAPTER TWENTY-SIX~

Visions

Della and Porter had sat in the living room talking about everything under the sun while chowing down on the most disgusting pizza ever until they finally grew tired. Things were awfully blurry in her mind, but somehow, they had both fallen asleep on the couch, leaning against each other both physically and in spirit.

Della was awake now, sitting there on the couch, trying to fall back asleep. Her pounding head had woken her up just before the sun had come up. Della's head flopped to the side, resting perfectly against Porter's shoulder. He was snoring softly, his head now resting on top of hers. She sighed, crossing her arms tightly against her chest as her tired eyes shut.

The facts were straight, the case as wobbly as a flag in the wind. The missing children were all abused, their abusive parents or guardians were killed, and Jed could have been the first victim several weeks ago. Porter was her top priority, and there was so much she wanted to do and tell him, and to lecture him about staying safe, but this, right here, bathing in the early morning light, was exactly what they both needed.

Her head was filled with pain, but she was too tired to care. She was freezing cold like she was standing out in the snow that fell in thick blankets back in Sycamore Heights. Another wave of pain filled her head, right at the front where it was said the third eye should be.

They had left the television on, the bright light stinging her retinas through her thin eyelids. A dull ringing filled her ears. She winced as another wave of pain hit her in the forehead. The pain was white-hot, making her glasses feel like cold steel against her face.

Suddenly, as if she had jumped off a diving board into a warm pool, she was plunged into spinning darkness.

Whether she knew it or not, she was dreaming.

~ ~ ~

She was once again running through the forest, but this time she didn't trip and fall, she kept on running until she got to a clearing where the town of Moss Hollow should have been. It was just a clearing in her mind's eye, full of thick brambles and mud. She spun around at the sound of snapping twigs, finding that she was surrounded from all sides by eight groups of eight crows.

Another snap of twigs caused her to turn back around.

A gigantic Grunch stood before her, it's claws dripping with blood, it's misshapen face breaking into a smile. Behind the Grunch, stood Theodore Heiser. He was looking down at his shaking hands, which were also covered in blood, slumping to one knee. He looked up to meet Della's eyes, terrified. He whispered something, and Della's eyes were filled with darkness.

She could hear a voice in the distance calling out to her. The voice was soft and familiar, but she couldn't quite focus on it.

As her head split with pain again, she heard herself cry out, the expanse of blackness beginning to swirl and fold in on itself until she was in a room full of bright, burning color.

Theodore was kneeling on the floor, clutching his bleeding stomach, trying to stand.

"Theodore!" Della screamed, falling to the floor beside him, helping him up. "What happened?!" She screeched.

His face was white and sweaty. He swallowed, wrapping an arm around her shoulders for stability. Somehow, she was in his jail cell early in the morning.

"Listen to me. He *knows*." He said weakly, wincing with pain. "He knows I'm trying to help, and thats why—"

"What's happening?!" Della asked in absolute terror.

He shook his head. "Listen, Delphee, it isn't your fault—it was—" He cried out in pain.

"I don't understand," Della said, helping him sit down on his cot.

He reached up with his bloody hands and held her face. "*Jimmie.*" He breathed.

Della was crying, trying to cover the wound on his stomach with her hands. No matter what she did, it was like she couldn't fully touch him like there was an invisible barrier separating them. "Stop, stop, *stop.*" She cried.

"Delphee listen to me—no, stop, *listen!*" He screamed at her.

"Do not let me die in vain, do you understand me? You have—got—to—find—him." He began sputtering blood, coughing and choking as he leaned back onto his cot. Too weak to keep his arm up in the air, it slid down her face and to her hands. "It's—not—your—fault." He choked.

He inhaled sharply, then relaxed, his lifeless eyes staring up at her. Della stepped away, muttering nonsense under her breath. Besides the puddle of his blood on the floor, his cell was normal. No sign of a break-in. Except for the vase of monkshood. They were slowly wilting.

Della screamed for help, but none of the guards heard her. None of the inmates could discern her voice. She was just a shadow to them.

She reached out to the bar, but her hands went right through them. Screaming in anguish, she fell through, landing hard on the floor. An alarm went off somewhere, the ringing filling her ears. Her head exploded with pain, feeling as if someone was pushing a knife through her skull. She was gasping for air, clawing at her ears for it to stop.

Something was shaking her.

She felt warm hands on her shoulders, but no one was there.

~ ~ ~

Her eyes shot open as she stood, falling into Porter's arms. She breathed heavily, her vision swirling, her head pounding. She could still hear the sirens, still see Theodore in the back of her mind.

". . .Della, answer me. . ." Porter's words sounded like they were miles away, as if she were hearing them from the bottom of a pool.

She ignored him, wiping a trickle of blood away from her lips. The pressure in her forehead and nose was deafening.

"Mmm. . . *help*." She choked out, clutching onto Porter's arm as if it was the only thing keeping her from slipping back into wherever she had just come from.

He pushed her off him gently, steadying her between his hands. He was completely white, staring at her like she was dying. Which, in a way, she felt she was. His lips were moving, but she couldn't hear a thing. Her eyes were filled with red liquid, making everything a dull shade of morbid curiosity. Porter's eyes widened, catching her before she fell back. She could feel his rapid heartbeat as they fell to the floor together, feeling his chest rising and falling with panic.

The last thing she remembered was him squeezing her to him, whispering softly that everything was going to be okay.

~ ~ ~

Porter just sat there, shaking all over, looking madly around the room. Della was limp in his arms, her unsteady breaths cold. She had woken him up with a scream, lying there on the couch, her face screwed up in pain, crying out in agony. Her nose began bleeding first, then her ears and finally her eyes. Her skin was ashy and hot to the touch. Her body felt like it was going to break in his hands.

He swore several times as he pushed her chin up to look at her face. She was out cold, looking quite peaceful despite the gore on her face. Using the back of his sleeve to clean up her face, he picked her up off the floor and set her on the couch, fluffing the burlap cushion behind her head as he did.

"Come on Della. . . Wake up." He whispered.

Why he thought she would listen to him was beyond him. She never listened to him when she was perfectly fine, why would she listen when she was lying unconscious?

He reached into his back pocket and dialed Max's cell, but it went to voicemail.

"Dammit!" He swore, pacing back and forth for a moment, still shaking.

He turned back to her limp body, making the conscious

decision that Max and Mavericks weren't going to be able to help. He ran to the door, struggling to unlock and open it, then picked Della up off the couch, filled with a sudden urge to knock down anything in his path that dared try to harm her. He made his way down the stairs to the lobby, pausing as he watched Richie Ambrose biting the neck of some unsuspecting, dazed tenant. They looked at each other with confusion, both forgetting the gravity of the other's situation.

Porter shook his head, looking back down at Della. "Not a word of this, Ambrose, or I swear to God—"

"Hey," Richie said, smiling at him with his glistening white fangs. "I don't care what you do at five in the morning on a Wednesday, as long as you can offer me the same courtesy." He said, pretending to tip his hat to him.

"You *disgust* me," Porter said as he brushed past him but nodded his approval of the deal. He had known Richie for years, though not by choice.

"Thanks." He heard Richie say as he continued to munch on his early morning snack.

As the sun rose, casting the world in purple and pink light, Porter put Della in the front seat of the hearse and peeled out of the driveway, making his way to the nearest hospital. His hearse looked exactly like the caskets it carried with Della's limp body inside it.

It seemed like it took days to get to the emergency room, the only sound in the hearse coming from Della's erratic breathing. The nurses and receptionists had been less than cordial, awfully confused at what had happened to poor Della— especially since Porter didn't have a plausible lie.

He looked over his shoulder, the sound of footsteps echoing through the empty hospital as he paced back in forth in the waiting room. Max was marching towards him with increasing speed, looking like he had seen a ghost.

"What happened?" Max asked.

Mavericks was a few feet away, chatting with the nearest nurse, most likely trying to persuade her to let them see Della.

"It's Della," Porter said dumbly, the words getting stuck in his throat.

Max rubbed his eyes, looking around with an air of sarcasm to his blank expression. "Ei can see that, ya utter floorboard, *what happened?*"

"She passed out about an hour ago." Porter said, explaining everything that had happened as soon as Mavericks joined them.

Max's eyes widened. "Bloody Hell! What did ya do tuh her?!" He tried to whisper.

Porter rolled his eyes, squeezing the bridge of his nose, whispering inaudibly in Portuguese. "I don't know, okay? I was crashing at her place, and I woke up to her screaming." He said awkwardly.

Max was staring at him, open-mouthed. He swallowed hard, pushing down all his worries. "Well if Ei woke up next tuh ya—"

"*It wasn't like that!*" Porter hissed.

Max rolled his eyes, moving his hand to Porter's words. Sarcasm was the only way he knew how to cope, and Porter knew that. However, it didn't stop him from wanting to tear that pint sized Irish man apart.

"Oh, you wanna go? We can go *right* now." Porter said, his eyes full of rage. Every ounce of his being wanted to put his fist through something, and Max was as good a target as any.

Mavericks cleared his throat. "Gentleman, as much as I love a good catfight, we have other problems to deal with." He said dully, adding a yawn for effect. The boys glared at each other but returned their attention to the grueling situation at hand. "Did she say anything?" He asked, gesturing for them to follow him out of the waiting room.

"She asked for help, then passed out." Porter said for what felt like the hundredth time. Who cares what happened? Why wasn't anyone trying to fix her?

Mavericks scowled deeply, scratching the back of his neck. "I'm sure she will be fine." He said, more to himself than to the boys.

Max nodded, wringing his hands and chewing on his right sleeve. Porter shoved him, rolling his eyes.

They followed Mavericks in silence for a little while until they came to Della's hospital room. They all hesitated, afraid of what would happen, what they would see, before they opened the door.

Della looked like something out of a fairytale, lying motionless on that hospital bed, the sun seeping in through the thin linen curtains. They'd hooked her up to a machine, her slow heartbeat echoing throughout the silent room. A steady flow of oxygen was hooked up to her nose, the tubes moving ever so slowly as she breathed.

Porter swallowed hard, slowly sitting down on the crinkling bed. He lifted Della's hand into his, squeezing it tightly. Max stood at the end of the bed, his fingers gripping the footboard so hard his knuckles turned white. Mavericks stood in the doorway, lost in thought, an odd look of concern on his face. It was almost a look of regret, though Porter hadn't a clue why he would feel that way.

The door opened again after a while, the doctor coming in, looking over a clear clipboard. He nodded to them all, trying to act cordial, though worry was written all over his face like some cruel prank.

"So, you three are her family?" Dr. Whitcomb, Porter deduced by the faded nametag on his scrubs, asked skeptically.

An awkward pause.

Porter cleared his throat, speaking for them all. "Yes, we are her family."

Dr. Whitcomb smiled kindly, checking something off on his papers. "Blood relation?" He asked.

The three of them shook their heads, awaiting further questions.

"Are you aware of the medication she takes?" Dr. Whitcomb asked, squinting at his papers with great confusion.

"Uh, yeah, sumatriptan, right?" Max asked.

The doctor shook his head. "It's an awfully odd brand of sumatriptan." He laughed. "We did some blood tests and checked the records, but Miss Coleman here has been prescribed a placebo for her migraines containing trace amounts of oleander, lemon verbena, and betony. Do any of you have any clue why?"

Mavericks paled, staring at Della with a questioning look. "Don't those things—excuse me, I'm awfully superstitious—aren't they meant to block out nightmares?" He asked.

Dr. Whitcomb nodded. "If you believe in herbal remedies, yes. I do believe that oleander is also used to help with headaches, but that's some seriously risky business."

Porter looked over his shoulder at Della, several things finally clicking in his head. He had seen many things in his time alive here in Moss Hollow, and no one with magical powers of any kind obtained them randomly. Most of the time, their abilities were suppressed. Sometimes, weary parents would cast spells over their children to dull their powers when they were young, so their child wouldn't cast a spell that would hurt them. What if Della's parents had done the same thing?

"Does she have seizures often? There aren't any reports in her files, but then again this is the first time we have seen Miss Coleman." The doctor explained.

"She's had a seizure?" Max asked.

The doctor nodded, looking at the three of them with suspicion. "Yes, a very serious seizure. I've never seen it this bad before. . . People don't just start bleeding out of their noses, eyes, and ears for fun Mr—"

"McGregor-Mavericks." Max said sourly, giving questioning looks to Mavericks and Porter.

"Right. I'd like to hold her for a couple days for observation. I'll get a hold of—" He looked down at his files again, squinting. "—Looks like Sycamore Regional and be back to you. Please inform one of the nurses if she wakes." Dr. Whitcomb bowed, then swept out of the room, leaving them all to ponder Della's situation.

Mavericks finally moved away from the door, plopping down in a cheap armchair in the corner. "Oleander is serious stuff; only four grams can kill a person. It attacks the heart and digestive system. . . Who—Why would that be in her medication?" He thought aloud. "And why now of all times it this happening?"

Porter shrugged, watching Della's chest rise and fall with increasing worry. He looked up at the monitor, watching her heartbeat dance across the screen.

"Ei mean, when ya think about it, it makes sense." Max began. "She stopped takin' it, her appetite increased, and she's been awfully sickly. Maybe it's a shock tuh the system? Maybe cuttin' herself off cold turkey caused some sort of reaction?" He shrugged.

Porter shook his head. "I have a feeling this isn't as simple as that." He said glumly.

Mavericks nodded his agreement, standing. "I'm going to head back to the office, you two stay with her. Call me if anything changes. For better *or* for worse."

"Can't you do anything to help her?" Porter asked, still squeezing Della's lifeless hand.

Mavericks thought for a moment, walking over and placing a hovering hand over Della's forehead. He stared at the monitor as golden light began to pour out of his fingers, seeping into Della's skull. Max and Porter watched in silence as Mavericks shook his head.

"There's nothing I can do." Mavericks said sadly, sighing heavily.

"But—But she's gonna be okay, right?" Max asked.

"That's not exactly my forte, Milliano. Dr. Whitcomb knows more than I do, and I suspect even he has his worries and doubts." Mavericks said, making his way to the door. He turned around, a fierce look on his face. "She needs rest. When she wakes, don't bombard her with questions. She will talk when she is ready." He said, clicking his tongue on the roof of his mouth, sweeping out the door.

~CHAPTER TWENTY-SEVEN~

Porter bit his fingernail as he stared at the flower arrangements in the gift shop before him. He couldn't sit there
and watch her lay unconscious. His heart was already in pieces, he couldn't bear to have it shattered anymore. So instead,
he was sitting here, picking up bouquets and vases, rearranging petals and sighing to himself over and over again.

Max was less of a mess. The only thing bothering him
was the poison in her veins. She said she'd been taking that
medication all her life, so how long had the poison been in
it? Had it been like that her whole life? Surely her parents
wouldn't have allowed it. Porter sighed again, breathing in the
sweet smell of peonies. He was praying that she was going to
be okay. Praying with every ounce of his being.

"Hey, dude." The scrawny boy at the cash register called.
"If you aren't going to buy anything, would you move out of the
way? We have a shipment coming in."

"Yeah, sorry," Porter said distractedly but did not move.
Maybe he should get her daisies. *Those are pretty and cheerful,*
he thought, *perhaps she'd like them.*

"Dude." The boy barked.

"It's all right, Mr. Garroway can take as much time as
he needs." A familiar voice rang. Porter turned; a small pot
of daisies clenched in his shaking hands. It was Clara Dixon,

dressed in a bright orange sweater, tortoiseshell sunglasses resting on her head, a cart full of flower arrangements before her. She smiled widely at Porter, waving.

Porter regarded her with a curt nod, more intrigued by the flowers wrapped in cellophane she was handing over to the boy at the cash register. He made his way over to her, nearly knocking over a rounder of stuffed animals as he went.

"No monkshood today?" He asked jokingly, his eyes resting on a mason jar filled with hydrangeas.

Clara scowled, crossing her arms. "Contrary to popular belief, I don't grow the flowers I sell. All I do is make them look nice. My supplier had some extra monkshood, and I asked if I could have some. She gave me some sprigs for free." Clara explained hotly, though there was kindness in her eyes.

"Who's your supplier?" Porter asked, setting the daisies down on the counter and reaching for the mason jar of hydrangeas. Some of the petals were bright pink, others a deep blue. Porter knew these colors meant heartfelt emotion and wishing an apology, two things he would love to express to Della.

Clara watched him as he fingered the petals, her demeanor softening.

"Eloise Heiser." She said softly. An odd feeling of betrayal swept through him at the sound of that name, though he had no idea why. It was a similar feeling to what he felt every time he had seen the Grunch. "Who are you visiting?" The way she was staring at his face made him slightly uncomfortable. Her eyes were resting on his bruised cheek, her mouth hanging open slightly. Almost an accusatory position.

"Della," Porter said, his voice shaky.

"Oh my! What happened? Is she all right?" Clara asked, her eyes as wide as dinner plates.

Porter nodded, then shrugged half-heartedly. "I think so. She's comatose upstairs." He said, telling her what had happened.

Clara looked absolutely horrified to find that Della was incapacitated. That warmed Porter's heart a little. Like the hydrangeas he held in his hand, it seemed Miss Coleman was often forgotten about. Most seemed to forget that hydrangeas could be placed indoors as well, to let their beauty shine twenty-four-seven, not just when you walked by them outside. It was nice to know that someone other than him or Max or Mavericks cared about Della. And of course, the flowers.

"How much for these?" He asked suddenly, cutting off Clara as she tried to ask another question about Della's wellbeing.

"Oh, uh, ten." She smiled.

The cashier rolled his eyes.

Porter smiled, balancing the jar of flowers in one arm, and reaching for his wallet with the other. Clara watched him struggle, a look of pity on her face. Porter smiled feverishly, trying to hand her his money, she took it, but then handed it over to the boy behind the counter. Porter blushed.

"She's got you up in a tizzy, doesn't she?" Clara asked, leaning casually against the counter.

Porter nodded. "I feel like I can't function."

Clara chuckled. "I can see that. She's going to be okay; I promise."

"I know, I just can't help but think this is somehow my fault." He whispered.

"Why would this be your fault?" Clara asked. "Sounds to me like this whole thing was a long time coming. If anything, you are the hero here. Just think if you wouldn't have been there, she could be dead."

Porter looked up, staring her dead in the eyes. "You are a good person, you know that?"

Clara blushed, waving away his praise. "I try."

Porter nodded, looking around the gift shop once more. He knew it wouldn't do much to help, but buying these flowers seemed like it was fixing everything. Della meant so much to him, especially now. She was the one person he knew wouldn't judge him for being what he was or think of him as anything less than good. He owed her his life. He owed her *everything*, and if he wasn't broke, he would've bought the entire gift shop to prove it to her.

"Find anything out about my sister?" Clara asked, her tone darkening.

"We have a few leads," Porter said. He was going to say something reassuring, something about how everything will work out in the end, when it hit him.

Eloise Heiser.

He'd seen that name before, somewhere. He bit his lip, trying to remember where. It was almost as if something was blocking his memories. But then he saw it; all the reports he had looked up at MHPD had had one thing in common; a name. Eloise Heiser was the school counselor, that's why she was vouching for the kids at court. She knew everything about what went on in their homes.

"Uh, you said Eloise Heiser grew the flowers?" He asked, containing the odd excitement he felt.

Clara nodded. "Yeah, why do you ask?"

"Do you mind if I get her address? I need to talk to her." Porter said nervously.

"Eloise didn't kill anyone if that's what you're asking," Clara said, wringing her hands.

"I'm sure she didn't, I just need to talk to her. We have found the same flower arrangements at several crime scenes, and I want to know if she has sent them." Porter explained.

Clara thought, then pulled a business card out of her pocket along with a pen. "Ellie takes custom orders every once in a while—she used to own my shop before she became a counselor. Maybe whoever has committed all the crimes is the person who ordered the flowers?" She proposed as she wrote an address on the card and handed it over, still looking skeptical. That odd feeling of betrayal returned to him, followed by a burst of anger.

"Thank you." Porter smiled, nodding to her and the boy behind her.

"Oh! Porter!" Clara said, stopping him before he left the gift shop.

"Yes?"

"If you find my sister, don't you dare let anything happen to her," Clara warned, tears stinging her eyes.

"I won't, I promise," Porter said. They held eyes for a long moment, Clara searching his, Porter fighting off this odd feeling that was growing in his chest.

~ ~ ~

Clara struggled through the parking lot, the wheels of her flower cart getting stuck on the many potholes in the pavement. She smiled to herself, unlocking the trunk of her car, struggling to heave the trolley up into the back. The back wheel was caught somewhere she couldn't see. She ducked under the tailgate, trying to see where it was stuck.

Footsteps echoed through the empty parking lot, startling her. She jumped, hitting her head. A sudden sense of foreboding filled her. She knew she shouldn't have parked this far away from the entrance to Moss Hollow General. . .

"Hey! Let me help you with that!" Porter's voice rang as Clara crawled out from under the tailgate.

"Oh, you almost gave me a heart attack," Clara said, laughing nervously.

Porter laughed too, but it wasn't a happy-go-lucky chuckle, it was low and disembodied. He offered her his hand, pulling her off the ground with little effort. She thanked him, watching as he placed the trolley in her trunk. Clara crossed her arms over her chest nervously, looking around. The sun was beating down on them, not a cloud in the sky, but there was something off. The birds weren't chirping, there wasn't a butterfly in sight. Too quiet for such a busy bayou town.

"There we go," Porter said, turning to her. His eyes looked empty to her, but then again, what did she know? Clara Dixon was just a scared girl whose parents had abused her. She suspected everyone of having ulterior motives.

"Thanks, well, I should get going. Tell Miss Coleman I said to get better." She smirked. He stared at her, nodding. Clara turned, reaching for her keys in her back pocket, but they weren't there.

Porter jingled something between two fingers. "Looking for these?" He asked.

Clara turned slowly, her throat closing in fear. Her keys, the ones with the rusty daisy keychain, hung from his fingers menacingly. She nodded. "I must've dropped them, thanks." She choked out, holding out her hand for him to place her keys in.

Surprisingly, he did. She gave him a little thumbs-up, then turned back to shut the trunk. She knew Porter was still standing there, his hands in the pockets of his army-green denim jacket. Shaking with fright, she locked up the trunk, walking away from him. He reached out for her, his cold fingers squeezing her wrist.

"So, you heading home?" He asked.

She nodded, trying to pry his fingers from her. He wouldn't budge. No human being should have this much strength. Not even her mother had been able to keep a grip on her for this long. Slowly, she stopped trying to remove him from her, looking up into his eyes. He smiled maliciously, his eyes flashing from gold to white. Clara squeaked, stamping her foot onto his toes, trying to get away.

Everyone hears the stories of the things that truly lived in Moss Hollow, but Clara had never believed them. Not until now.

"Let me go!" She cried.

Porter shook his head, reaching behind her neck and slamming her head into the back of her car far more times than necessary. A thick splatter of blood was now on the cracked back window, an unconscious Clara on the ground. He sighed, rolling up his sleeves. His bandages were falling off, flakes of dried blood and scales dusting his pants. Those were his favorite pants. . .

He picked up Clara's form, ripping the keys from her fingers, and unlocking her car. Haphazardly, he threw her in the back, slamming the door shut.

"Very good." A voice hissed.

Porter shrugged, pulling his bandages tight, feeling a searing pain shooting up his arm. "Protect the queen and all that." He said with a yawn.

A figure to his right nodded. "Go back to your friends, don't forget to wash up."

"Has he been taken care of?" Porter asked as sirens filled the air.

"That should be him now." The figure said, an ounce of sadness in his voice.

"Was it necessary to take the girl?" Porter asked, disgusted.

"She ratted out Eloise!" The figure hissed. "Of course, it was necessary!"

Porter sighed heavily. "You know, they'll figure out that I'm under your control." He said.

The figure nodded. "Exactly. That means they will have something else to worry about. Because you are an Ahool, the bite doesn't take fully. You're just under my control, it's just a spell. They'll think it's something worse."

Porter rolled his eyes. "See you around, then."

~CHAPTER TWENTY-EIGHT~

Benched

Della's heavy eyes flickered open, bright white light stinging them as she tried to move. She was aware of a small beeping noise, and soft voices, but other than that, her senses were all over the place. Her eyes finally adjusted, Max and Porter's faces swimming in and out of her sight. She groaned, slowly reaching up to touch her forehead. Her fingers were as cold as ice cubes against her hot skin, sending electricity through her veins. Her fingers traveled across her face, bumping into some sort of plastic in her nose. She went to pull on it when Porter quickly grabbed her hand.

"I'd leave it." He said softly, taking her hand.

She was too weak to speak, but she was able to look around, suddenly realizing she was in a hospital room. Panic began to rise in the back of her throat as she tried to force herself up off the bed.

"Hey, hey, hey, just—everything's okay, just calm down." Porter whispered, gently pushing her back down.

Della stared forward, observing her hospital room. There were thin floral curtains on the windows, a vase of flowers next to Porter, and several cheap teal armchairs.

Max—who had been standing at the foot of her adjustable bed—came to sit on her left, while Porter sat on her right. "How are ya feelin'?" He asked wearily.

Della shrugged weakly. She had the vague feeling that she had been crying, but other than that, she couldn't remember what had happened. Looking down at her hands, she saw they were covered in dried blood.

"You gave us all quite the fright." Porter said, gripping onto her free hand for dear life.

". . . Sorry." She whispered back, letting her arm drop to her side.

Her vision was still swimming, but she realized it wasn't from her headache, it was from the stream of morphine being pushed into her veins. She blinked several times, picking at the needle in her arm.

Porter smirked, patting her leg. "Pretty heavy stuff they got you hooked up to."

She nodded, the colors before her eyes dancing like fairies. "How did I—What happened?" She asked, her voice hoarse.

"We were hopin' ya could tell us." Max admitted.

"But only when you're ready." Porter added quickly.

Della, being Della, didn't want to be babied. She waved away Porter's grip on her leg, shakily sitting up. She rubbed her eyes, pulling the needle full of morphine out of her arm, much to the boys' chagrin. Her head was swelling with pain, but it was nothing compared to what she had experienced back in the confines of her apartment.

Her vision came flooding back to her. She shut her eyes tightly, sinking back into the pillows behind her. She reached a hand up to her forehead again, running her fingers through her greasy hair.

"I saw some stuff." Della whispered, feeling the boys awkwardly get comfortable next to her.

"W—What kind of stuff?" Max asked.

"*Max.*" Porter scolded.

Della shook her head. "It's fine." She lied. "I had another vision, whose-it-what's-it, or whatever." She said, confused by her lack of vocabulary.

"*Another?*" Max asked.

She nodded weakly, waving her hand through the air dismissively. "This one means three." She said, holding up two fingers, then three, opening her eyes, blinking against the light.

"Why didn' ya tell us?" Max asked, brushing a piece of hair out of her face.

"I told Porter." Della said simply.

"I thought you knew." Porter shrugged, receiving a glare from Max. "Obviously not."

Della nodded, sitting back up and swinging her legs over the edge of her bed. It was all she could do to stay upright and not fall over onto Porter. She was still in her clothes from yesterday, scorched shirt and all. She sat lost in thought for a minute, trying to find the words she so desperately needed.

". . . I saw—I *spoke* with Theodore in my vision. He was going on about how it's not my fault, and that I have to find someone." She explained. "Jimmie, I think. . ."

Max and Porter exchanged a look.

"What? What happened?" Della asked, worry flooding through her fragile body.

"Did Theodore die in your vision? Again?" Porter asked.

Della's heart felt like someone had crushed it, causing the monitor behind her to freak out. Porter inhaled sharply, rubbing her back comfortingly. He looked at Max, who shrugged and nodded.

"Not long after I brought you in, they brought in Theodore. No one knows what happened, but he was—he was. . . stabbed. . ." Porter explained.

"Is he okay?" She asked, already knowing the answer.

Max shook his head once. "He was gone before the wardens got tuh him."

Della's heart skipped a beat. She tried to stand up, but they held her down, exchanging strange looks they thought she couldn't see. Her mouth was dry. She looked to Porter, then to Max, and back down at her feet. Her hands were shaking. No, her entire *body* was shaking.

"I'm fine." She said, more to herself than to the boys.

She didn't care about Theodore.

She had to believe that.

He was just a lead and nothing more. He wasn't a friend, he wasn't an acquaintance, he was someone she used to get answers.

So why did she want to cry? Why was the fact that he was dead so hard for her to swallow? Why did this feel like it was her fault? *Maybe. . . maybe because it is,* she thought. She stared blankly straight in front of her at everything and nothing at all.

She stood briskly, breaking free of the boys hold, the pit in her stomach widening. She turned to them, her face set in an indifferent expression. This seemed to set them on edge.

"We need to go talk to his brother, Jimmie." She said, her voice scary calm.

"Absolutely not. You need your rest." Porter said, looking quite horrified that she thought she could do more than take two steps out of this room.

"I can decide what is best for me, thank you very much." Della said. There was no emotion in her words. They were just words.

Meaningless.

Fleeting.

Words.

The boys exchanged another look.

"Della. . . You've just seen something traumatizing. We can take a break. We understand if you need to rest, we will take care of everything." Porter said softly. He held her eyes with a passion that dared her to do something he would deem wrong, to see what he would do.

"I'm fine." She said breathlessly, wiping the dried blood on her hands off on her jeans.

"We can take five seconds tuh just sit, Della." Max whispered, reaching out for her arm.

She jerked herself away, still not exercising any emotion as she did so. "No, we can't." She insisted.

"Even if we wanted you to leave, you're on house arrest—er—hospital arrest, I guess." Porter said. "You had a seizure; the doctor wants to keep you for a bit to make sure you're okay." Della rolled her eyes, sitting heavily back down on the bed. Porter gave her a knowing look, reaching out for her hand. "You can help us from here, okay? We have phones, you can text and call us and tell us anything we need."

"But—" Della began, Porter shaking his head angrily.

This wasn't their fight. This wasn't their mess to fix. No matter what Theodore had said, she drug them into this, and she was going to be the one to finish it. She clenched her fists around the sheets beneath her, tears stinging her eyes.

"We realize how important this all is to you, but *you* are important to *us*. You said it yourself, we can't do anything without you, and if you die, well guess where that lands us?" He said sternly.

Della crossed her arms over her chest, she couldn't meet their eyes. She hated being benched like this. If this was what being the brains of the operation felt like, she hated it. She hated having them fawning all over her, acting like if she moved, she'd fracture into a thousand pieces.

Maybe she would. Maybe she should, but that's not who she was. She had learned early on that you *never* show your pain. You muddle through it, you keep on fighting, and you don't let others see you weak. So that's what she was going to do, she was going to push everything down like she always did. She was going to laugh it all off, pretending like she was just as cold-hearted as the rest of the world thought she was.

"You have to talk to Jimmie Heiser, he lives three doors down from the Dixon's. He's jumpy, and he only gives you half the truth, but he knows something. Tell him I sent you, and I'm sure he will talk to you." She explained.

"Can we use yer notebooks?" Max asked, trying to hide his excitement. They all knew that Mavericks hated letting him go out and investigate.

Della nodded reluctantly. "Don't do *anything* cool without me." She said sourly, eyeing Porter out of the corner of her eye.

Porter smiled, planting a kiss on her forehead. "Wouldn't even dream of it."

~CHAPTER TWENTY-NINE~

Jumpy Jimmie

Half an hour and a cheeseburger later, the boys were sitting in Porter's beat-up hearse outside Jimmie Heiser's home. They knocked on the front door, noticing that there were long scratch marks on it.

Max pulled out Della's notebook, cross-referencing the scratch marks to her notes. "Dear *Lord*, she writes too much. . ." He breathed. "As far as I can tell, those are new."

Porter nodded. He was out of place here. He'd much rather be at the hospital with Della, but he was here just in case. Max wasn't known for his strength. Or having a—well to be quite frank, he wasn't known for having a *friendly* demeanor. . .

The old man rushed to the door, pulling it open. His old face was covered in tear stains. He looked around his house, looking just as nervous as Della had said he would. There was something about his face, something familiar about him, but Porter was sure they had never met before.

"Hello?" Jimmie asked, examining the two boys before him.

Porter pulled out his wallet, flashing his visitor pass from the morgue at MHPD. "Hello, my name is Porter Garroway, and this is Maximilian McGregor, we are friends of Delphee Coleman."

"Oh, right, right," Jimmie said, roughly wiping his face. "How can I be of service?"

"Mandatory follow up," Max explained.

Jimmie seemed to understand but looked confused. "Where is Miss Coleman? I would've thought she'd be here."

"She's out of commission at the moment," Porter said.

Jimmie paled instantly, looking terrified. His eyes darted down to the scratch marks on the door. "I—Is she alright?" He stuttered.

The boys shrugged.

"She's definitely been better," Porter said darkly.

"Well," Jimmie said, seeming to make up his mind about something. "Come on in." He said, holding the door for them.

He led the boys into the kitchen, taking a basket full of muffins off the counter and setting them on the table. "Feel free to take one." Jimmie smiled, sitting down at the table. "Ellie made them."

"Ellie?" Porter asked, though he already knew whom he was referencing.

Max flipped through Della's notebook. "Theodore's wife, Eloise." He said correctively, smiling cheekily.

Jimmie sobbed into his handkerchief.

The boys exchanged a look of profound disgust. "We are very sorry for your loss." They assured him.

"Thank you," Jimmie said.

Max cleared his throat, his finger tracing over the questions Della had wanted them to ask. "We know this is a difficult time, but we have some crucial inquiries. . . ?" He looked up at Porter, who shrugged. Della's eloquent writing was awfully confusing to the two of them. That girl used the words 'penultimate', 'acrimony,' and 'cloying' far too much. "Were either of you abused as children? You and Theodore? Or Eloise?" Max continued.

"No," Jimmie said in a perplexed tone.

Max wrote a very large 'no' under that question, moving onto the next. "Do you know anyone who *was* abused?"

Jimmie thought for a moment then shook his head. "Why?" He asked politely.

"It's just routine," Max assured him.

Porter opened his mouth to shed a little more light on their situation but thought better of it. If Theodore had told Della to talk to Jimmie before he died, that could mean a multitude of things. He could be the villain, or he could be a victim.

Jimmie sighed heavily. "Not that you heard it from me, but Theo used to get a bit riled up when he got drunk. Poor Ellie used to come and stay the night here a lot."

Porter and Max shared a look. Spent the night, huh? Time to add the Heiser's to the list of unfaithful spouses that roamed the streets of Moss Hollow.

Jimmie nodded to himself. "Ellie retired this summer; she was the district counselor for Moss Hollow. She's mentioned that a couple of the kids talked about their abusive parents. I imagine they tell awfully tall tales." He explained nervously.

Porter clenched his fists. There was a special place in Hell for people who didn't believe kids when they told them they were being abused.

"You should really go talk to her about all this," Jimmie said, wringing his hands. "Or Eric Steiniger. He was Theo's best friend; they grew up together. He and Ellie hang around a lot."

Porter furrowed his eyebrows. He hadn't heard Steiniger mention them until recently. Why was he suddenly filled with doubt?

Max looked down at the notebook, then over his shoulder at the front door. "Mr. Heiser—"

"Please, call me Jimmie."

"Right, *Jimmie*, what happened to your door?" Max asked, putting the notebook away. Porter had a horrible feeling about going off-topic.

Jimmie looked between them nervously. "You know how teenagers are." He laughed. "First it's egging houses, then it's trying to break into them."

Max sat forward, crossing his arms on the table. "Really? There were no reports of vandalism on the radio this morning, were there, Porter?" He looked over his shoulder at him.

"What? Oh, uh, no." Porter stuttered, trying to discern Max's tactic. Was this good-cop-bad-cop, or was this Max being Max? It was impossible to tell.

"What really happened here, *Jimmie*?" Max asked, leaning forward, crossing his arms over the table.

Jimmie scowled at him. "There was no report because it's not a big deal." He assured them.

"Breaking and entering is a *massive* deal. Especially in a small town like this! Egging houses, breaking and entering, theft, *murder, kidnappings*? What's next?" Max laughed cynically. "Socialism?"

Porter smiled apologetically. "Sorry about my partner, he forgets the difference between thoughts and words. How about you have a muffin and calm down, Deputy McGregor." Porter said, snatching Della's notebook from him.

Max glared at him but took a muffin out of the basket.

Max was right, Della had written far too much information on the tiny pages of her notebook. She wrote sideways, upside down, backward, in the margins, and on the cover.

"We. . . We understand you have practiced witchcraft." He began. Jimmie stared at him. "Have you been practicing recently?"

"Like I told Miss Coleman, no." He said. There was something off-putting about his eyes. Porter wondered if the old man was hiding something.

"Right," Max said. "But have you been *summoning* anything?"

"*Max.*" Porter hissed. He wanted to solve this mystery as badly as the rest of them but that wasn't the way to get information.

"What kind of cops are you?" Jimmie asked, standing.

"Just mandatory questions, sir," Max said again, biting into his muffin.

"I would like it if you mandatorily left my house," Jimmie said, ripping the basket of muffins off the table.

"I'd kindly like it if you—" Max began, but Porter cut him off.

"We are very sorry to have bothered you, Mr. Heiser. We'll be on our way." Porter said, pulling Max out of his seat by the collar of his shirt and to the front door.

Jimmie followed, opening the door for them angrily. A woman was outside, her fist raised, ready to knock on the door.

"Oh dear, Jimmie, what's going on?" She asked.

She was stunning for her age, her brown hair dotted with streaks of gray. Porter knew her face from somewhere, but he couldn't quite figure out where. She eyed the boys with trepidation, sending an odd wave of shivers through Porter's body.

"Nothing Ellie, dear, they were just leaving," Jimmie said

coldly.

Max made to leave, but Porter was lost in thought. He stared at the woman a little longer before it finally clicked in his mind who she was.

"Mrs. Langeland?" He inquired, thinking back on his school days.

She nodded, her eyes lighting up a little. "Well, thats what I called myself back then. I used my maiden name for a while since. . ." She cleared her throat, most likely thinking back to when Theodore got arrested and the shame she undoubtedly had felt. "I'm Eloise Heiser." She explained.

Jimmie scowled deeply, gesturing for Porter to leave. Porter bowed in apology, sweeping out the door, smiling widely at Eloise.

"Do you remember me?" Porter asked.

There were many a day when Porter would come into Mrs. Langeland's office, divulging all his secrets to her. He had shared everything with this old woman, besides Della and Max, she was the only one who knew about Jed. Not even Max knew everything that Jed had done to him. Mrs. Langeland—or Mrs. Heiser as she was known now—had been his favorite person on earth, and he had forgotten all about her.

"Porter Garroway. . ." Eloise breathed. Her eyes fell upon the yellowing bruise on his nose, sadness filling her eyes. "Yes, I do remember you. You dropped out after the old school burned down, right? After everything happened with Robbie?"

Porter went red with embarrassment, rubbing at his nose. He nodded sadly. Eloise smiled sympathetically, winking at her old student. Max looked between the two, his eyebrows furrowed. He inhaled slowly, then cleared his throat again. Eloise looked over her shoulder, her eyes lighting up in recognition.

"And if it isn't Maximilian!" She exclaimed.

Max seemed to recognize her as well, but he seemed less than happy to see her. "Yeah, hi," Max said, waving sarcastically. "Come on, Porter." He said, glowering at Jimmie.

Eloise smiled, pulling Porter in a hug. "It was nice to see you again." She said, squeezing his shoulder. She turned away, sweeping inside her brother-in-law's house, waving to the boys.

The boys stood on the front porch, staring at the door in disbelief. Porter closed Della's notebook, tapping it lightly.

"That was weird, right?" Max asked, raising an eyebrow.

Porter nodded. "Della's going to be *so* pissed she missed it.

~CHAPTER THIRTY~

Dire Situations

Della's phone rang next to her. A number she didn't recognize lit up the screen. She grabbed it, making to answer when a knock on the door startled her out of the magazine she had her nose buried in. "Come in." She called, expecting to see Max and Porter. Instead, carrying a bouquet of flowers wrapped in yellow cellophane, Nicoletta greeted her eyes.

"Hey!" Della said, tossing her magazine to the side.

"How are you feeling?" Nicoletta asked, looking around the hospital room in disgust, wrinkling her nose. "Bad I bet, seeing as you are stuck in this dreary room."

Della shrugged. "I'm okay."

Nicoletta nodded to herself, placing the flowers on the nightstand next to the mason jar of hydrangeas Porter had bought her. "I brought you some reading material." She said as she pulled out a thick book from her carpetbag. A book of dreams.

Nicoletta handed the thick book to Della, smiling at how intrigued she was. The way she smiled reminded Della of her mother. She had a feeling that they would be fast friends, even though their ideologies differed greatly.

"Thanks." Della said, flipping through the book absentmindedly. The pages had silver gilding around the edges, the cover a rich purple.

"It will help you discern your visions." Nicoletta explained, smiling weakly. They stared into each other's eyes for a minute, a deep sadness floating behind Nicoletta's endless brown eyes. "Did my tea help?"

Della shrugged, holding the book to her chest. "I had a massive seizure—"

"So, it did?" Nicoletta said, an ominous tone to her voice.

"I guess so." Della said.

Nicoletta nodded, sitting down on the edge of her bed, taking Della's hand in her own. "Things get worse before they get better." She smiled, once again looking around the hospital room. "Where are the beastie and the monster?"

"Running a couple errands for me." Della said sourly, leaning back into her pillows.

"Premature cabin fever?" Nicoletta laughed, rearranging the flowers in the vase, adding a few of the ones she had brought.

Della nodded.

"What was it like when you saw Theodore Heiser die?" Nicoletta asked bluntly.

"How did you know that?" Della asked, looking at the old witch in disbelief.

"Dear child, I know all things." Nicoletta winked.

Della looked away, pulling at a loose thread on the bedding beneath her. "Can we not talk about it?" She asked.

"You will need to eventually." Nicoletta said.

"I was there." Della whispered. "He talked to me, I could feel him cling to me for help, but when I tried to touch the bars of his cell, I couldn't do anything." She said, choking back tears she swore she didn't need.

"Astral projection is a tricky thing. I wouldn't try it again if I were you. You could have gotten stuck in the metaphysical." Nicoletta said, looking somewhat disappointed.

"But I didn't do it on purpose, it just sort of happened." Della explained.

"Did you have your tea last night?" She asked. Della nodded. She had had a glass on the couch while she chatted with Porter. Nicoletta lightly furrowed her eyebrows. "Well that does cause some problems, doesn't it. . ."

"I'm not going to die, am I?" Della asked.

"Everyone dies eventually." Nicoletta said.

"That's not the answer I was looking for." Della said, but she was pretty sure she knew what Nicoletta had meant.

"It never is." Nicoletta said. "I'll let you get some rest. Leave the spell work to beastie for now, alright?" Nicoletta winked at her, placing a hand on her forehead.

Della felt all tingly where the old witch's hand touched her, suddenly feeling exhausted. Before she could stop it, her eyes closed softly, forcing her to drift off into her dreams.

Della didn't realize that Nicoletta stayed with her for many hours, watching the screen that was monitoring her heartbeat with great concern, until she sensed that the boys were back.

"Stay with us just a bit longer, Della. You have unfinished work to do." Nicoletta whispered before the door opened.

"Nicoletta?" Max's voice rang. "What are you doing here?"

She stood up off the bed, turning to address the boys. They were staring at Della, debating their options. "Visiting Miss Coleman." Nicoletta said simply, brushing off her long silk sundress.

"She okay?" Porter asked.

"Oh yes, just resting her eyes. I'm sure she will wake before long." Nicoletta smiled, watching Della sleep peacefully.

The boys breathed a sigh of relief, finally pacing through the doorway. Nicoletta was happy to know just how much they cared for Miss Della Coleman. The more people the young woman had in her corner, the better things would be, though Nicoletta still had her doubts. She had seen many powerful creatures die that were older and far more experienced than Della.

"Well, I'll be on my way." Nicoletta said. She looked directly into Max's eyes, giving him a knowing look. "When she wakes, would you mind leaving our little exchange out of the conversation?"

Max stuttered but ultimately nodded. "Yes, of course, ma'am." Even the beastie knew when to abide by Nicoletta's rules.

Porter eyed them but nodded too. She hadn't had the pleasure of meeting him now that he had grown out of his emo phase. It seemed to her that he was as good a choice as any to protect Della. She nodded curtly to him, then left.

~ ~ ~

"I can't believe it! Why does all the cool stuff happen when I'm not around?" Della asked, shoving a spoonful of butterscotch pudding in her mouth when the boys had finished filling her in on everything Eloise and Jimmie had said.

Porter shrugged, scraping the bottom of his own pudding cup. "What do you think? Do you think Mrs. Heiser has something to do with all of this?"

Della shrugged, pulling her knees up to her chest. "I don't know, but now I have my doubts about Jimmie. Innocent people don't act guilty on purpose." She said simply, pointing her spoon at them.

Max nodded his approval of Della's theory. "So, what now? Jimmie didn' seem too keen on having us coming back to visit. Ei don' fancy any more arrests on my resume."

"I second that." Porter sighed.

"Same." Della agreed, finishing her pudding.

The boys stared at her, funny little smiles playing across their faces.

She rolled her eyes. "I spray paint when I'm angry." She said, very matter-of-factly.

Porter chuckled, shaking his head. "Alright, so now that you are officially part of the Arcane Exiles, what's our next move?"

Della shrugged. "See if Eloise Heiser will talk? Maybe don't mention me, she didn't seem to like me much last time I met her."

"Right, back with the birdwatchers?" Max asked.

"Yeah." Della said, biting her lower lip. "What about this, Eric Steiniger?"

Porter's eyes flashed with rage. "He wouldn't hurt anyone." He said angrily, staring at her with death in his eyes. He inhaled sharply; his eyes fluttering closed for a minute. "What I mean is that he is like a father to me, he wouldn't do anything like this. I know him too well."

Max and Della exchanged a look. Porter crossed his arms over his chest, staring out the window.

"Well, I guess we'll go talk to Ellie." He exclaimed half-heartedly.

The boys had been staring at her strangely ever since she had woken up from her nap, they kept skirting the question when she asked how long they'd been watching over her. Now it was her turn to stare at them, wondering how to word this.

"I think you should hang back." Della said to Porter as the boys made to leave.

"Why?" He asked.

"If either of the remaining Heiser's are behind this, you are a walking target." Della said.

"Why is—" Max began, but it was clear a moment of realization had dawned on him. "Jed's not still—*Porter.*" Max breathed. "Why didn' ya tell me that he was still like that? Ei thought when ya stopped drinkin' so had Jed." He said, poking Porter's bruised nose.

Porter waved away his hand, looking utterly embarrassed. "Not important right now." He said.

Della looked back and forth between them. An unspoken tension seemed to disappear between them, like years of questions had been answered. She smiled to herself. She loved seeing them happy, loved seeing them act like actual friends.

"Ei always thought you were just growing out of me." Max laughed darkly. "If Ei would've known that—"

Porter shook his head. "I was just a kid. I thought that if I told anyone other than Mrs. Lange—Mrs. Heiser, that Jed would do something horrible to me and my mom." Porter explained. "Max you were my closest friend back then. Why would you ever think that I was growing out of our friendship?"

"Among other things, you turned fourteen, and suddenly you were this cool punk rocker with a blue streak in his hair and an attitude." Max said lazily.

"You had a blue streak in your hair?" Della laughed. Porter turned an even deeper shade of red.

"I have pictures." Max said, pulling out his phone.

Porter snatched up Max's phone, his face so red Della could feel the heat coming off it. "There's no need for that, I'm sure she has a good idea of what I looked like." He laughed nervously.

Della snorted with laughter, imagining a young Porter with an oversized leather jacket and an electric blue streak in his hair walking around the town of Moss Hollow, acting like he owned it.

"Shut up, I'm sure you had your moments too." Porter said, though he smiled.

Porter looked at both of them for a minute, his green eyes filling up with a passion Della had never seen. Even from him. "All these years, I've searched for things to fill up the void in my heart. I always thought that I wouldn't get to have the family I wanted, but I do. I got a brother and I've got a Della and that's more than what I could've asked for." He said with the biggest smile she had ever seen. "People say that family is who you are born with, not who you choose, but I choose you two. If you'll have me."

"I doubt we'd be able to shake you loose if we said no, so sure." Max joked.

Della nodded her agreement, looking at her friends in awe. She smiled weakly, wondering what she had done to deserve people like them. People that could distract her from the things that upset her, people who loved her undyingly and unconditionally. These two idiotic boys had so many things that they could be doing with their lives right now, but instead, they chose to help her. They chose to sit here in this musty old hospital, eating crappy pudding with *sporks* and chatting about their lives. Never in a million years would she have thought she would have friends like them.

~CHAPTER THIRTY-ONE~

Max's Mission

Left to his own devices, Max made his way to Eloise Heiser's house. He had always hated anything that had to do with therapy or counseling. He knew he had flaws, knew he was different, knew that he was doomed to be bullied, but that had never stopped him from being the person he was. He was proud of his flaws, proud of the color of his skin, proud that people were intimidated by him. He had never needed the relationship with Mrs. Langeland that Porter had.

But here he was, acting his part as he knocked on the door, scowling at the blue monkshood that grew in flower boxes under the windows.

Eloise opened the door. "Oh, hello, Max." She said, smiling brightly. She looked even older than Nicoletta, and not nearly as pretty.

"Yeah, hi." Max said, nervously rocking back and forth on his heels. "Mind if Ei nip in?"

"Of course!" She said, opening the door.

The first thing Max noticed was how bare the house was. Other than a TV stand and a couch, the living room was empty. There was only one picture on the wall, one of what he assumed was young Theodore and Eloise. There were no rugs, not a dust particle floating through the air, no shoe at the front door out of place. As Eloise led him through to the kitchen, Max saw boxes piled up in the hallway.

"Are ya unpackin'?" He asked, trying not to step on the tail of an old corgi as he took a seat at the kitchen table.

Eloise shook her head. "Theodore was going to be transferred to the state jail in November. I've been trying to get everything cleaned up, I thought I had found a place to move to. So, I could still be close to him." She explained, sitting across from him.

Max nodded to himself. He could smell something in the air, something familiar, something from his childhood. It was the smell that followed Mavericks and Nicoletta after they cast spells. Something crossed between sulfur, smoke, and perfume.

Either this woman desperately needed to move, or Eloise Heiser was a grade A liar. But most importantly, a witch.

"So, how is the investigation going? Is that why you are here? Jimmie told me all about it." Eloise asked.

"Uh, yes. We wanted to speak to ya alone." Max said, trying to find any other signs of witchcraft. "Well, Ei guess *Ei* wanted to speak with ya alone." Max was far from happy about being out on his own. There was a reason behind why Mavericks hated him out and about.

Eloise smiled. "Where are Porter and Delphee?"

"Della's in the hospital, Porter is. . . around." Max said, not wanting to say too much. Just in case.

"Oh my, what happened?" Eloise asked.

"She had a seizure." Max explained absentmindedly as his eyes fell upon a box of tarot cards that had been haphazardly hidden on a bookshelf.

"Oh well, thank heavens it wasn't something else." Eloise laughed nervously, placing a hand over her chest in relief.

Max nodded slowly, wondering what exactly he should be doing. He hated fieldwork, hated interrogating people. He even hated writing, that's why he was the IT guy. He sighed heavily, shaking his head to himself.

Eloise was silent for a while, fiddling with the thin string of pearls that hung around her neck.

Max squinted at her, trying to be nice. "Uh, we—er— *Ei* know that ya knew the Dixon's—specifically their daughters—but did ya know a girl by the name of Charity Boldt?" He asked, trying to act like he wasn't terrified about being alone in this house with her. "Or a boy named Angus Cummings? Sidney Oliver? Elmer Chapman? Lillie Hill? Kristin Fuller?" Max asked, listing off all the missing kids that supposedly had abusive parents or guardians.

Eloise looked very uncomfortable. "Aren't all those kids missing? Half of them used to come into my office like you and Porter." Eloise smiled at him again. "All in the same boat as your friend, I might add."

"Right. Did any of the kids mention anything to ya about their parents or guardians having any enemies?"

"No. I'm pretty sure that to the rest of the town, their families were perfect." Eloise said, scowling deeply.

"Are you aware that not only are the Dixon's dead but so are the Chapman's and the Fuller's? Angus's father died too; his mother was attacked."

Eloise's eyes widened. She shook her head, glancing out the window. As far as Max could tell, this was the most real expression the woman had had. He really wished that Porter and Della were here. He hated to admit it, but he was horrible with people skills.

"What happened to them?" Eloise asked.

"The Fuller's were found at a hotel in New Orleans, the window broken, stabbed to death. The Chapman's story goes that they were attacked by some sort of animal while camping. They all died within a week of their kids being kidnapped." Max explained, looking through Della's notebook.

Eloise was speechless, staring out the window in fear. "I had no idea. I haven't been getting the paper these last couple of weeks." Eloise shook her head in sadness. "I've got no use for the Moss Hollow Tribune in another town." She explained.

There was a moment of silence in which Eloise began to cry silently. Max began panicking deep down inside, hoping he wouldn't have to console her too much.

"I miss him greatly." Eloise whispered.

Max nodded, awkwardly reaching out to pat her on the shoulder. Yes, the old woman seemed sad, but there was something off about Eloise, something that Max couldn't quite put his finger on.

She sniffed a couple times, reaching for a box of tissues nearby. "Do you know who has been committing all these *horrible* crimes?" Eloise asked.

"We are getting closer." Max admitted, pretending to write something in Della's notebook. He cleared his throat, looking her dead in the eyes. "Those flowers ya grow, they were found at almost every crime scene. Do you have any clue why?"

Eloise looked awfully ashamed of herself. "I sent them. They're pretty aren't they? They don't exactly mean nice things."

Max nodded. "Clara Dixon told us."

Eloise pulled at the chain of pearls around her neck, blowing her nose. "I knew I shouldn't have sent them. I knew it. I just hated the way those people treated their kids. People like them shouldn't be aloud to breed, or at the very least shouldn't be aloud to see their children."

Max agreed whole-heartedly. He had the utmost hatred for his birth parents. Anyone who had the audacity to leave a crying baby on the side of the road was doomed to Hell, no matter what the reason.

He shook himself from his thoughts. "When your husband was convicted, do you know what happened?" He asked.

Eloise paled. "All I know, is that my husband was a good man and he was framed. He was a good person! He loved me with all his heart, and he *never* would have done anything like that."

"But he did." Max said, though not unkindly.

"That's what everyone believes." Eloise said, looking away. "If the three of you need anything, I'm here." Max took that as his cue to leave.

Max smiled apologetically, reaching for his phone to check the time. "Well, I'll leave you be. Once again, I'm very sorry for your loss, and so is Della and Porter." He said, standing.

"Tell them thank you." Eloise said, shaking his hand as she led him to the front door.

~ ~ ~

Max sat across from Della on her hospital bed, thanking his lucky shirt—his favorite blush pink one—that he had gotten out of Eloise's house in one piece. Della was lost in thought as he finished telling her everything that he had seen, while Porter was passed out in one of the teal armchairs in the corner, snoring softly.

"The only thing Ei don' get is why." Max said quietly as not to wake Porter.

"What do you mean?" Della asked. She flipped through Max's spell book, her eyes widening as she read something. "Abusive husband goes to jail for a crime he didn't commit, ruining all chance of Eloise having the happy life she wanted. Husband's brother tells her about this little thing called magic, Eloise finds a summoning spell, uses that to kidnap kids' blah, blah, blah, let's kill this psycho witch—"

"Well when ya put it like that." Max said, rolling his eyes. Della stuck her tongue out at him. "But what about the people that died before Theodore was convicted?"

Before Max, was the components of a special spell, something he was hoping he could use on Della. A black teddy bear, a jar of ashwagandha, a sachet of nutmeg, and a sprig of rosemary lay on the hospital bed.

"Maybe this isn't the first time Ellie has messed around with something she shouldn't have." Della smiled, winking at Max.

"Or maybe it's Jimmie." Max laughed as he opened the jar of ashwagandha. He wrinkled his nose, the room filled with a smell akin to horse sweat.

Della nodded to herself, itching to get back into the real world and help. "Thanks for going to speak with them."

"No problem." Max scoffed, taking a leaf from the jar, setting it ablaze. The ashes fell onto the teddy bear, making it shimmer.

"Seriously." Della insisted, her eyes scanning over another page in the book. "Hey, do you have a knife blessed with demon blood I could borrow?"

Max choked on his words, shaking his head. "I'm sorry, what?" He asked, setting the sprig of rosemary ablaze, letting the ashes seep into the teddy bear as he sprinkled it with nutmeg.

Della shut the book, tossing it aside. "Never mind." She sighed, her eyes lingering on Porter.

Max followed her gaze, giggling to himself. "You really like him, don' ya?" He asked, picking up a bright blue candle.

"Of course, I do." Della said. "But I can't have him."

That was *very* far from the answer Max was expecting. "Why not?" He inquired.

"You know how I never talk about my parents?" Della

asked. Max shrugged. "Well, it's because I didn't grow up like you guys."

"What? With a lovin' mother and father, a roof over yer head, food on yer plate, and loads of warm blankets? Wow, ya sure had it rough." Max said, his tone slightly too harsh.

Della scowled, returning her gaze to him. "*Loving* is a strong word." She began, clutching her knees to her chest. Suddenly, her face broke out into a smile. A cruel, capricious smile. "My mother, Kimi, taught me how to find beauty in everything. That there is light in even the darkest situations. But my father, he taught me that to love someone made you weak. That's obviously why he looked at me with that bubbling hatred in his eyes."

"Della, that's horrible. I never—"

"Oh, cry me a river, putty cat." Della said that unnerving smile still on her lips. "My older brother, Quincy, he may have been the social outcast, but at least he tried to make a life for himself. I'm just the disappointment." She chuckled to herself. "My daddy was a cruel man, one who taught his children that to love someone was something to be ashamed of. But thanks to him, thanks to me trying to impress him to get him to at least *pretend* to love me, I know cyanide smells like almonds, how to take apart a fifty-caliber, and that grown men flinch under the gaze of a girl like me."

"So that's why yer into everythin' yer into?" Max asked nervously. "Because of yer dad?"

Della nodded, pushing her hair behind her ear, fiddling with a piece of the teddy bear's matted fur. "He's a very Christian man, so I read the Bible inside and out. I would fill my vocabulary with verses to try and make him smile." Her smile darkened further. "That didn't work. So, I scrapped that and tried to up my grades. If I came home with a report card filled with 'A's,' then maybe he would be proud of me. He wasn't. He accused me of cheating. So then, I tried finding other ways to impress him. He always loved those cop shows, right? Loved watching people solve murders, so I thought maybe if I tried to solve a murder then, I would be as loved as those stupid buddy-cops. He didn't love me any more, in fact I think he ended up loving me less, but I found something to distract myself from the void in my heart. Yeah, I got into a lot of trouble, but I helped a lot of people. Or at least I *thought* I did."

Max stared at her, lost in thought. How could someone

treat their children like that? Sure, Mavericks was strict and at times overprotective, but he had received nothing but kindness from his adoptive father. Max had been nothing but a juvenile delinquent until Mavericks found him. Max could have broken into a thousand other cars that night, and a thousand other people could've caught him, but it had been Mavericks. Without him, he never would have met the two lovebirds he was now watching over. Max owed Mavericks his life, but his adopted father never asked for it.

"I know Porter is close to this. But I am too." She said quietly. Della pulled at her fingernails, opening and closing her mouth a couple times. When she spoke, her voice was broken in two. "Sometimes I stop and think that if it wasn't for him, would I be who I am? Would I have been a normal child, or would I still end up here? The only reason I believe in ghosts, is because I got trapped in an old house following some guy who was stealing from the tithes every Sunday. I saw things, Max, I swear to it." She shivered. "But would I have ever stepped foot in that house if Jasper Coleman wasn't the man he was?"

He shrugged. Max suddenly had the utmost respect for Della Coleman, the girl the world had wronged. She could be using the talents she had to hurt people. She could be the youngest mob boss in the world for all Max cared, but here she was, *solving* crimes. *Helping* people.

"Yer father sounds like an ass, and Ei hope that he can never wrong ya again." Max said with the sincerity of an old man who was promising his wife that he would love her forever.

Della's face reddened. "Well, that's enough of that. Carry on with the spell." She said, wiping away a single tear that she thought Max couldn't see.

"We love ya, Della, ya know, that right? Ya don' have to be ashamed of it." Max whispered, rolling his eyes as Porter grunted his approval even though he was asleep.

"I know." Della said, an air of finality to her words. The conversation was over, and it wasn't meant to be brought up ever again, that Max knew for sure.

He cleared his throat, holding the candle to his chest, his energy focused on the teddy bear. The wick on the candle sparked into a white flame. *"Eder bel hog ettskybes."* He whispered, opening one eye. The black plastic beads that made up the teddy bear's eyes glowed the same blue as the candle, the fur rippling with an unseen breeze. Max smiled to himself, shaking away the weakness he felt. He reached up and plucked a hair from Della's head, setting it ablaze and dropping it onto the bear. "*Ettskyles vil Delphee.*" The teddy bear's eyes stopped glowing.

"Did it work?" Della asked, taking the bear and holding it to her chest.

Max nodded. "It will grant you protection from nightmares. Hopefully." He said kindly.

"Thanks, Max." Della said quietly, gripping the bear as tightly as she could.

"No problem." He said, stretching. "I need the practice anyway."

They were silent for a minute, listening to Porter's snores and the echoes of the hospital; tiny beeps, the click-clack of footsteps, hushed voices. It was almost peaceful.

"Clara's husband called me." Della said out of the blue.

"When?"

"While you were gone. Clara didn't come home tonight; he was asking if I had seen her."

Max paled. He should've picked up on it earlier. "After he got ya flowers," He began, pointing at Porter, his voice barely a whisper. "He mentioned he had seen Clara and was acting really weird."

They stared at him, both thinking the exact same thing.

"He got bit." Della said, her voice shaking. Though she seemed scared, there was a hint of relief in her voice.

"Do you think he is turning?"

Slowly, she hopped off the hospital bed, setting the teddy bear aside, reaching into her book bag and pulling out a silver and gold flask with an intricate cross on it. Carefully, she made her way towards Porter, opening the flask and dropping water on him.

Nothing.

No sizzling, no burning, no smell of sulfur.

Max let go of the breath he'd been holding. "That was anticlimactic." He whispered.

~CHAPTER THIRTY-TWO~

The Future for An Ounce of Your Past

Della had never liked hospitals. Not because they cost too much, or she disagreed with the prescribed prescriptions, or the simple fact that nearly thirty-two people die in them a day. No, she hated hospitals because, like with many things, they make you think you know nothing about yourself or why you are the way you are. They take your clothes, tell you to put on a gown, and shove you full of morphine and someone else's blood. Ridiculous.

However, Della did quite enjoy hospital food. And she should know, this wasn't the first time she had to grace a place like this with her presence. Tripping down a flight of stairs and impaling yourself on a rusty piece of barb wire while hunting monsters was apparently something worthy a trip to the ER. Especially when you get tetanus. She may have to spend a week in the hospital, but at least she had free pudding and meatloaf galore.

She sighed, her hands in the pockets of her baggy gray sweatpants, squinting at a slice of cake behind the cold case in the empty cafeteria. Her tray was set out before her, adorned with two cups of *Jello* and a turkey sandwich. Technically, she didn't *need* the cake, but boy she *wanted* the cake. She shook her head, turning away.

"Self-control, Coleman, self-control." She whispered to

herself.

As she walked along the corridors, the smell of hand sanitizer and rubbing alcohol stinging her nose, a flash of a memory burned away at her brain.

She knew she was going to get hurt that day she fell down those stairs. She remembered having a dream about it. A very twisted vision, one where she kept on falling and falling down those stairs in that creepy old barn. She remembered telling her parents about it, remembered her *father* freaking out.

She shook away the memory, continuing back on to her room, nodding at the passing nurses.

"Miss Coleman?" A voice rang. Della turned to see the insufferable Dr. Whitcomb standing behind her. Clutching her tray until her knuckles turned white, she nodded, edging towards him. The hall was quiet, everyone going about their business in sorrow.

"What's up, doc?" She asked nervously, adding a smile.

"I wanted to talk to you away from your family." He smiled, nodding towards a nearby bench. "Sit for a while?"

She shrugged. Hospitals took away freedom. You couldn't even walk back to your room without getting cornered. Dr. Whitcomb stared at her, watching as she picked up her sandwich and began to eat. Who was he to stop her from having a crappy breakfast?

"Have you contacted your parents?" He asked. He was younger than you would expect, maybe in his thirties, his hair still brown, his eyes still full of life despite what he had seen.

"No, why?" Della asked, picking the lettuce off her sandwich.

He nodded to himself. "I was able to access your files from Sycamore Heights Regional. Well, what was left of them."

Della furrowed her eyebrows, studying him. "What do you mean?"

"Everything about you is gone, minus the fact that you were in the ER in April of two-thousand-and-seven. Do you know why you were there?" He asked, his eyebrow raised in suspicion.

"The only time I ever remember going to the ER was when I got tetanus, and that time I broke my elbow," Della said, absolutely confused.

"Your charts say you had a massive seizure in the middle of the night, screaming about something that was going to happen?" He asked, searching her eyes.

Della thought for a minute. There was a pinprick of pain in her forehead. She winced, thinking back. "Uh, yeah, I think I remember telling my parents that my grandma was going to die?"

Dr. Whitcomb nodded. "Do you remember being in the hospital for a month?"

"I don't remember anything other than my dad telling me to shut up and go back to sleep," Della admitted, rubbing her forehead. Her vision blurred for a moment.

"Is your grandmother dead?" Dr. Whitcomb asked.

"Yes, but—"

"When did she die?"

Della stared at him. What was he asking her? *Why* was he asking it? When she had talked to him before, after she had woken up, he seemed to be a pill-pushing ass who only cared about money. Now, he seemed concerned and caring, and honestly quite odd. She made to stand, but her legs wouldn't move.

"When did she die?" He repeated.

"Two-thousand-and-seven." She said, surprising herself.

"How did she die?"

That pain in her forehead was swelling. She blinked, trying to clear her vision. The room was swirling. "She had a heart attack." She said quietly.

"How did she die in your dream?" Dr. Whitcomb's eyes were so lifeless, so empty as he spoke.

Della inhaled sharply, staring him down.

"How did she die in your dream?" He repeated, his tone angry. He reached out and shook her, his hands feeling ice-cold, even through her t-shirt.

"Uh, she—" She tried to pull away but couldn't move. "—she was in the garden at her house, talking to my grandpa, and she started to feel weird. All the birds started turning into crows. Eight of them. She clutched her chest and died." She said, her voice hoarse with tears.

"And you saw it. You could've stopped it. You could've saved her, could've saved Theodore." Dr. Whitcomb whispered, clutching her arms tighter and tighter.

"What are you—" Della began, tears streaming down her face. Suddenly, he let go of her and stood, leaving her to sit in a blubbering puddle of her own tears and confusion.

Her breathing was fast, her chest feeling tight. Quickly, she gathered her lunch tray and stood, making her way back to her room to find Max and Porter. Tears streaming down her face, she rounded a corner, walking straight into Porter, sending her lunch tray to the floor.

"Oops, sorry," Porter said, launching to the floor to pick up the cups of Jello and the remnants of her sandwich.

Della said nothing. She was too busy staring at Dr. Whitcomb, who was standing at the end of a dead-end hallway, in deep conversation. He had walked in the other direction. There was no way he could have gotten there. Unless, of course, the person she had just talked to hadn't been Dr. Whitcomb at all.

"We wondered where you had gotten off—" Porter began, looking up at her face. "You okay?" He asked, discarding the mess on the floor, slowly standing back up.

All she could do was nod.

Porter placed a gentle hand on her shoulder, following her gaze. "What?"

"I saw. . ." She swallowed hard, reaching up to rub her temples, pressure building up in the side of her head. "Never mind." She whispered, feeling her legs give out. Porter caught her, pushing back up.

He looked back and forth between her eyes, searching them. She noticed, with some concern, that his hands weren't cold like the fake Dr. Whitcomb's had been. Maybe it was nothing, but Porter looked more *real* to her too. Like she was seeing clearly for the first time.

"You okay?" He asked, his voice shaking.

"I don't know." She said shakily. "I think I need to lay down." She whispered, wobbling on the spot.

Porter squeezed her shoulders, his face full of alarm, though he was desperately trying to hide it. "Yeah, maybe that's for the best." He whispered back, leading her back to her room.

~ ~ ~

"Ya know damn well we have to talk to him." Max hissed.

"No, we don't! I know Steiniger, okay? He's a good man, he wouldn't do anything like this!" Porter hissed back. "And for

God's sake, keep your voice down!"

Max rolled his eyes. "Ei betcha if we wake her up, she'll agree."

"Let her sleep!" Porter whispered, angrily tying his shoes. "I'll go talk to him, okay?"

"Not alone."

"I don't want to leave *her* alone." Porter hissed, his worried eyes on Della. She had fallen asleep not long after he got her back to her room. Her sleeping features were screwed up in fear, a thin line of sweat on her forehead.

"Ei don' either, but there's nothin' we can do," Max whispered.

"Can't you cast a spell? Something to help her?" Porter pleaded.

"Right, right, let's ask the guy who set her on fire to try and heal her!" He whisper-yelled, gesturing dramatically. "Ei did the best Ei could, all right? Even *Mavericks*, the man who fixed yer broken nose twenty times a week, can' help her."

Porter squeezed his eyes shut, pinching his nose. No words could express the worry he felt in the pit of his stomach. "You could stay with her." He said after a minute of wallowing.

"Absolutely not, if anyone is stayin', it'll be *you*." Max hissed, struggling to articulate that last word.

Porter stood. "No, I can't sit here and watch her like this. I have to help; I have to do something."

"Then we have to go together. If somethin' happens to ya, she'll kill me. Probably slowly, probably with like, acid or something and probably when Ei least expect it." Max said, shriveling up his nose as he stared at her.

Porter sighed heavily, ripping his jacket from the back of his chair, angrily pulling it on. "Fine." He mumbled, stepping past him. "Let's just hurry it up, alright?"

~CHAPTER THIRTY-THREE~

"She'll be fine. Mavericks is watchin' over her." Max said, his eyes bearing into Porter's back. Porter nodded. "If something happens to her, they'll call." Porter nodded. "If things get worse, Mavericks will—Ei don' know. . . He'll look away as ya kill all the nurses." Max laughed nervously.

"Can we just shut up about it? Please?" Porter hissed.

Max nodded, stuffing his hands in his pockets.

The boys made their way through the woods, their footsteps echoing through the trees. Steiniger was out on the job, looking over the crime scene where the Chapman's had been found. The footpath was littered with fresh footsteps, the brush cut away to make room for gurneys. Even the birds were silently watching, terrified of what they had seen not three days ago.

"Heyo, boys!" Steiniger said, startling his entire crew as the two of them entered the clearing.

"Hey, Eric," Max called. Whenever Porter had skipped school, Max had come with, and Eric took them both out for ice cream. Porter was hoping that Max would hold onto those memories rather than jumping to conclusions.

Steiniger beckoned them over. "What're we thinking?" He asked, showing them the mutilated tent before them like it was a prize on some sick game show.

Max wrinkled his nose, gagging at the bloody scene. "Ei

think Ei'm going to be sick." He whispered, using his sleeve to try and staunch the smell.

Steiniger laughed. His eyes were glossy, and he smelled of smoke. Porter rolled his eyes, walking around the tent. Gashes the size of baseball bats lined the bright yellow nylon, the fabric flapping in the wind like a surrender flag. Clothes and cutlery lined the scene. That definitely wasn't strawberry syrup smeared all over them.

"Victims torn to shreds, right?" Porter asked, kneeling to look inside the tent.

Steiniger nodded, crossing by Max to stand over him, handing over a pair of gloves to each of them. "If it wasn't for Jacobson running the teeth, we wouldn't have known who they were."

"Jacobson? He actually did his job right? Wow, I've missed quite a bit in three days." Porter said dryly, pulling the tent open, the smell of sulfur stinging his nose. Bloody green scales were stuck under the sleeping bags.

"Ei'm gonna throw up," Max said again. Porter glanced at him. He was looking awfully green.

"Just don't get it on the evidence." Steiniger laughed.

"Who found them?" Porter asked. Very rarely did anyone come out camping this far. The Chapman's had been adventurous, but Porter couldn't name another soul that would be out here.

Steiniger was silent. Max gave Porter a very judgmental look behind his back.

"Did you find them?" Porter asked, shooting Max a warning look.

Steiniger cleared his throat. "The weather has been getting worse and worse. I wanted to get one last jog in before it started to storm." He said.

Porter stared at him. "Really? How was that?" He asked, standing.

Steiniger locked eyes with him. He was smiling, but it wasn't his usual, happy-go-lucky smile. "Fine. I've been coming out here to smoke." He said heavily. "Not just cigars anymore. Stronger stuff."

Porter squinted at him, looking over every inch of him. He was lying. Blatantly lying to the person he loved most. Porter's heart broke. Max raised an eyebrow.

"Don't make me take you to rehab." Was all Porter could

say.

"Don't make me sing."

"Oh, Hell no, please." Max hissed, faking a laugh. Porter forced a smile.

"Well, I'll see you boys around then," Steiniger said, a hopeful smile on his face.

Porter was biting his tongue the best he could. He wanted nothing more than to rip Steiniger a new one, tear the truth out of him like the Grunches had torn apart the Chapman's, but he couldn't. Something deep in his brain was stopping him from doing so.

"Everything alright, boy?" Steiniger asked, his tone dark.

"Yeah, Eric, I'm good. Just a little torn up about everything." Porter lied. It was a pretty damn good lie too. Obviously, he hadn't learned how to lie from Steiniger.

"Good," Steiniger said, placing his arms behind his back.

Tears stung at Porter's eyes. He nodded to himself, stepping past Steiniger, gripping Max by the elbow and pulling him away.

"Ei'm sorry," Max said when they were out of earshot.

Porter shook his head, quickening his pace. "This doesn't prove anything; he could be lying about a thousand other things. This is just a—a—a coincidence." He snarled, not meeting Max's eyes.

"Okay," Max replied. "Okay, we will go with that. Ei just—He has seen what ya are like, seen how ya grew up. If it's not Eloise, then it would be him, Porter. Thats the only other option. I just want ya to be prepared for the—"

Porter stopped dead in his tracks, his arm searing with pain. He closed his eyes against the pain, filled with rage. "Shut up, okay?! It isn't Steiniger!" He roared.

Max stopped next to him, his eyes full of fear. "Okay, geez, Ei'm just sayin' that we have to look at all our options." He said, putting his hands up in defense.

The pain in his arm was burning, his veins rippling with heat. Porter squeezed his arm as tight as he could, trying to stop the pain. "You don't get it, do you? You have been given *everything* your *entire life.* You live with the richest man in town, someone who loves you more than he loves breathing. He buys you anything and everything you want or need and gave you a job in his *stupid* little law firm." Porter spat.

Max opened and closed his mouth a couple times, staring down Porter in mad confusion. "Okay, what's up with ya?" He demanded, taking a step towards him.

Porter recoiled, putting his hands through his hair. "Steiniger was the only person who ever made me feel like I belonged in this world. Without him, I'd be dead."

"Well, look here, mate, now ya've got Della and me. If ya lose him, it won' be the end of the world. Not this time."

"Yeah? What happens when I screw things up again? You going to leave me? What would've happened if Della had died, Max? Would you be standing here?" He asked, pointing an accusing finger at him.

"*Me*?! Ei didn't leave ya, ya left me. *Yer* the one who dropped out. *Yer* the one who stopped talking to me." Max hissed. "Ya need to stop being so damn codependent all the friggin time!"

"I dropped out so I wouldn't end up in jail, Max. I called you, I tried to make up for everything I did, and you ignored me." Porter hissed, shoving him backward a couple steps.

Max shook his head angrily. "Ei swear, *you* and Della. Ei didn' sign up to fix ya guys, okay? Stow yer shit, and quit takin' out all yer anger on me."

Porter swung his fist at Max's face, but Max was too quick. He dodged out of the way, grabbed Porter's arm, and pinned him up against a tree. He bit his tongue as best he could, scowling deeply.

"Ei know yer scared," He began, panting with the effort it took to keep him pinned. "But everythin' is gonna to work out in the end. She is gonna to be okay, we all will be."

Porter rested his forehead on the tree before him, shoving Max away. Max was right. He *was* scared, terrified even, of his world crashing down around him. He clenched his fists, trying to push down the anger and block it out. He didn't know what was coming over him lately. It wasn't like him to lash out like this or lose time. Wasn't like him to speak his mind.

"I'm sorry." He said shakily, pushing away from the tree, turning to face Max.

"It's fine, Ei guess," Max said sourly. "Let's just get back to Della, all right?"

Porter nodded, rubbing at his arm. It hurt like Hell. Every time he touched it, it got worse; the anger, the pain, the heat traveling through his body. He was sick to his stomach, feeling like something was wrong with him.

"Hey, Max?" He said, a ringing picking up in his ears.

"What now?" Max hissed, throwing his hands up into the air.

Porter pulled up his sleeve, tearing at the bandages on his arm. The skin around the bite mark was turning a grisly shade of green, flaking away like scales. The veins around the mark were twisting and moving like something was swimming around inside his bloodstream.

"What the bloody Hell?" Max whispered, briskly walking forward, grabbing Porter's arm and examining the bite.

Porter blinked a couple times, the rage he felt cementing in his chest. "I feel like I'm going to pass out."

"Okay, maybe don' do that," Max said, grabbing his shoulder to keep him from toppling over.

"Let's get out of here." Porter said weakly, leaning on Max for support.

~CHAPTER THIRTY-FOUR~

"We could try to exorcise it." Max proposed, showing Della the horror that was the bite mark on Porter's arm.

Della thought, shrugging. "He's not possessed, he's transforming. . . At least I think he is."

"You talk about me like I'm not here." Porter said, staring between them, a satisfied little grin pulling at his pale lips as Della poured Holy Water over his arm. He winced, watching his skin sizzle and steam.

"That didn' happen last time. . . Definitely demonic." Max said, ignoring him, using a magnifying glass that neither Della nor Porter knew how he got, to look over the wound. "How are ya feeling?"

"Better, I guess. Don't wanna kill anyone right now." Porter smiled. Della and Max paled. "I kid." He assured them. Della knew it was only half a lie.

"Well, until we figure out how to fix you, you need to stay put in your room, at your house." Della said, crossing her arms over her chest, staring him dead in the eyes.

"Ei love how ya were out cold, but yer still reignin' strong in your dictatorship." Max said sourly.

"Every Queen needs to know how to bounce back after a battle." Della sang.

Porter shook his head, laughing. "Well, this stable boy is happy you're feeling better. You friggin scared me—er—*us*." He said, his tone darkening.

Max nodded, flipping through his spell book, shooting Della a look out of the corner of his eye. "If ya die, we all die." He said dryly.

Porter nodded. "Which is why we want you to hang back. Let Max and I figure this all out. You can stay on the sidelines, telling us how to kill the monster, and we can get rid of it."

Della shook her head. The thought of them splitting up sent a wave of nerves through her. "If we do this, we do it together." She said sternly, looking at Max for help.

"We will. Just because ya aren' in the line of fire, doesn' mean ya aren' a valuable player." Max smiled, nudging her in the side.

She wanted so badly to tell them that she had seen Dr. Whitcomb, tell them how bad of an idea this was, tell them that she *needed* to be in the line of fire. But she couldn't. There were no words to explain what she was feeling. So, all she did was nod.

If there was one thing Delphee Chrysanthemum Coleman was afraid of, it was being seen as crazy, especially by the people she loved most. She had never cared what people thought of the way she dressed, or why her hair was the color it was, but she did care about how her loved ones viewed her. If she was crazy to them, then what was she to the rest of the world?

She'd be nothing but a sad case of insanity.

And Della hated that word.

~ ~ ~

Max spent the next few days pacing back and forth in Della's hospital room, nose to his spell book, trying to find a way to fix Porter. Nothing so far. The only thing that was working was wrapping the bite in towels soaked in Holy Water. Porter said the pain was unimaginable, but at least he was in control over his mind.

Something Della could not relate to.

Minus the mysterious hallucination of Dr. Whitcomb, she hadn't seen anything in her waking life, but her dreams were plagued with visions of the zombie-like Porter and the missing kids. Soon, it was too much to fall asleep. It was either she stayed up all night, then slept in the mornings when her mind was too exhausted, or she listened to podcasts meant to put you in a trance.

The boys wouldn't approve, but they had other things to worry about.

To ensure that Porter was safe, and that he couldn't hurt anyone, he was forced to be locked up in his room with a 'high fever.' It wasn't an ideal situation, but at least it meant Crystal would be fawning all over her 'sick' son, leaving no room for Jed to come and bother him.

Della was terrified something would happen to him. If something happened to him, she would never be able to forgive herself. Max promised to keep an eye on him, but what could he do to protect him? Every time he practiced spells, they backfired or simply didn't work. The only thing that kept her from losing her cool was the fact that Porter had promised to wear the necklace Nicoletta had made him wherever he went.

At the same time, Porter and Max had strictly forbidden Della to leave her house without their knowledge or permission. Dr. Whitcomb had sent her home with new pain medication—one that was free of poisonous flowers and herbs—though Della was keen on not taking it. Yes, she was shaky. Yes, she kept running a high fever. Yes, she felt like she might as well be dying, but at least she could stand up and walk across the room without toppling over.

Both Dr. Whitcomb and Mavericks had told the boys to keep a close eye on her. When Max wasn't at the library, Garroway Mortuary, or The Courier, he followed her around everywhere she went, holding open doors, carrying her bags, and doing little things Della was perfectly capable of doing. Not to mention that Porter texted her every ten minutes to check up on her.

Of course, in their eyes, they weren't being helicopter parents at all. No, in their eyes, they were being *sweet* and *endearing.*

As soon as she was released from the hospital, Della had taken advantage of the 'freedom' she now had. She didn't do much, but she could at least exercise a little self-care. At least she could *fake* being happy. Pretending to be numb was better than wallowing in self-pity and grief.

Much to her chagrin, the boys had done as much re-search on the current suspects as they could, reporting to Della every time they found something new.

Just like her husband, Eloise had a clean record. Her coworkers spoke highly of her, saying that she wouldn't even hurt a fly. Jimmie had a couple parking tickets and a DUI, but other than that, he was clean too. Steiniger was still a mystery, the only thing tying him to this whole thing was his friendship with the Heiser's and how he had been the one to lock Theo-dore away. And of course, Porter. . . Still, there was something off about him. Not to mention he had been avoiding Porter's calls, cementing Della and Max's worry. Porter was still sure he had nothing to do with any of this, but what did he know? He could be being controlled to think that way.

Not that it made any difference to Della or the boys. They trusted their own instincts more than they trusted any-one else.

Which was why Della was making a very irrational deci-sion early Saturday morning.

Today had been the only day all week the boys had let her be. Max was at Porter's, checking up on him and making sure Jed hadn't done anything to cause him to flee, and they were distracting themselves famously.

Being alone made her feel very free, a little too free Porter would say, but then again, he wasn't here. She smiled widely as she hopped off the stairs, marching towards the door of Ambrose Apartments, an idea brewing in her mind.

"Heading out, Miss Coleman?" Richie asked from his customary position at the front desk of Ambrose Apartments.

Book-bag slung over her shoulder, an actual pair of clean clothes on, her makeup done up nicely, she nodded. "Mind telling the boys if they show up?"

Richie shrugged, kicking his feet up on the counter. "Yup. Where you heading off to?" He asked, blowing his hair out of his eyes.

Della hesitated. "Mrs. Heiser's house." She said finally.

Itching for adventure, she knew she was recklessly jumping at any lead that fell into her lap. However, they were at a point of stagnation, and they needed more information. She had a feeling today would prove her theories one way or another.

In her eyes, Max hadn't been the most reliable source

of information, due to the fact his place in this team-up was to be the fiery arsenal. Maybe Eloise would have somewhat of the same mindset? Unquestionably, she'd believe that Max hadn't done a good enough job taking notes, and Della had to clear some things up?

Richie yawned, giving her a thumbs up. "Sounds good, just don't come back on a stretcher. Garroway will kill me." He said, an ounce of fear in his empty eyes.

Della nodded, sweeping out the front doors. She hadn't been this nervous since that time back in seventh grade when she snuck into the school to recount all the votes for class president. Guess who had been right about the fact that the English teacher purposefully miscounted?

~ ~ ~

Della knocked several times on Mrs. Heiser's door, cautiously eyeing her surroundings for any signs of snooping passers-by. She didn't want a repeat of what happened at the Dixon's house. Della knocked again, satisfied by the lack of people walking their dogs. No answer.

She had one of two options; she could go home, order a pizza, watch a movie, and act like everything was under control, or she could break into a house. Option one would have been the superior choice if it wasn't for the anger that Della had been trying to hide all week.

There was one thing about this whole situation that was bothering her; what was the point in killing Theodore? From what she gathered from him, Theodore and Eloise had been happy back then, so what had changed? Surely Theodore hadn't been as abusive as the parents of the missing kids? And what of Jimmie? He seemed as out of the loop as anyone. He barely seemed to care about the abused kids.

She sighed, looking over her shoulder one more time as she pulled on a pair of latex gloves and wiggled a bobby pin from her hair.

"Not like I haven't done it before." She whispered to the garden gnomes staring at her, shoving the sparkly purple bobby pin into the lock. The longer she looked at them, it seemed like their faces were melting into judgmental scowls. She remembered feeling that same way about a painting in her parents' bedroom many years ago.

The door unlocked much easier than it had back at the Dixon's, and as far as Della could tell, Mrs. Heiser had no cameras or security alarms. Something she wished she would have checked for on that fateful day this mystery truly began. Porter still hadn't told her exactly who or how someone caught her sneaking around. She had been positive she was alone.

"Mrs. Heiser?" Della called to the empty house, her heart beating so loudly, it echoed throughout the house. No answer. She released the breath she had been holding, shutting the door behind her and walking throughout the house.

The house was just as Max had described, almost entirely bare. She shrugged that little point away, making her way through the hallway, careful not to trip on any boxes.

Della's goal here was to find the spell book, an altar, a stone with an odd marking—something that could tie Eloise back to summoning the Grunches.

Della made her way towards the open door at the end of the hallway, which she assumed was the bedroom. This seemed to be the only room the old woman hadn't packed up. The bed was made, the walls decorated with painted canvases full of cherry blossoms, jewelry was littering the dresser, and a book was even laying on the nightstand. Too bad it was a self-help book and not a spell book.

Closing the door behind her, Della began looking through everything, leaving no metaphorical stone unturned.

"If I had a spell book I was trying to hide, where would I put it?" Della asked as she opened Eloise's dresser. Strangely, the dresser was empty. Della checked the nightstand. Same thing.

Maybe it was just her, but Della would've begun unpacking to try and distract herself from the fact that her wrongfully accused husband had died. There'd be no need to move anymore. Unless, of course, Eloise was planning to move for an entirely different reason.

Turning away from the dresser, Della threw open the doors to the closet, expecting to find some evil altar with pictures of the missing kids and their families taped to it, but of course, it was empty. Della swore, examining the room. Everything else was untouched, where were all of Eloise's clothes? Surely, they couldn't be packed up?

Just as she was going to check the living room, she heard the front door click open. She swore by accident, covering her mouth. If Della could hear the door, then whoever had come in could hear her.

She panicked, looking for an escape route. There wasn't a window in Eloise's room, the only way out would be the way she came in. There was nowhere to run.

Della dropped to the floor, hoping her skinny body would fit underneath the bed, thinking that maybe she could slip out if she heard Eloise go into the bathroom. As she tried to crawl underneath it, her head collided with the sharp corner of something shoved between the box springs.

A book.

Della reached up to touch it when the bedroom door opened. Eloise screamed, dropping her purse to the floor. Startled, Della hit her head on the bed as she crawled out from underneath it. Her vision sparkled with flecks of orange for a minute as she crawled out from underneath the bed.

"WHAT THE *HELL* ARE YOU DOING IN MY HOUSE?!" Eloise screamed, snatching her bag up off the floor and taking out her phone, dialing nine-one-one.

Della jumped up off the floor, slightly dizzy from hitting her head. Was it just her, or did everything in the room suddenly have an odd glow to it?

"I'm sorry, Mrs. Heiser, the door was unlocked. I thought you were in danger." Della stammered, putting her hands up in defense.

Eloise ignored her, turning away and speaking with the first responder on the other end of her call. "Yes, there has been a break-in. The perp is still in the house, send help immediately, she's armed."

"I'm not—" Della began defensively, but she understood immediately. It wouldn't matter to the police if Eloise was lying. Who would take the strange outsider's word over the beloved school counselor?

Eloise hung up on the first responder, turning back to Della. She didn't have a vengeful look on her face like Della thought she would. She looked terrified, like how Jimmie had been when she tried to ask him about what was going on.

"Please don't hurt me." Eloise cried.

"I'm not going to hurt you, I swear. I thought you were in danger. With everything that has happened with Theo—" Eloise scowled. "*With your husband*, I thought something might happen to you." Della said. For once in Della's life, her lie sounded like a lie. She didn't know whether to be proud of that or scared she was losing her edge.

"My door was *not* unlocked." Eloise said sternly, pointing her phone at Della like a taser. She held her other hand behind her back, but Della could see her wiggling her fingers. Eloise glanced down at the bed the same time Della did, hearing a small squeaking noise. Like springs moving.

Della stepped in front of the bed, blocking it from Eloise's sight. Yes, everything was definitely glowing. Della's hand shot up to her forehead, her head filled with a dull pain, just as the lamp on the nightstand next to her began to shake.

"All right," She choked, realizing she wasn't going to get anywhere with Eloise, and scared of what might happen if she were to keel over before her. "The door wasn't unlocked, but I was still worried about you. Theodore was my friend." Della said, real tears welling up in her eyes. "I'll leave, okay?"

Eloise shook her head. "I didn't like you the minute we met; I knew you were trouble." She spat.

Della looked around, wishing she had just stayed home. She heard something cracking, the mirror above the dresser slowly breaking. Eloise looked at the mirror, looking as if she was wondering the same thing Della was; *Am I doing that?*

"The police will be here quicker than you can blink, there's no point in trying to run, I know your name and Jimmie has your card." Eloise said shakily.

Della sighed heavily as the sound of sirens filled her ears. She swore, nodding to herself. She'd have to add this to the list of the most stupid things she had ever done.

~CHAPTER THIRTY-FIVE~

The Curious Case of Della Coleman

"**S**o, what should I do with her?" Steiniger asked, following Porter's gaze, his worried eyes tracing the form of the girl he loved through the dark window.

"I don't know." Porter said. His voice was calm, but Steiniger knew better. Every syllable was tainted with anger.

"Scare her? Threaten her with a night in jail, or sympathize?" Steiniger continued, scratching his chin, smiling to himself. Porter glanced at him, giving him a questioning look. Steiniger shrugged.

Porter pinched the bridge of his nose, fury flooding through him. He threw his hands up in the air. "I don't know, Eric. I'm at my wits end with this one. I mean, I think I figure her out, then she does something stupid like this." Porter said, shoving his hands towards the window.

Steiniger whistled. "Take it easy, will you? You're giving me anxiety."

Porter whipped his head around, his eyes flashing a dangerous shade of pure gold. "You are a washed-up old seadog. Anxiety is kind of your thing." He snapped. His breaths were short, his arm aching.

Steiniger stared him down, his eyebrows furrowed. Concern was written all over his face. "Porter, is everything all right? At home?" He asked.

"Yes, why?" Porter asked exasperatedly.

"You seem off." Steiniger scowled, reaching out for Porter's arms, pulling up his sleeves to check his wrists for cuts. Nothing.

Porter ripped his wrists away, crossing his arms and staring back out the window. "One minute, this chick is a happy little *shit*; the next, she is a brooding mess of idiocy. All I want to do is help, but somehow that is a crime to her."

"Sounds like she causes you a lot of pain." Steiniger whispered, an odd tone to his voice. Porter gave him a questioning look which he returned with a smile. "Have you tried, oh, I don't know, *talking to her*?" Steiniger scoffed.

"No one likes a clever clog, Eric." Porter said darkly.

"Call me by my first name one more time, and I will show you a clever clog." Steiniger said, though he smiled.

~ ~ ~

Della sat in the police station, wishing the ibuprofen the Chief had given her would kick in.

I'd never been sentenced for all the things I did back in Sycamore Heights, why would here be any different? She tried to tell herself. Surely, she could charm her way out of this situation like always. But if she was honest, she had her doubts.

Although she did have to hand it to this strange little town. Sycamore Heights hadn't been this fancy. She'd never even seen the inside of a Sycamore Heights Police Department jail cell, all she ever got back there was a couple rides around in a police car and a lecture. Here she got handcuffs.

How flattering.

She chuckled darkly to herself, full of worry. Her own sarcasm wasn't even helping her.

"I'm going to ask you again, Miss Coleman, why did you break into Mrs. Heiser's house?" Chief Steiniger asked. He was not at all as she had expected. He had a kind aura to him, but most serial killers did. That's why they were so great at their jobs.

Della sat, hands crossed in front of her, in a room with a one-way mirror, a tiny smile pulling at the corners of her lips. *Come on, you can do this.* She thought.

"You going to talk to me, or do I have to start reading your file?" Steiniger asked, glancing at the one-way mirror.

"Go right ahead, copper." Della smiled. Yes, that was the tone that had gotten her out of so many sticky situations. *That* was the Della she needed to be right now. The Della that wasn't scared, the Della that didn't care.

Steiniger tapped the stack of papers he held in his hands on the table between them, eyeing Della with great curiosity. He pushed up the thin bifocals on his oily nose, squinting through the lenses.

"Twice arrested for vandalism—" He began.

"My principal's car and the old mayor's parade float." Della interjected. One of those things she had done to try and impress her father.

"Yes." Steiniger said.

The way he was looking at her unsettled her. Halfway between a grimace and a look of satisfaction. Like that time her father found her digging in the backyard at two in the morning. He was both disgusted but enjoying the fact she was going to be in trouble.

Steiniger cleared his throat, continuing on. "Warned several times about freedom of speech and how *not* to use it, you've got many accounts of breaking and entering, but of course, you were only ten back then." He said, looking at her for approval, making sure he had his facts right.

Della nodded, saluting him. "I've always had trouble with abiding by authority." Something deep inside her finally clicked when she heard herself say that, something that told her she needed to float back down off her cloud of recklessness. Of course, she ignored it. When had regret, remorse, and repentance ever helped anyone?

"I can see that. Says here you stole your father's car the same night you held a cheating man at pepper spray point." Steiniger said. Was that a smile playing across his lips?

"Same month I got paid two hundred bucks." Della said, nodding approvingly at her own actions.

Steiniger stared at Della for a long while. He seemed very disappointed in her. "Miss Coleman, you do realize you could be going to jail for this, right?" He asked finally, a smile on his lips.

Della nodded coolly. Deep down inside, she imagined a tiny version of herself running around, banging on her brain, wondering how the Hell she had got herself into this sort of situation. The angel on her shoulder had flown out of its grave and was now screaming in her ear, telling her she was a horri-ble, *horrible* person.

Steiniger removed his glasses and set them on the table. "I know a bad kid when I see one. Obviously, you ain't one of them. The only thing is," He began, handing her over her own files to look over. Della was delighted to see her nine-year-old self staring up at her in a picture akin to a mugshot. Steiniger was watching her as she sat there smiling. "The facts are against you. You are eighteen. It's time to start growing up. Next time something like this happens, you are going to get a proper punishment."

Della furrowed her eyebrows. "Next time?" She asked, an ounce of relief flooding over onto her facial features.

Steiniger sat back in his chair. "Someone who is far angrier with you than I am has vouched for you, and I trust his word."

Della swore as the door to her left opened, revealing a furious Porter. She had sincerely thought he wouldn't be here, hoping that Mavericks would be the one to walk through that door. Her face reddened, though she tried to hide it.

"Think she learned her lesson?" Porter asked angrily, though he was trying very hard to keep his tone light.

"Probably not." Steiniger said, returning his bifocals to his face. "You have it handled, or do I need to keep her over-night?" The way they looked at each other made her think this had been rehearsed.

"A night in jail would do her some good," Porter began. Della's heart sank. She was exhausted from her first day back on the job and she desperately wanted to be home. Porter stared at her, shaking his head. Then it hit her. No, her heart hadn't sunk because she didn't want to be here, her heart sank because he was disappointed in her. "But then again, she'd be eaten alive." Porter finished.

Steiniger nodded, walking over to unlock Della's hand-cuffs and take back her file. Della stood. Porter's eyes bore into her like lasers, just as deadly and just as penetrating. She smiled awkwardly, playing with a loose strand of hair. She was dead. So very dead. Her heart skipped a beat as Porter held the door open for her. She could practically see the steam blowing out of his nose and ears.

"Thanks, Eric." Porter said.

Steiniger nodded, pushing Della out the door.

The anger flowing off Porter was enough to keep Della from trying to smooth things over. All eyes were on them as they walked out of the police station, Della cowering behind Porter's massive form. When they were finally outside, he stopped, causing her to walk into him.

Despite the obvious, today had been pretty great. Today was a day full of sweet reminiscence, too bad those memories were about to be shot down.

"You know, I'm not even sure why I'm mad at you. Am I mad because you got caught, or am I mad you went there in the first place?" He snapped, trying to contain himself, rounding on her.

"Can we just not be mad? Because I found the book under Eloise's bed." Della said with a smile.

"I swear, I don't believe you sometimes." Porter said in disbelief. "Do you think I care about that? Do you realize how *friggin pissed* I am with you right now? Della, what if she kept the spell book on her and she killed you? You *promised* Max and me that you wouldn't do anything stupid! Why the Hell did you go after her like that?" He yelled.

Della stared at her feet, shrugging, feeling like a child. "I had an idea, and I just—I wanted to—"

"I don't care!" Porter screamed. "You could have at least called us! At least had the courtesy to communicate your absolute stupidity! It's like you don't even care what happens anymore."

Della nodded in agreement. "I can see why you might be swayed to believe that." She said quietly.

Porter shook his head, his hands on his hips. "Are you okay?" He breathed.

She stared at him for a minute before forcing herself to laugh loudly. "I've never felt better." She lied.

"That's why I'm worried." Porter said, reaching for Della's hands. "Your handling things *awfully* well since the last time we talked about—" He swept his hand through the air at a loss for words. "—everything."

Della shrugged. "I can't be optimistic?"

"*Not when your entire being is based on pessimism.*" Porter said hysterically.

Della rolled her eyes. "I was tired of being benched! How is that a crime? I wanted out of the house." She so desperately wanted him to stop talking. She was terrified of what might happen if she lost control of her emotions. What if she hurt him?

"It's a crime when you are acting recklessly." Porter hissed.

"I just want to go home." Della sighed weakly, rubbing her temples.

Porter pinched his nose, one hand on his hip, looking like a disappointed schoolteacher. "Not until you tell me what's going on with you. You've been acting off ever since you got out of the hospital, and I want to know why."

"I don't know, okay? I feel like everything I do screws everything up. I feel like this whole giant mess is on me, and I don't know how to handle it." Della blurted out, stomping her foot on the pavement. Tiny bolts of pain burst through her veins.

Porter stared at her, his mouth hanging open. Della clutched her arms around herself, wanting this whole conversation to be over.

"It's not on you. There are three of us in this mess, you do realize that, don't you? You're the one who keeps saying we have to fix this as a team. It's Pluto, Mars, and Venus, or whatever Max likes to call us. Three." He said softly yet sternly.

Della turned away, running her hands through her hair repeatedly. "I just want to go home, okay?" She said, her voice shaking.

Porter shook his head angrily. "Not until we fix this."

"There is nothing to fix." Della said, turning back around to stare him down.

"You have eighteen years of crap to unpack Della. Don't shoot the messenger, but I'm pretty sure there is *a lot* to fix." Porter hissed. "Out of everyone in the world, I am the *one* person who will understand whatever is going on in that crazy, beautiful, mind of yours. I get it, okay? You and I are two troubled souls with daddy issues. I opened up to you, now you have to do that for me."

Della shoved her hands in her pockets, staring at the ground. "I'm not ready to open up." She said, her voice ringing throughout the night. Every syllable was a firecracker.

"You sure open up to Max." Porter said.

"Oh, screw you!" Della said, turning to walk away. She could see the nearest bus stop glowing in the distance. "Screw him too! He couldn't even keep his mouth shut if it would save the world!" She called over her shoulder.

Porter's footsteps came running after, stopping her by the shoulders before she could get any farther. His face was red, his green eyes full of tears.

"Do you have *any* idea how much it hurts me seeing you like this?" He whispered.

"Shut up! Just stop talking to me! I'm trying to make a dramatic exit!" She screamed in his face. "You had your chance to run after me and fix things back at that stupid crab-shack! You had a chance to tell me that you love me, had the chance to—"

He pressed his lips against hers, pulling her close to him by the waist. Every fiber of her being wanted to pull away and slap him, kick him between the legs, ram his face into her knee and run. But she didn't. She let him hold her there, reveling in the taste of his lips. It seemed Porter had a thing for root beer flavored lip balm.

He pulled away for a moment, his shaking hand coming up to brush her hair from her face. "See what I mean? Shuts you up every time." He whispered, a sad little smile pulling at his lips—which were now covered in her sparkly black lip gloss. "I do love you, Della. You have no idea how much I love you."

His thumb traced the edges of her face, catching the stream of tears that were overflowing from her eyes. A pain in her chest that she never, ever, realized was there, suddenly disappeared, sending a wave of exhaustion through her.

It was a common thing. A girl's life changes when she meets a boy. Some would say it was an overused storyline that made women into objects. Up until now, Della would have agreed. Others would call it romantic. Porter would think that. He probably *was* thinking that.

She melted into him, pressing her lips back onto his, her salty tears mixing with the taste of his lip balm. Porter wove his hands through her hair, holding her gently. His hand traveled to her cheek, tracing her features like he was a sculptor. She went to wrap her arms around him, when suddenly, he jumped away, clutching at his arm, turning away from her.

"Porter?" She asked, wiping away her tears.

He straightened, shaking his head. "I'm fine." He choked out, his shoulders rippling like they always did. Della reached out for him, but he pulled away. "It's okay, I'm okay." He said, turning back to her, rubbing his eyes.

Della was so utterly confused about what had just happened. She had experienced every known emotion in less than ten minutes.

Porter finally looked at her, his eyes a little less colorful than they usually were. "What?" He asked.

"We going home now?" Was all she could say.

"At least buy me dinner first." Porter smiled, rubbing at his arm. Tiny streams of blood trailed down his wrist from his bandages. It was obvious that blood was meant to be ignored.

"Get your head out of the gutter." She said, her face red.

"My mind wasn't in the—Wait, what did you think I meant—*What did you mean?*" He asked, horrified.

"You're cute, you know that?" Della smiled, watching as he slowly wiped her lip-gloss off his lips.

"Thank you." Porter said, his eyes still full of concern.

Perhaps he didn't need to know that all Della meant by 'going home' was so she could rip off his bandages and squirt his bite with Holy Water again.

~CHAPTER THIRTY-SIX~

The Great Mistake

"**D**ammit." The first man swore, pacing back and forth. He hadn't been this angry in a very long time.

"Don't look at me! I didn't tell her anything!" The second man said, backing up against the wall, the pillars of the back porch situated painfully between his shoulder blades. "I couldn't find the book, but I didn't think *she* took it!"

"Now, I have to fix things so she isn't blamed." The first man said, snapping his fingers. Porter stepped out of the shadows, stepping up onto the back porch, staring at the other one with the deepest disdain.

"If you hurt her, I swear to God I'll never forgive you." The second man vowed, his voice shaking.

"You don't have a choice in the matter, but sure, pretend you have free will." The first said, smiling a little.

"Do you have any idea what you have done? You promised me that you would stop the Dixon's, and that would be it. That was where this was supposed to end." The second man cried, his voice full of self-loathing. "I should never have agreed to this. I should've known history would've repeated itself. One more, you used to say. One more death, then this town would be clean. Really? Because the way I see it, everything just got a *Hell* of a lot worse. Theo is *dead*."

"I know, I killed him!" The first man hissed.

"Why? He was your—" The second man began, before being cut off by a maniacal laugh.

"I don't care *what* he was. Better him than me. Isn't that what you said all those years ago? You'd rather see him locked up then go to jail yourself? You think I'm being selfish? You had a thing for his wife! You wanted him gone so she would come crying into your arms. Look where that got you." The first man said, shoving a finger down onto the second man's chest.

The second man shook his head, tears stinging his eyes. "I hate you." He whispered. "She shouldn't have anything to do with this. You should've left her out of it. She took the spell book to keep us from doing something stupid. She was trying to help. And frankly, I should've come clean to her."

"If you would've done that, I would've killed you." The first man hissed, nodding towards Porter.

"You're going to stick *him* on her?" The second man quivered.

"No, I'm going to stick him on *you*." The first said, shoving a finger into the other mans chest, his eyes ablaze with furry.

The second man screamed in pain, pulling up his sleeve to reveal an intricate pentacle tattoo. Inside of each point of the star inside the circle, were runic symbols for the elements.

"*Innlinkal fra rofen, Grunch.*" The first man whispered.

The pentacle tattoo began to glow, his veins filling with red light. The first man grabbed his hand and pointed his palm to the ground. Flames so hot they burned blue erupted from the ground as a grotesque figure crawled out of the flickering flames. When the flames died down, the first man pushed the second to the ground, turning his eyes towards Porter.

"Come on, boyo, take him to our special place." He winked, patting Porter on the shoulder.

Porter nodded, dragging the second man off, muffling his screams with his rough hands as the first man kicked down the door.

"Ellie, I'm home." He called, leading his newly summoned Grunch inside.

~ ~ ~

Pluto, Venus, and Mars marched up to Eloise Heiser's house the next morning, determined to wrap this up once and for all.

Della knocked on the door. There was no answer, but the door swung open on its rusty hinges. She threw a worried look over her shoulder, stepping aside so Porter could enter first.

"Moss Hollow PD!" He called through the house, nodding for the others to follow.

The carpet in the living room was ripped to shreds, bloodstains on the floor. Della swore, running to the bedroom, diving under the bed. The spell book was gone. Max's pointy dress shoes appeared next to her as she crawled out from under Eloise's bed. He offered her a hand up off the floor, looking around the room. The bedspread was torn apart, pillow fluff lining the floor like snow. The dresser was on its side, the drawers ripped out of it.

"It's gone." Della breathed. She swore several times, running her hands through her hair repeatedly.

"Hey, guys!" Porter called from the kitchen.

They ran to meet him, seeing Eloise tied to a chair, bloodied and bruised, seemingly unconscious. Porter was kneeling next to her, untying her hands.

"Is she breathing?" Della asked, horrified.

Porter nodded.

"*Uakopp.*" Max whispered, waving his hand over Eloise's face. His fingers glowed white, tiny sparks showering Eloise's face.

She inhaled sharply, sparking to life. She stumbled out of her seat, coughing, looking around wildly. Max and Della grabbed her by her arms, directing her back to the chair gently. Her eyes fell on Della, filled with fear.

"Do you know where you are?" Della asked, kneeling, taking her hands into her own.

Eloise nodded, gripping her hands tightly. "Where's Jimmie?" She asked, her voice breaking.

"He's not here." Porter said, placing a comforting hand on her shoulder. He was smiling kindly, though Della felt like it wasn't the time nor place for that.

"What happened?" Della asked.

Eloise shut her eyes tightly, swallowing hard. "Jimmie and I were having tea last night, and I heard something crash outside. Jimmie went to investigate, but he didn't come back. I went to check things out, when this—this—this *creature* attacked me."

"Did you get bit?" Max asked, carefully rolling up the

frilly sleeves of her nightshirt to check her arms.

She shook her head, her eyes filling with tears. Porter stared blankly at her, his eyes full of perplexity.

"Why did you have the spell book?" Porter asked sternly. Della shot him a look.

"I took it from Jimmie a couple weeks ago. I saw him messing around with it around my flowers. He swore to me it was to help them grow, but I didn't want him to go down that path." Eloise cried, letting go of Della's hands so she could fiddle with the chain of pearls around her neck.

"Did you use it?" Della asked.

"I flipped through it, but I only cast a few things. That book oozed evil. Jimmie knew I took it, so I hid it. I was the one who talked him into giving all of his stuff to Nicoletta, but something happened, and he wanted that book back. Said he had to fix something." Eloise was shaking with fright as she spoke.

"Do you have any idea why?" Max asked.

She hesitated. "He's been hanging around Eric Steiniger again. Nothing good ever comes from that."

Della pulled at her fingernails, lost in thought. "Did he hang around Steiniger when Theodore was sentenced to jail?"

Porter straightened, looking betrayed.

Eloise nodded, glancing at the boys. She reached for Della's hands, pulling her closer. "Theodore was innocent, I swear! *And* Jimmie! Jimmie just wanted to help his friend." She shut her eyes tightly, tears streaming down her face. "Jimmie never truly gave up on magic. He loved the rush, loved how powerful he felt. I remember one night Eric, Theo, and Jim were all huddled around the kitchen table, drunker than they usually were, reminiscing on the old times. Eric had been assigned a case involving the death of a local realtor. Jim was so intoxicated he let it slip he had cursed that man. Theo and I panicked. Theo got angry and started screaming at his brother. Eric, however, asked how Jim had done it.

After a brawl in the front yard, Jim and Eric left, and next thing we know, some guy who owned a law firm here in town died. Theo wanted to believe it was coincidence, but he knew deep down it was his friends doing. A few more deaths later, and he confronted them. They got in a fistfight." Eloise shivered. "Eric was in over his head. People who aren't born with magic are corrupted by it, Theo used to say. Soon, he started killing off whoever he deemed was less than the law. Teachers who were mean to kids, some tourist who was rude to me—anyone. Jim backed out, but Eric continued. He got sloppy, someone saw him standing over a dead body and called the cops. He killed that person and pinned it on Theo.”

Porter clenched his fists, walking away, shaking his head angrily. Della and Max exchanged a look. Things just got a thousand times worse.

“I saw Della hanging around Jimmie, I thought she was helping him. . .” Eloise cried.

“Okay, we are going to get you out of here, alright? Get you cleaned up and take you somewhere safe.” Della said, gesturing for Max to help her get Eloise to her feet.

They picked her up, carrying her to the front door. Della realized Porter wasn’t following, so she let go of Eloise, assuring her that she was in good hands with Max. Della turned on her heels, quietly walking into the kitchen to see Porter leaning over the sink, gripping onto the counter, his knuckles white.

“You good?” Della asked, her voice shaking.

He nodded. “I needed a minute.” He said, removing himself from the sink, squeezing his arm. He looked extremely pale and green.

“I’m sorry about Steiniger.” She said, reaching out to touch him. He tensed up, but as her fingers touched him, he relaxed.

He nodded to himself. “I don’t understand how he could do that to her. I’ve always known him to be such a kind, loving person.”

“If I’ve learned anything from my years in this crappy plane of existence, it’s that people are *never* what they seem. I thought you were a psycho murderer, remember?” She smiled weakly, grabbing his hand and pulling him outside and to Mavericks’ convertible.

Max was helping Eloise into the passenger seat, his phone to his ear. “. . . yeah, she’s got bruises and cuts all over her.” He nodded into the receiver, covering the speaker as Della walked up to him. “Go check Jimmie’s house. Ei’m gonna get her tuh the hospital. Meet up at The Courier?”

Della nodded, glancing at Porter, then at Jimmie’s house across the street. They raced across, Porter reaching for his gun, checking how many bullets he had. Della picked the lock on the front door.

Jimmie's belongings were strewn across the floor like he had been in a hurry to get out of here.

"Stay here, I'm going to check out the rest of the house." Porter whispered, tiptoeing through the house, the floorboards creaking under his weight.

Della nodded, awkwardly rocking back and forth on her heels. She sighed heavily, feeling useless. Porter had a gun and super-strength, Max could cast spells, and here she was, hallucinating and trying to keep from moving things with her mind. Funny how the people who wanted magic the most, got the short end of the stick.

A phone rang somewhere in the house, startling her. "Porter?" She called nervously.

She heard his muffled voice, his heavy footsteps trudging back down the hallway. His cellphone was to his ear, his face screwed up in concern. "What do you mean he didn't show up?" He asked nervously to the person on the line. "Check his house. I—I'm not giving directions, Jacobson, I'm trying to help!" He yelled through the phone. He opened his mouth to say something else. Instead, he looked shocked, pulling the phone away from his ear slowly. "He hung up on me." He whispered hotly, briskly walking past Della.

"What's going on?" She asked, following him.

He stood on Jimmie's porch, breathing heavily, his hands in his hair. "Steiniger didn't show up for work." He said his voice breaking. "*Dammit.*"

"We'll find him. Maybe he's at his house?" Della proposed, reaching out for him again.

He pulled away, his eyes full of rage. "Don't. Don't touch me." He hissed, turning away to lean against the porch railing.

Della put her hands up in defense, then in her pockets. "Do you want to go after him?" She asked.

"Jacobson will handle it."

"Is that you or the bite talking?" Della asked shakily.

His eyes bore into her, sadness floating under the anger.

"What?" Della asked, taking a minuscule step back.

"I don't know what I did after I dropped you off at your apartment." He whispered.

Della inhaled sharply, nodding to herself. "You were tired, I'm sure you have nothing to do with any of this." She said, more to herself than to him.

He couldn't meet her eyes, tears rolling down his face.

The last thing he wanted was to be forced to use his powers like this. It was his greatest fear. He struggled with himself for a moment, then shook his head, walking away.

"Wait up!" Della called, skipping after him. Something was wrong.

"Leave it." His voice croaked.

"Porter—"

He stopped dead in his tracks, rounding on her. "I know you want to help me, but I need you to stop. Go to The Courier, I'll catch up. I promise." He said, his eyes pleading her to listen to him for once. She looked away, then nodded, taking a step back to try and show that she trusted him. He nodded. "I'll be there in an hour."

~ ~ ~

Porter knocked on Steiniger's front door. It was a simple cabin out in the woods, the windows crusted with dirt and grime, the thatching on the roof caving in over the garage. He knew this place like the back of his hand, knew that there was a key hidden behind the broken doorbell, knew that cameras were watching every side. He glanced up at the one in the hanging basket, taking the hidden key and unlocking the door.

The house was just as empty as Jimmie's.

Porter swore, filled with white-hot rage. He kicked over a side table, tore away at the couch cushions, ripped books from their shelves.

Steiniger should've been here. He should be sitting at the kitchen table, passed out because he had drank too much. He should be here to tell Porter that he was innocent, to say to him that Della was wrong, tell him that Max didn't have his facts straight.

Why was the universe like this?

Porter prayed every night to God, but God never answered his prayers. He had read the Bible, he wore a cross, he had angel statues in his room, but still, God was silent. He was a good person, deep down under his guilt, he knew that, so why were things the way they were? Why was he always given a bad hand of metaphorical playing cards during the poker game that was life? Why was *he* the one with this stupid, stupid bite on his arm? Why, why, *why?*

He heard Jacobson's sirens as he pulled up the driveway, parking next to Porter's hearse, breaking him from his thoughts.

Steiniger was gone, that's all that mattered. He shouldn't be dwelling on anything else.

As Porter exited the house he once called his sanctuary, he ran into Deputy Jacobson.

"Did you find him?" Jacobson asked.

Tears welled up in Porter's peridot eyes as he shook his head.

He and Jacobson had never gotten along, but the pain in the young deputy's eyes was that of a friend who knew how much you were hurting and wanted nothing more but to help.

Porter cleared his throat. "Did you?"

Jacobson shook his head once. "We've looked every-where, Porter. He's gone. I'm sorry."

With that, Porter left, ignoring Jacobson's many ques-tions as he climbed into the hearse.

~ ~ ~

Everyone returned to their normal lives over the next few days, acting as if nothing had happened. The only person who seemed to care was Della. No one wanted to talk about the fact that another kid had gone missing, no one wanted to help her hack into cameras and records to see where Jimmie and Eric had gone, no one wanted to believe that she was right and they were wrong, no one wanted to look for Clara.

Outside of that, everything was normal.

Excruciatingly normal.

Porter was quiet. He never met her eyes when they spoke. She had a feeling it was going to take a lot for him to get back to normal. And Max? He seemed perfectly fine, his only worry being whether his vampire costume was going to be politically correct or not.

Halloween.

When Della had first got here, that was all she could look forward to. Now it was a week away, and all she wanted was for that wonderful holiday to go away.

Della had finished her article for *The Utopian Courier* an hour before the deadline, and Norman and Irene had as-sured her she would make the front page. That was something the boys said she should be extremely happy about, but she wasn't. She felt she had stolen the spotlight from someone else. Someone who was capable of not being—as Max would say—an eejit.

But still, Della couldn't shake the feeling that everything had ended far too quickly. She kept researching little things behind their backs, tying up any loose ends.

The worst days were the ones Max told her to busy herself with her blog, the thing that her life used to revolve around. She had neglected her readers since she arrived here, and with everything that had happened, it was as if she wasn't worthy of them. She was tempted to delete that blog altogether, but that would raise suspicions back home, suspicions she'd rather not have to deal with.

So, she busied herself elsewhere, spending all her free time at the *Weeping Crow*, chatting with Nicoletta about everything. The old witch seemed to be the only one who allowed Della to romanticize the idea of the return of evil.

Everyone looked at her like she was going crazy, and maybe she was. Della was so paranoid that Jimmie and Steiniger would return that she hung witch bottles from the ceiling of her office and apartment, jumping at every little noise she heard. Even now, as Della laid in bed, half-awake, she squirmed at the sound of rushing wind. After all, Theodore had said that it was never truly the wind that howled.

She shook her head, rolling over, clutching the sheets to her. Everyone kept telling her to give it all up and move on, but she couldn't. She had made a promise to clear Theodore's name, find Clara and her sister, and she intended to keep it. No matter how long that took.

Fortunately for her, the universe wanted this conundrum solved just as badly as she did.

Della closed her eyes, falling into a deep sleep almost instantly.

~ ~ ~

As she dreamt, she ran through that same crooked forest again, this time with Porter at her side. He was scared, his eyes glowing brightly as if they were made from gold, as they ran, being slapped in the face by low hanging branches covered in thick moss. There was a beam of light coming from somewhere, but contrary to the normal, the light wasn't coming from in front of them. No, there wasn't a light at the end of this tunnel. The light was at the beginning. It was behind them. Della skidded to a halt, turning on her heels, face to face with a Grunch.

"Della! Come on! Keep running!" Porter's far off voice rang.

She shook her head. The Grunches mouth broke into a smile, pushing past her to get to Porter. Della tried to move, but she was rooted to the spot by growing vines. She looked down. She was in the shirt that Max had burnt, but it was still on fire, the flames burning her skin as they traveled over her. She looked to Porter who had stopped a few feet away, he looked sickly, his face red, his eyes puffy.

The Grunch sauntered over to him, dragging its arms on the ground, making a scraping noise against the roots of the trees.

Della furrowed her eyebrows in pain. Her head was splitting again. She shut her eyes tightly. "You're only dreaming." She told herself as pressure began to build up in her nose.

The Grunch turned to her, its disembodied voice filling her ears. "You could've saved him." He whispered. "You could've saved them all."

Panic flooded through as she looked back at Porter, seeing him cowering next to the Grunch. The flames on her shirt had reached her hair. She outstretched her hands towards Porter, hoping with all her might that she could do something, *anything*, to help him.

Della looked down at her feet, seeing the vines begin to shrivel away. "No." She said to the Grunch. "I can still save them. And I *will* save them." She said, her words the only magic she had ever needed.

The Grunches hissed at her, its voice so loud Della cried out in pain, feeling as if someone had stabbed her between her eyebrows.

"I CAN SAVE THEM!" She screamed at the top of her lungs. All she had to do was wake up.

Why wasn't she waking up?

~CHAPTER THIRTY-SEVEN~

Bad Habits Die Hard

Porter quietly unlocked the front door, thanking his lucky stars that Pops was asleep at the front desk. He kicked off his muddy boots and hung up his leather jacket, making his way up to his room. He plopped down face first on his bed.

Today had been utterly exhausting.

He and Max had been hanging out at The Courier, debating what to do about Della. They had to find a way to get her mind off their failure. It would be the death of her if they didn't. So far, the only good idea they had was an intervention, but that would fly over like a lead balloon.

He sighed heavily. All Porter wanted to do was lay here and go to sleep, but he couldn't. He knew he'd been in trouble for leaving without a word, but at least he had gotten home before midnight, and it wasn't like he was out being undesirable. He groaned, launching himself off the bed and changing into something he didn't mind getting bodily fluids on. It was so strange to him that so many people dropped dead in this town. It was like the soil he dug every day was cursed.

He opened his door, making to go back downstairs, pushing his untidy locks out of his face. The stairs creaked under his weight, sending eerie echoes throughout the house. His feet landed on the dingy tiles in what used to be the kitchen—before the house was remodeled the year before he was born—

grabbing the lavender embalming fluids out of an old cabinet.

"Where have you been all day?" Jed's voice rang throughout the silent house. It was nine o'clock at night, he should be asleep.

Porter turned to see him standing in the foyer, a sour look on his face. Porter's heart leaped. This was the last thing he needed right now. He bit his lip, gripping the bottle of embalming fluids in his hand so tightly the glass began to crack.

"I was at Max's," Porter said, glancing at Pops. He was a fool to think that the old man would be able to help him in any way.

"That boy is trouble," Jed said, taking a couple strides over to him.

Porter shook his head in disgust, biting his tongue.

"You have something to say to me, *boy*?" Jed asked, raising his voice as much as he dared, so as not to wake his wife.

"You know, you can do whatever you want to me, but don't you *dare* criticize who I keep as company." After everything Porter had been through the last couple of months, it was a miracle he kept what he really wanted to say buried deep inside him.

"What did you just say?" Jed asked.

Porter shook his head, turning away. "You heard me."

Something crashed to the floor behind him, causing Porter to turn. Jed had pushed a mason jar full of flowers to the floor, causing it to shatter with an ear-piercing *CLINK!*

"You know, most people would have kicked your disrespectful ass out of here by now!" Jed spat, marching over to him.

Porter set the embalming fluid down, clenching his fists. "Yes, because you are such a loving father figure."

Jed slapped him, leaving a red handprint on Porter's olive skin. He laughed as Porter stood there, gathering the strength to do something he had stopped himself from doing for thirteen years. Full of suppressed rage, Porter kneed Jedidiah Oye between the legs and pushed him to the floor. He stared at his abuser, surprised at himself. His arm wasn't burning with pain, his mind wasn't clouded with someone else's emotions. This was all him.

Jed regained his composure quicker than Porter would have liked, bouncing back up to two legs. He swung a fist at

Porter, but he dodged out of the way, planting his own fist into Jed's eye socket. Jed stumbled back into the counter, gasping.

Porter turned away, assuming that Jed had had enough when he felt two hands grip his neck, pulling him down to the floor. Jed pinned him against the tile, squeezing Porter's throat with all his might, as Porter tried to pry him off.

Porter had never wanted to kill someone before, not even Robbie had earned that, but right now, that was his only thought. He kicked Jed off, knocking the wind out of him.

"What the Hell is going on?" Crystal's terrified voice rang.

Porter, gasping for air, the impression of Jed's fingers on his neck, stumbled up off the floor, scowling at his ignorant mother.

"Your son attacked me!" Jed choked out, doubled over at the counter.

Pops snorted in his sleep.

"He threw the first punch," Porter said, not bothering to defend himself any more than that. He wasn't ashamed of his actions. Jed deserved far more than what Porter had done.

Crystal stood, pulling her fluffy robe tightly around herself. "Jed?" She questioned, her face going through a multitude of expressions.

"You going to believe him over me?" Jed asked angrily, sending another mason jar to the floor.

Porter rounded on him, winding up to cold cock him.

"PORTER NO!" Crystal shouted, running over to him, grabbing his arm. Porter shook her away, staring at her in disbelief. He was shaking with anger, backing away from his mother like a scared puppy. How could she treat him like this?

"I'm calling the cops." Jed hissed, reaching for the mortuary phone.

Porter didn't stay around long enough to see if Crystal tried to stop him, he ran to the front door, slipping on a pair of flip flops and fleeing to the confines of his hearse. He drove out of the parking lot, running to a place he swore he would never return to on a night like this.

~ ~ ~

The Burning Tankard greeted him with open arms as he sat down at the bar, waving to all the usual guests. His favorite pub was a small hole-in-the-wall building near the middle of the town. From the outside, it looked like a humble little restaurant, warm and inviting. The brick walls were white-washed, the neon sign depicting a tankard of alcohol on fire, flickering from old age. The inside was just as charming, the bar stood in front of shelves full of old gin and whiskey, a long mirror reflecting the appearance of the wretched souls that stared into it. The walls were painted a deep navy blue, the booths upholstered with a pattern of blue flames. Billiard tables stood in the corner, surrounded by rowdy patrons. This little bar was always packed with day drinkers and lonely vampires. Some might say it was more beloved than even *Bayou Gil's Crab Emporium*.

For years, this place had been Porter's second home. The owner—though he probably shouldn't have—always looked over the fact that Porter had been very underage. Then again, Elrod Kelly tended to overlook a lot of things. He had always said it was part of his job as a bartender.

Even now, as Porter took a handful of peanuts out of an old glass ashtray, Elrod walked over to him, grabbing a cup and Porter's favorite drink, *Jack Daniels* whiskey.

"Platter of cheese to go with it?" He asked, sliding the glass into Porter's hands.

Porter nodded, swirling the whiskey in his glass.

"Haven't seen you in a while," Elrod said, ducking down behind the counter to grab some fine cheeses out of the mini-fridge Porter knew was below the bar.

"Bad habits die hard." Porter sighed, downing the whiskey. As soon as the amber liquid touched his lips, he felt his anger leave him.

"Amen to that." Said Elrod, holding out his hand for Porter's cup, trading him for the platter of cheese.

Porter reached for his favorite, Roquefort, the most expensive one on the plate. Roquefort an acquired taste; the French cheese was so rich and multi-layered it made his throat burn as he swallowed it. Elrod handed him back his glass, now full of whiskey again. This place was a bottomless pit of enablers, and Porter was more than happy to be surrounded by them.

"So how are things, Elrod?" Porter asked, popping some peanuts into his mouth.

"Pretty good. Three days since the last brawl." He

smiled, twisting his handlebar mustache. "Werewolves won."

Porter smiled, shaking his head. "That's good." He said, downing his second glass.

Porter sat and chatted with Elrod for a while, watching as the bar slowly emptied, the sounds around him dying just like his mental welfare. He was filled with a sense of euphoria, laughing at commercials that cut in between some soccer game on the nearest TV. Elrod had begun drinking too, his choice of beverage being shots of tequila.

By his seventh glass, Porter had gotten up to play a game of pool with the remaining patrons. As he walked—or rather stumbled—through the tavern, he caught sight of one Eloise Heiser sitting in the corner, a glass of wine in hand. His arm burned at the sight of her, but he ignored it.

"Hey!" Porter said excitedly, making his way over to her.

"What are you doing here, at this hour, Mr. Garroway?" Eloise asked, looking him up and down. Her eyes lingered on his neck, gasping quietly as she realized what must've happened to get those bruises.

"Ah, you know, just hanging around," Porter said, doing an awkward little jig. He had always been a happy drunk. That was partially why he loved this horrible habit of his. He could be happy, truly happy. "What about you, you young whipper-snapper?" Porter asked, leaning against her booth.

"Mourning," Eloise explained, raising her wine glass.

Porter took that as an invitation to clink his glass against hers. He chuckled to himself at the noise, smiling dumbly at Mrs. Heiser.

She smiled back at him in pity, seeming to suddenly enjoy the idea of wine a little less.

"Hey, sorry my friend broke into your house," Porter said, staring into his glass. "She was just trying to do her job."

"I don't hold that against you, dear," Eloise assured him, discarding her glass.

"I'm glad you're okay," Porter said absentmindedly, taking a swig of his drink, wincing against the strong taste.

"Yes, well, I best be going home now," Eloise said, standing.

"What? No, stay! Stay!" Porter said, wrapping his arm around her shoulders.

"As much as I would love to dear, that would be highly inappropriate," Eloise said, pulling away. "I'll see you around,

Mr. Garroway."

"Damn, well, have a safe ride home!" Porter called after her, downing the last couple drops of his whiskey.

He had a feeling it would be a great night.

~ ~ ~

Della snorted awake, finding her nose was bleeding. She sat up, startled by her newest premonition. She wiped the dried blood from her nose, laying back down. She groaned; something was making an awful ringing noise. She looked around, realizing it was the sound of a ringing phone. *Her* ringing phone. She reached out across her nightstand, trying to grab it. As her fingers touched her phone, it fell off the nightstand and to the floor. She moaned, crawling out of bed, rubbing her temples. Porter's number lit up her screen as she made her way out of her bedroom.

"Mmm. . . wassup?" She answered groggily.

"Hey!" Porter's voice rang. His voice sounded weird, but Della couldn't figure out why. "Is Maxie there?" He asked.

"Maxie?" She whispered, shaking her head, forgetting he couldn't see her. Not once had she heard Porter call him that. "Uh, no, why?" Della asked, her eyes stinging as she turned on a light.

Porter was silent, the only noise coming from his breath against the speaker. "I'll get back to you," Porter said. His voice was low and rumbly, and over it Della could just make out the low melody of a country song.

"Wait, where are you?" She asked, the image of the Grunch trying to attack him flooding her mind.

"Uh. . ." He hesitated. Della heard the clink of silverware, and someone asked Porter if he wanted another round. "Please." He responded to the person.

"Are you at a bar?" She asked.

He couldn't be. Not now. Not after everything that had happened. That was the absolute *last* place he should be.

"Pfft," Porter said, laughing a little. "Why would I be at a—" He sighed. "Yes. . ." He laughed sadly. It sounded like he banged his head on the table.

Della looked around her apartment in disdain. *Thanks. Thank you, I'm so delighted I have to deal with this today.* She thought, hoping God, her guardian Angels, and whatever else was listening would hear.

"Are you okay?" She asked slowly.

"Yeah, I'm super great. Hey! I ran into Eloise! She's so sweet!" Porter said happily.

"That's nice. Did she say anything to you?" Della asked, entertaining him the best she could.

No answer.

"Porter?"

No answer.

"Porter Garroway!" Dell hissed.

"What, *gosh*!" Porter hissed back.

Della thought for a moment, rubbing her temples. "Are you drunk?" She asked angrily.

"Define drunk," Porter said groggily, his tone less than cheerful.

Della rolled her eyes. "Do you need me to come get you?"

"Yes—NO! No, no, call Max! I don't want you driving. What if you pass out at the wheel? I don't want that on my conscious." Porter said quickly. She heard him swallow.

"I always take the bus. I'm coming to get you." Della said impatiently, marching back into her room to get dressed. She hadn't bothered to wash the mascara off her face, nor comb her hair as she made her way downstairs. "Where are you?"

No answer.

"Let me come get you, and you can spend the day on my couch," Della said, making her way down to the bus stop.

"Fine." Porter sighed.

~CHAPTER THIRTY-EIGHT~

Accidents Happen

Della glared at Porter out of the corner of her eye as she paid the man behind the counter at *The Burning Tankard*. Porter was shaking all over, pulling the thin material of his zip-up hoodie tightly around his body. His eyes were bloodshot, his hair a mess, his lower lip swollen, bruises shaped like finger-prints around his neck. She had never felt so much like the 'mom-friend.' She was so disappointed in him. How could he let this happen? She shook her head as the cashier handed her a receipt for an entire bottle of *Jack Daniel's*, grabbing Porter by the elbow and pulling him out of the bar.

"Thanks." He breathed into the morning air, reaching into his pocket and procuring his keys.

Della ripped them out of his hands, clenching her hand into such a tight fist, the sharp, rusty keyring broke the skin on her hand.

"I can't believe you." She whispered, marching him over to his hearse and unlocking the door. She hadn't expected him to be this intoxicated. She opened the door for him, scowling at him as he drunkenly crawled into his seat.

"Sorry," Porter said weakly. He pulled up his hood, staring out at the street.

Della climbed into the driver seat, angrily starting the car and peeling out of Porter's parking spot. She was absolutely fuming now, the silence like sharp daggers pointed towards Porter.

"You going to yell at me?" He asked groggily. "I don't want you to explode a fire hydrant or anything."

Of course, she wanted to yell at him. Of course, she wanted to lecture him, to scream her head off at him. But she didn't say anything. Not a word. Because he had a massive point. Della was in a very fragile state of mind. Who knew how much power she had and what would happen if she lost control? She had a feeling that the results would conclude in a catastrophe.

"No," Della said finally, taking a deep breath to calm herself down.

"Why?" Porter asked, twisting around in his seat to look at her. It was only one-thirty in the morning, the sun hadn't even graced their presence. The streetlights and shop signs were still lit up, casting their glow on the side of his face in all the colors of the rainbow, the rain casting shadows on his cheeks.

Della said nothing, but she couldn't help but grip the steering wheel a little tighter. She had never been a great driver. She always got too distracted by the things around her to focus on not getting into a car crash, but tonight, keeping her eyes dead set in front of her was the only thing keeping her from biting off her own tongue.

"Okay," Porter responded to the silence. There was an air of finality to that single word.

After Porter had finished scrolling through the radio stations, failing to find something that piqued his interest, the rest of the car ride was silent, the only noise coming from the rain hammering down on the hood and the occasional clicking sound of the blinker.

Della decided as she helped Porter up the stairs, that he could have the couch and a blanket because she was going back to bed. Porter didn't seem too surprised by her decision. He looked just as exhausted as she felt.

He waited patiently for her to unlock her door, then made for the couch, plopping down face first on it, kicking off his sneakers. He felt around for one of her pillows, stuffed it under his head, and sighed heavily.

"Oh yeah, no, no, make yourself at home." Della sighed, tossing her purse on the counter.

". . . fanks." Porter said, his cheek squished against the pillow. "I like vhat you've fun vith the pace." He said, his voice wistfully sincere.

In reality, the only thing Della had changed about her apartment since the last time Porter had been here, was that she had hung up the witch bottles—bottles of nails and herbs that protected against witches, ghosts, and black magic. Nothing else had changed.

"Awe, thanks." She said facetiously.

Porter leaned up off the couch, punched the pillow a couple times, then rolled over, staring up at the ceiling. He reached his finger up and traced the lines of the popcorn ceiling, smiling to himself like a little kid.

"So," Della said, hopping up onto one of the kitchen stools so she could stare at him. It gave her a feeling of superiority she didn't need, but boy did she revel in it. "You wanna talk about anything before I get back to sleep?"

Porter bolted upright, his eyes wide. "Do you think Sigmund Parrish is happy? Like, do you think that he thinks that he made the right decision?"

Della squinted at him in confusion.

"And what about Jupiter?! What happens to her, and what's his face?!" He continued.

"A—Are you asking me about plot holes in *Vanish and Despair*?" Della asked. "The book?" *Vanish and Depsair* was a book Della had read many years ago that consisted of crappy vampires and an even worse plot.

"Do you know anyone else named Sigmund?" Porter asked with so much salt on his tongue he could've turned all the freshwater rivers to sea.

Della closed her eyes tightly, chewing on her lip. "As much as I would love to chat about all the reasons I hate that book—trust me, I would—" She said, shooting him a look as he tried to object. "—What I meant was, do you want to talk about why you called me at one in the morning to come pick you up from some bar?"

"Well, actually, I called you to tell Max because I know he'd listen to you and not brush off the gravity of my situation if it came from your lips." He said blankly, laying back down on the couch, shaking his head. "If New Orleans is new, where is Old Orleans?" He asked. "That's what I want to talk about."

Della jumped off her stool, grabbing her purse and making her way towards her bedroom. "Well, this has been fun." She said with a very forced smile.

"Are you going to bed?" Porter asked.

"Given as it is now two in the morning on a Sunday, I'm going to say yes." Della yawned.

"Okay," Porter said sadly.

Della rolled her eyes. She grabbed a pair of clean pajamas, brushed her teeth, combed her hair, and climbed back into bed. She had just begun to feel drowsy when a tiny knock startled her out from under the warm sheets.

"Della," Porter whispered. Well, *he* thought he was whispering. It was more of a strained screech. "Pst. *Dellaaa. . .* Hey! Hey, Della!"

Della peeled the covers off herself, stomping over to the door and ripping it open. Porter stood before her, his hands deep in his pockets, his hood pulled over his face.

"Della." He said sternly, still trying to whisper.

"What, Porter?" Della asked, thoroughly irritated.

"Della, I'm cold." He said, shivering violently.

"There's a blanket on the back of the couch," Della said, beginning to shut the door.

Porter leaned back so he could look down the hallway, a dumb look on his face. He thought for a moment then put a hand out to stop the door from closing.

"Can I have *another* blanket?" He asked.

"What if I said no?"

He looked very sad but only shrugged. "Well, goodnight." He said, turning away.

Della tapped her foot on the floor a couple times, debating whether to give in or go back to bed. She sighed angrily, grabbing a very large, very fluffy blanket from the hall closet. She followed Porter back to the living room and gestured for him to lay back down on the couch. He complied, and she draped both the blankets over him, tucking in his feet.

Porter smiled, yawning. "Thanks, Miss Coleman." He said quietly, wiggling around on the couch to get comfortable.

"Don't mention it." She shrugged.

He stared at her for a moment, his smile fading. "If you save everyone. . . then who saves you?" He asked.

Della rocked back and forth on her heels, shoving her hands in the pockets of her black and pink fleece pajama pants, the tiny love hearts looking like they were beating as she fiddled with a loose thread.

"I guess that's why I have you, huh?" She smiled, sitting down on her wobbly coffee table.

". . . But I'm everyone." He replied with confusion.

"Porter Garroway, you are *not* everyone," Della said. He furrowed his eyebrows, yawning. "You know, I misjudged you and Max." She smiled. "I thought Max was going to be a weak little errand runner—"

"Ouch," Porter said.

"—and I thought *you* were going to be the resident jackass." She finished. Porter raised an eyebrow as he turned his whole body to face her. "I've been pleasantly surprised by you people."

". . . Was that. . . a compliment?" Porter questioned.

She nodded sincerely. "Yes, Porter. That was a compliment."

He closed his eyes slowly, smiling. "I thought you were going to be a freak. Just another reject trying to act all high and mighty. But I was wrong. You're actually really sweet when you get to know you. And funny, and kind, and—" He yawned. "—and I'm really happy I met you."

"Am I still a reject?" She asked.

"Yeah. . . but you're still a high-functioning member of society despite it. I respect that. . ." He admitted.

A normal person would've been deeply offended by that comment, but not Della. She smirked at him, tucking the blankets into the couch as he began to doze off.

"G'night, Della." He whispered softly.

"Goodnight, Porter."

~ ~ ~

"You can go to work or whatever," Porter said later that morning as Della stepped over him, trying to get comfortable on the couch.

"Let a boy stay at my house? Alone? In this day and age? What are we? Neanderthals?" Della asked. Porter was staring at her in disgust as she scrolled through the different channels on her TV, bowl of popcorn in hand.

"I don't know, are we? You aren't seriously going to eat that for breakfast, are you?" He asked.

Della shoved a handful of popcorn into her mouth, tossing an un-popped kernel at him. "Do you have a problem with that?" She asked.

Porter stared at her for a moment, then rolled his eyes and set the popcorn bowl between them. After a while, he began listing the reasons why the show she was watching was both stupid and implausible. It seemed that he was very cranky when hungover.

Della was just about ready to tell him to be quiet when she heard a scraping noise. Her eyes darted to the shutters as a low wind made them flap. Out of nowhere, a sense of foreboding washed over her.

"Do you hear that?" Della asked, slowly standing up and edging towards the window, grabbing her smaller machete—which was wedged between the wall and the couch—as she went.

There was no way anything magical could get in. She had stuck every manner of beast, witch, vampire, werewolf, and monster repellent into the cracks of the shutters, but that didn't make her quit worrying. She peered through the shutters as Porter went quiet, bracing for impact.

Alas, there was nothing.

He swore in Portuguese, showing just how cranky he was. "You're paranoid—ish—ness has rubbed off on me," Porter said, hiding his concern behind a smile.

"You haven't seen me paranoid," Della said matter-of-factly, tossing the machete onto the coffee table and sitting back down.

"Obviously," Porter said sarcastically. He had stolen the remote from her side of the couch and was trying to find something better to watch.

"So, I like to be prepared, what's the harm in that? I could be—" The scratching returned; this time louder.

Porter went white, his ears pulled back. "You're sure nothing can get in, right?" He asked.

"Vervain, salt, wolfs-bane, silver, iron—you name it, it's somewhere in the house," Della said, though she had her doubts about how safe they were.

Porter nodded slowly. They sat in silence for a minute, staring at the TV.

"Wait." He said straightening. "If the Grunch is a demon spawn, and not necessarily made purely of magic, would witch bottles repel it?"

"Why would you say that?" Della asked. "In what world would you decide it was okay for you to jinx us—" *BANG!* Something crashed in Della's room. "—like that. Dammit." Della and Porter shot up off the couch, edging towards the hallway.

Before Porter had time to craft some sort of witty response to the mortal peril they were in, Della's bedroom door swung open, the drywall cracking where the knob hit the wall. There, standing before them in infamous glory, was the Grunch. Or rather, *a* Grunch. Only one. Porter looked at Della, who was brandishing her machete, then swallowed hard. This was going to be the fight of their lives.

The Grunch roared, two more Grunches appearing before them. Instead of attacking, the Grunches began to fuse, melting and stretching together in a heap of blue flames until its form was something much bigger, and so *very* much uglier.

More Grunches appeared as the bigger one lunged at Porter and Della. They dodged out of the way just in time, making it all the angrier. Porter cried out in agony as a smaller Grunch grabbed him by the arm, its sharp claws digging into his thick skin like butter. His eyes flashed gold.

Della ducked under one of the swinging arms of the giant Grunch, rushing to Porter, slamming her machete down into the skull of his attacker. The Grunch let go, spasming into a heap on the floor.

As Della opened her mouth to say something, one of the other Grunches lunged at her, sending her to the floor too.

Porter stood shaking, holding his head in his hands. When he finally looked up, his eyes were white, just like the Grunches. The bigger Grunch had gone to attack him, but stopped, its arm hanging over him. It sniffed the air, then turned towards Della.

Della swung her machete at her attacker, cutting one of its thick little arms in half. It squealed, spattering blood everywhere. The creature's arm had no skeleton, just fractured pieces of animal bones—maybe some human too—which were held together by a thin, sparkling thread.

Porter blinked a couple times, trying to regain control over his mind. He kicked and scratched at the bigger Grunch, but he quickly learned that an out of practice monster like himself would do little damage to the rapidly growing thing before him. Instead of fighting it head-on, he grabbed it by one of its arms, trying to see how much it weighed and if he could throw it.

"MOVE!" He shouted, the muscles in his arm rippling painfully, his eyes flashing from white to gold and back again.

Della didn't second guess his command, ducking out of the line of fire, watching Porter throw the creature halfway across the room. It collided with her television—which ironically had been left on a channel entitled 'Peaceful Music Videos'—the TV erupting with shattered glass.

The rest of the Grunches paused, staring at their fallen ally. The one closest to Della screeched, turning towards its friend. The other Grunches followed suit, launching themselves at the fallen warrior.

All the Grunches had now fused with the bigger one, it's skin rippling with the force of the magic it was made of. It towered over Della, so tall that even Porter looked like nothing but a cheap action figure. Its ugly head scraped across the ceiling, showering itself in loose pieces of drywall.

The apartment was filled with an otherworldly shriek.

Della looked to her left, feeling as if someone had stolen the breath from her lungs.

The act of the Grunches fusing into each other had just been a distraction; there, pinned against the breakfast nook by a medium-sized Grunch, was Porter. The Grunch had its claws in his chest, ripping his skin like some sort of cheap fabric. As he struggled against it, the necklace Nicoletta had made for him bounced around his neck, the gemstones shimmering. Porter cried out in anguish, the claws of his attacker cutting deeper and deeper into his thick skin.

Della tossed her machete from one hand to the other, focusing all her energy on the Grunch, trying to remember the spell Max had used to set the coffee cup ablaze. She had only a small window of time before the giant one to her right gained full consciousness.

"*VARMET!*" She screamed, waiting for a plume of flames to erupt from her hand. As she had sadly expected, nothing happened. She cursed the universe silently, then made to run at Porter and his attacker.

The other Grunch rounded on her with lightning speed, roundhouse-kicking her out of the way and to the floor, shoulder first. Something crack inside her as she fell. Della cried out as she tried to stand back up. Her machete had been thrown a few feet away—if only she could get to it. She reached out her thin fingers, watching the blade wobble. The giant Grunch had regained full consciousness, lumbering over to her and stepping down on her hand as her fingers brushed the hilt of the machete.

"NO!" Porter screamed. The smaller Grunch still had him pinned, its claws buried deep inside him, but the two beasts were struggling against each other, fighting for control over the situation.

Della bit back tears as she heard—and felt, for that matter—her finger bones in her left hand get crushed. She reached around with her other hand, trying another spell she remembered.

"*NEMMORTIS!*" She screamed at the top of her lungs. All she felt was a searing pain in her forearm. Nothing happened to the Grunch.

A sickening, terrifying thought took over her brain as she watched Porter finally throw the smaller Grunch off him and lunge in anger at the one stepping on her hand; she was useless.

She couldn't do anything to help. She was a liability, not an asset. Theodore had been right, she should've stayed out of this and went home, left this crazy town when she had the chance. If Max was here, he and Porter would have taken care of the situation within seconds. Even her visions were useless. She hadn't warned either of them of what she had seen. She couldn't even get that right.

Fear, pure fear, erupted inside her skull for the first time in what felt like years, attacking her heart when she needed it most.

Porter went to attack the monster again, when he fell to his knees, holding his head in pain, crying out.

The Grunch forced its crooked face into a smile, moving quickly to grab her by the throat. It was making an odd noise, something akin to a laugh, as its giant fist squeezed tighter and tighter around Della's neck, cutting off her airways, turning her face a gruesome shade of purple. With strength it shouldn't have had, the Grunch slammed her hard against the wall behind her. Her head hit the hardest, causing her vision to blur in and out. Everything had gone quiet except for the dull ringing in her ears.

She tried to focus on everything around her, sending a

message out into the universe to break anything worth breaking. She heard something crash in the kitchen, saw the chintzy coffee table break in half, but it did nothing to help.

The Grunch moved her away from the wall, holding her in midair. It squeezed its fist around her throat tighter and tighter, pops of orange flashing in Della's eyes as she kicked against it. The more she tried to fight it off, the weaker she felt, she couldn't even gasp for air. Her legs went limp against her will, the Grunch shaking her, still laughing in its choked voice.

She couldn't see Porter or the other Grunch; she couldn't hear anything over the rush of blood in her ears.

So, like any rational person, she gave up.

"He thought you were the one this town had spent years waiting for. He thought you were better than this, little one. Obviously, he was wrong." The Grunches voice rang in her ears, the room around her settling into darkness.

The Grunch squeezed its hand one more time before sending her to the tattered carpet. She was out cold before her head even hit the floor.

~CHAPTER THIRTY-NINE~

Elementary, My Dear Porter

Porter's hands were bound behind his back, painfully stuck beneath him as he laid, staring up at the ceiling. His chest was burning hot with pain from where the Grunch had plunged it's claws into him, but when he looked down, the only way you'd be able to tell he'd been attacked was that his shirt was ripped to shreds. His vision kept swirling, but he was pretty sure this was a classroom at the old Moss Hollow Elementary—now it was nothing more than a health hazard. He was still very hungover but not nearly drunk enough to be back here. He struggled to roll to his side, his bruised and bloodied face feeling hot against the cold floor.

The necklace Della had given him, the one that old witch had made, dangled from his neck, the black gemstones now white. He had a sneaking suspicion that if he hadn't worn this necklace, he'd be dead.

He looked around wearily, trying to shake his hair from his eyes.

Wait, he knew where he was, this was the cafeteria. From what he could see, he was alone. The last thing he remembered was being hit over the head and the sense that he was swimming in a whirlpool. He couldn't see Della, his last memory of her was seeing the Grunch crush her fingers.

He rolled back over, groaning angrily. He hated this

place. The happiest day of his life was when Max had accidentally burned it down; it meant no matter what, he didn't have to go back to it.

Boy, was he wrong.

His vision had settled, his eyes resting on the ceiling again, staring at the burn marks. To his left, there was someone tied to a chair. Clara Dixon.

"Clara." He whispered. She grunted but didn't move. "It's me, Porter. I'm going to get you out of here, okay?" He asked. She rolled her head to the side, revealing a cut on her cheek and a black eye.

His ears picked up on the click-clack of footsteps. Anger surged through him faster than a lightning bolt. He tried desperately to pull his hands apart, but he was not bound by normal means, he was bound by magic.

"You don't have to fight, Porter. I won't hurt you. I'd never hurt you." Steiniger's voice rang.

"You sent one of your things to attack us, pretty sure you're failing at that." Porter spat as Eric stepped into his line of sight.

He was dressed from head to toe in black, looking like some sort of demon priest. He held his head high as he walked towards him and knelt. He smiled sympathetically, running a hand over Porter's face.

"I admit, I shouldn't have done that boyo, but I thought she would be alone. Those little abominations have trouble listening to me." He whispered. Steiniger roughly ran a finger over the eye that Jed's fist favored. He smiled again, standing. "See? Fixed."

Porter felt his skin pull and stretch. Steiniger had fixed his face; he had healed his black eye and all his cuts.

"Where are the kids?" Porter spat.

Steiniger glared at him like a disappointed father. "They're safe."

"What about the parents? You going to tell me you didn't hurt them either?" Porter snapped.

Steiniger's face fell. He shook his head. "It's only collateral, boyo."

"And you think that's right?" Porter asked, finally strong enough to sit up.

"I know it's not, but don't you dare pretend that you haven't wished terrible, terrible things upon Jedidiah!" Steiniger screamed, the magical binding on Porter's hands tightening. "Yes, I killed them, but the people I have killed are monsters! Monsters far worse than you or I. I am saving these kids! Without me trying to break the cycle, they would become the same! Do you have any idea the kind of person you would be with out me?" Steiniger asked, raw emotion in his eyes.

"Save me the eloquent tongue and give it to me straight, Eric. The real monster here is you, and you know it." Porter said as he examined his surroundings, the words that flew from his mouth, hurting him more than they did Steiniger.

The old lunch tables had been pushed up to the wall, blocking off all but one doorway. The only light came from a small crack in the wall on the right, showing weakness in the structure he loathed. If he could just gather up the strength to bust through it, he could get out of here.

"Where is this coming from?" Steiniger whispered. "Porter, you are like a son to me. How can you turn on me like this?"

"My whole life," Porter began shakily. "You have lied to me. You made me idolize you, made me trust you, made me think that you were the only good person in this whole town."

Steiniger sighed heavily. "Yes, yes, two wrongs don't make a right and all that. Just because I go to Church doesn't mean I planned on going to Heaven." He laughed, waving his hand through the air, Porter's binding disappearing. "You have two choices right now," He began, sounding like a court judge.

Porter quickly stood, holding a hand before him, ready to attack. He wanted to lunge at him, rip him limb from limb for putting Della in danger, for bringing him here, for kidnapping and for killing, but something kept him where he was, waiting for Steiniger to continue speaking.

Steiniger began walking around him in a circle, like a mountain lion surveying his prey. "You can come with me and the rest of the kids like you, get far away from this town, and all the horrible people in it, or you can leave and go right back to the one thing you are afraid of." He continued, stopping back in front of him. "I'm trying to help you. You know I am. You used to run to me when you were little, oh the things that you said Jedidiah did to you. Do you know how hard it was to sit by and watch, not able to do anything?"

Porter let his shoulders relax, instinctively rubbing his wrists. He hated what he was thinking, and he hated that

Chapter Thirty-Nine

Steiniger knew he had gotten to him.

"You can't expect me to believe you are going to let me leave." He said sternly.

Steiniger shrugged. "The truth is always the hardest pill to swallow."

Porter rolled his eyes. With his bindings free, he would be able to grab Clara and get out. *If* he decided that's what he wanted to do. He opened his mouth to speak when Steiniger held up a hand.

"Let me put it like this," He said, sauntering over to him. "Come with me for an hour or so, see what life would be like with the children I have rescued, and then you can make your decision. How does that sound, boyo?"

Porter shifted his weight from one side to the other, startling him. The way he saw it, he had three options; flee, go along with Steiniger, or play along until he figured out how to save all the kids he had kidnapped.

"Fine." He said. There was no use trying to hide the scowl on his face.

Steiniger's eyes brightened. "That's a good boy." He waved him over, glancing at Clara, a scowl on his face. "The others are waiting in the art room. You still like to paint?"

Porter nodded, sticking his hands in his pocket, feeling around for his phone.

"Looking for this?" Steiniger asked, spinning his phone between two fingers. "You can have it back when I trust you aren't going to call our friends back at the station."

He should be running in the opposite direction. He should be fleeing; he should attack him. But something told him not to, so he walked through the halls he hated so much, following him in silence.

Porter had always loved art class. Getting to sit here, buckets of paint before him, brushes of every size, pencils in all the colors of the rainbow, all sorts of paper—it had been his happy place. He had never been able to draw a flower, and God cried whenever he tried to paint, but he loved art anyway. Of course, this town had to ruin that for him too.

Steiniger tossed him a canvas and a couple tubes of paint, sitting him down between a small redheaded girl and a young girl with blonde hair and oil pastel smeared across her face. The girl smiled, offering him a palette knife. Porter took it carefully, wondering why all the kids—eight of them to be exact—looked so happy. Didn't they know they were in danger?

"Kids, this is Porter. He hasn't made a decision about staying with us yet, please make him feel at home." Steiniger said happily, gently taking a paintbrush from the toddler next to him and cleaning off the poor kids' hands.

"Are you leaving again, Mr. Steiniger?" A young boy asked.

"No, I've got to see to our entourage." He winked. "Charity, you are in charge."

The girl next to Porter smiled to herself, quietly reaching for the bright pink oil pastel next to Porter's foot.

"Well all right, then." Steiniger nodded, standing. "Feel free to grab anything from the cafeteria, I'll be bringing back dinner so don't gorge yourselves." He said, laughing kindly. He waved to them all then swept out the door.

This was going to be easier than Porter thought. He turned to Charity, smiling widely. She smiled back, waving sheepishly.

"Hi." She said.

"Hey there." Porter replied. "What do you say we get out of here?" He asked.

Charity furrowed her eyebrows, looking quite appalled at the thought of leaving. "Why would we do that?" She questioned, drawing a crude rose on her construction paper.

Porter looked around. "You all do realize. . . that you've been kidnapped, right?" He asked the room. There was a collective nodding of heads.

"Just because we are kids doesn't mean we are stupid." The young boy that had spoken earlier said. He was wearing a pair of headphones with bright green cat ears on them. Porter recognized him as the boy he wasn't able to save.

"Angus, be nice." Charity said softly.

"I bet you all are smarter than I am," Porter said, opening a tube of blue paint for the quiet redhead next to him. She smiled up at him thankfully. "So, why do you not want to leave?"

"If you are here, you know why." Charity said. Her eyes glazed over for a moment as she dazedly reached up to touch her neck. There were yellow bruises that looked like fingerprints around her wrists.

"What happened?" Porter asked, painting a wobbly tree on his canvas.

Charity watched him paint for a moment, then shook her head. "Mr. Steiniger says it's best not to talk about what bothers us since we won't have to deal with it ever again. When we leave this town, we can all start new lives." She smiled.

Porter furrowed his eyebrows. "Aren't you going to miss it here?" He asked.

"I for one," Angus said. "Am going to pee on my porch when we leave tomorrow night, so no, I won't. Screw this town." He said, holding up his middle finger.

"Angus!" Charity scolded.

"That bad?" Porter asked with a small smile.

Angus rolled his eyes, replacing his headphones. A couple of the older kids laughed.

"Don't mind him, he's—" Charity began.

"Yeah he's punk." The redhead finished matter-of-factly.

"Anna." Charity hissed, but she smiled.

"Okay. . . What about your friends? Aren't you going to miss them?" Porter asked, addressing them all.

"What friends?" Charity scoffed. "My 'friends' left me for dead, Mister Porter. I'm pretty sure they don't care what's going to become of me."

Porter smiled despite himself. Charity reminded him of a certain green-haired someone who he was trying not to worry about.

"In my experience, there is always someone who cares about you. Like Wesley." Porter said, reaching across Anna Dixon for a fan brush.

"Yeah, and there is someone who cares, and he's given us a chance at a new life." Charity said, raising her voice a little. A couple of the kids winced. "Listen," She said, turning towards Porter with a very pained expression on her face. "You obviously have a choice, how old are you? Thirty? The rest of us don't have the luxury of being able to leave the people who have hurt us. If you don't want to stay with us, that's fine, but don't try to make us leave." She said sternly.

"All right, let's make one thing clear, I'm only twenty." Porter said. Charity smiled a little, rolling her eyes.

He sighed heavily, painting another leaning tree as he pondered the situation he was in. He was going to get nowhere by forcing these kids to leave, they didn't know how much danger they were in, and even if he tried to explain it, they wouldn't listen. Hell, if he was their age, he'd be just as happy as they were. The eight of them had already formed a friendship that he wished he would have had at their age. His eyes lingered on Angus, who was chatting with an older boy with blue hair.

Porter was struck with a thought, smiling to himself.

"Hey Angus?" He asked.

"What do you want, dumbass?" Angus asked, whipping his head around.

"Do you have a phone?"

Angus rolled his eyes, digging his phone out of his pocket. "I'm fourteen, of course, I have a phone." He said sarcastically.

"Can I use it?" Porter asked.

~CHAPTER FORTY~

Saving Venus

Once again, Max knocked on Della's door. He sighed heavily. "Della! It's me! Open up!" She'd texted him, saying Porter had called her drunk and decided she probably needed back up. "Della! Don't make me use my powers!" He screamed.

Nothing.

"Fine, be that way." He whispered. "*Seå opp.*" He said, waving his hands through the air as the door unlocked.

He took two seconds to take in the state of her usually pristine apartment, his eyes traveling over the scratch marks on the ceiling, before rushing to Della's side. She was lying on the floor in a heap of limbs, her chest rising and falling weakly. His fingers had barely grazed her shoulder when she shot upright. Her eyes were full of fire as she struggled against him, not realizing who was holding her.

"Hey, hey—it's me, Della it's me." Max said softly, pulling her up off the floor.

Her eyes softened as she scrambled to her feet, wrapping one of her arms—the one that wasn't hanging loosely from her side—around him. She squeezed him tightly, tight enough to make it hard for him to breathe, but Max hadn't the heart to push her away. He squeezed her back, once again looking around at the room.

"What the bloody Hell happened here?" He asked, fear-ing the answer. He hated himself for thinking that things would be able to return to normal.

Della pushed herself off him, wiping her face with the back of a very bruised and broken looking hand. She looked around, looking like barely half the person she was. Max held her face in his hands, brushing bloodied strands of hair from her eyes. His heart broke for her as she tried to speak.

She blinked a couple of times, reaching up and touching her shoulder, shutting her eyes against the pain she felt.

"He's gone, they took him." Was all she could manage, her voice barely audible.

Max swore, pulling her to him. "We'll get him back, Ei swear." He whispered.

She shook her head. "This is my fault."

Max pushed her face up so she would be forced to look at him. Her eyes were so dull, the light stolen from them.

"How is this yer fault?" He asked.

She laughed dryly. "I couldn't—"

"Ya did yer best, and ya went down with a fight. That's obvious." Max said sternly, shaking her. She winced, cradling her hand against her chest. Max looked her over, lightly putting a hand on her shoulder.

~ ~ ~

As Della packed what little weaponry she had into her book-bag, Max scoured the messy apartment for something of Porter's. Della's broken shouldered ached as she reached inside the dishwasher for a crowbar.

"Ya keep yer crowbar in the dishwasher?" Max asked, peering over the breakfast bar.

"It's old and rusty. I want to make sure it's sanitized." Della shrugged.

"Wow." Was all Max could say.

"Just, hurry it up, all right? I wanna find him." Della said, angrily shoving the crowbar into her bag.

"Magic takes time and patience," Max said, glancing at the couch. "Hey, Ei think Ei found somethin'." He darted to the floor, sticking his hand under the sofa, pulling out Porter's keys.

Della swallowed hard, watching Max as he held the keys up to the light. "You sure that will work?"

Max nodded. "Tuh cast a locator spell, ya need somethin' that holds emotional leverage. For *you*, Ei would use yer laptop or one of yer notebooks. Porter loves that ugly old hearse more than life itself, so this is as good a bet as any." He snatched his spellbook off the couch and sat down at the breakfast bar. "Ya wouldn' happen tuh have some quartz lying around, would ya?"

Della looked around, crossing her kitchen and peering inside the cabinet that held all her herbs. She reached around to the back, procuring a rather large piece of white quartz. She handed it to Max, who held it in front of him.

"Quartz amplifies magic and helps with manifestation. We are tryin' tuh manifest the location of our dear Venus, so this will be perfect." Max explained, flipping through his spellbook with one hand.

Della watched him nervously, her mind racing. Nothing Max could say to her would keep her from thinking that this was her fault. She wished she could help in some way. It seemed all she was good for was her crystals and her brain.

"Here we go. . ." Max whispered, looking back at the crystal. "*Finne, rof finne, Porter.*" Max said, then blew on the crystal.

The crystal began to shimmer, its clear facets filling with a cloud of black smoke. Soon the crystal started to depict a place. It looked to be a school.

"Shit." Max breathed, then blew on the crystal again, the scene disappearing.

"What?" Della asked, taking the crystal from him, holding it up to the light.

"That's the old elementary school. Dammit, we should have put that all together." Max said, running a hand through his thick curly hair. Della gave him a questioning look. "The year Porter dropped out, we got in a huge fight. Ei was so damn upset with him for killin' that boy, Robbie, that Ei lost control of my powers, and Ei set fire to the school. If it wasn't for Eric, Ei would have gone to juvenile detention. Ei had a huge list of offenses pending. That would have been the icing on the cake. Afterward, Eric closed down the place. No one ever goes there. It would be the perfect place to keep the kids!"

"Thank God for magic." Della breathed, setting the crystal aside.

Max sat lost in thought, staring off into space. He

cleared his throat, looking around at the chaos that was Della's apartment. "We should go. We don' know what state Porter is in, and what Eric has planned."

Della nodded, walking around to Max as he hopped off one of her bottle cap bar stools. She pulled him into a hug, wincing as she lifted her arm.

"W—What was that for. . . ?" He asked when she let go.

Della brushed her hair behind her ear. "You're always here for me. Even when I don't deserve it. I'm sorry I was such an ass when we first met; you didn't deserve that."

Max opened and closed his mouth a couple times. "Della, Ei've come to realize that if ya like someone, ya flick 'em shit. Ei see it as a great honor that yer an ass to me." He smiled.

"I don't deserve you." Della laughed tearfully.

Max shrugged, pretending to brush his hair behind his shoulder. "Now, let's go get our boy."

~ ~ ~

Porter paced back and forth in the hallway, staring at Angus's phone. No reception. Of course. How convenient. Every little thing had been setting him on edge. It was too quiet. Where were the Grunches? Why had Steiniger left them all defenseless? Was he that stupid, or was there a bigger picture he couldn't see?

"Do you have a death wish?" Angus asked as Porter tried for the seventeenth time to call Della or Max—or anyone for that matter.

"Not anymore." Porter said in a detached sort of whisper. He roughly handed Angus back his phone. "We've gotta get out of here Angus, can you round up the others?"

Angus thought for a moment. "As much as I don't like Charity, I'm going to go with no. I want your head on a platter, not mine. Thank you very much."

"Angus, you don't understand—"

"No, I understand perfectly." Angus snapped, scrolling through his phone, not bothering to meet Porter's eyes.

"Do you understand that Steiniger killed the Dixon's? Do you understand that he murdered people? Killed your dad? Attacked your mother?" Porter snapped, ripping his phone out of his hands.

Angus stared at him with a worried expression. "I—Well, now I do."

Porter rolled his eyes, kneeling, so he was at eye level with Angus. "I know better than anyone what having abusive caretakers are like, but leaving them for Steiniger is not going to fix your problems. He is a very evil person, Angus. Trust me, I don't like that truth any more than you do, but you have to help me make the others understand that."

"But. . . but I don't want to go back. . ." Angus said, a pleading tone to his voice.

"I have people coming for me, people who can help. The three of us will make sure nothing happens to you guys, okay? We have enough evidence on the people who have hurt you. We'll plead your cases, okay? I promise." Porter swore to that.

Angus nodded. "What do you need me to do?"

~ ~ ~

Max and Della stood outside the old elementary school, dark rain clouds looming in the distance. Again, Della swung the crowbar down on the chains binding the door, ignoring the searing pain in her shoulder. Her mind was set on Porter and his safety, that's all that really mattered to her right now. She swung again. Who would lock up an old school? Okay, yes, the place was nearly burnt to a crisp, but the chains on the doors were excessive. And inconvenient. *Very* inconvenient. She went to swing again when Max grabbed the crowbar from her hands.

"Aye, that's enough of that." He said. He reached into his pocket and produced his tiny green spellbook. He rifled through the pages for a moment, squinting in concentration, then smiled, holding his hand above the chains. "*Eksbryte.*" He whispered, and the chains shook and shattered.

"Show off." Della said sourly, throwing the doors open. Why couldn't she have done something like that?

"Yer just mad because the beastie is better at magic than *you* are." Max laughed.

"No shit." Della scoffed.

"Honestly, Ei haven' a clue what Ei'm doin' half the time." Max smiled, picking up the discarded crowbar and holding it like a sword. "But Ei know Ei'm good at it."

"And you're very humble, too." Della laughed darkly, reaching for her machete.

"Ei'd rather be annoyin' than insufferable." Max said. "Keep up, Pluto." He smiled at her over his shoulder, stepping past her.

They walked on in silence for a little while, both too nervous to continue the witty banter. The halls of the old school were covered in soot and moss, the cracking walls giving insight into the rooms that had been destroyed. The whole building looked like a scene out of some movie set in post-apocalyptic times.

"Ei hated it here." Max whispered, using his crowbar to move a burnt backpack.

"Really? Seems like such a charming little place." Della said darkly. Sarcasm. Such an underappreciated trait when it came to keeping yourself from exploding with terror.

Max laughed nervously. "Ya know, Ei wish ya would have been with us back then. Ei feel things would have been a lot different." He admitted.

Della had a flash of a memory, thinking back on all the days she wished she had had actual friends in school. She nodded in agreement. She would give anything to go back in time and change everything, to have grown up here and be with Max and Porter. It would have been Heaven to her. She silently vowed to make up for all the lost time.

As they walked along, they heard what sounded like laughs. Tiny little child laughs. Those disembodied laughs sent shivers down Della's spine. Creepy, like the sounds of child ghosts stuck in the school. They glanced at each other than ran in the direction of the noise, skidding to a stop outside of an open classroom. Seven kids sat coloring with crayons, markers, paints and pastels. Not the scene they were expecting by any means.

A girl with long blonde hair stood, looking alarmed. "Who are you?" She asked.

Della opened her mouth to speak when she heard footsteps echoing through the hallway they had just come from. She turned, ready to strike down Steiniger or one of the Grunches; instead, Porter's glorious face filled her line of sight.

~ ~ ~

Charity shook with anger, looking at Porter with tears in her eyes. "What did you do?" She asked. "What did you do?!"

Porter ignored her, wrapping his arms around Della and Max. Angus was at his heels, staring at him with a perplexed expression.

"Who are they?" Charity demanded, walking over and ripping Angus's phone from his hands, tossing it to the floor. The screen shattered into tiny pieces. The room was silent.

"Friends." Porter said finally, releasing them from his grip. His eyes lingered on Della's swollen hand, which Max had haphazardly wrapped up. It looked like she had shoved it in a waffle iron.

Charity just stood there, tears filling her eyes, shaking her head.

"This is Max, he's going to get you all out of here, okay?" Porter announced to the room. There was an odd look on Della's face as he said that.

The kids hesitated, looking at Angus with fear and anger.

"It's okay," He said. "I trust them." Angus nodded at Porter, smiling brightly. "Let's gather up our stuff, everybody." He said.

Porter hated that Angus had to grow up so fast, but he was proud of him for stepping up.

Della began to herd the children out of the room, a glum smile on her face.

"I'll stay here, get them all out of harm's way. You and Max take care of the bigger problem." She said.

"Max can stay behind." Porter said utterly confused. Usually, Della jumped at any opportunity to put herself in harm's way.

"I don't think I would be of much use." Della said. Her magnificent brown eyes looked very empty.

Porter eyed her carefully, but nodded, taking her book bag. Inside, all the weapons she had packed clinked against each other, an ominous ringing sound filling the art room.

This was it, the final battle.

"Okay, call the cops and I'll—"

"NO!" Charity screamed. "He's trying to help us, why can't you see that?" She yelled, running past them and out of the art room.

"Charity! No, come back!" Porter yelled.

"*Oooh draaamaaa. . .*" Angus whispered, edging past Porter to gather his things. Wesley and him would make great friends.

"Take care of everybody, we've got to go get Charity." Porter exclaimed, slinging Della's bag over his shoulder. Max tightened his grip on a very rusty crowbar. "Everyone listen to Della and Angus, all right?" The room nodded, though reluctantly.

He and Max raced out of the art room, hopping over burnt memories from the days they had spent here. Neither of them wanted to stay a minute longer in this damned place, but alas they had to.

"Charity!" Porter called, running the length of the hallway, opening doors, and looking behind overturned desks.

As he left a classroom, he saw the door to the gym swinging shut. The boys ran, bursting into the gym, the familiar smell of gym socks and sweat piercing their noses. It had been nearly seven years, and it still smelled the same. Charity stood in the middle of the room with Steiniger, who was muttering something beneath his breath. Jimmie stood off to the side, looking horrified. The old bleachers had been drawn out, sleeping Grunches snoring somewhat peacefully on them.

"I gave you a chance." Steiniger said, waving his hands in the air. The doors to the gymnasium slammed shut, the glass windows inside them shattering. "You could have come with us and lived a peaceful life, why did you have to go and ruin it all?" Were those tears in his eyes?

Max brandished his crowbar as the Grunches began to stir. "Ei don' think we thought this through." He whispered, his voice cracking with fear.

Porter swore, turning his attention towards Charity. "Charity, I know you don't want to hear this, but Steiniger is—" He shook his head, biting his lower lip hard. "Steiniger is an evil person. He killed some of these kids' parents! You can't—" Porter began.

"Don't listen to a word he says, he's just like the rest of them, lying little ba—"

"*EMRAV!*" Max shouted, a plume of blue-hot flames shooting forth from his hands.

Steiniger put up a hand, an invisible shield protecting him and Charity from the flame. He snapped his fingers several times, holding out his hand. Jimmie pulled something out from his jacket, rushing over to him. He shoved a book into Steiniger's hands, cowering behind him.

Steiniger flipped through the pages, but he didn't seem to have a clear vision of what to do. Max's plume of flames disappeared, and as he went to fire again, Steiniger found a spell that piqued his interest.

"*NEMMORTIS!*" He cried, a jet of water blasting Max in the chest.

Max fell to the floor, but other than being soaking wet, he was unscathed.

"Oh, two can play at that game." He said, spitting water from his mouth and digging into his pocket.

He fumbled with his spell book, he had marked the different sections with sticky notes so he could easily find what he was looking for.

"*Elkiv rekarniv!*" He shouted, pointing his finger at Steiniger's feet.

Two vines burst through the floor, wrapping themselves around his feet. Max stood, balling his hand into a tight fist. The vines tightened, crawling over Steiniger's frame as fast as snakes. He held the book out before him, trying to flip through it as the vines wrapped around his forearms.

"*Idilavin!*" Steiniger shouted.

"OH SHI—" Max began as he slumped to the floor, unable to move.

Steiniger snapped his fingers, causing Jimmie to run up to him, rolling up his sleeve to reveal a pentacle tattoo. As Steiniger held his hand over the mark, Porter's mind was filled with buzzing, the bite on his arm searing with pain like never before. A memory of helping Steiniger drag Jimmie away filled his mind, the rest of his thoughts melting together.

Porter's eyes glowed bright white, anger flowing through him as he stared at Max. He screeched, instantly regretting it. The Grunches had awoken, beginning to circle. Porter's instincts were to follow them, but he stayed where he was trying to fight off the feeling in his chest.

Steiniger now had his own stream of flames coming out of his hand. The flames wrapped themselves around his legs, burning the vines that Max had grown.

From behind, a Grunch jumped onto Porter's back, digging its claws into his shoulder blades, ripping his thick flesh. Porter screeched again, shaking violently to get the Grunch off. It was days like this when he wished he could cast spells or move objects with his mind like his friends.

The crippling spell Steiniger had placed on Max was wearing off. He sat up, reaching for his spell book and looking through the pages.

While he was preoccupied, Steiniger brushed himself off, shoving the giant spell book he had into Charity's hands and telling her to run. The scared girl complied, running out the doors on the other end of the gymnasium, followed by Jimmie, leaving the others to fight. Steiniger returned his attention to Max, an evil smile on his face. That was no longer Steiniger. He had been corrupted by magic for who knows how long, and it was finally taking its toll.

He lifted his hand, whispering something Porter couldn't quite understand. A ball of crackling lightning erupted at his fingertips. With his spare hand, he pointed two fingers at Max.

"*Elkiv rekarniv.*" He said calmly. Twenty thorny vines grew up from the ground, pulling Max back down to the floor and pinning him in place. The thorns dug painfully into his wrist, blood seeping through the thick vines.

Max tried to choke out a spell, but nothing happened. The vines were closing around his throat. He cried in agony, trying to fight the vines, but they were too strong. He couldn't move. He looked to his left; Porter was fighting off three different Grunches. He wouldn't be able to help.

The rest of the Grunches had fused together, creating three giant ones that stood behind Steiniger menacingly. He strolled over to Max, the lightning crackling in his hand. He clenched his fist, baring his teeth, the vines tightening, then threw the bolt up at the ceiling.

Once again, the school was up in flames.

Max was just happy that it wasn't his fault this time.

~CHAPTER FORTY-ONE~

Della herded the kids out of the school, entertaining whatever questions they had. She dug in her pocket for her phone, dialing those three simple numbers that would send help. She loosely explained the situation they were in, ultimately just yelling for the operator to send help immediately. She stuffed her phone back in her pocket, nervously pacing as she made sure all seven kids were with her.

"Charity!" One of the older kids screamed, pointing to the trees.

There stood Jimmie Heiser, pulling a screaming Charity towards Della, tears welling up in his eyes. He had the spell book in his other hand, gripping it tightly. Della scowled at him, running over. He let go of Charity, pushing her in the direction of the other kids.

"What happened?" Della demanded angrily.

Jimmie shook his head, shoving the spell book into her arms. "I did something horrible." He whispered, weeping into his hands. "Eric, he said he wouldn't harm her, but you got too close. Is she all right?"

"Eloise? She's fine, she's staying with Clara Dixon's fiancé." Della hissed, taking a step back from him.

He looked up from his hands, his eyes full of self-hatred. "I never meant for this to happen. Theo wasn't supposed to die,

I swear. Neither were the parents." He cried, shaking.

Della's eye twitched in anger. She was about ready to rip him a new one when Angus cut her off.

"Hey, D?" He called, pointing to the sky. Della looked up, nodding. "Is that smoke?"

Della looked up into the dull blue sky. A dark cloud of smoke was presenting itself, illuminated by the mid-day sun, mixing with the coming rainclouds like a potion in a cauldron. Della swore thickly, shoving the book back into Jimmie's hands, running to the door of the school.

"Where are you going?!" Asked Angus, his eyes full of fear.

"I've got to go save them, stay here, keep everyone safe." Della said, putting all her trust in a fourteen-year-old.

Angus gave a little thumbs-up. "Hey, uh check the cafeteria on your way out. I think some woman named Clara is in there?"

Della swore as she ran inside the school, wishing she still had her bag of weapons. She was utterly defenseless without them. She heard a screech that sounded like a bat, a wave of fear rushing through her. She ran faster, forgetting to breathe as she tried to find her friends. She came to a stop a few feet away from two double doors with smoke billowing out from under them.

Della swore, ducking under the smoke to get to the door handles. She pulled and pushed them, but they didn't budge. Through the smoke, she could see Porter's figure fighting off Grunches and Max lying on the floor. She tried to open the doors again, inhaling far more smoke than she should have.

She took a step back, coughing wildly. She shut her eyes tightly, trying to tap into her anger, her sadness, her guilt, channeling it all into power. Her eyes shot open. From somewhere deep inside, she felt power like she had never felt in her entire life, yet it was familiar. She screamed, throwing her hands out in front of her. The doors shot open, bending and cracking against the force of Della's abilities. Della ran inside what she realized was the gym, overtook by a dazed feeling.

Steiniger was standing over Max, his fist clenched tight. Della looked down, seeing Max spasming under the thick vines Steiniger had conjured. Della thrust her hand towards Steiniger, sending him flying backward. He crashed into a gigantic Grunch behind him, slumping to the floor.

However, it was obvious the fight wasn't over. Steiniger clutched his side, rolling back and forth on the floor. His focus had broken, the vines around Max loosening and retreating into the ground. Della rushed to him, helping him up off the ground. He was covered in oozing pinpricks and cuts. He shook her off, pointing at Porter.

He was pinned to the floor by one of the Grunches, trying his best to fight it off. His eyes were white.

"Where's the spell book?" Della asked.

Max shrugged, swallowing hard. "Lost—it." He choked, rubbing his neck.

Della darted to the floor, ignoring the fire above her, and the spells Max was shooting at the three giant Grunches around Steiniger. The flickering orange light from the flames lit up a glistening brick a few feet away. Della ran to it, picking up the spell book and tossing it Max.

After all, she wasn't going to need it.

Max looked through its pages, placing two fingers in the air. "*Neginbindi tau.*" He said breathlessly, sketching a bow in the air with his finger. The Grunch closest to him now had thin, glistening silver ropes around it. Though the Grunch could have broken any ordinary rope, this mystical binding kept it occupied while Max looked for something a little more powerful.

Della set herself the task of keeping the other two Grunches at bay, putting up her hands, feeling waves of energy leaving her palms. She had created some sort of invisible barrier between the two sides of the battle. She looked over her shoulder, seeing Porter rip the last of his attackers in half, sending their bloodied corpses to the floor. He fell to his knees, holding his head in his hands, crying out in pain.

Max groaned, shoving the thin spell book in his pocket. "Ei've not a good spell! Damn Nicoletta and her practical magic!" He screamed over the crackling flames.

Della lost focus, her mind slipping from keeping Steiniger and the last Grunch at bay to help Max.

For an old man, Steiniger was exceptionally fast. One hand pointed at Della, the other pointing at his temple, he cast his spell. "*Etsmerte!*" He screamed.

Della's head exploded in pain. Not white-hot pain like she had when she had visions, or anything like a migraine, just pain. She tried to fight it, but she didn't know how, falling to her knees, gripping at the broken floor beneath her.

"Della!" Max screamed, running to her side. "*Emrav skjolden*—ARGH!" He screamed.

A weak shield of fire burst before Della's eyes, but that wasn't what she was watching. Porter, his eyes white, his mouth dripping with foam, had attacked Max, sending him to the floor, his hands covering his mouth and nose. Max kicked and clawed at Porter's hands, but nothing was working. His movements became smaller and smaller, the life draining from him.

Della staggered to her feet; her hand pointed at Porter as Max's body went limp. Through the pain, she focused her power on the boy she loved. He looked at her in mild surprise before being flung off of Max, colliding with Steiniger.

The pain in Della's head ceased.

She raced to Max's side, shaking him. He laid there on the floor, his face screwed up in a surprised expression. She shook him, but to no avail. For all she knew, Porter could have killed him.

As she stared at him, an idea struck her mind. Every spell that Steiniger or Max had cast had required them to have a clear line of sight regarding their target. She looked up, watching Porter stir from the floor. She grabbed the spell book out of Max's pocket, jumping to her feet. She knew she wouldn't be able to do anything, but she had to try. She flipped through the spell book, tears streaming down her face, mad emotion surging through her. Porter would never hurt Max. Never. The hold on his mind was obviously much stronger than they had originally thought.

As she flipped through, her eyes landed on a spell that was meant to bring light. There were instructions and a warning saying that if the spellcaster wasn't careful, they could blind everyone within a ten foot radius.

And thats *exactly* what Della aimed to do.

She looked to Steiniger, focusing all her anger and fear on him. "*LYS!*" She screamed at the top of her lungs just as Steiniger looked up at her. Della covered her eyes as an explosion of cold white light filled the room.

An eerie silence followed the explosion of light. Slowly, Della let her arm drop, looking around at the sight. Steiniger sat on the floor, holding his head in his hands. Small streams of liquid light were trailing away from his hands and down his face.

Della looked to Max, the taste of revenge sweet on her tongue. She stepped past him and over to Steiniger, glancing at Porter, who was stumbling around, rubbing his eyes, blinking madly. She held up one hand to keep the last Grunch at bay, and with the other, she drug Steiniger to his feet by the collar of his shirt. He struggled against her, but ultimately let Della hold him by his forearm. His hands dropped from his face, revealing two scorching holes where his eyes should be.

"Tell us how to get rid of the Grunches." Della said sternly.

Steiniger scowled at the floor. He looked like a mad man standing there, a ring of flame encircling them, the orange light turning their clothes an odd shade of Hell.

"Tell me." Della insisted, shaking him a little.

"You can't," Steiniger said wistfully. "Not without doing something unspeakable." He smiled. "And from what lover boy has said, we both know you won't do it. Both know you hold yourself in too much pride. You think you're the hero." His lips pulled into a smile, his teeth drenched in his own blood.

Della let go of him. "What do you mean?"

Steiniger laughed.

There was a deep hatred burning in Della's body, a hatred she did not know how to control. She let go of her hold on the Grunch and instead focused her power on Steiniger. She heard the old man's tiny bones break and crack under the force of her power, but Della was too far gone to feel remorse. It was like every emotion inside of her had been shut off. She felt no joy from breaking this horrible man, but she felt no sadness either.

Suddenly, Nicoletta's words filled her ears. *Two paths.* Which path was she on right now? Good or evil?

From what felt like miles away, she heard Jimmie say her name. She glanced over her shoulder at him, seeing him standing over Max, tears overflowing from his eyes, but she couldn't break away from Steiniger. Slowly, she clenched her fist, expecting him to cry out in pain. Instead, it was Della who cried out. She shut her eyes against the familiar white-hot pain of her visions, blood filling her eyes. She had no doubt that her ears were filling with blood too.

Steiniger laughed again. "They warned me about you." He whispered sourly. "*Our savior.*"

Della's veins were rippling down her forearm with pain. She focused all her energy on Steiniger's neck, squeezing it like he had done to Max with the vines.

"You—wouldn't—dare." Steiniger choked out as Della tightened her hold on his neck. She could hear the fear in his voice. The same fear his monsters had forced onto the people he had attacked.

Once again, Jimmie screamed her name, this time it felt closer, but not close enough to break her out of whatever trance she was in.

"Tell me how to call off the Grunches." Della demanded, loosening her grip just a bit.

Steiniger laughed again, looking up with his holes for eyes, his lips pulling into a smile. "Kill her." He whispered.

Della furrowed her eyebrows, confused for only a split second, before feeling something plow into her, knocking the wind from her lungs. Porter was on top of her, his hands around her neck, an evil smile on his lips, his cold eyes filled with joy. With one hand, she reached up towards his face, trying to claw at his eyes, trying to push him off her with her legs, the other hand searching his side for his gun. It wasn't there. Of *course*, it wasn't there. When had anything gone the way Della had wanted it to?

Porter rammed her head into the floor, his eyebrows furrowing in sadness, though the rest of his face was still shrouded in evil.

"Jimmie, the book." Steiniger said, pulling himself to his feet. He stood tall, cracking his knuckles, rubbing away at his neck. His loss of vision didn't seem to bother him.

Jimmie said nothing.

"I said the book, Jim! Give it to me now!" Steiniger hissed.

"I'm done following you! Look at yourself, Eric! You have pinned the person you love the most on one of his closest friends! You've killed people in the name of justice, in the name of doing what is right! Look around! This isn't the way things were meant to be!" Jimmie screamed.

Della's eyes flickered with darkness as she grabbed on to Porter's arm. As her fingers touched his skin, his grip relaxed. His eyebrows furrowed, his eyes flashing gold for a fraction of a second. He looked confused.

"Porter—it's—me." She choked out, trying to inhale

as much air as possible. "You—have—to—fight—him." She coughed, the back of her throat stinging with the effort it took to speak.

His fingers loosened an ounce more, his eyes squeezing shut, his expression pained. He launched himself off her, holding his head in his hands. Della inhaled sharply, coughing blood onto the floor, wiping her face off, staggering to her feet. Porter looked up at her, watching her try and steady her feet on the ground.

"Sorry." She croaked, then kicked him in the face, sending him into an unconscious heap on the floor.

She wobbled for a minute, then looked over her shoulder. Jimmie had her bag of weapons in his arms, searching it for who knows what, his eyes on Steiniger.

"You are a horrible, *horrible* person, Eric." He said shakily, pulling her smaller machete out of the bag, sending the rest of the weapons to the floor. He weighed it in his hands, stopping himself from crying any more. "You put Eloise in harm's way, you killed my brother, you tried to frame Ellie and me. I hope you rot in Hell." He hissed, then plunged the machete into his own stomach.

"NO!" Della screamed, rushing to him as he collapsed to the floor.

Steiniger had fear written all over his face. Jimmie sputtered blood, the blade falling from his hands. The pentacle on his wrist was sparkling, slowly disappearing. The last Grunch fell to its knees, shining with Hellfire, screaming in pain as it burned.

"WHAT DID YOU DO?!" Steiniger roared. "WHAT DID YOU DO?!"

Jimmie coughed a couple times, pulling Della's face down to his. "Tell Ellie I'm sorry." He whispered. He coughed again, his hand falling from her face, his eyes staring lifelessly up at the burning ceiling.

Della panicked, looking to Steiniger, who was shaking with rage. He seemed to feel her eyes on him as he turned in her direction. She stared him down, clutching Jimmie to her chest. Max was probably dead. Theodore *was* dead. *Jimmie* was dead. Clara was hurt. Porter was. . . She wasn't quite sure what Porter was, but she knew it was all on Steiniger. Hot angry tears spilled from her eyes, that same dizzying rage flooding through her veins again.

"This is all *your* fault." She hissed, standing confidently, thrusting her hand in his direction, forcing him to his knees. Imaginary wind blew her hair out behind her. "You *KILLED THEM!*" She screamed, twisting her wrist, breaking his rib cage.

Steiniger's face was filled with surprise. The burned cavities where his eyes should've been were bleeding. So were his ears and nose. He reached up, clawing at his throat, crying out in pain. The hatred inside Della grew, if only she could see herself, she could see the color her eyes had gone. They were no longer the color of wet tree bark like Porter had said, they were a deep, dangerous shade of violet.

Again, Nicoletta's voice spoke in her ears. *Two paths.*

"Why did you kill Theodore?" Della demanded, her voice breaking. She needed answers.

Steiniger spit at her feet. "That man was horrible to his wife, and she let it happen. She let him scream and yell at her. I watched my best friend turn into something he wasn't every time he lifted the bottle to his lips, and she did nothing to stop it. I was *saving* her, saving Jimmie!" He screamed. "She sent him flowers! Sent him care packages! Sent him love letters! She was so blind! I took matters into my own hands. Studied a few voodoo spells in my free time, trying to learn everything I possibly could to rid this world of all the evil people in it. Ellie was going to send flowers out to the parents of the abused kids, so I cursed the flowers to be a beacon for my Grunches. Those people *deserve* death! Those people deserve to rot! I don't!" He sputtered.

"That is not your choice to make!" Della screamed.

"Then whose is it?" Steiniger spat. "I don't see anyone here trying to do whats right. I saw your files, I saw the kind of person you are! You aren't any better than me!"

"Why did you take Clara?" Della demanded, pulling him closer to her, ignoring those words.

"Clara had her doubts about a lot of things. I knew if she confided them in Eloise, Ellie would tell her I wasn't who I said I was. I did what I had to do to protect the operation." Steiniger explained nonchalantly.

"You could've killed her!" Della screamed.

"Collateral." Steiniger sighed.

That was the final straw. Della had made her decision. She snapped her wrist again, Steiniger's neck snapping with it. He fell to the floor, his eyeholes pointed up at the burning ceiling. Della finally snapped out of her trance. A weakness like none she had ever experienced swept through her. Her head was pounding, but she could fight through it enough to move. She turned, staring at Porter. The flickering light of the flames made it hard to tell if he was breathing or not. She took a step forward, watching the arm with the bite twitch. He shot up-wards, squeezing at his arm, rolling up his sleeve. The bite was foaming and sizzling, but most importantly, it was healing.

"Porter?" She choked out, rocking back and forth on the spot.

He looked up, blinking away the pain in his arm. He took one look around then bolted to her side.

"What—" He began, his eyes tracing something behind her. "Oh shit, Max." He breathed, pulling her towards their friends' body. They knelt beside him, Della fighting back tears and exhaustion, Porter shaking Max's broken and bloodied frame. "Dammit, Max, quit the dramatics." He pleaded, patting the side of his face.

Della looked up at him. There was no sadness or worry in his eyes, just confusion. He pounded on Max's chest, his face changing to irritation. Della opened her mouth to tell him to stop, when Max shot up, his head colliding with Porter's.

"STAND BACK! EI'M ARMED!" He screamed. "LEMME AT 'EM, LEMME AT 'EM!" He shouted fighting against Porter. "ABRAKA—FRIGGIN—DABRA!"

Porter rolled his eyes, shaking him gently. "What's this? Five lives left?" He asked, lightly patting the side of Max's face to try and get him to snap out of it.

Max stopped trying to rip Porter limb from limb, looking around dazedly. "What happened. . .?" He asked.

Della scrambled to her feet, finally understanding, relief flooding through her as she wiped tears and blood from her face. Max was a familiar whose form was a cat. He had nine lives. Well, apparently only five now.

Porter cleared his throat, pulling Max to his feet. "We saved the day." He said darkly. He glanced around, dusting Max off. "We need to go. Like, now." Although the flames had finally died down, the smoke around them was as thick as syr-up.

Max yawned and stretched, looking as if he only had been sleeping. "Yay us?" He asked as Porter pushed him towards the door, pulling Della out by her elbow.

Della smiled weakly. She tried to speak, but no words could force their way out of her mouth. Della looked over Porter as they walked. His nose was crooked, his shirt was ripped to shreds, covered in blood. A fresh cut on his side made her heart do another somersault.

"Is that blood?" She gulped, at a loss for anything else to say.

Porter laughed. "I love that you care and all that, but you look like you're going to keel over." He said seriously, a struggle to his voice. He knew that it was partly his fault she looked the way she did, knew the red splotches around both her and Max's neck were from him. He swallowed hard, his eyes falling on Jimmie then his former father figure. He took a step back, running a hand through his hair. "Oh no. . ." He whispered, stopping as he glanced over his shoulder.

"What. . . What did we miss?" Max asked.

Della staggered, doubling over, playing it off like she was picking up her bag of weapons. She heaved them up onto her shoulder, swallowing hard. "Talk later." She coughed, her eyes following Porter's to where Eric lay lifeless. "We've got to get Clara and get out of here." She said, her voice weak.

The boys hesitated, but nodded, leading the way.

"It's a little early for vows and whatnot, but Ei swear to God Ei am never settin' foot in this place ever again." Max coughed as they walked out of the burning gym, looking like the heroes in an action movie.

"I second that notion, Milliano." Porter laughed darkly. Neither of them argued over the fact that he had the nerve to call him that.

Despite everything, Della smiled to herself as Porter pushed open the door to the cafeteria. Clara sat tied to a chair, her head lulling to the side. Porter ran to her, startling her awake.

"Hey, it's okay, no one is gonna hurt you." He whispered, untying her from the chair, sweeping her up into his arms.

Della's vision was blurring, her heartbeat erratic in her chest. She shook it away. There were more pressing matters than her well-being.

It seemed like it took hours to reach the outside world. The sound of sirens sounded like a symphony, blinking red and blue lights like atom bombs in their eyes. Porter took Clara to the nearest ambulance, explaining to the paramedics that there were two bodies inside the school. Max nudged her, pointing to the yellow convertible where Mavericks was screaming at a police officer.

"Go, I'll find the kids, make sure they are okay." Della said weakly. Max hesitated, then ran to his father. Mavericks pulled him into a giant hug, tears streaming down his face.

Della smiled, feeling her heart do another somersault, feeling like someone had ripped the floor out from beneath her. She coughed a couple times, clutching at her chest. Her heart felt like it had stopped, her lungs feeling like they were next. She blinked, and suddenly she was on the ground, staring up at the sky. Everything seemed to slow, playing out like a movie before her eyes. Porter's face was suddenly above her. He was shaking her, screaming at her. Two sets of paramedics were at his side, Max following close behind. She was numb all over, physically, emotionally—everything.

Della lay there, ignoring her friends shouting at her. An odd sense of calm flooded through her. Her body felt like it was floating in the middle of a sea made of her own worries.

This town had made her question everything she had ever believed. If the guardians of these kids were evil, and Steiniger killed them, what did that mean? In every storybook Della had ever read, the good guys always killed the bad guys. So why was she questioning her role? Was Della now the bad guy because she killed Steiniger? Should she have let him live?

Delphee Chrysanthemum Coleman felt broken.

Everything around her felt like a lie. How did she know what was right and what was wrong anymore? How did she know that things were going to work out? If she was meant to be the heroine in this story, why did she feel like she had lost everything?

They stopped a murderer, but what if those sweet kids were being damned to a fate worse than what they had already lived through?

They stopped a murderer, but Theodore Heiser was still dead. And so was Jimmie. So was everyone else Steiniger had killed.

They stopped a kidnapper, but Nicoletta said this was only the beginning.

They stopped a supposedly evil man, but did they do it

without weighing all the options?

No, not *they*.

She.

She was the one who stopped a murderer without weighing all the options.

Her eyelids twitched as she fell into the pit of her own brain. She felt Porter shaking her, but she was spiraling too quickly to care.

The more Della thought about it, the more she felt that everything over the past eighteen years was her fault. How many lives had she ruined with her 'unique' set of skills? How many families split because she wanted to prove herself or make a quick buck? How many more lives was she going to ruin? When did it all stop? What was going to be the final straw?

Della inhaled softly, hyper-aware of everything around her, aware of the way the cold, wet grass beneath her soaked her jacket, aware of the feel of every crack on Porter's hand as he patted her face, aware of the smell of smoke, the sounds of the ambulances, children crying—everything. Maybe the most important thing she was aware of, was that Eric Steiniger wasn't the only monster she had found the last couple of months.

No, this story didn't have one monster, it had two.

And one of them was her.

~CHAPTER FORTY-TWO~

Della woke with a start, feeling tears rushing down her face, though she had no idea why. Her words caught in the back of her throat. She tried to stand, but instead, she fell out of a hospital bed, her head colliding with the floor. She groaned, all the colors dancing. Porter stood over her, offering her a hand up.

"You worry me, you know that?" He asked, pulling her up off the floor, forcefully shoving her on to the hospital bed.

Confusion flooded through her. She had no idea how she had gotten here or where she had been before, but this didn't feel right. Something was wrong. She was shaking all over, a cold sweat penetrating her skull. Someone was in danger. Someone was dying, she had to get to them. She stood.

"Whoa, whoa, whoa, hang on there," Porter said, catching her as she stumbled forward. She hated feeling like this, hated her lack of balance. She'd felt it before, though she couldn't remember where.

"Where's Max?" She demanded. Maybe he was the one in danger.

"With Mavericks, why?" Porter asked. He was studying her face, watching her with an emotion she couldn't pin.

"He needs to be here," Della said, trying to stand.

"Why?" Porter questioned.

Della shrugged, running a hand through her hair. "He's in danger. At least I think he is."

"Danger of what?" Porter questioned without blinking. "Becoming an ass? Sorry, but *that* ship has *sailed.*" He laughed.

Della opened and closed her mouth a couple times, ignoring his joke. "I don't know." She whispered.

Without warning. Porter laughed maniacally, his face contorting into what looked like a demon. He tried to grab her, but she ripped herself away from his grip.

Her vision danced, that familiar feeling of the floor dropping out from underneath of her returned, though she had no idea where she had felt it before. She ran from the hospital room, crashing into nurses, ramming into patients. Everything was swirling like a whirlpool, the colors mixing like a four-year-old's paint palette. She stumbled into a wall, gripping onto it for dear life. She steadied herself, shutting her eyes tightly. Everything was going to be okay. She'd find Max and save him.

Or maybe it was Porter who needed to be rescued? She pinched the bridge of her nose, trying to remember who needed her help.

She opened her eyes.

She was sitting in the reptile chair at *The Utopian Courier*, watching Mavericks as he moved chess pieces across an intricate board that hovered in front of him. The last six pieces on the board were shaped like bats, cats, and rats. Laying on the desk were several other animal pieces, each broken beyond repair. Mavericks looked up at her, smiling, his teeth sharp and white, glinting in the candlelight in his office.

"Care for a game?" He asked, his voice distorted.

The chair tilted to the left.

Suddenly Della was sitting on an ottoman in the *Weeping Crow*, watching the witches cry. They all wore their best lacy black garments, their makeup smearing across their faces. A picture of her was on the bar, surrounded by decaying monkshood flowers and candles with blood-red flames.

The ottoman pouf lurched forward.

Now she was standing in the middle of *Bayou Gil's*, overseeing a group of vampire's chow down on the local werewolves. She walked through them like an unseen ghost, terrified. Hadn't they been at peace?

She stumbled, falling to the ground. Her hands gripped

onto soft carpet. She stood, looking around. She was in some sort of house. The windows were wide open, a warm breeze blowing in, but there was nothing outside. Just black. She turned. Someone was singing a low, broken song as they rocked back and forth in a rocking chair a few feet away. She stepped forward, reaching out.

This was the person who needed help. The name was on the tip of her tongue, like some far off memory. Her hand clutched around the back of the chair, she spun it around to see a man in a straight jacket, a brightly colored scarf tied around his eyes.

Della recoiled, watching as the sweet beach bungalow she had been in transformed into a padded room. The man was still humming.

Della shut her eyes, covering her ears. When she opened them, she was once again at *The Utopian Courier*. Mavericks was staring at her with a drawling expression. He rolled his eyes, gesturing to the floating chess board.

"It's your move, Delphee. Your choice." He yawned. "You going to win, or are you going to lose?"

Della stared at the chess board.

"You do remember how to play, don't you? You were always so good at chess." Mavericks said, leaning back in his chair, kicking his feet up on to his desk.

"Why are we playing?" Della asked without thinking.

Mavericks said something, he explained everything, but Della could not hear it. All she could hear was a loud beeping. Her ears filled with pressure. She looked down at her hands, a drop of blood falling from her nose. Before she knew it, she was face down on the desk, unable to move.

~ ~ ~

"CLEAR!" A voice screeched.

Electricity flooded through her veins, filling her with adrenaline. Her eyes shot open, but all she saw was a bright blue light. There was a massive pain in her chest, her lungs ached as she breathed, her body weak. She blinked. No, it wasn't light, it was the sky. She was lying on the ground, looking up at the sky. Her vision swam, settling on four people who looked to be paramedics. One held paddles, another had a stopwatch. They were all staring at her, their faces a mix of relief and surprise. She blinked at them, ignoring the one who asked if she knew where she was.

The guy holding the paddles was pushed aside, Porter's face filling her view. He was as white as the clouds above him, his face stricken with tears. Max appeared next to him, screaming at the nurses to give them all some space. The nurses moved unwillingly, looking terrified of the tiny African-Irish boy before them.

Porter fumbled around for words before lifting Della off the ground and squeezing her to his chest. His tears soaked her hair, his cold fingers squeezing around her shoulders, as she heard him gasping for air.

"EI SAID BACK THE BLOODY HELL UP!" Max screamed at the top of his lungs. Della heard hurried footsteps.

Porter refused to let go of her, his hands in her hair, chin resting on the top of her head. He was barely breathing now, sitting there listening to her breathing, afraid to let go. Della was too weak to shove him away—not that she wanted to. She felt Max place a hand on her shoulder, then launch himself into the hug. She forcefully looked up to meet their faces, searching their eyes.

"What happened?" She whispered.

Porter was whispering inaudibly in Portuguese, blubbering like a beached whale.

Max carefully brushed the hair from her face, his head resting on Porter's shoulder. "Ei don' know, Della. Ei look up, and Porter is screamin' for help, and yer on the ground." He whispered, his voice cracking.

Porter squeezed her tighter, stroking her hair, rearranging himself on the ground. "Don't—do—that—ever—again." He choked. "I thought you died."

Della nodded into his chest, shutting her eyes, though she was afraid to do so. "Sorry." She whispered. She suddenly realized that neither of them were the one she was trying to save; she had been trying to save herself.

Max choked out a laugh, reaching around to ruffle her hair, following Porter's lead and squeezing his arms around them tighter and tighter. They sat like that for a while, listening to the conversations around them, waiting for someone to move them. Della was pretty sure no one had the guts to.

Finally, Porter pulled away. Roughly brushing Della's hair from her eyes, a sad little smile on his lips. Max let go of them, sitting next to Della, his arms crossed, chewing on the collar of his sweater. They looked like quite the sight, all bloodied, and bruised, and beaten.

"What happened?" Porter asked shakily. "Did you see anything?"

Della blinked a couple times. "I guess I went into shock." Her voice was small and broken.

She closed her eyes against the emotional pain she felt. Too much had happened today. Far too much.

Porter swore, his voice breaking. Max stared at her, studying her face, a deep scowl on his lips, his eyes full of sadness.

"Ya wanna talk 'bout it?" Max asked darkly.

She shook her head. The thought of speaking, of forcing her brain to form words then send them to her lips was exhausting.

"Okay," Porter whispered, nodding to himself as he wiped the tears from his face. "That's okay. Let's go get your hand and shoulder checked out, shall we?"

~CHAPTER FORTY-THREE~

The Fall of Man

Halloween had always been Della's favorite holiday. Even Sycamore Heights had celebrated it. She had always loved dressing up as a witch or a fairy, getting free sweets, tormenting her younger siblings, and carving pumpkins. Imagine how she felt being in the spookiest state in the spookiest month? Before everything had happened, she had been looking forward to experiencing a genuine Moss Hollow, Louisiana All Hollow's Eve. Not today. Not even Halloween could cheer her up.

Funerals shouldn't happen on Halloween. Even Della couldn't handle that much darkness.

"How do you tell if someone is a monster?" Della asked the sea of seats before her.

Behind her were two freshly dug graves, and a handful of people dressed in black sat before her. Eloise sat in the front row of chairs, Max on her left, Porter on her right, nodding at Della to continue. Della looked over her shoulder, her eyes scanning Jimmie and Theodore's names. The clouds above the funeral attendants mirrored their emotions as Della cleared her throat and rearranged her note cards. Max and Della were dressed in their best, while Porter was covered in dirt, looking like an old grave-robber.

Della hadn't spoken much since everything happened. She was too scared of what would happen. She had to keep herself locked inside her head. That was the only way she could keep everyone safe. She hadn't slept much either, awaking in the middle of the night plagued with dreams and visions. She wished she could pass these powers on to someone else, but then again, she wouldn't wish the pain she felt on her worst enemy.

Porter gave her a questioning look, making to stand, but she shook her head. She smiled kindly at Eloise, turning her attention to the crowd.

"What makes that person a monster?" She said loudly and clearly though her hands were shaking. The words written on these bright note cards needed to be spoken, and she was the only one who could say them. "Green scales? Pointy horns? Sharp teeth? Are monsters made of darkness and evil intentions? Are they made of Hellfire and kisses from the Devil?" The funeral attendants looked at each other. "No. Monsters don't have scales, or horns, or sharp teeth."

She looked to Richie and Lenora, who stood at the back of the group. They smiled weakly at her. Della nodded to herself, walking around to the front of the pedestal, discarding the note cards. She knew the words already. It was like they were burned inside her brain.

"They don't hide under kids' beds or come out when the lights are turned off. They walk among us every day, in broad daylight. Sometimes we don't see them, sometimes they make us think that someone else is the monster." She looked at Porter, who looked down at his feet. "Monsters hide in plain sight. No one should beat themselves up about not seeing them, they never wanted to be found." Della stared down at her own feet, thinking about everything that she had gone through in her time here.

She cleared her throat again, returning to her place behind the pedestal. "People don't do things because they think they are bad. Theodore was a good man. He may have had a temper, he may have gotten angry when he was under the influence of alcohol, but when he wasn't, he volunteered at the hospital, and he planted flowers for his wife."

Eloise broke down into tears, clutching onto Porter for support. Max squeezed his eyes shut, rubbing away tears.

"He wasn't a monster, he was a man with flaws." Della continued, nervously flipping through her note cards. "Jimmie was another story. He wanted power, yes, but he was forced to be something he wasn't. He wasn't a monster, he wasn't evil, he was corrupted, controlled.

The real monster manipulated an entire town. He killed people in cold blood because he thought he was righteous. He sentenced Theodore to a life in jail, away from his wife, and forced Jimmie to be the bearer of a horrible, *horrible*, burden. There is nothing we can do to fix that. Nothing. What's done is done. However, everyone here can tell the real story of what happened. A story of a man who blurred the lines of law and justice, proving that two wrongs never make a right." Della said, swallowing hard, tears stinging at her eyes.

With that, she stepped away from the pedestal, returning to her seat next to Porter, mindlessly listening to what the rest of the people had to say.

The funeral had been small. Just a few family members, a couple friends, and the entirety of *The Utopian Courier.* No one seemed too upset about the fact that the two brothers were dead. Mavericks took it upon himself to help pay for things. His heart ached for Eloise. He sat quietly near the back, lost in thought next to Nicoletta.

The cat, the bat, and the rat were one of the last to leave. Rain pouring down on their heads, they stood shoulder to shoulder-ish due their height difference, staring at the graves.

Max nodded to himself, sticking his hands in his pockets and chewing on his lower lip. "Have fun in Valhalla." He whispered in the direction of Theodore's grave.

Della stared at the headstone. It was so plain. So empty.

The boys eyed her. Neither of them knew what to say to her. Neither of them knew how to help her. They didn't even know how to help themselves. Porter reached out for her hand, interlocking his fingers with hers. She squeezed his hand tightly, never wanting to let go.

They stood out there in silence for quite some time, letting the rain soak them through. None of them had ever thought something like this would have happened. Even Porter, who had dealt with death his entire life, never thought this would happen. After a while, Max detached himself from them, silently walking away.

Porter swallowed hard. "I don't think I would've been able to do what you did." He said to Della.

Della stiffened, biting back tears. "If you tell me you're

proud of me. . .” Her voice trailed off.

Porter glanced at her, looking like someone had stabbed him through the heart. “I am proud of you.” He said darkly. “But not in the way that you think I am.”

Della nodded. She wanted to tell him so bad that she lost control over everything, but what would he say? What would he do?

“I’m really sorry you have to carry this.” He whispered after a while, squeezing her unbroken hand as hard as he could. “I wish I could take it from you. . .”

“Can I—” She started, the words getting caught in her throat.

Porter turned to look at her, his heavy shoes squishing in the mud over Jimmie’s grave. He looked her over, taking in the sight of her dripping wet hair, and the sling and cast on her arm. “Promise me you won’t let this drive you insane.” He said sternly.

“It won’t.” She said, forcing her cheeks to pull up into something that resembled a smile.

Just like that, everything she had learned, everything she had taught herself while she was here, escaped her. Hope ran from her like a scared animal, understanding flew the coop, happiness died. That’s how she could tell that it was getting bad again.

Porter looked over his shoulder, his face darkening. “I’ll catch up with you later.” He whispered, then placed a kiss on her cheek before walking away.

Footsteps belonging to Mavericks and Nicoletta squelched through the mud. They stood at her side, Mavericks’ hands crossed behind his back, Nicoletta staring at the graves in deep sadness.

“Eric and the Grunches said I was marked for a different fate,” Della began. “Eric said someone told him—that someone warned him about me.”

Nicoletta and Mavericks exchanged a look.

Mavericks cleared his throat, nodding. “Assume everyone knows who you are, Delphee. Assume your name is written everywhere we look.”

There was a long drought of silence as they stared at the graves, each lost in their thoughts.

Della had a feeling that Moss Hollow was not the only place that harbored magic. If she was honest, she knew that even her home town had its secrets. Why else would she be the person she was? Where had her powers come from?

"Why did you bring me here?" Della whispered.

"Because." Mavericks said simply. "Because there was no one else who could have done this."

"You are more important to this world than you may think," Nicoletta said quietly.

Della looked to Mavericks, studying the side of his face.

"Did you know?" She asked.

"About which part?"

"About me."

He nodded. "We all did. . ."

Nicoletta placed a hand on her shoulder. "We will be here if you need us." She said, then walked away.

Mavericks lingered, crossing his hands over his chest. "I am four hundred years old, Miss Coleman. I have seen evil in every form but this. . . this surprised me. . . You, Max, Porter— you surprised me. . ."

"Did I do the right thing?" Della asked.

"You have a capacity for unimaginable good, Delphee," He said, turning to smile at her. "That is the thing that drew me to you. Ever since you were young, you have seen how the world beats people down, and you have wanted to fix it. You *have* fixed it."

"That's not an answer, Mavericks."

He nodded. "I never give answers, Della." He said, then patted her on the shoulder. This surprised her. Mavericks hated touching even Max. "All you need to know, is that everything will be okay."

Della grimaced.

Oh, how wrong he was.

Before her was a puddle, reflecting her face in a very poetic sort of way. The light rain made her face bend and contort, the mud in the water portraying how dirty her soul felt. A bitter reminder of the feelings she was trying to hide. She smiled sadly at her reflection, her broken shoulder stinging with pain as she tried to move it.

So, this was it? This is what being a hero felt like?

Or was this the best part of being a villain? A single tear dropped from Della's lifeless, cold, brown eyes, mixing with the rain. She sighed heavily, looking over her shoulder. She forced herself to smile up at Mavericks, watching his face twist in sadness. She had a feeling that she would never be able to let go of that little skill of hers, the way she could so easily fake being happy.

She looked away, turning towards Garroway Mortuary, carrying the weight of the world with great difficulty.

One way or another, she would fix this.

One way or another, she would right a few wrongs.

. . . . TO BE CONTINUED

~EPILOGUE~

Mavericks paced back and forth in his office, a feather quill hanging loosely from his lips, his tattered spiral-bound notebook in his hand. He took a sip of his coffee, smiling slightly. Things hadn't gone to plan by any means, but at least they were alive.

For now, at least.

He set his coffee on the edge of his desk, turning to face Lenora, Richie, and Nicoletta.

"What's another word for 'happy'?" He asked.

The three exchanged a look. Richie shifted his weight from one foot to the other, discreetly whispering something in his cousin's ear.

"Joyous." Nicoletta yawned, flicking the reptilian chair she sat in as it growled.

Mavericks rolled his eyes, writing that word down in his flowery handwriting. He stared at it for a while before crossing it out, shaking his head with a sigh.

"That's too cheerful." He said absentmindedly, scanning the room for inspiration.

"You have a phone, look it up on *Google*." Nicoletta scoffed, stringing beads onto a piece of thin gold wire. Jewelry was her true passion, not witchcraft. Richie snickered.

"You three are supposed to be helping me," Mavericks said, tapping his foot on the floor, turning to stare her down.

Nicoletta did not return his gaze, instead grabbing a bright blue bead from a box, holding it up to the light. "I'm not a writer, Percy."

"Obviously."

"Bubbly is a good word." Lenora smiled, playing with a

piece of her hair. Richie smacked her up alongside the head,
Nicoletta shriveled her nose in disgust. Lenora sighed heavily.

"Did you have your fun, Mavericks?" Nicoletta asked,
replacing the bead back in her box, reaching for a purple one.

"Quite." Mavericks smiled, pushing up his glasses.

"The girl could've died," Richie said, his voice dry.

Mavericks nodded, rolling his eyes. "Yes, yes, yes, moving on." He smiled. "So we have joyous. . . bubbly. . . What
else?"

Nicoletta stared him down. It irked him so that he was
scared of her. He was far older than her, far more powerful. He
shouldn't be trembling under her gaze.

He straightened, returning to his book. "Fine." Mavericks whispered. "Are we not going to talk about who *helped*
Miss Coleman with her powers?"

"No. Are we going to talk who invited her here in the
first place?" Richie asked, crossing his arms over his chest. He
smiled playfully. "And oh, I don't know, *why he invited her*?"

"Obviously not. He thinks he's done 'the right thing.'"
Nicoletta said, laughing darkly.

"Nicoletta." Mavericks said softly, making a clicking
noise with his tongue. "Next time you want a protege, ask
Nick." He quipped.

She rolled her eyes. "This isn't about having a protege,
this is about the girl's powers. From the minute she stepped
foot on this unholy ground, we felt her presence. She isn't like
the rest of us. She had a right to know."

"Just like Milliano has a right to know who his mother
is?" Mavericks smiled.

Nicoletta clenched her fist around her needlenose pliers,
biting her tongue as best she could. "They'll figure it out eventually." She spat.

"How old am I? What is it this December? I can handle
a couple teenagers." Mavericks said. Richie reluctantly nodded
his approval as Mavericks brushed a dust bunny off his jacket.
"It is my job to protect everyone, and that is what I am doing."

Nicoletta shook her head angrily, ignoring that last
statement. "Why didn't you listen to Richie? He's just about as
old as you, he's just trapped in a lesser form. He has your best
interests at heart, you know that."

Richie nodded again, puffing out his chest. Mavericks
rolled his eyes, acting as if the only people standing there were
him and Nicoletta.

"Richmond is. . ." Mavericks thought for a moment,
picking at his fingernails. "Richmond is an extraordinary kind
of idiot." He finished.

Nicoletta rolled her eyes again, holding up her hand to

stop Richie from saying anything as she carefully discarded her work and stood. She crossed her arms over her chest, eyeing Mavericks mischievously. "They are better than us. They always have been, always will be." She smiled. "They are better than the *others* ever were. Better than everyone you have tried to use."

Mavericks' face brightened, nodding proudly. "I chose well."

"You chose nothing." Nicoletta corrected, still smiling. "You don't get to take credit for saving the world. Not this time. It was the three of them, and you know it."

"I still curated it. I still pushed and pulled them in the right directions." He smiled hopefully.

Nicoletta opened and closed her mouth a couple times, anger filling her. Richie shook his head, grabbing Lenora by the sleeve of her puffy polka dot shirt and pulling her out of his office. Nicoletta nodded at them, grabbing her things and making to leave. She heard Mavericks laugh, felt his eyes roll as he stared at her.

She stopped in the doorway, holding her head high. "I know they can save a lot of people. I know *she* can. But Della has the prospect of being the exact opposite of what we want. That's what I'm scared of. She has visions. She's seen things she shouldn't have. Her mind is breaking, Percy, and when it does, that's on you. Whether she dies, or worse, it will be on you."

"No, my dear, that is on her parents." Mavericks said, an audible smile on his lips.

"And are we ever going to tell her why we know it's her parents fault?" Nicoletta snapped.

Mavericks was quiet, his face full of sadness. "Not yet. Not now. She's had enough heartache for today. . ."

For updates on the cat, the bat, and the rat, follow me at:
Twitter: @AmeliaRikstad
Instagram: @utopian_courier_press

Thank you to all who purchased this book, its merchandise or any of
my other artistic endeavors. I couldn't have done this with out you.